OVERCOMING THE BETA

FROM THE WARRIOR SERIES

KRYS STRONG

BOOKS TO HOOK PUBLISHING, LLC.

ISBN: PB: 978-1-957989-68-6

ISBN: eBook: 978-1-957989-6

To find out more about the author and her upcoming work, please visit www.krysstrong.com.

Cover design by: Kasmit Cover
Printed in the United States of America

This book is dedicated to my daddy, the late and great Earnest D. Pittman.

In which the character, Gamma Earnest, was based from.

Thank you for your unconditional love and support, as well as gut checking me when I needed it.

Not a day goes by that I don't think of you.

I know you'd be my biggest fan and how proud you'd be that I'm pursuing my dreams.

I love you and I'll see you later.

CONTENTS

BOOKS BY KRYS STRONG

Warrior Series

Warrior: Sins of the Past

Warrior Book 2 – Releasing Fall of 2022

INFORMATION

Trigger and Content Warnings

This book may contain some scenes that are not suitable for all audiences. Please review the list below before proceeding.

Bullying – **Cheating** – Depression – Emotional abuse – Hospitalization

Profanity – Weapons – **Sexually Explicit Scenes** – Violence – War

Playlist

I created a Spotify playlist of sounds that go well with this book. Please keep in mind, I'm not a professional DJ. I hope you enjoy.

https://open.spotify.com/playlist/70uWCuWfVKhgHEoJOHHhO3?si=207a9d8a5dc74d95

CHAPTER ONE

THE CITY THAT NEVER SLEEPS

February 2004

Kate

IT'S BEEN A LITTLE over two years since I left the only place that I have ever called home. I had no other choice but to leave everything I have ever known and loved to break free of him. When I first arrived in New York City, everything was so unfamiliar and scary. Some call it the Big Apple, but I prefer to call it the city that never sleeps. Back home, nights are filled with the peaceful silence of the sleeping forest, insects chirping, and the howls of my people. Here? It's so noisy all the time. Sirens at all hours of the night, the sounds of people's voices, shouts, loud music, sounds of people moving around, horns, and non-stop traffic. For a werewolf like me, whose hearing, sight, and smell are enhanced, this city was almost too much for me in the beginning. Now, it's home. My wolf, Sasha, and I have learned to tune out the distractions of the city and blend in with our surroundings. To keep Sasha settled, once a month, we take about a three-hour car ride into Connecticut to spend the weekend camping in the Cockaponset State Forest. It's werewolf and shifter friendly, and even though I keep to myself, I have made a couple of friends along the way. While camping for the weekend, I allow Sasha to run free, allowing her to run, hunt, and play in her wolf form.

We have adapted to city life, the best we can. Even so, I miss home. I miss the smell of my mom cooking blueberry muffins every Sunday morning. I miss being squeezed so tightly by my dad that I think he'll break one of my ribs. Pack life is what I miss the most. Hell, I even miss my annoying brother and his constant teasing. There is one person I'd like nothing more than to forget. As hard as I try, I still can't get him off my mind. The man I fell in love with at fourteen, the man who helped me through my first shift at eighteen, the man I gave my virginity, and the man that shattered my heart into a million pieces. As much as I miss home, I can't go back... not just yet. I can't afford to run into him, not while my heart is still healing from being crushed by him.

You'd think that after two years I'd be over him, moved on, but no. I haven't been able to just simply move on. It's harder than I ever thought it would be. My human friends say that your first love is the hardest to get over. Maybe that's true, but it's not something that is often experienced in the werewolf world. Humans seem to fall in and out of love many times in their lifetime. In the werewolf world, we mate for life. There is only one love. When we meet the one Moon Goddess designed and made for us, an invisible bond that only true soulmates share pulls us to each other. It's that bond that binds the two souls for life. Sure, there are exceptions to the rule. Mates get rejected or die, and in those cases, we can only hope that the Moon Goddess shows us mercy and grace and grants us a second chance mate.

Missing home is especially hard today as I go through my mail and see an invitation to my brother's wedding. I've known about the wedding for several months, but this invitation sets it in stone, and I'm dreading going home. Since moving to New York City, I've been able to avoid going home, and haven't seen my family at all. But my mom will skin me alive if I miss the wedding. She has already expressed that. Weddings are abnormal in our world; most don't see a point in a wedding ceremony since the mate bond binds us together. My brother, Kelsey, is the future gamma for our pack. He will take over for my dad when he retires in two years. Anyone can have a marriage, but in our pack, the Alpha, Beta, Gamma and their mates are married in a very public ceremony that is noted mostly in the human world. The Alpha, Beta, and Gamma all work the pack businesses alongside humans, being married helps them to blend better in their world.

Looking at the blue and white invitation with gold embossed lettering, memories flood my mind. I wonder what my life would be right now, had my heart not been crushed. What would my wedding have been like? Would I be a mom by now? I can't let the what if's get to me… not now. I'm finally at a point in my life where I think I have found someone I can spend the rest of my life with. He's perfect on and off paper. His name is Darren McCall and comes from a very influential family in Manhattan. He just passed the bar and is working for his father's law firm. His father is a well-known attorney to the rich and elite, and his mother is a socialite and philanthropist. We've been dating for three months, and things are progressing in our relationship. I explained I come from a conservative family and have lied that I'm a virgin and want to wait until marriage. He says he understands and will wait, but lately he seems to push the envelope a bit more where sex is concerned. I'm pretty sure that I love him, but I have this nagging feeling that I can't get past where intimacy is concerned. My birthday is in two weeks, and he says he has a special surprise. Thinking about what kind of surprise he might have in store makes my stomach flip and knot up... that can't be normal. The wedding is six-weeks from Saturday. Maybe the apocalypse will happen between now and then. That's the only way I'll get out of going home.

My cell phone rings, jolting me out of my thoughts. I look at the display on the front of my flip phone... mom. *Great.*

"Hello?" I answer with a smile on my face and a light voice, so I don't get asked fifty million questions.

"Hey sweetheart, get the invite?" Mom's voice is so sweet.

"Yes." I answer back, waiting for the shoe to drop and the interrogation to begin.

"Well? What do you think?" She asks.

"Why did you send me one? It's not like I have a choice of going or not." I look at the invitation.

"I meant, what do you think about the invitation? Pretty, right?" She sighs.

"Oh... Yeah, it is." I push the invitation to the side.

"Did you get your dress yet?" Mom asks, and I don't answer. "Kate?" I remain silent, trying to decide what to say. "Oh, my goddess, Kate!" She shouts.

"Yes, mother, got my dress." The lie falls so quickly out of my mouth.

"Good." She sounds relieved.

"Do I really have to go?" I whine.

"YES!!!!!" She growls, clearly getting irritated at me.

"Ok... Geez." I roll my eyes.

"You don't have to talk to him, Kate." My mom's voice is soft.

"I know. Look at the time... well, got to go, headed to dinner with the girls." I blurt.

"Fine," she sighs. "Love you, sweetheart. See you soon." She blows kisses into the phone.

"Bye, love you too." I giggle and blow a kiss into my phone. It seems silly to blow kisses through the phone, but it makes my mom happy, so I do.

I close my phone and put it on the counter, next to the wedding invitation. No, I don't have dinner plans. I have my nose stuck in a book in my pj's plan. I hate lying to my mom. She and I both know I haven't bought the damn dress. I know exactly where that conversation was going, and I don't want to hear it. She'll tell me how much he's changed, and that he is always asking about me, blah, blah, blah. It's as if she doesn't remember the pain he put me through, and why I'm studying art so far from home.

After a nice, long, hot shower, my Chinese delivery is at my door, and I can't wait to sink my teeth into some roasted duck. I take the food and place it on the table next to the door when I notice some kids playing in the hallway. A little boy pushes his sister down and another boy is there to help her up. It brings back a memory from seven years ago, when a fourteen-year-old me realized she was in love with the future beta of our pack.

April 1997

"Go away, Kate!" Kelsey shouts at me.

"No!" I stand my ground, crossing my arms and stomping my foot.

"Go away, Kate!" Kelsey shouts and shoves my shoulder.

"No, it's a free country and I can do what I want, Kelsey." I stick my tongue out at him.

"It's cool, man, we're just fishing." Zane steps between Kelsey and me.

"It's not your bratty little sister that's always following you around. Besides, Stacey said she'd come by and hang out. I'm trying to get to second base, and I don't need *that* ruining it." Kelsey points at me.

"What's second base?" I question, tilting my head at him. Zane and Ian both roar with laughter.

"I can show you, if you like." Ian steps forward and leans down so he's eye level with me.

"Dude, that's my fucking sister!" Kelsey shouts at Ian.

"Relax, man, I was just kidding." Ian raises his hands in a mock surrender, then turns and winks at me. I wrinkle my nose and blush. Ian seems to make me blush a lot lately.

"Ommmmm... I'm telling dad you said the F word and that you're going to second base with Stacey." I stick out my tongue, taunting my older brother. Satisfied seeing Kelsey's face turn red, I turn and walk away. Suddenly, I feel two hands hit the middle of my back before I fall to the ground. I hiss in pain as both of my knees hit the gravel pathway hard, scraping them both badly.

"Damn, Kelsey. Not cool, dude. Both our dads are going to kick our asses." Zane shouts behind me. The pain from my knees causes tears to fall down my sweaty cheeks.

"Hey," Ian helps me off my knees and sits me on the soft grass next to the gravel path. "Let me look at that." He inspects my knees, cleaning the dirt and rocks from the scrapes with water from his newly opened bottle. The water is cold, causing me to flinch and hiss a little. "It's ok, please don't cry." He wipes the tears from my cheeks, then gently brushes the hair from my face. "It's just a couple of scrapes. In a couple of hours, you'll be good as new. I'm sorry your brother pushed you. He's kind of an asshole. Have some water." He hands me his bottle of cold water and I take a sip. As the cool water hits my throat, a new feeling hits me, a feeling I'm unfamiliar with. I'm seeing a different side to one of my brother's best friends, a gentle and sweet side. He rests his hand on my thigh and it sends a series of shock waves through my body, making my heart skip a beat. "Come on, you can go fishing with us. I'll even bait your hook. What do you say?" He smiles sweetly at me. I'm at a loss for words and only nod. He stands, then offers his hand to help me to my feet. As we walk past my brother, Kelsey protests, but Ian stops him.

"Dude, her knees need a couple of hours to heal before your dad sees them. Understand?" He puts his arm around my shoulder, and we continue to walk away from my brother. It was in that moment I realized I was in love with the sixteen-year-old boy next door, one of my brother's best friends, and our pack's future beta.

February 2004

"Ma'am?" The annoyed delivery man shouts, snapping me out of my thoughts.

"Huh, what?" I look at him, confused.

"Fourteen-fifty. I only said it five times. Geesh." He snarls at me.

"Sorry, um... keep the change." He snatches the twenty from my hand, turning away, mumbling something in Chinese under his breath.

CHAPTER TWO

TWENTY-FIRST BIRTHDAY SURPRISE

February 2004

Kate

"MELISSA, WHERE ARE WE going? I thought we were going to your folk's place for dinner?" I follow my friend through a set of large wood and glass doors into a crowded bar. It's eight p.m. and we're already pushing our way through the thick crowd. The smell of beer, whiskey, and bad decisions fill the air. We come to another door that opens to a spiral staircase that leads to an Italian restaurant below.

One thing I love about New York City is the history. There are many stories about buildings all over the city being hangouts for some of the most notorious Italian gangsters. I can imagine this building in the Bronx as one of those seedy little hangouts. You can see the history in every aspect of this building. From the tall, tiled ceilings, the exposed brick walls, and the massive amount of ornate dark woodwork throughout. I imagine the finest carpenters building out each piece in here by hand. I can almost hear the sweet jazz music filling the air while they smuggle illegal booze in from below and up the spiral staircase to thirsty patrons in the bar. When the heat got too close or a rival gangster paid a visit, the spiral staircase made for a quick escape. I bet if these walls could talk, the stories they'd tell.

"We are, silly. My uncle owns this place. Ma didn't feel like cooking tonight, so change of plans." Melissa looks back and smiles at me. She was one of the first people that I met when I first moved here. I met her in a class at the university and we hit it off right away. Her big personality balances my shy side. Actually, over the past two years, she has rubbed off on me a little. I'm not as shy as I used to be, but I'm far from being as loud as her. Melissa comes from a big Italian family and was the one who taught me how to eat pasta properly. She was dumbfounded and thought it was hilarious how I ate spaghetti. She said I look like a cow eating hay.

"What the hell?" Melissa shouts as we walk into a pitch-black private dining room. "Wait right here. Let me find out what's going on." I can hear her walk away, but I hear something else. Multiple different heartbeats. I steady my breathing and concentrate on the sounds of the beating hearts. I sniff the air and realize that I'm not alone.

"SURPRISE!!!" A crowd of friends shout as the lights turn on. I jump with excitement and squeal with joy. I can't believe it; they threw a surprise birthday party for me. I'm not a fan of surprises, especially the ones where people jump out at you. However, I'm thrilled that they went out of their way for me.

"Happy twenty-first birthday, baby." Darren wraps his arms around me.

"Did you do this?" I look at him and smile.

"No, this was all Melissa." He points at Melissa as she walks up. "You can be mad at her. I tried to tell her you don't like surprises," he winks at me.

"Really? Shut up! You said you didn't want me throwing her a surprise party, because you had your own surprise. And you didn't want my surprise to outshine yours." Melissa rolls her eyes at Darren, then smiles at me. Melissa doesn't like Darren at all. She tells me all the time that I can do better than the khaki wearing prep schoolboy. I ignore her because what best friend approves of her best friend's boyfriend?

"I should have known." I laugh and squeeze her around the neck, trying to defuse the tension between Darren and Melissa.

"Hey, I hate to break this up, but some of us are starving. What? Did you two take the scenic route here?" Melissa's father asks.

"Stop it, Al." Melissa's mom, Patti, slaps her husband on the shoulder. "Here sweetie, your first legal alcoholic drink." Patti hands me a martini and guides me over to the table. Over the last two years, I have come to see Melissa's parents as my own. They welcomed me into their big family with open arms. Melissa's dad, Al, talks loud and sounds grumpy most of the time, but he really is a sweetheart that gives great hugs. Patti reminds me a lot of my mom and has shown me nothing but love and kindness. Not to mention, she is one hell of a cook. I'm surprised I haven't gained a ton of weight from devouring her cooking every chance I get.

We feast for hours on some of the best Italian food the Bronx has to offer. Tonight, my heart is completely full for the first time in over two years. I'm truly blessed to have each one of these people in my life, but it makes me miss my family even more. The past two years have been rough, being so far from home. I jumped headfirst into a scary and unfamiliar world, but each person at this table helped to make the city that never sleeps a little less scary. With all the joy I feel in my heart right now, I'd love nothing more than to be with my family back on pack land. However, the thought of being back on pack land ties my stomach into knots of anxiety. As much as I miss my family, I'm not looking forward to dealing with *him*.

After dinner, we make our way from the private dining room up the stairs to the bar. Where Melissa insists I wear a sash that reads, 'Buy me a drink, I'm twenty-one', and a crown that has twenty-one in cheap plastic jewels that lights up. It's completely cheesy but hilarious, so of course I go along and wear it. This fits so well with Melissa and her family's larger-than-life personalities. We drink, dance, and laugh. The shots and drinks from complete strangers are flowing. I'm having so much fun.

"Excuse me, ma'am, can I buy you a drink?" I'm tapped on the shoulder and a familiar voice fills my ear. I turn and come face to face with my brother.

"Kelsey!" I scream and leap into his arms. I squeeze him so tight around his neck, I'm sure I'm cutting his oxygen off. "You're here?" I pull away, holding his arms and taking him in before pulling him in for another tight squeeze. I don't want to let him go. My brother is here in the flesh, and I feel like I'm floating on cloud nine. My heart is overflowing with love that I think it might burst. Is this the surprise Darren was talking about? I pull back from the hug again and look at my brother. Since I've been gone, Kelsey has aged some... looks more mature since the last time I saw him... taller too, I think. I can't believe how much he looks like our dad.

"Of course I am. Do you think I'd miss my baby sister's twenty-first birthday?" He brushes the hair out of my face. "I didn't come alone, though. I'd like to introduce you to someone special. This is Sonia, my m... fiancée." Sonia steps into view and I let out a breath, thanking Goddess it wasn't someone else.

"Hi," I hug her. She's tall like me, with a slender build. She is so beautiful, with red hair and porcelain skin. Her smile is so infectious that it can light up the room. Kelsey is a lucky fella.

"Don't be pissed..." Kelsey's face turns serious as he grabs my arm and whispers in my ear. I look at him with a confused look. *What does he mean by that?* He steps aside without letting go of my arm. Suddenly, I'm staring into a familiar set of eyes. Eyes that I never wanted to see again, because they're attached to the man who ripped my heart out and stomped it to death two and a half years ago. *What the hell is he doing here?* I understand why Kelsey is still holding my arm. He's keeping me from running away.

I take slow and shallow breaths. My heart races as I fight back emotions. I stand frozen in place, not too sure how to handle this situation. I've thought many times about what I'd say to him when I saw him again, but every scenario ended with me running away, unable to face the man who hurt me so badly.

Our eyes stay locked on to each other's as he steps forward from the shadows of the dimly lit bar. When his smiling face comes into the light, his fresh scent hits my nose and I'm transported back to happier times with him. He takes his place beside me, across from my brother, who still has a firm grip on my arm. Sonia is standing in front of me with her arm wrapped around Kelsey.

"Hi, angel." He places a gentle kiss on my cheek, and I swear there is the tiniest spark there. *How can that be?* I rejected him; the bond is severed.

"Ian," I gulp and say with a quivering voice. After so much time apart, he still makes my heart skip a beat. Ian slips his hand under my elbow and Kelsey releases my other arm. Ian's hand is rougher than the last time he touched me, but his touch is still gentle. I look down at my elbow in his hand and back into his eyes. The familiar haze of the mate bond fills my mind, and the world disappears.

"I missed you, angel." He closes the space between us and leans down into my neck. His warm breath teases my skin, and I instantly want more.

Someone bumps into me from behind, breaking the haze and jolting me back to reality. I pull my elbow from his hand before I completely lose control of my mind and body. "Where's Zane?" I clear my throat and hold my head high. Ian can't know how much he still affects me. "Where there's one, the other two are usually around." I purse my lips, looking at my brother. Ian snorts under his breath. He's either disapproving of me removing my elbow from his hand or he knows exactly the effects he still has on me. I know one thing, any buzz I had going on is long gone.

"Home. Rebeka's parents came down to spend time with the twins." Kelsey smiles at me apologetically.

"Oh, how old are they now?" I steady my gaze on my brother, not paying attention to Ian. Although I can feel his stare burning into my skin.

"Sophia and Carina will be three in four months." Kelsey wraps his arm around Sonia's waist, glancing at Ian.

"Three already?" I'm taken aback.

"You've been gone far too long, angel." Ian whispers in my ear. "Can we talk privately, please? I have a gift for you." The sweet smell of whiskey lingers on his lips.

"Hey, babe." Darren puts a drink in front of my face from behind. "I brought you another drink. Can't let the birthday girl go without a drink in hand. Who are your friends?" He pushes his body into mine as if he is making his claim.

"Thanks... babe." I side glance at Ian, then take the drink from Darren's hand. "Guys, this is my boyfriend, Darren." I take a sip and wait for the ball to drop.

"Babe..." Kelsey laughs.

"Boyfriend?" Ian growls.

"Well," Kelsey clears his throat, "Darren, I'm Kelsey. Kate's older brother." He extends his hand to Darren.

"Nice to meet you... wow, that's some grip you have there." Darren pulls his hand from Kelsey's grip.

"I'm Ian. Kate and I go way back. She was the girl next door." Ian shakes Darren's hand.

"Nice to meet... ouch. Wow, you have quite the grip too." Darren stutters. His free hand moves to my hip. Ian's eyes glance down to where Darren's hand is resting, and a low growl escapes his lips.

"Yeah... sorry about that. We workout daily." Ian looks at Darren's face, offering him a fake smile. The tension between Darren and Ian is so thick you can cut it with a knife. The only thing separating the two men is me... literally, my body is the divider between the two. *Great!*

"Hey! This is a party! Shots on me!" Kelsey shouts.

I walk into the diner and immediately see my brother, Sonia, and Ian sitting in a booth. Of course, the only place to sit is right next to Ian. *Great!* Annoyed, I slide into the booth next to Ian.

"Look who's finally here. The birthday girl herself. Don't tell me you got drunk last night?" Kelsey says, waving the waitress over.

"I can't get a hold of Darren this morning." The waitress pours me a cup of coffee then walks away, "is he alive?" I bring the cup up to my lips.

"He was, when my men dropped him off at his place." Ian laughs and puts his hand on my thigh.

"Poor guy can't handle his liquor, can he? Whatever do you see in him, Kate?" Kelsey laughs.

"He doesn't have the same metabolism as us." I pick up Ian's hand and drop it in his lap without looking at him. "What you did, jackass, wasn't fair." I snap at Kelsey. Werewolves have such high metabolisms that it is almost impossible for us to get drunk. I mean, we can, but the amount of alcohol it takes would kill a human. Last night Kelsey bought Darren shot after shot, and like an idiot, Darren didn't say no. The only thing that stopped him from drinking was the floor when he passed out. That's when Ian had a couple warriors load him up in their SUV and take him home.

"Do you love him?" Ian asks, rubbing the back of his hand along my arm.

"What difference is it to you? You lost the right to be concerned with my personal life years ago." I snap and pull away from him. I'm annoyed at him, but unlike before, I'm not afraid to show him my anger.

"I am your personal life, in case you forgot." He leans in and whispers in my ear. The waitress puts four plates of greasy eggs, bacon, pancakes, and hash browns in front of us.

"I hope you don't mind, little sister. I took the liberty of ordering your food, too." Kelsey speaks up.

"Thank you, Kelsey." I turn to look at the waitress, "thank you, it looks delicious." I say in an attempt to distract myself from Ian.

"You're welcome, sweetie, but you can be honest with me. It looks greasy as hell, and will sit in your gut like a brick for hours. Probably clogging your arteries just looking at it." She lets out a husky laugh. "Let me know if you need anything else, sweetie." She refreshes our coffee, then walks away.

"No, you're not my personal life. I rejected your cheating and lying ass in case you forgot." I snap. "Thanks for breakfast, brother, but suddenly I'm not hungry." I stand to leave.

"Wait, wait... I'm supposed to take you dress shopping. If I don't, your mom is going to kill me," Sonia squeezes over Kelsey's lap.

CHAPTER THREE

WE NEED TO TALK

March 2004

Kate

IT'S BEEN A WEEK since my birthday. Kelsey, Sonia, and Ian returned home a few days ago with the dress that my parents bought me for the wedding. I enjoyed spending the afternoon with her. She is sweet and funny. She never asked what happened between Ian and me, and I'm so thankful for that. We meet up with Melissa for a late lunch and drinks. Sonia and Melissa get along great. What's not to love about Melissa, though? She has an enormous heart with a personality that is larger than life. I wish I could tell Melissa about who I really am and where I come from, but by law, I can't. We can't tell humans about our existence, and for good reasons. We are a hunted species by some humans, and if others found out about us, we'd be handed over to the scientific community. There's no telling what experiments they'd do to us in the name of science.

This week has been crazy at school. It's finals and then the end of the spring semester. Being an art major, you'd think my course of study would be easy, but no. Dad says it's a bullshit degree that won't get me a job in the real world. Maybe he's right, but I don't care. I love art and the bullshit degree that I'm getting. Tomorrow, Darren is taking me out on his sailboat, but tonight belongs to me.

By the time I make it home with my Chinese takeout in my hands, it's well after dark. After the incident with the takeout the last time, I thought my food would be safer if I picked it up. I'm exhausted from school and the emotional rollercoaster I've been on since Ian showed up here. All I want to do is soak in a hot bath, slip on my jammies, then get into a good book. My apartment is dark, and I don't turn on any lights. I see just fine in the dark. I put my bag and food down on my kitchen table, then walk into the bathroom and draw a tub of water.

After pouring myself a glass of wine and grabbing my book, I head back to the bathroom. Undress, then add a bath bomb to the water before slipping into the tub. The bath bomb bounces, bobs, and swirls in the water, releasing oils and fragrance. I sip my wine and read my book, but I can't concentrate long enough to get drawn into it. I keep thinking about my trip home in a few weeks, and how Ian showed up here. What is waiting for me when I go home? Did I feel the tingles of the mate bond? They were so light, but I swear they were there. Surely not. That bond was severed years ago. I soak in the tub until the water is too cold and my wine glass is empty. I let the water out, watching as the last bit of water swirls down the drain, then I stand and rinse off.

After I dress, I head to the kitchen to fill my wine glass and grab my takeout, but something is off. I'm sensing a presence that wasn't here before. *Shit!* Someone is in my apartment. I stand still, letting my wolf control my senses. I listen, then sniff the air. There's something so familiar in the air. Something that calls to me… luring me closer.

"How did you get in here, Ian?" I turn and see Ian's figure sitting in a chair in the living room.

"I was wondering how long it was going to take you to sense me." He speaks but doesn't move.

"How did you…" Ian interrupts.

"You should lock your balcony door. The security in this building is shit. I figured you'd be in a better place with daddy's money." His voice is low and husky while his alluring scent is filling my lungs as I breathe.

"You need to leave." I demand.

"We need to talk, angel." Ian adjusts in his seat.

"We have nothing we need to talk about." I snarl.

"That's where you're wrong, angel." Ian chuckles under his breath.

"Don't call me that. Angel died a long time ago. Every woman you screwed behind my back murdered her." I shift from one foot to the other. I'm angry that he has the nerve to show up here and to use a pet name he had for me. The woman I was two and a half years ago would have just backed down and let him sweet talk his way back into her bed. But not this woman. This woman wants him gone… to be rid of him once and for all.

"What would you like me to call you?" His tone is soft, reminding me of when he helped me shift.

"Nothing. Please leave." I point to the door.

"Do you love him?" Ian questions.

"What? Who?" I'm confused by his question.

"Your boyfriend, Darren. Do you love him?" Ian stands.

"What difference does that make to you?" My voice shakes as I watch him stalk slowly to me.

"The fact that you can't answer that question speaks volumes." Ian stands directly in front of me.

"Please go." I beg, not too sure how long I can fight the pull of the mate bond. It's almost like he's a drug and I'm a junkie seeking my next high.

"There it is," he brushes the hair away from my neck. "My mark is still there. It's faded, but it's still there. Just like yours." He pulls his tee-shirt over his head, showing me his neck.

I lightly gasp at the sight of his bare chest. His muscles are more sculpted now. He looks more like a man than the boy I rejected and walked away from. His chest and arms are broad and well defined. I want to reach out and touch his perfectly sculpted abs. My eyes follow from his abs to the V that dips into his pants. His body is sculpted to perfection, and I can't take my eyes off it. "See something you like?" He chuckles and closes the gap between us.

"Please..." I step back.

"I'll do anything for you, Kate." He begs and steps forward.

"Go..." I step back.

"Except that. I need you. Please." He steps forward.

"I can't." I step back again. The closer he gets, the stronger the pull of the mate bond becomes. I'm fighting the pull, but the haze is creeping into my mind.

"Why? Because of the frat boy who can't hold his liquor?" Ian steps forward and his scent fills my nose.

"Not because of him." I back into the wall. *I'm trapped.* My hands are at my side with my palms flat against the wall.

"Then why?" Ian closes in on me, resting his hands on either side of my head.

"Because I can't handle you causing me any more pain." Tears fill my eyes.

"Oh, angel." He presses his body into mine. "I'm here begging you for one last chance. I'm a changed man. Let me prove it to you. You are the only woman for me. You're the only one I want to wake up to in the morning and the last thing I taste at night." He brushes his cheek against mine. "Let me prove it to you… please," he whispers in my ear, then kisses my neck.

I hate how much I'm enjoying feeling his body pressed up against mine and how it's responding to his lips. My mind is screaming stop, but my body is begging for more. A haze of lust fills my mind, and any rational thoughts are gone. I move my head to the side, giving him more room. My body takes over, moving on its own accord. A soft moan leaves my lips as Ian's tongue trails up and down my neck, then up to my jaw. He kisses his way to my lips, and instinctively I kiss him back. Something inside me wakes up for the first time in years. Something primal, and craving the taste of his lips. I open my mouth, welcoming him to explore every inch. Our tongues collide and dance together.

"I've missed you, angel," he whispers into my mouth before taking it again for a deep and passionate kiss. No man has ever kissed me the way he does. He is the only man that can make my body purr with ecstasy. I would be lying if I said that I didn't miss him, too. "I want to taste you; it's been too long and I'm starving." He pulls my top over my head, tossing it to the ground. My breasts are on full display for him. "Mmmm..." he groans out before taking one of my hard, erect nipples into his mouth. I moan and fist his hair as he takes his time and savoring the taste of my flesh. His tongue swirls circles around my nipple while his teeth nibbles, before switching to my other breast. "Can I please taste you, angel?" I pause. My mind screams no, but I can't form the words. I can't deny him what we both want, and he knows it.

"Please," I whisper and nod my head. He drops to his knees and pulls my panties down, slipping them into his pocket.

"Mmmmm," he lets out a low growl, running his nose along my slit, taking in my scent. He puts one leg over his shoulder and runs his tongue along my slit. I gasp and throw my head back, moaning. His tongue works its way through my core's lips and into my core, moving in, out, up and down. Devouring me like a starving man. He moans and groans as his tongue moves up to my nub. His lips latch on to my nub, sucking and licking vigorously. I rock my hips grinding my core on his face, "that's right, angel, ride my face."

Fisting his hair, I shove his face hard into my core. I don't want to hear him speak, just the sounds of him sucking and licking me. He slips two fingers inside me and massages my sweet spot. I ride his face and fingers hard, moaning loudly. It feels so good, I can't get enough. Pressure builds and my core pulsates. Soon, I explode from a powerful orgasm that overtakes my entire body. I tremble as the waves of my climax roll over my body.

Ian stands, allowing my exhausted body to rest against his. "Such a good girl. Let's get you to bed so you can rest." He picks up my limp body and carries me to bed, laying me down gently, then covering me. "You rest, angel. I've got some things that I need to take care of. Don't worry, I'll lock up on my way out." He kisses me before walking out of my bedroom.

Chapter Four

IAN'S GIFT

May 1999

Kate

"Jessi, I'm kinda freaking out." I flat iron my hair.

"Oh my gosh, Kate. If Ian finds his mate today, then you know it wasn't meant to be." Jessi applies her lip gloss.

"Jessi, if he finds his mate today, I'm going to die. DIE!" I put the straight iron down and clinch my heart overdramatically and gasp. "I could never love anyone else."

"You're so dramatic." She laughs and throws her lip gloss at me. Jessi and I have been friends since the first grade. We know each other like the back of our hands. Jessi's dad is a warrior, and her mom is a nurse, and she is a spoiled only child. "Ya know, even if you're not mates, you can still use him for his hot bod." She wiggles her eyebrows at me.

"Oh, my goodness, don't be gross." I throw her lip gloss back at her.

"Don't be a prude. It's just sex. You're sixteen and he's eighteen. What's the big deal?" She stands and adjusts her very short leather miniskirt. Even though Jessi and I are very close, sex is the one thing we don't agree on. She has been sexually active for a year now and always has a new and hot boyfriend. Many of the girls in our pack are very experienced... sexually, and that's fine for them. I'm still very much a virgin. That's the way I plan to keep it, too. I want to wait for my mate, even though I'm sure he's not waiting for me. That's something that Jessi constantly points out. She is always asking why wait, you know he's not. But to me, my virginity feels like a gift that I only want to share with someone who was made for me. Maybe I read too many romance books and they've made me some hopeless romantic, but I'm fine with that.

Standing next to Jessi, I take a long look at myself in the mirror. I love my floral pink babydoll dress. It makes me look more like a woman and less like a little girl. It has a deep plunging neckline with a tie front, hugs my waist and hips, then flares out. Yes, it's short, but not nearly as short as Jessi's skirt. My dad had a fit when I came home after shopping for it. He hated the fact that he could see cleavage and that it was short. Luckily, mom intervened. Whatever she said to him worked, and he allowed me to keep the dress for Ian's eighteenth birthday party.

Ian is the son of our pack's Beta; therefore, a gigantic party was planned for him. Turning eighteen in our culture is huge. We meet our wolves and shift for the first time, it's also when we can feel the pull of the mate bond. Everyone usually gets a party of some sort for their eighteenth birthday, but those of us who are ranked... it gets made into a pack affair. Many other unmated females from other packs will be in attendance as well, hoping he will be their mate. I hope he doesn't find his mate; I really want it to be me. Since I'm only sixteen, I won't feel the mate bond for another two years. It's going to be a torturous two years.

"Girls!" My Dad shouts from downstairs, "We need to get going, put it into high gear!" I grab Ian's gift and head downstairs with Jessi in tow. Waiting for us at the bottom of the staircase are my parents. Mom's face is glowing with pride as we descend the stairs... dad looks like he's constipated or something painful like that.

"Shit," dad mumbles under his breath, triggering an elbow to his side from mom.

"Kate, you're simply breathtaking. Where did my little girl go?" She rubs my arms lovingly with her hands. "Jessi... you look... beautiful," mom squeaks out. I can tell she is not a fan of Jessi's outfit of choice, but my mom is so sweet and wants to make everyone feel loved.

"Beautiful, sugar." Dad pulls me into a hug. "I'm going to have to fucking kill someone tonight." He mumbles under his breath. Mom gives him the side eye and dad calms down. He releases me and steps to the side, taking a last look at himself in the large mirror in the living room.

I find myself looking into the most exquisite brown eyes. Ian. He is dressed in a black form fitting suit, my cheeks flush at the sight of him. The fresh scent from his signature cologne is intoxicating. I wasn't expecting Ian to be here, but I guess he, my brother, and Zane want to make their grand entrance together, just like they did at Zane's eighteenth birthday party last month.

"Wow, Kate..." Ian puts his hand on his chest and breathes out.

"Bro... that's my sister." Kelsey snarls.

"I guess this is where the body count starts." Dad mumbles, causing another side eye look from mom.

"We need to get going. I need to do a final security sweep before too many guests arrive." Dad says, looking at mom.

"The girls can ride with us... if you're in a hurry. We have the Alpha's six-seater golf cart." Ian looks between my mom and dad.

"Yeah, it's really no big deal. My father told me to take the big golf cart in case you were too busy to give the girls a ride. Actually, if anyone needed a ride. If we take the girls, we'll be full and can go straight to the party." Zane, our pack's future Alpha, says with authority. My dad looks intently between Zane and Ian. My guess is he is trying to detect an ulterior motive.

"Okay," Mom breaks the silence. "Um, girls, can you ride in the golf cart with the boys, so we can get going now?" Mom looks between Jessi and me. My heart just about jumps out of my chest at her suggestion, but I play it cool.

"Yeah... I guess." I sigh out as if I'm annoyed.

"Good, thank you, sugar." Mom pats my arm before turning her attention to Ian. "Oh, Ian, I almost forgot. This is for you, from us." Mom hands Ian a small box that was beautifully wrapped by her. Mom has such a talent for wrapping gifts, she has a workspace dedicated to it. She has all kinds of different wrapping papers, ribbons, and trinkets to put on each gift. She wrapped Ian's gift with a simple yet elegant paper. He rips into the paper and into the small box containing cufflinks with his initials. "Every man should have a beautiful pair of cufflinks." She smiles and pats his cheek.

"Thank you so much. I love them." Ian gushes over his gift.

"Bro, we match." Zane shows Ian his cufflinks. My parents leave for the party, and I watch as Zane helps Ian put his cufflinks on. I can't take my eyes off Ian. He is so beautifully built. After they finish with Ian's cufflinks, Jessi nudges me with her shoulder, almost knocking me off balance. Ian takes notice of the interaction between the two of us, then turns his attention to me.

"Hey, Kelsey..." Jessi makes her way to my brother. If you ask me, she has always had a little crush on him.

"Oh... um, this is for you. It's silly really, I made it." I nervously hand him a badly wrapped gift, compared to mom's. He enthusiastically takes it from my shaking hands and rips into it. "It's a paracord bracelet."

"I love it, Kate. Thank you. Help me put it on?" Ian flashes me a smile that instantly melts my heart.

"Now? But you're wearing a suit. This doesn't go with it." I protest, tilting my head at him.

"It goes with everything." He smiles and hands me the bracelet, pulling the sleeve of his shirt up. With trembling hands, I put the simple two-row black paracord bracelet around his wrist and clasp it shut. I look up at his face and smile. He cups both of my hands in his and holds them, rubbing my knuckles with his thumbs. "Thank you for making the bracelet for me. It was so sweet of you. You really are an angel on earth." He makes my heart race and my knees weak.

CHAPTER FIVE

MARRY ME KATE

March 2004

Kate

"EARTH TO KATE." DARREN stands in front of me with a glass of wine in each hand. He sits on the lounger next to mine and hands me a glass. "Where did you go?"

"What?" I sip my wine.

"You looked like you were a thousand miles from here. What were you thinking about?" He sips his wine.

"Oh, nothing really." I lie, "I was just enjoying the fresh ocean air, the sunshine, and the rocking of the boat. And I was thinking about my friend Jessi from back home. The time we went sailing like this with her family. She's due with her first child any day now." I smile, hoping that he doesn't know that I'm not being one-hundred percent honest with him.

"Well, you'll get to see her next week." He studies my face.

"Maybe... she lives two-hours from where we grew up, and with a new baby, I don't expect her to be at the wedding. Maybe, I'll make a special trip to go see her. I haven't met her... husband yet." I sip my wine and watch the seagulls in the distance.

"You should." He rubs my leg. "I have missed you this week. I'm sorry for that, but I was hungover for three days straight. How the hell does your brother drink so much?" Darren laughs.

"My entire family is like that. I think it has something to do with our metabolism... or something like that." I smile and nod.

"Are you sure you don't want me to go with you?" He questions while sipping his wine.

"I'll be there for a month... and you already know how conservative my parents are. They'd never approve of me bringing a boyfriend home." I smile, trying to avoid this conversation yet again. I haven't told Darren about me being a werewolf. Honestly, I'm not too sure how he'd take it. There are no rules about having a human as a mate, but there are laws forbidding us from telling humans about our existence. The few humans that know of our existence are sworn to secrecy. I'm not too sure if we are to a point in our relationship for me to tell him my biggest secret.

"I don't have to stay for the month. I could come down on the weekends, or every other weekend." He removes his hand from my leg.

I give him a sideways look and sigh out. "Conservative parents..." I say in a low tone that begs him to drop the subject.

"So, they'd be against a boyfriend..." he digs in his pocket. "What about a fiancé?" He holds up a single stone diamond engagement ring. "Marry me, Kate." I sit up straight and gasp, staring at the ring. My heart pounds, my palms get sweaty, and my breathing is fast-paced. I can't believe this is happening. "Careful, you'll hyperventilate." Darren leans into me, putting his hand on my thigh.

"This is happening so fast." I look at his hand on my thigh, oddly his touch doesn't ignite a fire inside me like Ian's touch does. I'm confused and terrified. Shouldn't I be excited right now? But I'm not. What is wrong with me? I'm terrified of making the wrong choice and getting my heart broken again. "Darren, we've only been together for three months. Don't you think this is moving too fast?" I breathe in deeply, blowing it out slowly.

"Yes... I think we're moving fast, but Kate, I love you. You'll make the perfect-looking wife. I want to spend the rest of my life with you."

"I... need more time." I look down. Two weeks ago, I would have jumped at the chance to marry Darren, but now I'm not too sure. He is perfect. Comes from a well-off family, has a wonderful career, and he treats me well, but I still have doubts. Will I ever be able to tell him the truth about me? How do I handle the pup situation? Werewolves only carry for six-months, where humans carry for nine. Wouldn't he have questions about that? Our pups will have to know who they are before their first shift. Marrying him means continuing to live away from my parents and the pack. Is that something I'm willing to give up? Then there's Ian. Him being here has confused me so much. He broke my heart, but what we did last night... the way his touch ignites a fire with in me. I'm not sure Darren can ever make me feel that way. But have I given him a fair chance? My mind swirls with a million more questions and my chest is tight. I feel a panic attack coming on and all I want is to get off this freaking boat.

"Hey... relax. How about you give the ring a test drive? When you get back from visiting your family, we can talk more about it. Who knows, maybe being apart for a little bit will make your heart grow fonder." He slides the ring onto my hand.

"I don't feel good. Must have been something I ate. Can we head in now?" I'm nauseous and am feeling light-headed. This is definitely not the way a newly engaged woman should feel.

Soaking in the tub, I stare at the diamond ring on my left hand, playing back the events of yesterday, and earlier when Darren asked me to marry him. His words keep playing on a loop in my mind. You'll make the perfect-looking wife. What the hell is that supposed to mean? Like his status in life depends on appearance, and I have the correct look... or I'm trainable to fit the role? I don't want to just look the part; he can hire a hooker or actress to play the part of wife if that's all he's looking for. I want to feel a lifetime of passion and I want my husband to woo me until death. I don't want to be some trophy wife that he keeps on the shelf, pulling her down when he needs to parade her at some gala event.

"Damn..." Ian whistles as he strolls into the bathroom.

"What are you doing here, and how do you keep getting into my apartment?" I snap and shake my head.

"I found your spare key last night." He waves a bottle of wine at me.

"Remind me to change my locks." I lift my glass and he fills it.

"What's that?" He points to Darren's ring on my left hand.

"I'm engaged." I say in a monotone voice, staring at the wall in front of me.

"Wow, you sound so excited about it." Ian says sarcastically.

"Yeah... Ian, about what happened last night." I look at him.

"It was fucking amazing." He kneels beside the tub.

"It can never happen again. I'm serious. We are through." My voice shakes. As the words come out of my mouth, doubt sets up in my head. Will we ever truly be through?

"Your body tells me something different. I can smell how much you want me." His fingers play in the water.

"I want you to listen to what my mouth is telling you." I sit up and look at him.

"Hurry, dinner is getting cold." He walks out of the bathroom. *Why won't he listen to me?*

I finish up in the bathroom and slip into a light sundress. I walk into the living room and see Ian unpacking food containers onto the table. He insists on being a part of my life and I am annoyed that he won't listen to me. I sit on the couch and rub my head.

"You want me to bring the food to you?" Ian asks from the kitchen.

"No... I'm not hungry. We need to talk." I turn and look at him.

"Ok," he pops a cucumber into his mouth and walks over to me. "I'm at your service, my love," he sits down close to me. Having him this close to me is making my body buzz. If I don't put some space between us, I'm afraid we'll have a repeat of last night, so I slide away from him. He chuckles under his breath. "What do you want to talk about?"

"I'm going to marry Darren." I say as a matter of fact.

"No, you're not," Ian laughs and leans back.

"Don't tell me what I am or am not going to do." I growl, getting tired of his arrogant attitude.

"Look," he slides closer, "I know you haven't let him touch you, past a kiss. If you wanted him, you would have let him by now." He puts his hand on my thigh. "Frat boy will never make you feel like I do." He runs his fingers up and down my thigh. I can feel the slightest trace of a tingle, so faint, but it's there. A primal feeling arises in me, the need for him to touch my entire body. I fight the need to touch him back. My heart races with excitement as the lust haze takes over my mind. "I can smell your arousal. I know you want me too." He grabs the back of my neck, bringing me in for a hungry and demanding kiss. We both moan as our tongues dance and explore each other's mouths. There's something about his kiss, almost like his lips are laced with some sort of magical potion that makes me crave more of him. He pulls away and I'm lost and saddened at the sudden loss of his touch. "You want me? Come get me." He leans back on the couch and pats his lap. It's like I'm under some sort of spell. I leap onto his lap as if he has an invisible rope that is pulling me to him. My body has a mind of its own and my mind is no longer in control. "Such a good girl." Ian's voice is low, sultry, and sexy. Everything about him is beautiful and sexy, and I can't get enough.

I attack his mouth with mine, taking control. I suck his lips and his tongue, moaning into his mouth. He massages my ass with his hands, moving my hips and grinding his hard member into my wet entrance. The light tingles turn into electric currents that race through my veins and straight to my core. I'm so wet for him. He kisses and nips my neck; then pulls my sundress down, exposing my breasts. "Mmmm, so fucking perfect," Ian moans. He massages both breasts with his hands as he takes each nipple in his mouth, one at a time. "Mine," he growls.

"Yes, Ian. Yes, like that..." I moan as he bites down on my nipple. It feels so good, and my core is throbbing for him to be inside.

"WHAT THE HELL IS GOING ON HERE!" I hear Darren shout from the doorway. I gasp and look up to see him standing there with flowers and wine in his hand. "What the fuck, Kate, you fucking slut!" The flowers and wine slip from his hands, hitting the floor. I scream, jumping from Ian's lap quickly covering my bare breasts. Ian jumps to his feet with a wall shaking growl and rushes to Darren.

"No one calls her that!" Ian shoves Darren's shoulder.

"Oh yeah? What are you going to do about it? Huh?" Darren pushes his chest into Ian's.

"Back off, frat boy, you don't want any of this." Ian shoves Darren back. Darren is furious. He pulls back his right arm and swings towards Ian's face. Ian grabs Darren's fist midair and pushes it back to him, squeezing Darren's balled up fist with his hand. "What did I tell you?"

"Stop it! Stop it!" I run in between the two men, separating them. I put my back into Ian's body, using my hands as I release Darren's fist from Ian's grip. With my hands, I push Darren back.

"I knew it! He's why you've been distant lately and why you weren't excited when I asked you to marry me. One hundred women would kill to have a chance with me, but you... you're fucking some gym bro behind my back." Darren is red faced and full of rage, shouting and pointing at my face.

"Like she's the only one with a side piece." Ian laughs.

"Fuck you, man," Darren steps closer.

"Nah, man, you're not my type." Ian continues to laugh while I push him back with my body.

"Yo bro, you see whose body she's pressed into right now?" Ian laughs. Darren's angry eyes move from Ian to me. I have never seen him so angry before. This is a side I've never known of Darren, and it's a little more than scary.

"What's the matter, Kate? Afraid I'm going to hurt your boyfriend?" Darren snarls and snaps at my face.

"No. I'm afraid he'll kill you." I regret my words as soon as they leave my mouth.

"Wow!" Darren runs his hands through his hair. "That's probably the most fucked up thing you could say to me."

"I didn't mean it like that." I shout through tears. If he knew the truth about us, he'd understand that naturally Ian has the upper hand in a fight.

"Fuck it, I'm out. Have fun." Darren runs out of my apartment and down the hall. I notice several neighbors are now in the hallway watching the scene unfold.

"Let him go," Ian whispers in my ear, cupping my shoulders and bringing my body close to his.

"No Ian. This stops now!" I spin and face him. "I ran away from my home because of you. The fear of running into you has prevented me from seeing my family for over two and a half years. I ran far away to free me from the chains that bind me to you." The crowd outside my door grows, but I don't care. He needs to hear this. "You broke my heart every time you stuck your dick into another woman. I gave you my life, my love, and my virginity." I wipe the tears from my eyes. "You were my world since I was fourteen. You caused me physical pain with every woman you screwed. I was suffering because of you." I poke him in the chest. "You made promises you couldn't keep. In the end, you couldn't control your dick, so I rejected you and fled the fucking state, Ian. Now two... almost three years later, you waltz back into my life, confusing the shit out of me and flipping my world upside down. You need to go. I don't want to see you anymore." I shove him towards the door, then collapse to the floor in a crying mess.

"Fuck..." I hear him say before he walks away, slamming the door behind him.

I sit on the floor and sob. What have I done? I was finally ready to move on, to allow someone to love me like I deserve. Now? Now everything is a colossal mess, all because of my selfish feelings and cravings. I've hurt Darren in a way I never wanted to hurt anyone, causing him to feel the same pain I did. I've messed up my life. It's my fault. Worst of all, this time I'm the cheater.

Chapter Six

I DON'T WANT TO SEE YOU

March 2004

Ian

"IAN, PACK AN OVERNIGHT bag. We're leaving for New York in an hour." Kelsey says while I wipe the sweat from my face.

Today I trained extra hard, first with weights, then combat training with Zane. I'm over working my body and I know it. I can't help it; my body has been so numb lately since the spontaneous heartburn began three months ago. I'm not positive, but I think it's related to Kate finding someone else after all these years. I feel her getting closer to someone else. I don't think sex is involved because it's not the same pain she described to me. Knowing that there is someone else is driving me insane.

"What? Why are we going to New York?" I question, looking between Zane and Kelsey.

"Do you know what today is?" Kelsey hands Zane and me water.

Do I know what today is? Of course, I do. How could I forget Kate's birthday? How could I forget Kate? She consumes my thoughts and my dreams. She is the one that I drove away with my actions.

"Yeah man, Kate's birthday." I put my head down in defeat.

"Her friend, Melissa, is throwing her a surprise party, and I got an invite." Kelsey crosses his arms and smiles at Zane.

"YOU... you got the invite, not me." I shake my head. Kate has made it abundantly clear she wants nothing to do with me.

"Hey man, I think it's time you and Kate have a conversation. The heartburn is getting more frequent. Somehow, someway, you and Kate are still bound together. She'll feel it if you're in the same room together. Show her how much you've changed since she's been gone." Zane's words and tone are softer than the future Alpha normally is. Maybe he is right, maybe I just need to go talk to her.

"You coming?" I ask Zane.

"Sorry bro, Kelsey is your wingman on this mission. In-laws are coming into town." Zane pats my back.

Kelsey, Sonia, and I arrive in New York City to surprise Kate for her twenty-first birthday, since she won't come home to celebrate it with us. I might look calm and put together on the outside, but on the inside I'm a ball of fucking nerves. Her friend Melissa contacted Kelsey a few weeks ago and invited him to a surprise birthday party for Kate. Apparently, Kate gave Kelsey's name as an emergency contact when she enrolled at the university, and Melissa was able to get his information from a friend of a friend, as she put it. Kelsey told Melissa he wouldn't miss his baby sister's birthday for the world, and that we wouldn't be there in time for dinner, so we'd meet them in the bar upstairs from the restaurant.

We arrive earlier than expected and decide to head to the bar and order food there. Actually, Ian's mate, Sonia, was starving and decided for us. She's normally very sweet and quiet until she gets hungry and if she isn't fed immediately, she turns into a raging, screaming banshee. It's funny, watching Kelsey cater to his mate; hungry or otherwise. He has changed so much in the year they have been together. Watching him and Zane with their mates makes me wish I hadn't royally fucked things up so badly with Kate.

"Man, that Kate of yours is a fine piece of ass. I bet she rocks your socks off in the bed." I overhear one man say to the other while Kelsey and I wait at the bar for a table while Sonia visits the lady's room.

"I wouldn't know. I've had to work extra hard for it." The second man laughs.

"You mean you two haven't?" The first man makes some sort of hand gesture out of my line of sight.

"Nope... get this. She's still a virgin. Comes from a very conservative family down south. She's saving herself for marriage." At first, I don't think they are talking about Kate, but my gut is telling me otherwise. *Why would she say she's a virgin?*

"Damn, seriously... virgin... those are scarce these days. You lucky son of a bitch." The first man punches the second man in the arm, "wait so you haven't gotten laid in three months?"

"I've gotten laid... I see her friend Melissa at least once a week." The second man laughs.

"Yeah, me too. That ass of hers is too irresistible to pass up. So, I guess wedding bells are in your near future?" He finishes the last of his drink. These two remind me of frat boys back in college. They're using women and tossing them aside like Kelsey, Zane, and I used to. They look to be in their late twenties. You'd think these two clowns would have outgrown their womanizing ways by now.

"Hell no. There are too many hot women around that I haven't fucked yet." The second man waves down the bartender.

"Man, do what our dads do. You keep the trophy wife at home and two or three chicks on the side." The first man laughs, then orders another drink. They've learned to treat women this way from their fathers, great fucking role models they are. Anger builds up inside of me at this filthy conversation about Kate between these two pigs.

"My parents say she's not the one, that her family is unknown in the circle, but I have a plan for that virginity of hers." The first man says. Anger turns to rage and I ball my fists at my side. Kelsey is hearing the same conversation and is sensing the rage rise inside me. He puts his hand on my shoulder.

'Calm down. This is not the place.' He mindlinks me. I know he's right. Kate will never forgive me if I attack the frat boy. I need to play this cool.

"Is that a fucking engagement ring?" The second man laughs.

"Yeah, it's just a cheap piece of glass. Just enough for her to believe we have a future together. Once I get what I want... she'll wake up in an empty, blood-stained bed and I'll be long gone." The two men laugh and knuckle bump each other. Kelsey pulls me to a table in the corner where Sonia is waiting for us.

Just before we order our food, I see the frat boys leave the bar quickly. I'm assuming that they're headed to the restaurant downstairs and Kate should walk through the doors at any moment. What feels like hours pass, then I see her. The world slows down as she moves gracefully in slow motion through the bar. She looks more mature and is even more beautiful than she was two and a half years ago. Damn, she's filled out in all the right places. She's wearing thigh-high boots, a black miniskirt, and a pink top. I have always loved her in pink. I'll never forget seeing her on my eighteenth birthday, walking down the stairs in her pink floral dress. It was like she went from a little girl to a woman in a blink of an eye. Her sweet floral scent hit my nose before I saw her, and it was the most intoxicating smell ever. In that moment, I thought she might be my mate, and I confirmed it the moment she put the paracord bracelet on my wrist. I felt the sparks radiate off her fingertips on to my skin. I wanted to kiss her so badly, but she was only sixteen and too young. Looking at her now is a reminder of how badly I messed things up between us.

"Bro, don't worry, frat boy isn't asking her to marry him tonight. I'll make sure of it." Kelsey looks from his sister to me. I hope he's right; I can't lose her forever.

"Kelsey! You're here?" Kate screams as she jumps into her brother's arms. I can only hope she is as excited to see me, but I doubt it. Kelsey moves aside and I step up to her and our eyes meet for the first time in over two and a half years. I see pain in her eyes, but not hate, and I take that as a good sign. I rub her elbow and feel a light spark. This is conformation that the bond isn't completely broken. She looks down at my hand and pulls away from my touch. I'm disappointed with the loss of contact, but I'm sure she felt the spark just like I did... which is why she pulled away. I watch her as she speaks to Kelsey and Sonia, ignoring me. She still feels something for me. It's undeniable.

Frat boy comes over like a jealous pup trying to claim his toy from others. It pisses me off that he's touching her. She is mine. I don't see her reciprocate his actions, and that brings a smile to my face. Her body is stiff, and both her hands are gripping her glass like she's afraid someone will come to steal it from her. I can't help but to wonder if she is always like this with him. Or if it's my presence, that's making her act like this towards him. Kate never had a problem touching me in anyone's presence. We would have been all over each other.

"Shots on me!" Kelsey shouts. So, this is his master plan. We know frat boys and we know they don't turn free drinks down. He's planning on getting frat boy so drunk he'll be shitting himself. Classic Kelsey... fucking bravo, bro. I laugh in my head.

"Bro, I can't go." I look at Kelsey. "I can't leave her." We're at the airport waiting for our flight home.

"Took you long enough." Kelsey bends his Wall Street Journal down to look at me. "Go get your girl and try not to fuck it up any worse than it is."

I race out of the terminal, not sure about my next move. All I know is that I need to get Kate alone so we can talk. I go straight to her apartment, but she is not there. It's the middle of the day, so I figure she's in class. I decide to check into a nearby hotel and wait for an opportunity to talk with her. I laugh at my nervousness about seeing and talking to her. Some male werewolves would just toss their mates over their shoulder and chain them to the bed until their mate listens to reason. Our culture can still be a little barbaric. I'm choosing the more gentlemanly approach. I want her to see that I have changed, that I can be soft and loving, the mate that worships the ground she walks on, the mate that she deserves.

It's been three days that I have watched and waited for Kate to be alone, but she's always with a female or two. Luckily, I haven't seen frat boy at all. I hope we didn't kill the poor bastard. In the diner by her apartment, I overhear two females talk about finals, and I'm guessing finals go for Kate too. I guess she and these other females are studying for tests.

It's late. I'm waiting in the shadows for her to arrive home. I finally see her; her hands are full of bags and some sort of takeout. She walks in her building up the three flights of stairs, then into her apartment. I can see her window from the street. She doesn't turn any lights on, but I can see candles flickering. I see another person with full arms struggle to unlock the outside door, so I offer to help him hold the door as we both make our way into the building. Following her scent up the stairs to her door, I stand there for a moment, not too sure if I should knock or what. I put I put my ear to the door and can hear water running. She must be drawing a bath. She loves a hot soak when she is extremely stressed out. I turn the knob... locked.

I make my way out of the building and look up to her second-floor apartment window. Then I see the balcony door that has curtains hanging out of it. I look around and see that the street is unusually quiet, so I seize the moment and scale the wall up to her balcony. Just as I thought, the door is unlocked. I slip in as quiet as a mouse, trying not to make a sound, and take a seat in a chair in the darkest corner of the living room. Finally, I hear her draining the water from the tub, then turn the shower on. Moments later she walks from the bathroom to the kitchen, and I'm disappointed that she is fully dressed in pj's. She stops dead in her tracks and without moving; she calls me by name. I smile, knowing that my mate is still familiar with my scent.

I can tell my presence annoys her, but she's not screaming or running from her apartment. She knows I won't hurt her. I tell her we need to talk, but she doesn't want to talk. She wants me to leave. I can't leave, not without her hearing me out and remembering the bond we share. Then I see my faded mark on her neck. It's a beautiful sight and something special just between her and I. I take my shirt off to show her mark to her. I know she is feeling the pull of the mate bond, the same as me. One second, she can't take her eyes off me, the next second she is trying to escape.

She backs up against the wall, still fighting the pull. Her voice is strained, and tears fill her eyes. She's afraid I'll break her heart again, but that couldn't be further from the truth. I beg her for another chance, just one chance to prove my worth to her... to prove I can be the mate that she deserves. I close off any distance between us, pressing my body into hers, kissing her neck. Her breathing changes and she tilts her head to the side, giving me more room to run my lips and tongue along her skin. Her body responds to me and my touch. She is not fighting the pull but giving in to it.

We kiss passionately, as if our lives depend on it. I have missed the taste of her lips; and want to taste all of her. I remove her top, exposing her perfectly round breasts. My mouth teases her hard nipples. The smell of her arousal awakens my beast. To claim it as my own, I need to taste her sweet pussy. She gives me permission to taste her and bring her to a place of euphoric ecstasy. I drop to my knees and take her with my mouth. With every stroke of my tongue, I'm claiming her as mine and only mine. As she climbs higher and higher, she takes control riding and grinding her wet pussy onto my face. Her moves are rough and forceful, taking what I alone can give her. Pleasuring her only excites me more, and my cock is rock-hard. She explodes into a screaming orgasm; her body shakes as her juices cover my face. She continues to ride until she fully comes down from her climatic high. Fully sated, her body goes limp in my arms. I pick her up and carry her to bed and put her under the covers. I give my exhausted mate a sweet but lingering kiss and promise to be back tomorrow before leaving.

I spend the day rehearsing what I plan on saying to Kate. It has to be perfect. She needs to know that I've changed, that I'm no longer the womanizing asshole she knew before. That I plan on spending every day of my life worshiping the ground she walks on. I know that with my actions I abused... not physically, but mentally. With every woman I bedded, I caused my mate physical pain, pain that I can never imagine. I abused her trust with every lie I told her. After she caught me many times, I promised to be a better man. I let lust and greed control my mind, and it cost me something so special. *Kate.* I finish booking our flight in first-class for our trip home in two days and I pack up my overnight bag. I don't plan on leaving my mate tonight or any night after that. On the way over to Kate's, I pick up dinner from the little bistro around the corner and a bottle of wine from the neighborhood bodega. I'm so happy that I'm practically skipping because tonight is the night I plan to fix the damaged mate bond I destroyed years ago.

Standing at her apartment door, I can hear water running. Not wanting to bother her, I let myself in with her spare key I found in her apartment. I set my overnight bag just inside the door and close it. I set our dinner down on the small kitchen table and open the bottle of wine. Walking into the bathroom, I find my sexy mate soaking in the tub. She is such a beautiful sight. I pour her another glass of wine. It annoys her I keep getting into her apartment, but she isn't running or screaming, so I feel like I'm still winning. I see that cheap piece of glass on her left hand. Hmmmm, she must have been with the frat boy today. Funny, I didn't have heartburn today or any day since showing up here in New York.

She doesn't seem like a woman who just got engaged. She should be thrilled and overjoyed. But she looks melancholy about the engagement. She tells me last night was a mistake and can never happen again, but her body tells a different story. She leans into me as I kneel next to the tub and freely exposes her breasts to me. I rush from the bathroom before lust can take over, telling her to hurry before dinner gets cold. I have so much I want to say to her.

She emerges from the bathroom in a light short dress. She sits on the couch and insists we talk, which is fine with me. I sit so close to her on the couch our legs touch. The energy between us picks up and the air around us buzzes. She breaks the connection by moving away from me, which causes me to laugh a little. Kate feels the bond too, and she is once again fighting it. She tells me she is marrying frat boy, which we both know is a lie. I could tell her what Kelsey and I overheard at the bar the night of her birthday party or that the ring on her hand is only a cheap piece of glass, but what good would it do? Would she believe me? It would turn me into a jealous villain in her eyes. I simply slide closer to her and run my fingers along the bare skin of her thighs. The haze of the mate bond swirls around us. I bring Kate in for a hungry kiss, and we are both overtaken by the haze of the mate bond.

Kate straddles my lap and attacks my lips with a dominating kiss, grinding her wet pussy into my hard cock. I pull down her dress, exposing her erect nipples. I take each nipple into my mouth while Kate moans my name. Hearing her say my name in ecstasy almost makes me cum in my pants.

"What the fuck, Kate, you fucking slut!" I hear the frat boy scream, followed by the sounds of shit hitting the floor. Hearing him insult my mate like that sends me into a rage. I rush to him and tell him to back off, then that fucker throws a punch. Kate quickly steps in between us, breaking up the fight before it got started. I laugh as I take notice of her body language. Her body is pressed into mine and she is pushing him away with her hands. He's not amused when I point this out to him. He storms off when she admits she is afraid that I will kill him, and he won't cause injury to me. Kate cries out for him, which breaks my heart, then turns to me and the words she says next will forever be etched in my mind.

"I ran away from my home because of you. I haven't seen my family in over two years because of you. I ran away to free me from the chains that bind me to you. You broke my heart every time you stuck your dick into another woman. I gave you my life, my love, and my virginity. You were my world since I was fourteen. You caused me physical pain with every woman you screwed. I was suffering because of you. You made me promises you couldn't keep. In the end, you couldn't control your dick, so I rejected you and fled the fucking state, Ian. Now two... almost three years later, you waltz back into my life, confusing the shit out of me and flipping my world upside down. You need to go. I don't want to see you anymore."

It was the last words that stung the worse. *I don't want to see you anymore.* She collapses to the ground and cries for another man as I stand there in shock. I look up and see a crowd of people in the hallway watching the drama unfold. "Fuck." I mumble before grabbing my overnight bag and slamming the door. *I've made more of a fucking mess out of things.*

CHAPTER SEVEN

IT'S GOOD TO BE HOME

****March 2004****

Kate

'IAN,' I CALL THROUGH my mindlink, but his blocks are up. 'Ian,' I call out again... still nothing.

"Kelsey?" I walk up to my brother, who is making out with some she-wolf sitting on his lap.

"What?" He snaps, "Can't you see I'm a little busy?"

"Yeah... I see that. I'm looking for Ian. Have you seen him?" I grab my chest and take a deep breath as the pain intensifies.

"He stepped outside to get some fresh air." Kelsey says, before waving me off.

Walking out a side door, I head towards a garden shack about thirty yards away. The pain is extremely intense, but Sasha is able to push the pain aside. As we get closer to the garden shack, I can hear grunting from both a male and female, causing my heart to sink.

'He's in there,' Sasha cries. We both know what is going on behind the garden shack door, but I need to see it with my own eyes. I fling open the door and hit the light switch.

"What the fuck!" Ian shouts. The shock of the bright lights in the shack causes him to close his eyes as he removes his dick from a she-wolf's mouth.

"How could you?" I whisper as tears spill down my cheek. My breathing becomes shallow as my chest heaves up and down with every breath. My heart races at the sight of the two of them together.

"Kate," Ian says as he tucks his dick back into his pants, quickly zipping up before rushing to me.

"No," I shout, backing up. "How could you, Ian?" I say through tears.

"Please... let me explain." Ian walks towards me.

"Explain what?" I shout, "I know the truth now... all these months... these pains... all because of you." I turn and run.

Jolting up straight, I gasp for air, waking from the same nightmare that caused so many sleepless nights. Realizing that this was only a dream, I rub my face with my hands and take a cleansing breath. It's been some time since the memories invaded my dreams like this. I'm in a bed I haven't slept in since just after my eighteenth birthday, in the house I grew up in. It's not surprising that the nightmares have started again, now that I'm home.

My bedroom is exactly how I left it two and a half years ago. The delicious and sweet smell of blueberry muffins waft from the kitchen downstairs, permeating every inch of the house. I stretch my tired, aching limbs, still feeling the effects of jetlag. I make my way to the window and take in the sights of home. Pups playing soccer, moms sitting on park benches with strollers parked in front of them chatting with other moms, a group of elderly practicing tai chi. *Home.* I've missed this place so much.

After breakfast, I take a casual walk around our village. Welcoming in the sights, sounds, and smells. I can smell the orange blossoms from the orchard, roses in the flower beds, and jasmine that climb an arched trellis that Alpha Nathaniel's grandmother had built. Alpha Nathaniel's grandfather, Alpha Ezekiel, worked tirelessly to build a large, formidable pack, and his mate Luna Scarlet made our village the picturesque place it is today. You'd never guess by the beauty of our territory that the outside world views us as nothing more than a bloodthirsty and ruthless pack.

Walking further, I see they've added a diner and pizzeria next to the grocery store since I've been gone. I love the progress they've made, and the way the pizza smells. I wonder how it compares to the pizza in New York. There is peace and tranquility here. No horns honking, traffic noises, or people noises; just the sounds of pups playing, birds chirping, laughter, and the peace of nature. I finally make my way to the tree line and excitement fills my soul.

'I could use a run,' Sasha speaks in my mind. Here we are safe to run whenever we want, no hiding and only running by the light of the moon.

'Me too,' I reply. *'Dad, I'm going for a run along the west border, heading east.'* I mindlink my dad to let him know about my plans. Although I'm a member of this pack, the patrolling warriors may not recognize my wolf since I've been gone for so long. Better to be safe than sorry, that's what I always say.

'Ok sugar, I'll let patrols know. Have a good run. Love you. It's good to have you home.' I feel his love through our mindlink and it makes my heart swell and brings a smile to my face.

'Love you too, dad. It's good to be home.' I cut the link and step behind a tree to undress, then shift into my chocolate-colored wolf with white paws.

I give Sasha complete control, stepping back in my mind to enjoy the ride. Sasha stretches, then bounces and takes off towards the east. She is so fast; the forest is just a blur as she races through it at top speeds. Jumping over stumps and fallen trees, ducking under low-lying branches. Her white paws make a thunderous roar on the forest floor. She spots a rabbit, and the race is on. Instantaneously she is on its heels and just before she chomps down; it escapes by ducking into a hole under some fallen branches. I laugh as she frustratingly paws and scratches at the branches, then movement from the tree canopy catches her attention. *Squirrel.* She loves the taste of fresh squirrel. Sasha chases it as it jumps from tree to tree, but she knows that she'll never catch it unless it falls. Giving up on the squirrel, she decides she needs a dip in the artisan-well fed lake.

When we arrive at the lake, she dives in. The cool water washes over her fur and is so refreshing. She swims and even tries to catch a fish. I giggle at her antics, as she enjoys her freedom. Soon she is tired of swimming and exits the lake shaking vigorously, shedding water from her soft fur. Exhausted and happy, she lies down on the bank next to the lake for a quick nap.

Mom's voice calling us home for dinner at the packhouse wakes us up. Sasha stands and stretches before heading back home. She trots along for several minutes before picking up another presence.

'We are not alone,' Sasha nervously looks around, then picks up the pace. Suddenly we hear the sounds of paws hitting the ground. *'They're getting closer, but I think I can outrun them.'*

'Hurry, we're still a good way from home.' I nervously reply. Sasha takes off in a full run, running as fast as her legs will take us. She doesn't dare look back, only forward. The sounds of the stranger's paws pick up. They're closing in.

'Da...' before I can finish calling my dad for help, we're hit from behind and tackled to the ground. We tumble and roll with the strange wolf rolling with us. All I see is my chocolate-colored fur mixed with the beige fur of the strange wolf. When we stop tumbling, Sasha is quick to get on her feet. She takes a quick look but sees nothing.

Before she can run again, an excruciating pain comes from our tail. Sasha yelps. The strange wolf is biting our tail, and it hurts so damn bad. Without warning, it tosses us like a rag doll. We hit the ground... hard, knocking the wind out of us. We lay on our side and play possum. Maybe the strange wolf will think we are dead and leave us alone. Then the bastard stands over us, growling and snapping his teeth. Sasha and I are not fighters. We have trained our minimum requirement, but we have no fighting skills to speak of. Right now, if we don't do something, we might just end up dead. My fight-or-flight instincts kick in. The wolf looks away from us for a moment and we seize the opportunity and latch on to its hind leg with our jaw. We chomp down hard, shaking our head and growling. If it's a fight you want, it's a fight you'll get. The strange wolf whimpers and lets out a pain-filled howl. Then we notice the hind leg turns into a human leg. The wolf has shifted.

We look up to see my brother's laughing face. Irritated, we chomp down harder, trying to inflict as much pain as we can for scaring us like that. He tries to push our head away from his leg, but we tighten our grip. When we release him, we shift into our human form. I take control. Kelsey is sitting there with a bloody ankle, laughing at me. I stand up and punch him in his stupid head as hard as I can.

"Asshole! You scared me!" I sit down next to him.

"Sister, your senses are dull. I tracked you for ten minutes before you sensed me." Kelsey is still laughing and rubbing his ankle.

"Is it broken?" I look at his ankle.

"Nope, just a scratch. I'll be healed up by the time we make it back home." He nudges my shoulder. "Your teeth are freaking sharp, though."

"How did you know I was out here?" I look at him and smile. I can't stay angry at him. This is a game that we have played several times before.

"I heard dad tell the patrolling warriors your location, and I couldn't resist harassing you." He laughs.

"Asshat," I shake my head.

"Want to talk about it?" He leans his shoulder into mine.

"Nope." I shake my head.

"Sure about that?" He pushes his shoulder into me.

"What good will it do? I've messed up any chances I might have had with Darren, and for what? A cheating bastard... who made me a cheater just like him." I lay back on the grass.

"He's changed, I can promise you that," he lays down next to me.

"He's your best friend. Of course, you'll take his side like you always have." Tears fill my eyes. "Kelsey, can I tell you something, without you telling anyone else?"

"Of course." Kelsey turns his head towards me.

"I had such a hard time when I moved to New York. Anxiety and depression took ahold of me. I almost came home because of it. Then I reached out for help. For the past two years, I've been seeing a therapist, and I've been working on me. Without my therapist, I wouldn't be the woman I am today. I've made so much progress." I inhale and slowly exhale.

"Thank you for trusting me enough to tell me. I know that I haven't always had your back and have been a real shitty brother. Kate, I'm truly sorry about that. I know I should have stopped Ian from hurting you. You should have been a priority over loyalty to Ian. I know that now. I can't change the past or the way I have treated you, but I can assure you that moving forward I will be a better brother and protector to you." He exhales looking up at the sky.

"You're right, you have been a shitty brother." I nod my head.

"Yeah, I deserve that." Kelsey laughs. "There's a lot you don't know, and it's not my place to tell you. Here's the thing, if I didn't think he was worthy of another chance with you, I would have never brought him to New York with me. Do you really think you'd be happy living the rest of your life with humans? If you thought Darren was *the* guy, you wouldn't hesitate to tell him about our kind. That and the fact that he's not here with you speaks volumes." He leans up on his elbow, facing me.

"I don't know, Kelsey. I'm not too sure I can forgive him, much less trust him." Looking into my brother's eyes, I can tell he's being sincere. He believes Ian has changed.

"Give him a chance, Kate. You deserve to be happy, and I think Ian can make you happy." He smiles.

"Wow! When did you become so... sweet?" I laugh.

"You can thank Sonia for that. When she asked why my sister refused to talk with me, I explained everything to her. She scolded me for a month straight, telling me that I need to make things right with you because she wants our future pups to know their aunt." He smiles and laughs.

"This isn't weird at all, us lying here buck naked." I say sarcastically, so the conversation doesn't drift back to Ian.

"You've been around humans too long, little sister. This is just natural. Mom is mindlinking me now. We better get back before mom has a huge fit." He stands, offering me a hand up. "You are my sister and I love you. I will have your back. You have my word on that." He kisses my forehead before shifting to his wolf. I stand there watching him trot away, digesting the moment we just had. Did my brother just promise to have my back over his Beta? That's huge. So much has happened since I've been gone. Looks like I'm not the only one who worked on themselves.

'You coming?' He asks through our mindlink. I smile, realizing that my brother loves me, after all. Without answering him back, I shift and we run back home together, just a girl and her asshole big brother.

CHAPTER EIGHT

PICK ME UP AT FIVE

March 2004

Ian

I'VE BEEN BACK IN Blue Moon territory for five days now. Kate has been here for three days. I haven't run into her yet. I'm sure she's avoiding me. Avoiding someone in our territory isn't hard since the lands are vast. I heard her dad announce to patrols that she was going for a run yesterday and Kelsey said he snuck up and tackled her to the ground. I wish I had the nerve to go out and run with her. *I can't believe how nervous I am around her.* Maybe if our wolves could connect, she'd forgive me.

During our lifting session in the gym, I explained to Zane and Kelsey what happened back in New York. And how she cried after frat boy when he caught us and ran off. That's the part that baffles me. She doesn't seem like she's in love with him. Why cry for him?

"Bro," Zane laughs, "always lock the fucking door. Basics of not getting caught."

"Yeah, who are you trying not to get caught by these days?" Kelsey laughs and points at Zane.

"Twin girls who know how to turn a doorknob." Zane laughs and throws us each a bottle of water.

"I think it was the fact that she got caught, period. In an instant, she became what she hated in you the most... the cheater." Kelsey explains.

"You think?" I look away with a confused expression.

"Yeah, I do. She still feels the bond, and she is still in love with you. Everyone can see that. Bro, she just doesn't want to get hurt again." Kelsey takes a huge gulp of water.

Could he be right? She's more upset that she became the cheater, making someone else feel as bad as she did? As far as hurting her, it's the last thing I want to do.

"When the hell did you get so insightful?" I grin.

"Bro, I've been a mated man for a year now. That shit matures you fast. Well, it matures some of us." He tosses his empty water bottle at me.

Coming out of the weight room headed to the outdoor sparing ring, I catch a familiar sweet floral scent. *Kate.* I look around and finally spot her on a treadmill, unfortunately she sees me too. I'm sure she picked up my scent when I entered the room. She stops the machine, quickly jumping off and heads for the door. Trying to catch up with her, I pick up my pace. A couple of warriors attempt to stop me for a chat, causing me to lose sight of her for a moment. I maneuver around the warriors and through the crowd before catching a glimpse of her outside. She's already fifty yards from the gym, walking fast and with a purpose. *To lose me, I'm sure.* I run to catch up, jumping in front of her with my hands out.

"Please, Kate. Please stop and talk to me." I beg.

"Ian... I don't..." I interrupt her.

"Wait, let me go first. Things went down in New York and I'm sorry. I never meant for frat... Darren to get hurt. I wasn't thinking about anyone else's feelings, just hell bent on making you feel the bond that we somehow still share. Kate, I've had a thing for you since I was sixteen, and loved you since I was eighteen. Truth is, I'm still madly in love with you. I can't imagine the pain and trauma I put you through. I know it must have been unbearable. Three months ago, I started having heartburn occasionally. It would come and go. I knew it was because of you getting close and kissing someone else. If *you* kissing someone else after I had fractured our bond caused me discomfort, I can only imagine the genuine pain you felt with a fully intact bond." I slip my hands at the base of her head, "I'm sorry for hurting you with my lying and cheating ways. I'm begging you for another chance... please, just one more chance to prove to you I'm changed and worthy of your love. Let me show you I can be the mate that you deserve." I press my lips into hers. Tears fill her eyes, but she doesn't speak. "Go on a picnic this evening with me, please."

"You don't deserve another chance." Kate speaks through tears that roll down her face.

"I know I don't, but I'm asking, anyway. Please." I pull her hands to my chest. She stands still and quiet, contemplating her choices. If she doesn't agree, she'll leave me no choice but to resort to more barbaric tactics. Which is something I don't want. I want her to give me a chance of her own free will.

"Ok," she whispers, with her head bowed down.

"Ok, you'll give me another chance or ok you'll go on a picnic with me?" I smile, bending down to look into her eyes.

"Yes," she snaps her head up and looks me in the eyes, "pick me up at five." Without warning, she walks away.

Watching her walk away; I play it cool, in case she looks back. But on the inside, my wolf and I are jumping around. Finally, after all this time, I will have a chance at winning back my Kate. Let's just hope I don't royally fuck it up... again. After she's about thirty yards from me, I can't contain my excitement any longer. I jump up and shout YES!

Kate

I'm not too sure why I agreed to go on a picnic with him, much less give him another chance. *Yet again.* What number chance is this? Who knows, I lost track of them. I meant what I said about him not deserving another chance... he doesn't. I walk back to my parents' house in a zombie like daze. *What just happened?* I knew that there was a high possibility I could run into him at the gym. It's right next to the training grounds. By looking at his broad chest and rock-hard abs, I'd say he pretty much lives at the gym and training grounds. I needed the workout today to quiet my mind, and I know avoiding him forever is impossible.

I replay our conversation over and over in my mind, analyzing every word he said, looking for the lie. There didn't seem to be one. It was weird, because the man who was speaking to me today was not the same man that I rejected all those years ago. There was something in his voice, something sincere. Even Sasha thought so. He did something I thought he'd never do... he apologized for cheating on me, he never apologized in the past... not once. He simply did the same shit he did in New York and relied on the mate bond to pull me back to him. *Did he really change?* I walk into the backdoor of my parents' house; the sweet smell of freshly baked cake fills the air. I follow the delicious smell straight to the kitchen. My mom is mixing something and has her back to me, and on the kitchen island there are at least five dozen cupcakes. I lean down and take a huge whiff of them, and my stomach lets out a roar.

"Hey sweetheart, help yourself. There's plenty there." Mom says with her back still to me. I grab two cupcakes and sit at the table, ready to dive in.

"They're individual pineapple upside down cakes," mom says over her shoulder. "Nancy requested I make my famous pineapple upside down cake for bunco night, and I thought it'd be fun to have individual sized ones." Mom continues with her mixing.

"Why so many?" I say through a mouthful of cupcake.

"Simple... your father. Hey, I have a great idea," mom puts her whisk down, "come with me to bunco. All the ladies would love to see you." Mom turns and faces me, licking the batter off her thumb. Her smile turns to concern when she sees my face. "Honey, what happened? Your eyes are puffy and bloodshot." She walks to me, "Have you been crying?"

"Ian." I take another bite.

"Did he hurt..." I interrupt her as she sits next to me, rubbing circles on my back.

"No, nothing like that. I'm just... frustrated." I shove the rest of the cupcake in my mouth.

"I bet. He broke your heart and now he's back..." she has an evil smirk on her face, and I know what is about to come next. Thinking about it makes me cringe and sink into my seat. "From outer sp..."

"Mom..." I shout, narrowing my eyes, warning her, but I'm sure it will fall on deaf ears like it always does. I know what she is trying to do. She has done this my entire life. Sometimes it's to cheer me up, other times because it fits her mood. Frankly, I'm just not in the mood to hear her speak the lyrics to any song, just because it fits the moment... like it's some sort of profound advice.

Just as I thought, she continues her lyric speaking until she can't contain it any longer and starts belting out at the top of her lungs her own rendition of Gloria Gaynor's song *I Will Survive*. Mom loves to sing, but unfortunately for everyone around her, she can't carry a tune in a bucket. Listening to her sing, which is basically just her shouting to a tune at this point, and watching her dance her way to the cupboard, I can't help to have an appreciation for this woman.

I will say this: for what mom lacks in her singing abilities, she makes up for with her dancing. She pops her hips, shakes her booty, and rolls her chest. She'll do anything to make her pups smile and laugh. Two coffee mugs in one hand, she produces a bottle of white wine from the fridge, then sashays over to the table before returning to her seat next to me. I'm seriously hoping my dad doesn't walk through the door right now, because one of two things will happen. One, I'll get tossed out the front door on my ass so dad can have his way with his mate, or two, they end up doing some Sonny and Cher number. Either way, it's not good for me if he shows up right now.

I hate to admit it, but her antics are working and a smile creeps onto my face. *Damn it!* She pours us both a mug of wine and continues singing. If I don't stop her, she'll sing the entire song. When she sings the word key, I decide to throw her a bone.

"He didn't have one to begin with. He took my spare after he broke into my apartment through my balcony door." I shrug and unwrap the cupcake in front of me, revealing the rich, ooey, gooey pineapple and cherry layer. I take a bite and a giggle escapes my lips. *Mom has succeeded.*

"I hate when you do that." I laugh.

"I know. I felt the same every time my mom did it to me." She brings the coffee mug to her lips. "But sometimes, in order to see things clearly, you need to be in a good and calm headspace."

"Coffee mug, mom?" I question, looking in my cup as if she poisoned it.

"The ceramic keeps the wine cooler longer. Plus, no one is the wiser to my day drinking when I'm holding a coffee mug." She laughs and sips her wine. "What happened?"

"Nothing... everything." I pause briefly, not wanting to verbalize the thought that's going through my mind right this second. "Mom, I'm still in love with him. No matter how hard I've tried to forget him and move on... I just can't." I shake my head and sip my wine.

"Oh..." Mom sips her wine.

"Oh, is correct. Just when I thought I was ready to move on, he shows up, scrambling my brain and confusing my thoughts. Here's the strange part. I *think* I can still feel the bond." I say, looking up at her. She stares into my eyes, searching for the perfect words to say.

"How's that possible? I thought you said you rejected him." She puts her mug down.

"I did." I get up and get us both a cupcake.

"Interesting. I know you don't want to hear this," she rubs the back of my hand, "but I think there is hope for the two of you, after all. He has changed, whether or not you want to believe that. I think he had to lose you to understand what it was like to live without you." I look at my mom and absorb her words, "after you left for New York, we didn't tell anyone, including your brother, where you were. We knew you both needed space... to be apart, even if that meant your dad and I couldn't see you for a while. As expected, he came looking for you. He begged and pleaded with all of us for your whereabouts, and when that didn't work, he threatened your father. Of course, your father didn't take the threat lightly and the two of them got into a bloody fight right in the front yard. It was almost like Ian had lost his mind." The thought of Ian fighting and hurting my dad infuriates me. "Beta Charles came running. He was furious... at his son's actions. Beta Charles pulled your dad and Ian apart so he could fight Ian. He was angry at the way his son treated you. Ian was no match for his father and ended up in the hospital for a week." The thought of Ian hurt in the hospital saddens me. My freaking emotions are all over the place. "When he was released, your dad went to have a chat with Ian. He told him if he really loved you, he'd prove it to him and the pack first. When and only when, he felt Ian could be trusted with his most precious possession... *you*," mom smiles, "he would give Ian your location and his blessing." Mom takes a deep breath and exhales slowly. "Just before your twenty-first birthday, your friend Melissa called Kelsey inviting him to your surprise party. When Kelsey told us that him and Sonia would go to New York for the occasion, your dad simply said, take Ian." I lean back in my chair, still absorbing all my mom's words with tears in my eyes. So much has happened since I have been gone. Ian's own father was furious at what he did to me. My dad did see a change in him. Or is Ian the master manipulator that has fooled everyone around him?

"I told him I'd go on a picnic with him today," I put my head down. Feeling almost ashamed for agreeing to go with him. I've told myself a thousand times I would never give Ian another chance... and here I am. I feel like a fraud.

"A picnic? That's... sweet and romantic," mom smiles and nods.

"I'm giving him one last chance." I look up at my mom with tears in my eyes.

"Oh, honey, don't cry. Is that what *you* want?" She wipes my tears.

"Mom... I don't know what I want. I just... want to be happy." I hunch over, covering my face with my hands and sob.

"Sugar," she pulls me into a hug, "I hate this for you. I hate that you're having to make this decision. Sugar." She lifts my chin and looks me in the eye, "Your dad and I will support you one hundred percent, no matter the choice you make. I love you, baby girl." Mom's words are laced with love, understanding, and compassion. They're so comforting.

"I love you too, mom. Thank you." I squeeze her neck, not wanting to let her go.

"For what, sugar?" She whispers in my ear.

"For this... for holding me... for making me laugh... for being you." I pull back and look at her.

"Oh sugar, no need to thank me. It's my job." She pulls me in for another tight hug.

"Mmmm... smells good in h... what's going on? What happened? Did that mother..." Dad's voice booms behind me as he slams the door.

"Nothing dear," mom stands, "girl chat sweety. Have a pineapple upside down cake." Mom shoves a cupcake in dad's face. Her back is to me, but I can tell they are mindlinking.

"I'm going on a picnic with Ian today... to talk." I say just above a whisper with my head down.

"Oh... and the thought of that made you cry? Maybe you shouldn't go." Dad peels the wrapper back from the cupcake.

"No... I need to. He says he's changed... I need to see that for myself." I inhale sharply.

"I can just break his neck and be done with him once and for all." Dad takes a huge bite of his cupcake.

"No, thank you. This is something that I need to do. Can't have daddy fighting my battles for me for the rest of my life." I smile. "I'm going to go upstairs and soak in the tub. Ian will be here in a few hours."

"Oh, sugar, I put some bath bombs under the sink in your bathroom. I know how much you love them." My mom sips her wine.

"Thank you, mom." I turn and walk away. Practicing a calming technique that I've learned. *Calming breaths.* Slowly inhale, holding it for three seconds, and slowly blowing out the breath for five.

When I'm about halfway up the stairs, I hear my dad call out to me, "offer still stands."

I don't look back; I just wave my hand in the air.

CHAPTER NINE

MEMORY LIKE AN ELEPHANT

May 1999

Kate

"I CAN BAIT MY own hook, Ian." I put my hands on my hips and protest.

"Yeah, I'm sure you can, angel. I don't mind doing it for you." He looks up from putting the worm on my hook and flashes me the million-dollar smile that stole my heart two years ago. His smile is contagious, and I smile back, ear to ear. "There... all done." He hands the rod and reel to me.

"Thank you, Ian." I take the rod and reel and walk towards the area where my brother and Zane are fishing.

"Nope, angel, we're going over there." He points with his fishing rod, "that's where the big fish are."

"That's bullshit," Zane shouts, "fish don't just hangout in one spot."

"We'll see about that," Ian shouts back.

Ian guides me over to an area that he calls his honey hole. It's far enough away from my brother and Zane, which is probably the best, since my presence seems to bother my brother. He says that I'm a buzz kill, but we all know it's because the pack tramps won't come around if I'm here. I think it's funny watching my brother get so annoyed and then make lame excuses to sneak off into the woods. Like I can't hear his gross grunting. I like that Ian and I are separate from the other two. They can't hear our conversation without straining their ears. Not that we are having deep conversations or anything. I guess I just like it when it's just me and him. *Please let me be his mate.*

"How come we've never fished here before?" I cast my line out before sitting on the soft grass.

"I discovered this spot two weeks ago, when you and your mom went shopping." He takes his seat beside me.

"You remember I was shopping with my mom two weeks ago?" I smirk and give him an inquisitive look.

"Yeah, I have a memory like an elephant," he taps his head. "I don't forget the important things, angel."

"Do elephants really have good memories, or did you make that up?" I laugh.

"Elephants have huge brains and excellent memories. They never forget things when it comes to survival or things that are important to their needs." He leans back on his elbows, leaning into me with his legs stretched out in front of him. Our eyes meet and I'm lost in his soft brown eyes. For a moment, I feel a connection with him, and it feels like he might just kiss me. *My first kiss.* Then we blink and he sits up to check his line... the moment is gone. *Does he feel the same as me, or did I just imagine the entire thing?*

"It's going to be weird with all three of you gone this fall." I check my line as well, avoiding eye contact with him.

"We'll only be three hours away. We'll come home like every two weeks." Ian pushes a stray hair behind my ear.

"You better... you can leave *them* there." I giggle.

"I heard that," Kelsey shouts. Then the tip of my rod bends down and jumps violently in my hands.

"Woah!" I shout, pulling back just like Ian showed me to set the hook. We both rush to our feet and the battle begins. The line squeals as I spin the handle on the reel. Whatever is on the other end of the line is big and it doesn't want to come out of the water. I jerk forward as the beast tries to get away. My small arms are working overtime as I pull and spin the handle on the reel.

"You got this angel, take a step back... breathe... pull... reel... step back." Ian coaches me, "I'm right here, that fish isn't getting away from you, angel." His arms are out, like he is ready to catch me.

Zane and Kelsey rush over with the net. "Bro, take the rod before that thing snaps the rod and gets away," Kelsey shouts. Excitement is in the air. I'm in the biggest battle of my life. Then the water breaks and we all see the silver and white beast jump out of the water, trying its hardest to break the line and get away.

"Not in a million years. She has this." Ian's words give me the boost of confidence I need. Energy surges through my hands. I'm working hard, pulling and reeling. Sweat beads form on my forehead.

Soon the beast of a fish is close enough to the shore that the three of them rush into the water. Zane uses his net, and before I know it, I caught the beast. I throw down my rod, jumping up and down, screaming and shouting. Adrenaline still coursing through my veins.

"I can't believe it," Kelsey runs his fingers through his hair.

"Great job, Kate. This catfish has to weigh at least ten pounds." Zane brings the beast of the fish to me.

"I'm so proud of you, angel." Ian rubs my back. The thrill and victory of the battle has left me speechless, and all I can do is nod my head like a silly fool.

"You know what this calls for, Kate?" Zane asks, looking between Ian and me.

"What's that?" I tilt my head.

"Bonfire," Zane and Ian say in unison.

"I'll put the call out," Zane smiles.

Chapter Ten

PICNIC FOR TWO

March 2004

Kate

"YOU BROUGHT ME TO your fishing honey hole?" Looking towards the lake, I see he has set a picnic area up. Complete with a blanket, pillows, and a low table in the center. The table has place settings for two with candles. Next to the table is a wine chiller filled with ice and two bottles of wine. "Wait, you're not going to make me catch my own lunch, are you?" I spin to look at him.

"Nope," he laughs, "but if memory serves me correct, you're one hell of a fisherman... woman." He picks up the large picnic basket from the back of the golfcart. "I came prepared," he taps the basket and smiles.

"Ian, I'm not going in there with you any time soon." He follows my gaze to the fishing cabin.

"That was not my intention," he motions me over to the picnic area. "This place holds a special place in my heart and calms my spirit." We take off our shoes before walking onto the soft blanket. "I brought you here, because this is where you and I really began." We take our seats across from each other, and Ian unpacks the basket and places the food on the low table. "This place is where we got to know each other, where we connected." He pours a glass of wine and hands it to me.

"And the fishing cabin is where I gave you my virginity." I say as a matter of fact.

"This place holds so many wonderful memories for you and I." He gulps and takes a deep breath, "before I messed it up so bad." He lowers his head in shame.

"Rosé," I try to change the subject, "this is my..." Ian interrupts.

"Favorite. I remember. Memory like an elephant and all." He taps his head and sips his wine.

"I have a question," I swirl my wine.

"Okay?" He has a nervous look in his eye.

"Why didn't you kiss me? There were so many times that I thought you might, but you never did. Why?" I sip my wine.

"I couldn't." Ian states.

"Because of my age? You were eighteen, and I was sixteen." I look deep into his eyes.

"Not because of that. I stopped myself every time, because if I didn't... if I would have had a taste, there wouldn't be any turning back for me. I would have claimed you... subsequently, breaking the law. I wouldn't have been able to keep things between us a secret either. I would have shouted that shit from the mountain tops, and I knew

I wouldn't be able to leave for college either... not without you. That and your fucking brother was always watching us." Ian and I both laugh.

"So, it wasn't my imagination?" I smile, thinking back.

"Not by a long shot." He snickers, "trust me... I wanted to."

"Wow, everything smells amazing." I eye all the foods in front of me.

"It should. It took all afternoon to prepare." Ian smugly says.

"Wait... you cooked and prepared all this?" I put my hand on my chest in shock.

"No... I burn water. I meant it took someone on Chef Marcie's team all afternoon to prepare and like five minutes for me to pick up." He grins, "you wouldn't believe the favors I had to do to get this done." He pops a grape in his mouth.

"Sexual favors?" I ask in a monotone voice. Ian gasps and coughs as if he is choking. He hits his chest and coughs again, spitting out a grape into a napkin.

"Shit, Kate. You almost made me choke on a grape." He coughs again, taking a sip of his wine, "but no... no sexual favors were made."

I look at his red face and laugh, "did I embarrass you?"

"Pfft, no... I don't know, maybe a little bit. Definitely caught me off guard. I see my little Kate is grown up now. I better stay on my toes with you." We both laugh. It feels good to laugh with him. This is the Ian I fell in love with seven years ago.

"So, what are we having? I'm starving." I look between him and the food, catching a look in his eye that I hadn't seen in years. The look that makes me feel like I'm the only girl in the world.

"Roasted duck. Looking in your fridge back in New York and seeing all the leftover Chinese takeaway containers with leftover duck, I figured duck was a new favorite of yours." He points to the duck and looks at me.

"How many times were you in my apartment when I wasn't there?" I pour myself another glass of wine.

"Is that really important? I mean, what's a little b and e when you're trying to win the girl back?" He laughs and continues to give me a food tour, "roasted asparagus and cherry tomatoes, garlic and parmesan green beans, burgundy mushrooms, honey brown sugar roasted carrots, and my favorite..." I interrupt him.

"Deviled eggs." I smile and pick up a carrot.

"You remembered." He returns the smile and watches me intently as I take a bite of the carrot.

"Mmmm, so good." I tilt my head back, closing my eyes, savoring the sweet and buttery flavor of the carrot. I open my eyes to find Ian staring at me with a smile on his face. "What?" I giggle and take another bite of the delicious carrot.

"Nothing, I didn't say anything," he laughs, knowing I have caught him.

"You were staring." I take the last bite of the carrot and snicker.

"No, I wasn't," he scoffs, pretending to be offended.

"Liar," I laugh, sipping my wine.

"Ok... you caught me. You're so beautiful, I can't help but to stare." Ian smiles and raises an eyebrow.

"Wow, you slathered the cheese on thick with that one." I point at him, then drink the last of my wine. He takes the bottle and pours us both another glass.

"It may be cheesy, but it's true. I was such a fucking idiot for treating you the way I did." He looks down and bites his quivering bottom lip.

"That's definitely a true statement." I inhale sharply and exhale. "Ian... if I'm... if we're going to do this, we can't talk about the past. The past has kept my heart in turmoil for over two and a half years. I can't be reminded of the lying, cheating, manipulation, and broken promises. I want to concentrate on the future and forget about the past." A tear rolls down my cheek.

"Hey, hey, hey," he crawls over and sits beside me, cupping my cheek in his hand. I can feel a mild tingle on my cheek. I wonder if I will ever feel the full sensation of the mate bond on my skin again. "Ok, no more talk of the past." He pauses, then breathes in and out slowly, before speaking again. "I want you to know how sorry I am for the bullshit I put you through, Kate. I'm going to spend the rest of my life making sure you know how much you mean to me, and how much you are loved. And I promise to be the mate you truly deserve. Ok?" He pulls my hands to his lips, kissing the palms of my hands slowly and tenderly. His tone is soft and warm, and he seems incredibly sincere. He looks like he is apologetic about the past. I want to throw caution to the wind and put all my trust into his words, but the nagging feeling in the pit of my stomach is screaming danger, danger, danger, proceed with caution.

"How? A leopard doesn't change it's spots. How can I trust you, after everything you have put me through?" I look at him and gulp.

"Because I have done a lot of work to better myself and change." Ian shifts in his seat. He exhales sharply and runs his fingers through his hair. He seems agitated. "What I'm about to tell you, you can't tell anyone." He gulps, "I hope you still choose to give me a chance after I tell you."

"Go on." I inhale and brace myself for bad news.

"Each time I cheated, I knew I was hurting you. I felt bad for my actions after the fact. I tried to stop, but I couldn't. There were these urges, and no matter how hard I tried, I couldn't control them. After you left, I lost it. I thought I was going insane. In my crazed state, I challenged your father to a fight. He could have killed me that day, and I would have deserved it. As much as I wanted to change and to control my urges, I couldn't. With the help of my parents, I checked into a six week residential sexual recovery program for men." He pauses and looks at my face. There is fear in his eyes. "Kate, I'm a recovering sex addict."

"Wow," I breathe out.

"I've been in recovery for almost three years now. I still see my therapist once a week. He's helped me work through so many issues. Issues that I didn't realize I had." He chuckles. "I hope you don't think I'm weak."

"Weak?" I squeak out. "Why would I think you're weak?"

"My addiction." He reaches for my hand.

"Ian, I don't think you're weak. It takes a brave person to admit they have a problem. You did that. You admitted you had a problem that you needed help with... and got the help you needed. I'm so proud of you for that." I squeeze his hand. I've often wondered why I was never good enough for him, this answers so many questions. "I've also been in therapy... back in New York. Although mine was so I could forget you and move on." I wrinkle my nose and bite my lip.

"You have?" Ian pulls my hands to his chest.

"I have. Seems like we've both been working on ourselves over the years." I smile as he cups my jaw. "How are your urges?" I hate to ask and ruin a tender moment, but I need to know.

"They're completely controlled... with the exception of you. This is going to sound like I'm lying, but I don't see women like I used to. The thought of being with any other woman but you, makes my stomach turn." He looks down then back at me.

"You're right, that does sound like a lie." I laugh.

"Yeah, I know. I'm not going to lie, I can look at a woman and think she's beautiful, but the urge to conquer and have her isn't there. However with you... the need is very much there. It's not just about sex though, it's about love." He pushes a strand of hair behind my ear. "It's about showing you what it is like to have a mate that worships the ground you walk on." Ian kisses the palm of my hands. "I have an idea. Would you like to join me for therapy? We can work on us together."

"Yes, Ian. I would love to." Without hesitation I answer him. Trust is a hard thing to restore once it's been broken, but I think this is a step in the right direction.

We sit in a peaceful silence for a long moment, hand in hand. Just staring into each other's eyes. They say the eyes are windows into your soul and right now I'm searching his soul for the truth. Can I trust him with my heart? Will I be able to forgive the past? Before any more doubt rises in my mind, I push down all my emotions and lock them away. Ian worked so hard putting this beautiful picnic together for us. I don't want to ruin his efforts with my skepticism.

I pick up a strawberry and take a bite. When a little juice drips on to my chin, Ian wipes it away with his thumb. I love the way his touch makes me feel alive inside. He leans into me like he is going to kiss me. Just before his lips reach mine, I shove the strawberry into his unsuspecting mouth. We both laugh. I'm enjoying this time with him, but I'm not ready to kiss him. I need time... time to see if he really is a changed man.

We lounge around the picnic area long after we've finished eating. We talk about life over the past two and a half years. I tell him about studying art at the university and all the fun I have with my friend Melissa. I find it odd that every time I bring her name up, his smile turns into a frown. Why doesn't he approve of her? I can't help but to wonder if something happened between the two of them at my party. Thinking back to that night, Ian never left my side, so I really don't understand what his grievance is with her. When I asked him, he said he heard two guys talking about her and it didn't make her look like a good friend to me.

I drop the subject and he tells me about college, his time training at the palace with Zane, and the missions that he, Zane, and Kelsey have been doing over the last year. The three of them, along with pack warriors, have traveled to other territories helping other packs fight battles against rogues and blood hungry Alphas looking to take over territory. He even shows me some of his battle scars. I cringe and he quickly changes the subject, seeing my discomfort.

Now that he is finished with college and Beta training, he is back in Blue Moon territory to apprentice under his father. He will slowly take over more and more Beta duties from his father, as well as continuing missions. I'm not thrilled about the missions part, but I'm proud that they are helping others that are defenseless.

We talk and laugh for hours. This is the Ian I fell in love with. The man I can talk about nothing with for hours and never get bored. He makes me feel relaxed and calm, and I hope this feeling doesn't fade. The sun is setting and the sounds of birds chirping gives way to the insects singing their nightly song. I love the peaceful sounds of the forest at night with the sounds of moving water in the background.

"Hey, I have an idea." Ian leans into me.

"What's that?" I mimic his movements and lean into him.

"Let's go for a run. It's been a long time since Sasha and Alex ran together. What do you say?" He rubs my leg. I remain silent for a moment, "um… it's ok if you…" I interrupt him.

"I would have immediately answered you, but Sasha was screaming so loud I couldn't remember how to talk." I smile as a look of relief washes over Ian's face. "Last one to the tree line is a rotten egg!" I shout and jump to my feet and run towards the tree line.

"Hey! Not fair!" Ian shouts. I can hear his feet getting closer to me. I'm just inches away from the tree line when his massive arms wrap around me, and I giggle. "Caught you, you little sneak." He spins us around and he backs into the tree line, pushing me away. "I win!"

"Yes, you did. Too bad I was going to let you watch me undress as a second-place prize. Looks like I'll be watching myself." I stick my tongue out, teasing him.

"What? Wait, I demand a do over." He puts his hands on his hips.

"Nope." I shake my head.

"Wait! It's only fair that you get the second-place prize and watch me undress." He crosses his arms with a smug look on his face.

"Nope! Turn around, mister." I swirl my finger in a circle in front of me.

"You can't change the rules." He narrows his eyes at me.

"Oh... but I can, and I did. Turn around, big boy." I laugh. Ian is used to getting his way and not losing. I can see the thoughts are swirling around in his head by the way his facial expressions change. He finally accepts defeat and snaps his body around. He's sulking, which I think is hilarious. In the past, when he would sulk or get upset, I was the one who'd jump into action, doing whatever I needed to make him happy. Now? I simply don't care; he can sulk all day if he wants to. The power I found within myself over the past two and a half years has given me the confidence to stand up to him, and I love the new me.

I quickly undress, folding up my clothes, and putting them at the base of a tree. Then I shift into my chocolate-colored wolf. I turn to see Alex, Ian's wolf, looking at me. *How long has that sneaky rat been watching me?* The thought makes me giggle. Alex is a very large beige wolf; I think he might be bigger since the last time I saw him. I turn control over to Sasha, who is more than excited to see Alex.

Sasha cautiously saunters to Alex, showing off for him, but not allowing him to touch her. She sniffs him from head to rear, inspecting him to see where he's been and who he's been around. It wasn't just me who was hurt by Ian's actions, Sasha was hurt just as much as me. For months she whined and cried over her mate, and it was her who gave me courage to reject him. She couldn't handle the pain it was causing the both of us, and together we decided being alone or dead would be better than what we were going through. Alex has to earn Sasha's trust back in the same way Ian has to earn mine.

Pleased with the results of her inspection. she nudges her head under Alex's jaw. She rubs her head into him as if she is marking him with her scent. Happy, Alex closes his eyes and makes a low growl that almost comes out like a purr. She missed him so much.

Soon, she pulls back and nips playfully at his face. She lowers her front half to the ground, keeping her rear raised in the air with her tail wagging. Prepared to pounce. Alex readies himself, tilting his head with his legs stiff and tail pointed straight up in the air. There's a few tense moments before she pounces, springing all four of her legs off him before taking off into the forest. Alex stumbles a little from her weight hitting him, but soon enough recovers. *The race is on.*

He chases after her. They race through the dark forest, jumping over rocks and fallen tree limbs, and ducking under low-lying branches. Sasha jigs and jogs, keeping Alex on high alert for what her next moves are. Then Sasha catches the scent of a rabbit, and the hunt is on. Alex takes the lead on the hunt; he's doing his best to impress Sasha with his skills. Soon, Alex has the rabbit cornered and is moving in for the kill. Alex is completely focused on the rabbit; his body is tense and ready to pounce any second. Just as his back legs twitch, Sasha slaps his back legs out from underneath him, knocking him to the ground. The rabbit quickly makes its escape.

Alex jumps to his feet. Angry, he lets out a thunderous growl at Sasha. She simply looks at him with her tongue hanging out, tilting her head side to side, and laughing through their mindlink. Sasha is in a playful mood and a grumpy Alex will not spoil it, and to prove her point, she slaps his nose with her front paw. Alex stands stunned by her actions; she is not the same wolf she was two years ago. She turns and runs, leaving a confused Alex in her dust. Soon though, she can hear his paws hitting the forest floor, gaining ground on her. As she reaches the blanket where we had picnicked earlier, he tackles her to the ground.

Alex's beige fur and Sasha's chocolate-colored fur is all she can see as they roll and tumble. When the dust settles, Sasha shifts, giving me back control. Alex stands over me with his tail wagging as I open my eyes. I smile and rub his soft beige fur with my hands. I have missed him, too. He nudges his nose into my neck, causing me to close my eyes and giggle from his cold wet nose tickling my skin. Soft fur turns to naked flesh and the cold wet nose turns to Ian's lips, kissing my neck.

"We've missed you both so much." Ian whispers into my ear, sending a shock wave through my body straight to my core. "You and Sasha have changed so much. You're both... stronger."

I open my eyes, looking straight into Ian's handsome face. He makes me feel like I used to; loved and safe. The look he is giving me makes me feel like I'm the only woman in the world... like his one and only love. This is the boy I fell in love with all those years ago. I savor the moment while taking him in. I note the tiny lines on his forehead and a small scar just under his chin. How is it possible that he has gotten more handsome? I rub my fingers through his tousled hair. He licks his full lips and just like the sirens lure the sailors to their inevitable deaths, his lips lure me in.

Like waves on rocks, our lips crash into each other. Our kiss is not sweet or soft, it's passionate and fiery. Emotions wash over my body as we deepen the kiss, both of us ravenous. I moan into his mouth as he massages my breasts. The tingles and sparks radiate off our skin, almost as strong as the past. The mate bond seems to be mending. I run my nails down his back and he groans from both pleasure and pain. I'm enjoying his hands and mouth on me as he kisses his way down my neck. His hard member presses into my belly, snapping me out of the mate bond haze. Suddenly, I remember that I'm not ready to simply forgive and forget... that I need time.

"Ian... wait," I push his shoulders back.

"What... what's wrong?" He's breathing heavy.

"I'm not ready... yet." I breathe out and bite my bottom lip. Half afraid that I'll make him angry for stopping him. He pauses for a long moment, contemplating his next move. I know he can smell my arousal as well as I can feel his hard member. My body wants him, there's no doubt about that, but my brain needs time to trust him again. I need to trust him before I give him my body. I need to know what he tells me is real and not just a manipulative mind game.

"Ok," he smiles and nods.

"Ok?" I question.

"Yes, ok," He rubs my jaw with his thumb and looks at me lovingly. "I have the rest of my life to make love to you. We have a lot to work on and I have a lot to prove. We'll take this as slow as you like. You are the love of my life, and I intend to move mountains to prove it." He places a gentle kiss on my lips.

"Oh, Ian," I softly say as tears roll down my cheek. This is new. The old Ian would have been furious for having to stop. He would have pouted until I gave in. *Who is this man?* "Thank you for understanding."

"Anything for you, love." He kisses me gently; his words are soft and sincere, causing a wave of relief to wash over me. If this is his true self, I can see myself falling madly in love with him all over again.

"As much as I don't want to, I'm going to have to get up. Skin to skin contact with you is keeping my dick hard." We both laugh and get to our feet.

I forgot we were both naked from shifting after our run. It's funny how quickly I'm shedding the taboo thoughts the human world has on nudity.

"Wait," Ian pulls me into his arms, "thank you for today. Being with you is the most fun I've had in a very long time. Always remember that you are the love of my life, Kate. I love you." He gives me a soft, sweet, and lingering kiss.

CHAPTER ELEVEN

IT WAS ALL SO FAST

February 2001

Ian

"COULD YOU DRIVE ANY faster, Kelsey?" I question, annoyed that this trip home from school seems to take longer than usual.

"Relax, bro, we're almost there. The party doesn't start for another two hours." Kelsey taps the steering wheel to the beat of the music on the radio.

The closer we get to our territory; the more my wolf, Alex grows restless. Today is Kate's eighteenth birthday, the day she finds out she is my mate. I'm nervous and excited at the same time. A part of me wonders if she will accept or reject me. Although I'm pretty positive she'll accept me, but there's no telling what has happened over the last couple of years.

I've been away at college with Zane and Kelsey, and we haven't come home for visits very often, like I promised Kate I would. I had every intention, but life turned into one big party. We found out quick that human girls would do anything to get our attention... and I mean anything. I came home from class one afternoon to find a naked sorority sister in my bed. The night before was her roommate. I've taken full advantage of the partying and girls at school before Kate turned eighteen... sowing my wild oats, if you will. Now that her birthday is here, those days are behind me, and Kate is my future.

"Relax, bro, we'll be there in like ten minutes." Zane looks at me.

He knows exactly why I'm anxious. Besides my father, he is the only one I've talked to about Kate being my mate. I haven't talked with Kelsey about it because Kate is his sister. It just feels odd talking to him where his sister is concerned. Even though the three of us are close, the bond that I share with Zane runs deeper, just as an Alpha and Beta should. One we've shared since we were kids. More often than none we can feel each other's emotions. He knew that I've had a thing for her since I was sixteen and she was fourteen, and he witnessed the instant that I realized Kate was my mate. If Kelsey knows, he has said nothing... probably because it's weird as fuck for him, too.

"My mom called earlier and said that they've secured a cottage for you this summer, Ian." Zane looks up from his phone at me. By the look on his face, he realizes he spoke out loud instead of through our mindlink.

"Why does Ian need a cottage?" Kelsey looks at Zane and then me through the rearview mirror.

"Tell him..." Zane turns and looks at me.

"Tell me what?" He turns the radio off; the silence is deafening. "What? That my sister is your mate?" Kelsey grins.

"You knew?" I tilt my head.

"Bro, the whole fucking pack knows... except Kate. Apparently, she's not that bright." Kelsey laughs, "my dad told me to keep a watchful eye on the two of you when she was like fourteen, and again after your eighteenth birthday."

"Are you serious?" I shout in disbelief.

"Yeah. Bro, the way you'd follow her around... like a puppy dog. Pathetic." Kelsey and Zane laugh.

"Why didn't you tell me?" I ask.

"You want me telling you how hot your sisters are? Yeah, I didn't think so." Kelsey pulls up to the front gate.

"Finally," Zane groans out.

"Welcome home, boys. Your fathers are looking for the three of you. I have notified them you are here. Alpha has asked for you to meet them in his office." The warrior guarding the gate says, then bows his head as the gate opens. As we drive past, warriors bow their heads.

"What the fuck did we do now?" Zane frustratingly rubs his face.

March 2004

"Alpha Nathaniel." I walk into the Alpha's office; Zane and Kelsey are already here.

"Ian, please have a seat. We're just waiting for your father now. How's things with your mate?" Alpha Nathaniel sits up from his chair, resting his elbows on his large wooden desk, forming a triangle with his hands in front of his face. Alpha Nathaniel is a formidable man standing at about six feet three inches. He is intimidating, to say the least. He and Luna Martha are very much by the book and have a no-nonsense approach. Luna Martha comes off cold to many, that is because she was raised to be a Luna and is formal. Watching her as a mother to Zane and his sisters, it's apparent she loves them; however, she is not as affectionate as mine and Kelsey's mothers are. Alpha Nathanial is a strict and stern alpha who doesn't have a problem personally issuing punishments, especially where Zane, Kelsey, and I are concerned. Often I've felt sorry for Zane being raised in such a strict and cold household. Other times, I was happy to share my mother's affection with him.

"Kate is good, Alpha. We're taking it slow; I have a lot to prove to her." I exhale and shift my eyes from Alpha Nathaniel to Gamma Earnest, Kate and Kelsey's father.

"You know where I stand, boy. Do right by my daughter and we will have no issues." Gamma Earnest looks at me and pushes his shoulders back. Gamma Earnest looks like an older version of Kelsey. He is a large man, but he's not nearly as intimidating as Alpha or my father. I challenged him to a fight when he wouldn't give me Kate's location, a fight I thought at twenty years old I could win. I was grossly mistaken. He is one hell of a fighter, even in an Armani suit. The only thing keeping him from killing me that day was my father. No, he wasn't there to rescue me. He was just tired of my shit and wanted his turn at beating my ass.

"I have every intention of doing just that, sir." I have a great respect for Gamma Earnest. We have grown close over the past two and a half years. There are things that I have learned from him, that I never did from my own father. I guess it really takes a village to raise a pup.

"We have a fucking issue," my father burst through the door in Alpha's office.

"What's that, Beta Charlie?" Alpha Nathaniel tilts his head at my father.

"Fucking rogue king has already launched his attack on Crimson Tide. We need to move if we're going to save them." My father looks around the room, then back to Alpha, waiting for his orders.

"Do we know the numbers on the rogues?" Alpha Nathaniel leans back in his chair.

"Fifty, but scouts found the rogue encampment. Numbers look to be close to two hundred there." My father looks down at the papers he is holding.

"Gather one hundred warriors and prepare to leave for battle in fifteen." Alpha Nathaniel orders. The thrill of the battle races through my veins. Battles and wars are something Zane, Kelsey, and I thrive on. Especially when we can save the underdog, like Crimson Tide. They are a small pack, only about two-hundred members, with an exceptional territory. The rogue king has wanted to take over the territory for years. I suppose now he's gathered enough wolves and is making his move. The only thing he has not counted on is Zane, Kelsey, me, and our warriors.

"Excuse me Alpha, but my wedding is in three days…" Alpha Nathaniel interrupts Kelsey.

"Then you better make it quick and try not to get yourselves killed."
Alpha Nathaniel says with authority.

We all jump to our feet without another word or argument. Alpha
Nathaniel's orders are final. Rushing from the Alpha's office, the
three of us head to our rooms on the sixth floor to grab our battle
bags that we each keep packed and ready to go at a second's notice.
Crimson Tide is about two hours from us, which is why we need to
move so quickly if we're going to save them. I rush back downstairs
to the dining area, where all the warriors are already gathered. It is
controlled chaos as loved ones see the warriors off, while the kitchen
staff carries coolers of food and drinks to the awaiting SUVs parked
in the front. One by one, the warriors file out and load up.

"Ian?" Kate calls out while pushing her way through the crowd..

"Kate, I was just about to mindlink you." I pull her in for a tight hug.

"What's going on?" She nervously asks as she looks around.

"We're leaving to go help another pack from a rogue attack." I look
her in the eyes.

"But... Kelsey's wedding." She is nervous and breathing heavily.

"We'll be back in time. Trust me. Kate, I love you." I kiss her tenderly
and turn, leaving her standing in the same spot. I keep walking,
despite wanting to turn around and pull her into my arms. If I don't
keep walking, I may not leave here, and I'm sure Alpha will lock me
in the dungeon and give me daily lashings.

My chest tightens as I load into the SUV with Zane and Kelsey. I
know that I'm feeling her sadness and anxiety as well as my own.
As we pull away, I see her standing in the packhouse's doorway with

tears in her eyes and my heart sinks to the pit of my stomach. I hate leaving her.

"Bro, the first time leaving them behind is always the hardest." Zane pats my shoulder.

"The girls will take care of her," Kelsey adds.

"Yeah, this sucks." I press my head against the glass and look out the window. I need to get ahold of my emotions before we battle, or mistakes will be made. "Let's fucking make this quick. I have someone I need to get home to." I watch the world out my window as we zoom by at top speeds.

Kate

Stunned and with tears rolling down my face, I watch as Ian's SUV leaves. As they pass, I see the pain in his eyes. I'm honestly not too sure what just happened or where they're going. I just know they're going to help another pack. Does that mean he just left for battle? What if he doesn't come home? I just decided to give him a chance and now he may not come back at all. *What the hell?*

"Hey," Rebeka wraps her arm around my shoulder. "The first time is the hardest. He'll... they'll be ok."

"It was all so fast," I whisper through tears.

"Yeah, it happens like that sometimes." Sonia stands in front of me, rubbing my arms.

"How do you handle it so well?" I ask, holding my chest.

"First, we rid our mind of all nervous energy. They can feel our feelings." Sonia replies.

"Then we drink margaritas, watch chick flicks, and eat junk." Rebeka laughs.

Sonja and I spend the night locked away with Rebeka in her and Zane's family suite on the sixth floor. We spend the evening eating nachos, drinking margaritas, and watching our favorite chick flicks. At about two a.m. we sneak past Rebeka's sleeping twins and down to the kitchen looking for some peach ice cream that Chef Marcie put aside for us. We laugh and talk, and most importantly, we try not to think about the guys and their mission.

Since my dad is Gamma and needs to be closest to the warriors, I wasn't raised in the packhouse, so I'm unfamiliar with the family suites and who lives here on the sixth floor. It's basically a small two-bedroom apartment with a small kitchen, dining area, and living room. Kelsey and Sonia's suite is on the left and Ian's suite is on the right. Sonia tells me that all three suites are identical, and when I decide to move forward with Ian that we'll be neighbors. As excited as I am about being close to these two wonderful she-wolves, I still have my reservations about Ian and my future. This jumping and running off to battle doesn't sit well with me at all.

"I was thinking of calling Ian to see how it's going." I pick up my phone.

"NO!" Rebeka shouts as Sonia snatches it from my hands. "We aren't allowed to contact them while they're on the battlefield."

"You both are ok with not being able to contact them? That seems like a strange rule." I look between the two of them, bewildered.

"They need full concentration and no distractions from us." Sonia says with certainty while nodding her head.

"Their phones could give away their position as well. It could get them ki…" Rebeka looks down without finishing her sentence. I can tell from the look on both of their faces the possibilities of their mates not coming home is something they don't speak about.

"I understand." I lie, because I don't really understand fully. I don't remember my mom not being able to contact my dad while he was away on a mission. Why can't I remember a detail like that? I've either been away from pack life too long or maybe it's my lack of trust with Ian… I'm just not sure. "Can I have my phone back, please?" I hold my hand out.

"Promise me you won't call Ian. They will contact us when they can." Rebeka says in an authoritative tone that I've never heard from her before.

"I promise." I gulp and take a deep breath. Rebeka and Sonia exchange a look, then my phone is placed in my hand. "Thank you for trusting me." I smile at them both.

Ian has been gone for twenty-four hours now, and I haven't heard a word from him. I'm not too sure how I feel about it. Part of me is wondering if he is off with one of his many bimbos, the other part of me worries about his safety. I'm not a fighter, which is the complete opposite of Ian. You'd think being the daughter of the Gamma and being raised near warriors I'd be a fighter, but the truth is, it all makes me sick to my stomach. Plus, I'm my dad's princess. Between him and my brother, I've never been worried about my safety.

Today I'm running last-minute wedding errands with Rebeka, Sonia, and Sonia's three sisters. I'm really just going through the motions, because my heart is not into this today. I woke up late and missed my parents before they left for the day. Mom, Luna, and Ian's mom have their own day of wedding preps to take care of. Today, of all days, I really need to talk to my mom. I check my phone for the five hundredth time... still no Ian.

"Have you two heard from the guys?" I look at my phone again.

"No," they both reply.

"This isn't killing you?" I let out a frustrated breath.

"We try not to think about it," Sonia looks down.

"Sorry... I think I'm going to head back. I need my mom." I laugh at the last part... needing my mom, like a pup.

"Oh, hey Kate," I'm pulled out of my thoughts by the most annoying, nails on the chalkboard, high-pitched voice. "I didn't realize you're back from Chicago," she laughs.

"New York. I was in New York, Nikki," scoffing, "nice to see you too." I narrow my eyes and purse my lips. Nikki is the poorest excuse of a she-wolf with no moral compass. She is two years older than me and was one of the pack's tramps, as well as one of Ian's whores. Nikki enjoyed tormenting me with the fact she continued sleeping with him after she found out he and I were mated. *She didn't care.*

Chapter Twelve

GET A HOLD OF YOURSELF

March 2000

Kate

I STUMBLE DOWNSTAIRS, FOLLOWING the smell of bacon, sausage, eggs, blueberry muffins, waffles, and hash browns. Wonder why mom is cooking so much food? I step off the bottom tread and hear multiple voices coming from the kitchen. *What's going on?* I rub my eyes and step into the kitchen.

"Kelsey!" I shout seeing my brother standing in the kitchen with a piece of bacon hanging from his mouth. I jump into his arms, so happy to see my brother home from school. It's been six months, far too long.

"Hey, angel." I hear the sweet sound of Ian's voice from behind me. Pulling away from my brother, I turn into Ian's waiting arms.

I squeeze him tight, not wanting to let him go. "I've missed you, angel," he whispers in my ear.

"Oh, good grief, Kate. Go put some damn clothes on." My dad snaps, looking up from his newspaper. I look at my tank top and short shorts and giggle at my dad's reaction.

"Sorry dad," I slip from Ian's arms.

"We're going fishing after breakfast, so wear something comfortable." Ian holds my hands in his. I nod and take off for my room.

"Hey Zane," I say, running past him.

"What? No hug? I'm like chopped liver." He takes a bite of his blueberry muffin.

After we feast on the huge breakfast mom prepared for everyone, the guys and I cleaned the kitchen. I'm so excited to have them all home, even if it's just for the weekend. Kelsey complains that they're missing a raging kegger to be here, but I ignore him. He's always complaining about something.

Soon we load into two different golf carts and head for the lake, just the four of us. Just like the old days, Ian insists on baiting my hook. We cast our lines and sit on the soft grass at the lake's edge. We make small talk about school and what we've been up to. This is my third year attending the boarding school here in the pack's land. I live at school Monday through Thursday, coming home on Friday after school. Not everyone has the luxury of going home on the weekends, but when your dad is the gamma and you're his princess, you get special privileges. Ian is a business major, just like Zane and Kelsey, and he claims his classes are relatively easy.

"So, with such easy classes, what do you do with the rest of your time?" I adjust my line.

"Ummm…" Ian seems to be at a loss for words. Zane and Kelsey laugh. "Well, there are lots of things to do on campus."

"Like parties?" I look from my line to him.

"Yeah… there are parties." We hear Zane shout; I turn and see the water break as Zane reels in the massive fish. Ian jumps up and rushes over to help him. I find the entire interaction with Ian about parties odd, like he didn't want to talk about it. Just weird.

"Hell Yeah!" Zane shouts, lifting the huge catfish over his head. "You know what this means, right Kate?"

"Bonfire!" I excitedly shout.

"Bonfire!" The three guys shout back. I giggle. I'm so happy they're here, especially Ian.

We continue to laugh and fish the day away, each of us catching an enormous fish. Ian's mom brought us a cooler full of sandwiches, fresh fruit, and water. Slowly, our friends arrive and soon a gigantic pile of logs and fallen tree branches are intricately stacked ten feet tall. As the sun goes down, the silence of the forest is drowned out with loud music and laughter. They light the logs and prepare the fish to be cooked.

"Ian… babe… there you are." The most annoying high-pitched voice belonging to Nikki, one of the pack's whores. "I've been missing you all day. Your blocks are up, and I couldn't contact you." She whines and then pushes her body under his arm and wraps her arm around his waist. I purse my lips and cock my lips to the side. I hate Nikki.

"My blocks are not up. I was ignoring you." He wiggles out of her grip, staring at me.

"Oh, my goddess, don't be silly." She looks at him then follows his gaze to me, "oh, hey Kate." She whines my way. Bile rises in my throat, watching her filthy hands all over him.

"Nikki," I look down, so he doesn't see my lip quivering.

"Don't you have someone else you need to be bothering right now, Nikki?" Ian pushes away from her again.

"Funny..." she snaps, "I wasn't bothering you when I was going down on you yesterday." She crosses her arms and curls her lips in disgust at him.

"Excuse me," I feel like I'm about to puke, so I quickly turn to walk away when Ian grabs my arm.

"Where are you going?" He asks, pulling me into him.

"I just remembered that I have a paper due Monday that I haven't started yet. I need to go home and work on it." Looking at the ground, because I can feel the tears threatening to form and I don't want Ian to see me upset.

"I'll take you home." Ian leans down and whispers in my ear.

"No... I'll just take my dad's golfcart. Stay. Have fun." I pull my arm from his grip and walk away.

March 2004

"How's Ian doing these days?" Nikki giggles and looks at the two she-wolves she's with. She's still the horrible evil person she was before.

"How's your mate... Bruce, is it?" I push my shoulders back and cross my arms.

"Dante... we're so happy and in love. Not that you'd know what that was like since you rejected your mate." She laughs.

"Because you were so innocent in it all, right?" I cock my head to the side.

"Excuse me?" She scoffs, "can you believe she is blaming me?" She puts her hand on her chest and says, turning to her friends.

"Hmmm, I wonder what Dante thinks about being mated to the pack's doorknob?" I snarl out. In the past, I would run away from a confrontation with her; I'm not running anymore. *Bring it, bitch.*

"What?" She scoffs and crosses her arms.

"The pack doorknob... you know, cause everyone has had their turn." I laugh. Nikki's face turns red from anger, her fists are balled up at her side.

"Enough," Rebeka steps in between the two of us. "Nikki, Kate is your future Beta Female and, just like me, you'll show her respect. Please don't make me get Zane and Ian involved... I'm sure they will just escalate it to Alpha Nathaniel." Rebeka's voice is low, soft, yet firm. She's going to make a great Luna.

"Fine." Nikki and her friends turn on their heels and walk away.

"You ok, Kate?" Rebeka looks at me.

"I'm fabulous." I pretend not to be phased by Nikki, but I am. The sight of her brings back so many horrible memories. This is the bitch that I caught Ian with at the palace when I realized my chest pains were because of his infidelity. She seemed to enjoy causing me pain and has been the subject of so many nightmares. Funny how she is playing innocent in front of her friends. Seeing and hearing her awful voice, doubts about Ian being a changed man flood my mind.

"You stood up to her like a champ. I've never cared for her. She's kind of bullied me since I moved here." Sonia smiles and rubs my arm.

"Let's wrap this up and head home. It's margarita time." Rebeka laughs.

After coming back from running the last wedding errand, I go home, hoping to catch my mom there. There's no sign of her anywhere. I sniff around, and her scent is so faint, it's like she hasn't been here in days. I decide to take a shower and change into my pj's, hoping that mom will come back by the time I'm done.

After my shower, I come back downstairs and still no mom. This is just weird.

'*Mom?*' I call out through our mindlink.

'*Yes, sugar?*' She mindlinks back.

'*Where are you?*' I mindlink back.

'Pulling away from the main gate. Going to the city with Luna and Beta for dinner. Everything ok?' Mom has worry in her voice.

'Yes... no, I just needed to talk to you. I guess it can wait. Have fun. Love you.' I mindlink back.

As much as I could use my mom's advice, this might be better if I learn to control my doubts and emotions. Ian hasn't given me a reason to doubt his intentions... yet. He's been nothing but loving and caring. He genuinely seems remorseful about the past and has put me first. Maybe it's time I trust him. I push all my emotions down and make my way to the packhouse. Tonight, Rebeka has arranged a pajama girls' night to celebrate Sonia's last night as a single lady. Technically speaking, Sonia is far from a single lady, but we're trying to incorporate all human traditions for weddings. We'll be feasting on nachos and margaritas, which is Rebeka's go to junk food.

Minutes turn into hours as about one hundred she-wolves gather in the common area of the packhouse. My mom, Luna, and Ian's mom get back from dinner and join us. We all laugh, eat, drink, and tell stories about growing up with Kelsey... and yes, most of the ladies gathered here have some sort of story to tell about my brother. The best come from my mom, of course. It's a little past two a.m. and none of these ladies look like they're getting tired.

"I would love some pickles," mom says out of the blue.

"That's an odd craving. Am I getting a new sibling?" I tease.

"Ha! Nope, I'll leave the baby making to you and your brother." She crosses her arms in front of her in an X pattern.

"Ewww, mom. I'm not making babies with Kelsey." Sonia, Rebeka, and I laugh. It takes mom a minute to understand why we're laughing at her words.

"Oh, my goddess, Kate," she smacks me in the face with a pillow. "You knew exactly what I was trying to say. Now go get me pickles, young lady." She's giggling like a schoolgirl and pushing me off the couch.

"I'm going. I'm going." Mom playfully slaps me across the bottom because I'm still laughing. "Hey!" I jump and laugh.

Walking to the kitchen, I look at all the happy and smiling faces as I move past them. This was one of the main things I missed so much while I was living in New York. *Pack life.* Being part of a pack is the best feeling. We share amazing moments like this, but also help each other through the sad and heartbreaking moments as well. I'm honestly not sure how humans live their lives in solitude. They really don't know what they're missing.

Still with a silly smile on my face, I look in one of the large refrigerators in the kitchen area. Finding exactly what I came for, a familiar high-pitch voice causes my blood to curdle as I grab the jar from the fridge shelf.

"Oh, hey babe, how was Vegas?" Nikki speaks loudly into her phone. Knowing her, it's one of her lovers. I honestly can't imagine her being faithful to one man.

"I'm so glad you had a fun boys' trip, Dante. Can't wait until you get home. The things I want to do to you, starting with the way I'm going to su..." Nikki is interrupted before she can finish her filthy thought.

"Gross, Nikki, TMI." A female voice says.

"Babe, I've got to go. They're too many listening ears around. See you soon, lover." I hear her footsteps walk out of the kitchen and back to the party in the common area.

Dante? She was talking with Dante? Did she say boys' trip? Vegas? You've got to be kidding me. Ian lied again. He's the exact same... nothing has changed. How could I be so stupid? As the thoughts race through my mind, my breathing becomes heavy as I fight the tears back. The pickle jar slips from my fingers, shattering on the floor at my feet. Glass shards, pickles, and pickle juice fly everywhere.

"Damn it!" I murmur, "get a hold of yourself." I look for a broom and mop to take care of the mess that I've made.

I take my time cleaning up the mess, getting up every piece of glass from the floor. Once I've inspected the floor area a final time, squeals of joy and giggles of excitement fill the air. I can only assume that the guys are back from their trip. A fresh wave of anger washes over me.

"Kate... I'm home." Ian's voice booms from behind me.

CHAPTER THIRTEEN

SOMETHING FEELS OFF

February 2001

Ian

OUR FATHERS HELD US up in Alpha's office a little longer than I would have liked. They were mostly bitching about our three-point-zero GPA. They want a three-point-seven GPA or better and are holding our titles over our heads. *Bastards.* Sometimes I wonder if the three of us will ever be good enough in their eyes. We never seem to do anything right. They also inform us we will be required to attend meetings and formal functions with them, starting with the Autumn Moon Ball at the royal palace with them in September. This is a recent development. While we've attended certain functions with our parents over the years, we've never been required. Our fathers explain how important it is that the werewolf community gets to know us as the future leaders of this pack. In most packs, new alphas take rein between the ages of eighteen and twenty.

Our pack is different, reins change at twenty-five, after college and a year of training at the royal palace. This is because our territory and pack are the largest in North America, with around two thousand members. Our territory includes a growing city that is home to both humans and werewolves. Alpha Ezekiel decided that a certain amount of maturity was needed in an Alpha to handle such a massive pack.

After our meeting in the Alpha's office, Zane, Kelsey, and I make our way to the party tent set up in the garden behind the packhouse. I'm not surprised Kate's eighteenth birthday party is out here; she loves the roses and other flowers planted in this garden. So many times, I've watched her from the balcony of the packhouse; curled up in the rope hammock swing under the old oak tree just behind the garden reading. Simply lost in her own world. I could watch her for hours, her hair shimmering and being highlighted different colors by the rays of sun that leak through the heavy tree canopy. The way she'd lick her finger to turn the page as her hair gently moved with the breeze. She is so beautiful. Her dad had the swing added to the tree for her twelfth birthday, because the tree was her favorite place to read. She said being in the garden, smelling all the flowers, made her feel calm. I've had a thing for her since I was sixteen, but I didn't really understand what it was until after my eighteenth birthday. Not being able to tell her right away, I feel like I have lost years with her.

The party is in full swing by the time we make it out there, but there's no sign of Kate anywhere. I was hoping to meet up with her before the party started so I can give her a gift, but for now it sits safely in the pocket of my blazer. Leaning up against the bar with drinks in our hands, we note all the available she-wolves undressing us with their eyes. Most of the ones that are here are friends of Kate's, but like with any big function, unmated males and females travel from miles around hoping to find their mate. If they don't find their mates, they'll settle for a quick hookup in the woods later tonight.

Tonight, is a full moon. Full moons are exciting for us werewolves. We draw energy from the moon, and when the moon is full and high in the sky, it's at its most powerful. It's sort of like we are recharging our batteries while growing stronger. Emotions and hormones are always higher than normal during a full moon.

"Damn, look at all the fine pieces of ass that are here tonight." Kelsey says while eyeing a blonde, "looks like I'm having some fun tonight," he licks his lips earning a giggle from the blonde.

"That redhead looks like she might eat you alive, Kelsey." Zane laughs and takes a drink.

"Hey there's enough of Kelsey to go around." The cheeky bastard runs his hands through his hair and kisses the air towards the redhead. Zane and I burst into laughter, watching Kelsey's cheesy actions.

Before I know it, they surround the three of us. Twenty of the hottest she-wolves around. I quickly get lost in the moment with so many sexy women wanting my attention. Just like I've grown accustomed to, these women are all over the three of us. What can I say? I love the attention.

I'm not too sure how long we all laugh and talk, but apparently, we missed the arrival announcement of the birthday girl herself. I only realized it after I caught my parents glaring at me. *Shit.* I look around the tent and I see Kate staring at me as well. *Double Shit!* I recognize the look in her eyes... sadness and disappointment. *Did I do something wrong?* It was the same look she had when she ran from the bonfire...

that was just over a year ago. I've been home twice since then, but she's never around.

"Bro, we need to go wish your sister a happy birthday before our parents kill us." I look at Kelsey, then back to Zane.

"Will you excuse us, ladies?" Zane flashes the women his million-dollar smile and we make our way to Kate.

"Nice of you to come talk to your sister." Gamma Earnest snarls and sucks his teeth, looking at Kelsey.

"Happy Birthday, Kate." Zane hugs her. I breathe heavily, controlling Alex. He's not happy that any man is touching his mate.

"Thank you, Zane." She smiles at him.

"Kate... you look absolutely beautiful. Happy birthday, angel." I embrace her, pulling her fully into my arms. The electric tingles of the mate bond erupt on my skin. She hugs me back, but her body is stiff... something is wrong. She pats me in the middle of the back like you would a friend. *Wait! Am I in the friend zone? What the hell has happened since the last time I saw her?*

"Ian, thank you for coming," she pulls away from my arms. "I hope you all have a great time." She takes a deep breath. "Now, if you'll excuse me, I have guests to greet." She walks away, followed by her parents.

My mouth is wide open as I'm left standing there stunned and speechless, watching my mate walk away from me.

"What the fuck just happened?" I put my hands on my hips.

"Bro... no clue. Shouldn't she have felt something?" Zane puts his hand on my shoulder, "I've never seen her so cold before."

"Kelsey, is she dating someone?" I look at him.

"Not that I know of." He shakes his head.

"She is my mate. I know damn well I have felt the mate bond." I look between Zane and Kelsey.

"Wait... she's still seventeen. Her birthday is tomorrow. Today is just her party." Kelsey snaps his fingers and points like he's had some grand epiphany or some shit like that.

"What?" I turn to him.

"Yeah, since her birthday fell on a Sunday and she has school on Monday, my parents decided to have her party on Saturday." Kelsey winks at a brunette that's looking at him.

"So, she hasn't met her wolf yet?" I look at Zane, since Kelsey is obviously thinking with his dick.

"That explains a lot. Look, let's just have a good time tonight and things will be clearer to her tomorrow." Zane pats me on the back and leads me and Kelsey to a group of hungry she-wolves.

I've been watching Kate move around the tent, dancing and talking with everyone here. She is absolutely stunning in her blue dress with pink roses. The dress is short, form fitting, and is very low cut. I'm surprised Gamma Earnest let her out of the house at all. I'm surrounded by two horny wolves and a dozen she-wolves, but I couldn't care less. The only woman I have eyes for is my Kate. I just wish she felt the mate bond... or would just talk to me. *What the hell?* Kate and I used to be so close; we could talk for hours about nothing at all. Now she won't even look at me. I watch her as she dances with her friends... including male friends. Watching her dance and laugh with other males enrages me. That should be me out there with her, but she won't give me the time of day. I just sit and watch from afar.

Hours go by. It's a little after eleven p.m. and I have lost sight of her. She was here one second and gone the next. *Did she sneak off with some male?* That thought sends a pain straight through my chest.

"Bro, you see Kate?" I lean into Kelsey.

"Ha! You think I'm watching my sister? Bro, that's your job." Kelsey kisses the she-wolf on his lap.

"I'm going to go find Kate," I say to Zane before lifting the female from my lap and walk away.

I walk all around the tent looking for her, but she is nowhere to be seen and her scent is fading fast. *Where did she go?*

"Excuse me," I say to Kate's mom.

"Ian!" She turns to me still dancing, "are you having fun, sweety?" She is smiling from ear to ear.

"Yes ma'am, but I was looking for Kate. I have a gift for her." I pat my blazer where her gift is.

"Well, she has been dealing with a migraine all day and went home early." She spins and rocks her hips. I laugh because she is the opposite of Gamma Earnest. He's very strict and always stoic while she is the life of the party. I'm guessing Kelsey got his temperament from his mom rather than his dad.

"Oh, ok. Thank you very much." I bow my head and back away from her.

I make my way to Kate's house and can see Kate's bedroom light is the only light on in the house.

'Kate...' I call out through our mindlink, but she doesn't answer me back. 'Kate.... Kate.' I repeatedly try, but still no answer. *Something feels off.* Checking the front door... locked. I walk around the house looking for an unlocked window or something. There is a nagging feeling that I need to get to Kate. Luckily for me, the back door is slightly cracked. I walk through the kitchen to the living room and stand at the bottom of the staircase, debating whether or not I should walk up the stairs.

"Kate!" I shout from the bottom of the stairs... no reply. "Kate! It's Ian. Answer me or I'm coming up there." I wait and listen, but nothing. "Fine, you forced my hand." I take a deep breath and slowly make my way up the stairs.

I walk down the hall to her room; her scent is light. Her bedroom door is open, but I still knock before walking in. The dress she wore to the party is lying on her bed, but she is not here. I turn around and check the bathroom that she and Kelsey shared as pups. Again, I find the door open, and there is some water in the tub's bottom, but no Kate. I step into the bathroom and slip in a puddle of water. I hang on tight to the bathroom sink to keep from falling to the ground like a newborn baby giraffe. Looking around, the entire bathroom floor is covered in water, almost like she was dragged out of the tub. *What the fuck?*

I walk back downstairs, looking around the house again for her. The nagging feeling turns into panic and worry that sets up in the pit of my gut. I'm not too sure what to do. Part of me wants to call for help, but the other part wants to find her myself. I walk out the back door and onto the gravel path just outside her home. I look at my watch. It's just after midnight and the full moon is high in the sky. I hear howls throughout the territory, as many are shifting and running. Suddenly, I'm hit with the most excruciating pain that starts in my chest and radiates through my entire body. The pain is so intense that I drop to the ground, letting out a whimper and cry. I lay on the ground for a few minutes, trying to catch my breath, then another wave of pain hits and every muscle in my body tenses up. I can't move. My body is frozen in place. It's like I have rickets or something like that. Soon the pain releases a bit and I'm finally able to get back up to my feet. Alex cries in my head. He repeats mate over and over in my head. *Kate.* This pain is from her... I'm feeling her pain. *Is someone hurting her?* I need to find her, and fast.

'Zane... I need your help, bro. Meet me at Kate's place. Hurry,' I mindlink before another wave of pain hits and I drop to my knees. I'm not too sure how long I'm on the ground before Zane's shoes come into sight.

"Bro, what's going on? You okay?" Zane helps me off the ground.

"I came looking for Kate. I can't find her," I say through a heavy breath, "and I keep getting hit with these fucking horrible waves of pain. Zane, this pain is from her... I just know it. She's in trouble." I shake my head, trying to stay calm in between the waves of pain. "This feels like her body is sending me an SOS call." Looking at Zane, I can tell he's mindlinking someone. My guess, his father.

Another wave of pain hits and I groan as I hit the ground. Once again, my muscles stiffen up and my body contorts before I'm frozen in place. Soon I see several sets of shoes quickly approaching.

"Ian, honey, what happened?" My mom drops to her knees next to me.

"Kate," I say through the pain, "I... need... to find... Kate." My body finally relaxes enough, and my father helps me to my feet.

"Ian, look at me." Luna Martha holds my face between her hands. "I need you to concentrate. Do not allow the pain to overcome you again. Kate's wolf is calling out to you. Allow your wolf to track her. To do that, you'll need to block the pain out. Can you do that for your mate?" I nod, almost too weak to speak.

I close my eyes and inhale as another wave of pain hits, then I exhale, and the pain is numb. It's still there but numbed down enough for me to concentrate.

'Alex, we need to find Kate.' I give him control of my human form. With him in control, all our senses are heightened, making it easier to locate her. Alex smells the air and listens. His head snaps to the left as he hears her faint cries. He takes off running to the tree line, leaving everyone else behind.

The closer we get to the tree line, the stronger her scent is. *I'm coming Kate!* As we step into the tree line, we see something laying on the forest floor. *Kate.* She is moaning in pain and wrapped only in a towel. *What happened to her?* Alex vows to kill anyone who hurt her before giving me back control. My heart races as I rush to her. The faster I run, the further away she seems to get. My legs are heavy like I'm running through mud.

It feels like I run for miles and miles before I finally reach her. Her eyes are closed, and she is moaning lightly. Alex cries a pain-filled howl for his mate. I drop to my knees next to her and inspect her for injuries. She has a couple of cuts and scrapes on her knees, legs, hands, and arms. Her face has dirt on it, and there is grass and leaves in her hair. She looks like she has fallen and crawled to the spot where I found her. I hear the others as they catch up to me. Kate's mom cries out for her injured pup.

"Kate," I brush the hair out of her face. "It's me, angel," I stroke her cheek with the back of my hand.

"Ian," she mumbles, opening her eyes, "you came."

"Yes, angel, I'm here." I lean down to her, supporting her neck with one hand and rubbing her jaw with the other.

"Mate," she whispers before screaming out in pain. Her entire body goes stiff in my arms as her muscles lock up.

"Kate!" Her mom shouts and cries behind me.

Chapter Fourteen

TUNNEL OF LIGHTS

February 2001

Kate

"WAKE UP, BITCH!" JESSI shouts as she jumps on my bed.

"Uhhhh. Go away!" I groan as I'm violently jerked away from my peaceful sleep.

"Get up! Get up! It's time to get up!" The crazy she-wolf continues to use my bed like a trampoline.

"Who let you in my house?" I cover my head with my blanket.

"Your dad. Now get up. Guess who's coming home today?" She lands on her knees beside me, jerking the covers completely off me.

"Ian," I smile.

"I was going to say Kelsey, but yeah, I guess Ian will be coming here too." She laughs and hits me with a pillow.

"You're such a horn dog, do you know that?" I laugh and hit her with a pillow.

"Duh," she laughs. "But I'm eighteen now... we might end up sisters." She smiles from ear to ear, "if not, I'll just have some more fun with him."

"Ewww, gross. He's my brother. I don't want to hear about your gross escapades with him." With my hands, I cover my ears. I always knew she liked Kelsey, but I never knew that they have already done it. I guess she was one of the ones I heard him grunting with in the woods.

"I haven't seen Ian in so long, but after the thing with Nikki and him at the bonfire... I just couldn't." I sit up and stretch.

"You should've punched that bitch right in her nose." Jessi punches the air.

"Maybe..." I look down and play with the sheet on my bed.

"You'll find out today if Ian is your mate, after all." Jessi squeals.

"No, I won't. My birthday is not until tomorrow." I purse my lips and look at Jessi.

"That sucks." Her smile fades to a frown.

"Yeah," I sigh out.

"Girls," mom shouts from downstairs, "biscuits and gravy are ready! Come eat! We leave for the salon in one hour."

Jessi and I look at each other and smile, then rush downstairs, pushing and shoving each other out of the way. Biscuits and gravy are one of our all-time favorites, and mom only makes it once or twice a year. She makes everything from scratch, just like her mom taught her. I love the drop biscuits that she calls cat head biscuits, and if you ask her why they're called that, she'll simply say because they're as big as a cat's head. When I was about ten years old, I asked my grandma who was visiting why she didn't make biscuits like they do in the packhouse; rolled and cut into circles. My grandma just tilted her head at me and said, "dear sweet child... because I don't want to. You see, once I learned never to do things I don't want to do, my life improved by tenfold." Little advice like that has always stuck with me.

Jessi and I slide our way into the kitchen, narrowly missing mom as she walks from the stove to the table with her plate of food. My stomach lets out a loud roar, letting me know it can't wait to get the yummy smelling food inside my belly. Mom has plates waiting for us next to the stove, and we each take a baseball sized biscuit and split it in half. I pour on two huge ladles full of the delicious cream gravy with sausage mixed in. Jessi butters one half of her biscuit, then pours fresh raw honey from our pack's apiary over it. I love the honey from our territory this time of year. The citrus trees are in full bloom and the honey has a sweet orange blossom taste to it. She then pours two ladles of the creamy goodness over the other half of the biscuit. Jessi has said she can drink the gravy straight from a mug, and I believe her.

My mom watches the two of us shoveling food into our mouths like we haven't eaten in weeks. I can tell by the look on her face she is not approving of the way we are eating, so I sit up and elbow Jessi.

"You know," mom sips her coffee, "you both are not pups anymore. You're both women now and could meet your mate any second. Maybe it's time we act a little more... ladylike. You know, put the finishing classes your dad and I paid for to good use." She looks between Jessi and me.

"I didn't go to finishing school," Jessi looks down. Jessi's parents are not ranked wolves and because of that, there are differences in our lifestyles. Like finishing school. As a ranked wolf, it's expected that I will be mated to a ranked wolf and will be expected to attend different events where I will need to know proper etiquette. Even though Jessi is not ranked, my parents have always welcomed her into our home. My mom has even treated her like a daughter, teaching her things here and there.

"If you like, Jessi, I will be happy to teach you proper etiquette. A lady should always have good manners. You never know when you'll need them." My mom smiles and takes a bite from her fork.

"Really?" Jessi says through a mouthful of food. I put my head down and laugh to myself.

"First lesson," my mom puts her hand up to Jessi, "don't talk with a mouthful of food." Jessi simply nods as she chews. My mom really has her work cut out for her. Jessi is a sweetheart, but really rough around the edges.

Suddenly I'm hit with a sharp pain in my head behind my eyes. I hold my head in my hands and groan quietly.

"What's wrong, sweetheart," mom says.

"Sharp pain in my head." I look up at my mom.

"Migraine?" She stands next to me.

"No, it feels different." I rub my head with my fingertips. Unfortunately, I have had migraines since I was fifteen. The doctor's at the pack hospital ran a battery of test and could never pin point an issue. My dad told me that migraines run in the family, that his grandmother suffered from migraines before she got her wolf. So I'm hoping that once I get my wolf the migraines will stop. My triggers for my migraines seem to be stress or when I get my period. Right now, I'm neither of those two things. This pain is behind my eyes. My migraines usually start on top of my head. This pain is unusual and different.

"Let me grab your medicine." Mom walks to the cupboard where we keep medical supplies and medicine.

"Just something over the counter. The other stuff makes me drowsy, and I want to be wide awake for my party." I smile at my mom and breathe. I really hope this is not a stupid migraine, not today of all days.

"Come on honey, time to wake up and get dressed for your party." My mom strokes my shoulder. I take a deep breath and slowly open my eyes.

The pain in my head hasn't gone away all day. I took two doses of over-the-counter pain meds before my mom convinced me to take my prescribed meds. And just as I thought, they knocked me on my ass. I look at the clock on my nightstand and my party starts in less than an hour. I've been asleep for four hours.

"Mom, why did you let me sleep so long?" I shoot straight up.

"You're the birthday girl. The party doesn't start until you arrive." She smiles and tucks a piece of hair behind my ear.

"My hair and makeup..." I gasp.

"Are just fine. We'll touch everything up a bit and it will be good as new." She walks to my closet and pulls my dress out for me.

"How can you be so calm?" I stand up.

"Well, we both can't be freaking out now, can we?" She laughs. "How's your head?"

"Better." I nod and smile.

She helps me change into my party dress. This dress screamed at me when Jessi and I were shopping. It was love at first sight. I didn't want something in my normal pink color. I wanted something... different. The dress is a medium bright blue color with a pink rose print all over. It has half puffy sheer sleeves and a plunging sweetheart neckline. It's form fitting to my hips, then flares out in multi layers of the same sheer fabric the sleeves are made of and comes about mid-thigh.

"Oh, Kate. You look like an angel on earth." My mom has tears in her eyes. She slowly breathes in and out while looking at me from head to toe. "You're all grown up," she sniffles, "and so beautiful. Your future mate is so lucky." She puts her hands on her chest.

"Mom, don't cry. You'll make me cry," I fan her face with my hands.

"Sorry, sugar." She looks up at the ceiling and breathes. After she gains control of her emotions, she looks at me. "Look, all better. Ready to party the night away?" She smiles, then grabs my hands and does a little dance.

"Yes. I'm ready." I laugh at my mom. "Did Kelsey make it back to the territory yet?" I really could care less about Kelsey. What I really want to ask is if Ian is here.

"Yes, all three boys made it back a couple of hours ago. But they're in a little trouble, so they've been in Alpha's office since they got back. I'm sure being yelled at by their fathers."

"Oh. Sucks for them." I laugh.

"Dad should be here in a few to pick us up for your grand entrance." Mom walks into her bedroom. *Dad.* A wave of panic sets in. He hasn't seen my dress yet. I hope he doesn't get upset because it's short and low cut.

Mom, Dad, and I arrive in the garden where my party is being held. They set the tent up in the middle. We walk the red carpet and have our pictures taken in front of a wall made of greenery with my name written in roses. After we pose for like five-thousand pictures, we continue down the red carpet into a tunnel of lights. This tunnel is probably twenty feet long and has thousands of sparkling and twinkling white lights. It's so neat to walk through but seems to trigger my headache again. I ignore the pain behind my eyes. Nothing is going to ruin my night. As we make our way through the tunnel to the other end, I hear the music fade a little as the DJ introduces himself to the crowd.

"Okay, I'm going to need everyone on their feet." The DJ announces, "Come on now, on your feet." He waves his hands in the air. "Our guest of honor, the birthday girl herself, has arrived. She'll be walking through the tunnel of lights any second, and I'm going to need you all to make some noise. Let's hear it. Make some noise for the very special and beautiful Kate. Let's hear you make some noise for my girl, Kate." The DJ shouts into his microphone, pumping up the crowd.

As I walk through the tunnel followed by my parents, everyone cheers, claps, shouts, and howls.. I clap and wave to everyone. I'm so happy that there are so many from our pack here tonight to celebrate my birthday with me. It makes me feel so special. Then *In da Club* by 50 Cent plays. Mom grabs my hand and we dance our way to the center of the dance floor. I'm all smiles dancing with my mom; she so good at it. I turn and see my dad walking up to me carrying two dozen white roses.

I can't believe my dad surprised me with white roses. Even more surprising is the way he didn't react to my dress. I thought he'd be upset with it, but he didn't seem to be. With tears in his eyes, he told me how beautiful I am and how lucky my mate is. I found it odd that both Mom and Dad mentioned a mate to me. *Do they know something?* He squeezes me tight, kisses my forehead, and gives me a beautiful gold diamond tennis bracelet. Mom says every lady needs a simple yet elegant diamond tennis bracelet.

Everyone joins us on the dance floor, even my dad is dancing. Well, his version of dancing anyway. He's so stiff, which is the complete opposite of mom. I'm having so much fun. I look around the tent... looking for Ian. My smile fades to a frown when I see some whore sitting on his lap. There are probably two dozen tramps surrounding him, Kelsey, and Zane. I stop dancing and just stare. My heart breaks. Any hope of Ian being my mate fades. I don't want someone like him... someone who doesn't care to give me two seconds of his time on my special day. I'm not too sure how long I stand there watching him with his hands all over another woman, smiling and laughing. Completely in his own world. The crowd moves around me, almost in slow motion. Then Ian looks up and our eyes meet, and his smile fades to confusion when he sees the hurt written all over my face.

After the bonfire, I have purposely avoided him. I'm not a confrontational person and seeing Nikki hanging all over him and hearing the gross things she did with him hurt so badly. Deep inside, I always knew he was not waiting for his fated mate. Most everyone I know doesn't wait. I'm the oddball in the crowd. Even though I always knew, having it flaunted in my face just sucks. So, to keep from seeing him and his playboy ways, I've just avoided him. Seems he didn't miss me at all.

"Party is over here, sweetheart." Mom turns me away from Ian and back to my crowd of friends.

Chapter Fifteen

SASHA

February 2001

Kate

EVEN THOUGH I'M SAD and frustrated, I don't want my party ruined. My mom worked so hard on it. I push down all my feelings and continue to have fun with the people who want to be with me today. I dance for a while until I'm stopped by a guest wanting to wish me a happy birthday. This continues for a while until I hear my dad say, "nice of you to come talk to your sister." *Crap!* I turn and come face to face with Zane, Kelsey, and Ian. *Double Crap!*

"Happy Birthday, Kate." Zane greets me with an enormous hug. I squeeze him back; this is the second time I have ever hugged Zane; the first time was his eighteenth birthday.

"Thank you, Zane." I pull away and smile at him.

"Kate... you look absolutely beautiful. Happy birthday, angel." Ian pulls me into an embrace. He pulls me tight into his body. This is a different hug from him, almost like there are emotions to it. He's also wearing my favorite cologne on him. I love the fresh scent; he smells so good. Not wanting to get hung up on Ian again, I give him a halfhearted hug and a pat on the back like you would a friend. Then pull away.

"Ian, thank you for coming. I hope you all have a great time." I take a deep breath, "now if you'll excuse me, I have guests to greet." My head is pounding. I leave to get some fresh air.

As the night wears on, my head continues to pound, exhaustion takes over my body, and I feel lightheaded. The pain that first started behind my eyes has now spread to my entire head. The noise and lights are bothering me, and I feel like I might get sick. I've had migraines since I can remember, but this feels different.

"Mom," I tug on her arm.

"Oh sugar, you look white as a ghost." She presses the back of her hand to my forehead.

"Yeah, the headache has turned into a migraine, and it's getting bad." I close my eyes and rub my temples. "I'm going home to take some medicine and soak in the tub."

"Okay, I'll go with you." She loops her arm into mine.

"No, mom. You stay here. Have fun. I just need some quiet and rest." I pull my arm away from her. She looks disappointed. I'm not too sure if it's because I'm not feeling well, or that I'm leaving my party early, or that I just want to be alone.

"Okay, sugar. If you need me, I will be there in less than a minute, okay?" She holds my hand and brushes the hair out of my face with her other hand.

I walk through the back door of my house and brace myself against the wall with one hand as another sharp pain shoots through my head, radiating down my spine. Slowly I breathe in and out until the pain subsides enough for me to move again. For a moment, I consider mindlinking my mom, but I decide against it. She worked so hard putting the party together for me. She deserves to have fun. After all, I'm her last pup, no more big bashes. My mom loves to party. How could I deny her this? Besides, I know I won't be any fun after I take my medication.

Making my way up the stairs, I have to stop and rest halfway up. Normally I can run up the stairs in less than a minute, but today it feels like there are a hundred miles of stairs to climb. Once I reach my bathroom, I plug the tub and turn the water on. Then I brace myself against the bathroom sink as another wave of pain hits my head and neck. I breathe through the pain, then look into the mirror. Wow, mom was right. I am as white as a ghost. I study my face and see that dark circles have formed under each eye; it looks like someone punched me in both eyes. I walk into my room and take off all my jewelry, carefully placing it on top of my chest of drawers. I admire my new tennis bracelet from my parents. It sparkles in the light and is so magnificent. My mom has several tennis bracelets that I've always admired, and now I have one of my very own. I take off my dress and toss it on my bed. I remove my panties and bra and toss them into the hamper.

As I sink into the tub, I remember I hadn't taken my medicine yet. I know I should probably get out of the tub and go downstairs and take it, but the hot water feels so good against my skin. With a rolled-up wash cloth supporting my neck, I lay back in the tub. I'm relaxing and the tension in my head seems to go away. I close my eyes and feel myself drifting to sleep.

"Hey!" A woman's voice shouts. I open my eyes and sit up. *Did I just imagine that?* I sit quietly, looking out the opened bathroom door. Nothing... just darkness and silence.

"Mom?" I call out, "I'm in the tub." Nothing. I chalk up hearing the woman shout hey as my subconscious not wanting me to fall asleep in the bathtub.

Laying back, I breathe, trying to relax again. Suddenly I'm hit with another wave of pain, only this time the pain shoots through my head, down my neck, into my spine, and down my legs. I groan out in pain and pull myself up from the water. One hand is flat against the cold tile of the bathroom wall, the other hand is holding on to the side of the tub. I breathe in and out until the pain releases its hold on my head. I need to get out of the tub and downstairs to take my medicine. The pain has never felt like this before, but then again, I've never let a migraine go unchecked for so long.

I bend my knees and try to stand when another wave of pain hits. If I thought the last round was bad, this one is ten times worse. The pain quickly takes over my entire body and I slip, falling backwards. I catch myself on the wall and by the side of the tub. Every muscle in my body goes completely stiff and I can't move. My body feels like one big muscle cramp. There are ripples in the water caused by my body shaking. I'm not in control of my body, like some other force is at work here. Something is blocking me every time I attempt to mindlink my mom. It's like I'm hitting a brick wall every time.

By the time the pain passes, and I can move my limbs again, the water is cold. I use my toe to pull the plug out of the drain. I'm not too sure what happened, but I don't want to be in a tub full of water if it happens again. Feeling the need to get out of the tub, I try to stand, but my legs are too weak. I pull myself up on the side of the tub, then bend forward and let gravity do the rest. I slide out of the tub, landing on the floor mat in front of the tub. Water splashes out with me and now covers the entire floor. I rest on the floor mat for a few minutes. Getting out of the tub took so much out of me, and my energy is completely drained. Before I can regain my strength, I'm hit with another wave of excruciating pain throughout my entire body. Again, my muscles stiffen, and I can't move, completely frozen in place. I whimper as tears roll down my face. I don't know what is happening to me, but I just want it to stop. As I'm laying naked and cold on the bathroom floor, I'm hoping that someone will come home. Right now, I need my mom more than anything.

When the pain releases me, I pull myself up and sit on the toilet seat. I grab a towel and wrap it around my cold, wet body. I'm out of breath and my body aches from all the cramping. Something inside my head is continuing to block me from mindlinking my mom. *What the hell is going on?* I need to get to my mom. I slowly stand, keeping the towel tight around my body. Moving out of the bathroom down the hall, I brace myself on the walls. My body is so weak.

When I get to the stairs, I stand there and stare down. How am I supposed to get down the stairs in my weakened state? What if my muscles freeze up again and I fall to my death? I need help and can't wait in here until someone comes home. Remembering how Kelsey and I used to slide down the stairs as pups, I decide that is my best option. If my muscles freeze up again, I'll be on my bottom and can brace myself. I sit on the top step and breathe, then slide my bottom to the next step. Moving my feet a couple of steps below me and use them to pull myself down to the next step. I continue doing this until I reach the bottom of the staircase. Grateful that my body didn't freeze up again.

Slowly, I make my way out the back door and walk in the packhouse's direction when I'm hit with another wave of pain. I drop to my knees and roll to my side as my body freezes and contorts itself. I scream out in pain, but I don't hear any sound coming from my lips... just the sound of air escaping my lungs.

"Woods!" A woman's voice shouts. The same voice I heard while I was in the tub.

Suddenly, I feel my body move on its own. *What the hell?* I'm on my knees with my forehead resting on the ground. I stand and involuntarily move towards the tree line. *No! I need to go get my mom.* I fight my body, stopping myself from moving, causing another wave of pain to take over my body. I collapse to my knees again and drift off into darkness.

When I wake up, I'm walking and can see the tree line just ahead. My body moves on its own. I feel like I'm watching a movie or something. My vision is blurred, and my hearing is dull. It feels like I'm underwater. The world around me looks like it's moving in a wave pattern. It feels like there is cotton in my ears. I'm having a hard time hearing. *Did I slip and drown in the tub? Am I dead?* Just inside the tree line, I try to stop moving forward and am met with horrendous pain that forces me down to the ground. I fall, hitting the ground hard. My body contorts into different positions, and I can hear the same woman's voice screaming in pain. I drift back into the darkness.

When I wake up, I'm crawling on all fours with my belly rubbing against the cold, wet ground. I watch as my fingernails dig into the soft soil of the forest floor, and my hands pull my body forward.

"Moon," I hear the woman's voice say. Her voice is softer than before, she sounds weak.

I finally make it to a clearing in the forest where the strongest light from the full moon above is. My body is exhausted, and I collapse into the center of the clearing, rolling onto my back. Facing the moon, I can't help but to wonder if I'm dying and my body wanted to see the glory of the full moon just one more time. As I look at the moon, I fade into darkness.

When I wake up, I can't see anything. I raise my hand to my face and nothing. There is no light or sound, just darkness and nothingness. I hear whimpering and crying. I'm not alone.

"Hello?" I call out. My voice echoes. "Who's there?" I wait for a response. "What is your name?"

"Sasha," a woman's voice whispers.

"Hi Sasha, I'm Kate. Do you know where we are?" I turn my head, but all I see is black.

"Your mind," Sasha whispers.

"My mind? Then who are you?" I ask.

"Your wolf," she cries.

"What? Where are you?" I call out, desperate to meet her.

"I'm hurt and scared. I'm early and have been trying to come out all day, but something kept stopping me." She cries. My stomach drops, the over counter pain pills and my prescribed medicine kept her from contacting me today. "The full moon is pulling me... It hurts. I need mate."

"I'm sorry Sasha. I'm hurting and scared, too. We don't have a mate."
I close my eyes and put my head down.

"Yes, we do. He's close." She whispers.

"Kate. It's me, angel." I open my eyes to see Ian's gorgeous face.

"Ian, you came." I whisper.

"Yes, angel, I'm here." He leans down and shows me his million-dollar smile. But his eyes are full of fear and pain. He supports my neck with one hand and rubs my jaw with the other. Tingles and sparks radiate, and suddenly I'm hit with his fresh citrus smell.

"Mate," I smile and whisper before another wave of muscle cramping pain hits me. I scream as my entire body goes stiff and contorts. Ian grunts and breathes as if he is in pain, too.

"Kate!" I hear my mom shout and cry just before my world fades into darkness again.

Chapter Sixteen

FIRST SHIFT

February 2001

Kate

I'M NOT TOO SURE how long I've been asleep, but I wake up in Ian's arms. My head and back are pulled up on Ian's lap. He is rocking me, playing with my hair, and humming.

"Gamma Earnest, get your mate home. Kate doesn't need to hear her mother cry for her. She needs calm. Everyone go! I will stay and keep watch as she shifts for the first time. There's nothing anyone can do for her; she needs her mate. I will let you know." I hear Luna Martha say with authority.

"Hello, my angel." Ian says as my eyes flutter open. Hearing footsteps, I turn my head to see who's approaching.

"Hello Kate," Luna Martha kneels next to me. "It's Luna Martha, sweet girl," she sighs. "Honey, I know you're scared and confused, but you're shifting for the first time." Her voice is soft as she gently rubs my cheek with the back of her fingers. "I'm sure you've heard that first shifts are painful. Unfortunately, yours will be excruciating, just like mine was. My first shift fell on a full moon too and my wolf was pulled and forced out before she was ready… just like yours. Luckily for you, your mate is here to help keep you calm, making it a little more bearable." Her hand moves from my face to Ian's shoulder, then back to my face. "Your wolf is just as scared as you. Normally, first shifts can take hours. Yours will be relatively quick, because of the intense power of the moon." She pauses before looking up. "Ian, I know this is scary and you're not too sure what to do. Just let your instincts kick in. Alex will guide you. I will be right over there; in case you need me." She pauses before standing and walking away.

"Angel, I'm here. You've got this." Ian says before a wave of pain hits. I try to fight the pain away, but it quickly overcomes my body. Every muscle tenses up and I contort and freeze. "Don't fight it, angel. Breathe and relax." Ian inhales deeply before exhaling. He rubs my face and continues to breathe in and out. I follow his lead and soon my muscles relax. "Good job. You're doing so good, angel. I can't wait to meet your wolf." I smile, then I'm hit with another wave of pain. The pain is so intense I'm overcome by darkness. When I wake up, I'm still being rocked in Ian's arms. Everything about him is different from the Ian I saw just a few hours ago. He is so kind and caring, just like he was when I first realized that I was in love with the boy next door.

I continue to be hit with pain, and Ian continues to keep me calm. He looks like he is in pain as well, but he puts my needs over his. I fade in and out of consciousness and I can feel my body is wet. I'm not too sure if it's sweat or dew… maybe a combination of the two. My body trembles from being wet and cold. Noticing me shivering, Ian removes his blazer to cover me. I see he is wearing the paracord bracelet I made for him two years ago. I lift my hand and run my fingertips across the top.

"I wear it every day. It makes me feel close to you." Ian smiles and covers my body with his jacket.

Another wave of pain hits. This is the most intense yet. The pain hits me wave after wave. Ian tries to comfort me, and I try to breathe. The pain pulsates through my body. My body contorts, and I can hear strange sounds coming from within me. It almost sounds like dishes being broken. The throbbing pain and cracking sounds are too much. Once again, I'm overcome by darkness.

"Open your eyes, angel." Ian's voice guides me from the darkness that I have become familiar with tonight. "Open your eyes." I open my eyes and see the love in Ian's eyes. "you're so beautiful," he whispers.

I move my neck to look down and feel a weird sensation, like I'm wrapped in a soft fur blanket. Looking down, I see a chocolate-colored furry leg and white paw where my arm and hand should be. *I've shifted.*

"You've shifted, Kate. Can you stand?" Ian asks. I try to move, but my body is a little stiff. "It's okay, angel. You just went through a lot. Why don't you rest?" Ian rubs his fingers through my fur, and I drift to sleep.

'Hi Kate,' I hear a familiar woman's voice. I open my eyes and am surrounded by white light.

'Where am I?' I look around when I hear a giggle behind me. I turn around and come face to face with the most beautiful chocolate-colored wolf with white paws standing there. Her fur shimmers and shines in the white light. 'Sasha?' I rub my hands through her fur.

'Yes,' she giggles.

'You sound different.' I smile.

'I was weak earlier because you kept taking pills and fighting me. I'm much stronger now.' Sasha rubs her head into my chest. 'No more of those little red pills. They hurt. You won't need them now that I'm here.'

'I had no idea you where trying to contact me. I wasn't expecting you until tomorrow. Deal, no more red pills. I'm so happy you're here and I'm finally meeting you. Where are we?' I look around.

'We're in your mind.' Sasha laughs.

'But we were in my mind earlier and it was nothing but darkness.' I tilt my head at her.

'I was hurting and scared, and I didn't want to meet you for the first time like that.' Sasha stretches. 'I'm ready to meet my mate and run. Aren't you... ready to run?'

'Yes, but how does it work?' I cross my arms in front of me.

'You and I are one, Kate. We will know each other better than anyone else. Because we are one, we can switch giving each other control in both forms.' Sasha explains.

'How do we switch?' I ask.

'You just visualize taking a step back in your mind. That's when I will come forward. You'll be able to feel everything I do, and vice versa. If a time ever arises... like an emergency, I can push through... and vice versa.' Sasha stands. 'It will be hard at first, but it will get easy as time passes. Ready?'

'Ready.' I take a deep breath and smile.

I open my eyes and see Ian's wolf, Alex, sleeping next to me. He is such a magnificent-looking beast. Alex is beige with red undertones and a white chest. He almost looks like he's wearing a beige tuxedo. I've only seen him twice from a distance, and now he's here, up close and personal. I need to touch him. Bumping his nose with mine, he opens his eyes. His ears perk up as he sits up, staring at me.

'*Kate?*' A gruff voice that is unfamiliar to me fills my head.

'*Yes,*' I answer.

'*My name is Alex. I'm Ian's wolf. I'm so happy to finally meet you. I've been watching and waiting for you.*' Alex bows his head at me. '*can I meet your wolf now?*' My heart swells and it feels like a thousand butterflies are in my belly, fluttering around, hearing him say he's been waiting for me.

'*Yes,*' I concentrate on stepping back into my mind. Suddenly I feel like something pulls me backwards, and soon it feels like I'm sitting in front of a giant movie screen complete with surround sound.

At first Sasha is clumsy. She trips over her paws as she gets used to her body. I watch her learning how to use her new body in amazement. It's like I'm on a ride in an amusement park. I can feel the bounce in her step, running, jumping, and even snuggling into Alex for affection. Everything, I can feel everything. This is wild, freeing, and exhilarating. I giggle with excitement.

Alex and Sasha make their way through the forest. Soon the sounds of howls are heard from all around as members of the pack join us. My heart flutters as I see my parents' wolves. They both nuzzle into Sasha, showing her so much love. Soon Sasha is tackled to the ground by my brother's wolf. She quickly jumps to her feet and chases after him. They play and wrestle like young pups until Zane's wolf tackles him to the ground. Soon the three male wolves are play fighting while Sasha watches. She and I both laugh at the shenanigans.

We continue running and playing until the sun rises. Even though I'm having fun, I can feel Sasha's body getting tired, and I know the fun will need to stop so we can rest. Slowly but surely, everyone goes home and soon it's just Alex and Sasha. He guides Sasha into the lake next to the fishing cabin for a swim. The cool water is instantly refreshing and makes me feel like we can keep running for hours more, but I know we can't. We need to rest.

We exit the water behind Alex. He shakes, shedding water out of his fur, then shifts. It's almost instantaneous and effortless for him.

'Time to shift back to our human form, Kate.' Sasha says in my mind.

'How am I going to do that? I'm not even sure how I shifted into my wolf's form to begin with. When I woke up, I had four legs, paws, and fur.' I snap.

'You're so silly,' Sasha giggles. *'It's all about instincts. Some things will come naturally. You'll just know how to do them.'* I feel her lie down on the ground, *'Okay, so close your mind's eye and think of your human body. Visualize your legs, arms, hands, and skin. As you do, step forward in your mind to regain control.'*

'That easy, huh?' I question.

'Yes, that easy.' Sasha giggles.

'Will it hurt?' I ask, afraid of feeling the pain I experienced during my first shift.

'It may be uncomfortable the first few times, but soon it will be as easy as walking and talking.' Sasha replies.

I follow her instructions and hope that she is right about only experiencing a minor discomfort. Closing my mind's eye, I visualize my legs, hands, arms, feet, skin, hair, and my face. As I take a step forward, I feel a free-falling sensation. It's the same sinking feeling you get in your belly when you're on a rollercoaster. As I'm being pulled forward, the breath escapes my lungs as my internal organs push against each other. When the sensation stops, I'm in control of my body that is still shifting back to its human form. I can hear the sounds of dishes breaking, but soon realize it's my bones changing from one form to another. My muscles and joints ache, but the pain is nothing like last night. I take deep breaths and soon I feel cool air against my skin.

I open my eyes and see my human hands pressed flat against the ground. My body is laying flat on the cool ground. I can hear the birds singing and feel the warmth of the sun on my back. I raise my head and see Ian's smiling face looking lovingly at me.

"Welcome back, angel." Ian offers his hand to me. I lift my hand to his and he pulls me to my feet. "Did you have fun on your first run?" He brushes the hair out of my face.

"Yes, it was so much fun," I smile.

We stand still for a moment, lost in each other's eyes. My eyes drift from his shoulders to his arms, then down to his perfectly chiseled chest. My eyes drift further down to his... member. *Yikes!* Snapping my head up, I look straight up at the sky. I'm so embarrassed. I've never seen one of those before. To confirm if I saw what I thought I saw, I looked back down. *Yes!* His member is really out in full view. I snap my head back up to the sky. A hot flash moves across my face and body, and I'm almost positive that my face is ten different shades of red.

"What's wrong?" Ian laughs.

"You're... naked." I exclaim, still avoiding eye contact with him.

"Yes, that's normal after I shift. I hate to break it to you, angel... but you are, too." Ian steps back and looks me up and down with a huge grin on his face. I look down and am shocked that I'm standing there as naked as the day I was born. I use my hands and arms, trying to cover my private areas, which gets another roar of laughter from Ian. "Angel, why are you trying to hide your body? Nudity after shifting is normal and natural. Plus, I'm your mate. There's nothing you should hide from me, especially this delicious body of yours." He puts his hands on my lower back and pulls me into him.

"Ian!" I snap, looking around, "this is not funny! What if someone... or a pup sees us like this?" I'm still trying to hide my embarrassment and my body.

"Being daddy's princess kept you sheltered. I like that. Okay, angel, let's go inside the fishing cabin. I had the liberty of having some clothes and food dropped off for us." He motions with one hand to the door of the fishing cabin, while his other hand presses on my lower back, guiding me inside.

Walking through the door of the fishing cabin, the smell of bacon attacks my nose, and my stomach lets out a massive growl. I see takeaway containers from the packhouse kitchen on the counter next to the coffeepot. In front of the lower cabinets I see a couple of paper bags with other food items inside.

"The door on the right is the bathroom and the door on the left is the bedroom. A bag packed with your clothes and toiletries is on the bed. Why don't you take a shower and I'll make us some coffee and get breakfast on the table?" Ian walks to the coffee pot without looking at me.

I stand still for a moment; this seems so weird. Yesterday I woke up in my bed in the house I grew up in. Today I'm standing naked in the fishing cabin with my mate. *My Mate.* How did I go from a child to a woman overnight? I know that I have prayed to be Ian's mate, but I never really thought about what that entailed.

"How did my things get here?" I turn to Ian.

"Your mom sent them." Ian fills the coffeepot with water.

"My parents know I'm here... alone... with you?" I tilt my head, "and they're okay with this?"

"Yes, angel. Mates are normal and natural. There's nothing wrong here." Ian turns to me and chuckles under his breath, "you really are pure and innocent, aren't you?"

Frustrated, I don't answer him. I turn, and in a half daze, walk into the bedroom to get my bag. How can all this be happening so fast? Part of me knows this is natural and the other part just wants to stay a child with a crazy crush on the boy next door. I open my bag and find a note from my mom on top of my neatly folded clothes.

Choose to love each other every day.

Even when he annoys the shit out of you.

Love, Mom

I laugh at mom's note. I guess they really are okay with it. Maybe I'm not because I saw the way he was acting just hours before my first shift. Before I accept him as my mate, we need to talk, but for now I'm in desperate need of a shower. I stink.

After my shower, I dress in shorts and a tank top and head straight for the coffee. The events of yesterday and the night have left me drained. I sit on the small loveseat, sipping on my coffee, while Ian takes a shower. I giggle when he sings in the shower. There are two things I didn't know about Ian; he's a country music fan, and he sings in the shower. He's got a great voice. *Is there anything this guy is bad at?*

After Ian's shower concert, we eat breakfast in an awkward silence. Ian and I have known each other for as long as I can remember. We know each other well. We have spent time fishing and talking about everything. Still, this is just awkward. I'm nervous about what might happen after breakfast. *Am I ready?*

"You're the first girl besides my mom and sisters that I've ever had breakfast with. I look forward to a lifetime of breakfasts with you, angel." Ian rubs my leg.

"We should probably talk." I swallow the lump in my throat.

"Uh oh... about what?" Ian pushes his empty plate away.

"Us," I whisper out.

"Us?" He turns to me, placing his hands on my thighs.

"When did you know I was your mate?" I look into his eyes.

"My eighteenth birthday. When you put this on me." Ian looks at the paracord bracelet on his wrist, then back at me. I look down at the bracelet I made for him when I was sixteen. It looks a little worn and faded, like he doesn't take it off.

"I know that you've been with other women... even after finding out I was your mate. What you've done before I knew we were mates doesn't bother me so much. I never expected you to wait for me, mostly because nobody does... wait for their fated mate. But what I saw last night, all those tramps all over you. It hurt, really hurt. I was looking forward to you coming home and finding out if you were my mate or not. Something that I've wanted since I was fourteen. I should have been your focus, but instead of paying any attention to me... on one of the biggest days of my life, you had a tramp on your lap with your hand resting between her knees. Were you planning on screwing her in the woods before you came to me?" My bottom lip quivers as a frustrated tear escapes my eyes. I need answers.

"Shit." Ian breathes out, placing his hands on top of his head and sitting straight up in his chair. "Look, I know what you saw looked bad... really bad. I went there looking for you. You were the only woman on my mind. Then all these women surrounded us, and I... I got lost in the moment. I liked the attention that I was getting from them." He leans back down to me and places his hands high on my thighs. "I'm an asshole, Kate. I shouldn't have... Kate, I promise it will never happen again." He rubs my thighs. Everywhere his hands touch, sparks radiate off my skin through my body to my core. My core throbs for his touch and my nipples instantly get hard. Both are new sensations that I've never experienced before. "I'm sorry, angel, you'll never have to worry about me and other women again. You are the only one for me. The other half of my soul." His lips gently press against mine. *My first kiss.* "Wait here. I have something for you." He leaves me sitting at the table in a daze. I touch my lips... I just had my first actual kiss. He promptly returns to his seat, pulling me into his lap. "Happy birthday, angel." He puts a small golden box in my hands.

"You got me a birthday present?" I whisper, looking at the box in my hands. His scent fills my nose and I'm suddenly lightheaded as my heart beats faster. I want him to never stop touching me.

"Of course, I did. You're the only thing that's been on my mind lately." He wraps his arms around me and places his chin on my shoulder. "Open it. I had it made for you." I open the box to find a gold necklace attached to a charm that reads Kate.

"I love it, Ian." I gasp, "it's perfect."

"Would you like me to put it on you?" Ian kisses my shoulder.

"After I wake up. I'm mentally and physically exhausted." I look between him and the necklace.

"Let's go to bed and get some rest, angel." Ian presses his lips into mine. Our kiss is sweet and gentle. He breaks our kiss and leads me to the bedroom.

CHAPTER SEVENTEEN

WE'RE DONE

March 2004

Ian

'*THAT'S THE LAST OF them.*' Zane's voice floods everyone's mindlinks, '*We are victorious!*" Victory howls spread from the destroyed rogue encampment in Crimson Tide's territory.

'*Your father will be very pleased, Zane. You're becoming an excellent leader.*' My father says through our open mindlink. Both my father and Gamma Earnest joined us for this mission, while Alpha Nathaniel stayed in our territory. Originally, it was supposed to be Zane, Kelsey, and myself with one hundred warriors, but with some last-minute intel coming in, Alpha thought it best to send his Beta and Gamma as well. My father doesn't hand out compliments, so him complimenting Zane is huge.

'*Thank you, Beta Charlie, but this was a team effort.*' Zane mindlinks. I watch as Zane shifts his weight from one foot to another. He's uncomfortable with the praise he is receiving. To Zane, this is just another lifesaving mission, just like the others we've been on over the last year.

Our first mission was while we were training at the royal palace. We assisted the palace with removing a blood hungry and abusive Alpha. Unfortunately, about half of the pack sided with the Alpha and took up arms against the palace. It was our first war... and it was a bloodbath. The pack never stood a chance against the royal guard and the young Alphas and Betas training at the palace. The pack was half starved and grossly undernourished. We begged and pleaded for them to surrender to us and promised no harm would come to them, that we were just there for the Alpha. However, they stayed loyal to their abuser and met us head on. It was forty-eight hours of intense fighting. They used weapons against us and used women and pups as shields.

Until that point, I had never seen so much blood or experienced my first kill. I will never forget his eyes as the life drained from his body. It was my life or his. That was the only choice I had. The only reason I'm not haunted by what I saw and experienced is what came after. Seeing the innocent lives come out of hiding once we had made it safe for them and watching their eyes light up with hope for their future was pure joy. The oppression the pack members lived under was far worse than what the palace was told. They praised us as heroes, which lit a fire inside the three of us. We made a promise to ourselves to make it our mission to help as many werewolves as we can. It's a promise that our fathers stand behind and was the first time that my father offered me any kind of praise.

"Look at you, receiving praise from Cesar." I tease Zane.

"Shut up!" Zane throws a bottle of water at me. "Kelsey, what are our injuries and fatalities?"

"All our warriors survived with a few minor injuries," Kelsey proudly says, taking a swig of water.

The three of us train hard, pushing ourselves to be a cut above the rest. Zane and I train to fight side by side together. We have since we were about ten. And with each passing year, we become more of a force to be reckoned with. Kelsey trains and works directly with the warriors. Once he is officially the gamma, all the warriors will report to him and will be his sole responsibility. He currently leads training alongside his father, and you can see the pride in his face for his warriors.

"That's fucking awesome, bro. We need to get back to Crimson Tide territory and check in with our Beta and Gamma. Kelsey, leave twenty-five warriors here to help Crimson Tide clean this mess up. Just have them make one big disgraceful pile of rogue remains and their camp and burn it."

When we arrived here, the fighting in Crimson Tide's village was raging. The rogues were minutes from capturing the packhouse. Once we eliminated the threat in the village, we attacked the rogue encampment. We decimated the rogue camp, taking no prisoners. Unfortunately, the rogue king and some of his followers escaped us. We'll deal with him another day. Zane's take no prisoner and burn everything to the ground approach is giving him a ruthless reputation. He is following in his great grandfather's footsteps and werewolves everywhere are taking notice.

"Got it. I'll catch up with you two." Kelsey nods and walks away.

It's almost one in the morning when our SUVs pull away from Crimson Tide's territory. All of us are exhausted and filthy; we smell like rotten flesh just like the nasty rogues we've been dealing with. We've been away for thirty-six hours. None of us have showered and have only had an hour or two of sleep. Crimson Tide offered us a place to stay and rest, but all of us are eager to get home to our mates. *Mate.* I never thought I'd be able to say that word while referring to Kate. I'm excited to get back into her arms. I absolutely hated leaving her the way I did, but I plan on making it up to her. It's mere hours before Kelsey and Sonia's wedding, and we know from Alpha Nathaniel that the women are in the common area celebrating Sonia's last night as a single woman. So, we decide to surprise them by not letting them know we are headed home. I can't wait to see the look on Kate's face. Hopefully, she'll forgive the way I smell.

It's three-thirty in the morning when we pull up in front of the packhouse. I'm full of excitement as I make my way into the packhouse. At first, the women are shocked to see us walk through the door, and rightfully so, we're filthy and stinky. Then Sonia spots Kelsey and screams with delight as she rushes into his arms. As more couples reunite, I continue to search for my Kate. I follow her scent into the kitchen. Then I see her standing by the refrigerator, looking at the floor with her back to me.

"Kate... I'm home." I can hardly contain my excitement. She flinches at the sound of my voice, then stands still for several moments. "Kate?" She slowly turns towards me; her body is stiff and shaking. Kate's face is red and the veins on the side of her neck are protruding out, while her fists are in balls at her side. Her chest rises and falls as she scrunches her face, fighting back tears. *What the hell is going on?*

"How was the boys' trip? Hmmm? How was Vegas?" She shouts, pointing her finger at me.

"What?" I'm shocked, "Vegas? What does that mean?"

"Don't lie to me, Ian! I'm sick to death of your bullshit lies!" She picks up a coffee mug from the counter and hurls it at my head. I duck and the mug narrowly misses my head before crashing into the wall behind me.

"What are you talking about? I wasn't in Vegas." I look at the wall behind me, then back at Kate. "What's gotten into you?"

"You can't even tell me the truth when you're caught. At least tell me the truth!" She shouts. The tone in her voice is cold and harsh. This is not my sweet Kate.

"Look at me, Kate. Look at me! Do I look like I've been partying in Vegas? No, I don't. I look like I've been to hell and back, and I know I smell worse." I'm so confused. What should be a joyous time has turned into one gigantic pile of heaping steaming shit. I just wanted my mate to rush into my smelly arms and welcome me home. Instead, I come home to a possessed she-wolf who's throwing shit at my head.

"I'm done! We're done! I can't take the lies anymore." She walks away, then turns back to me. "Accept the rejection so I can move on with my life or die. Anything but this." She turns away.

"Kate!" Her mom attempts to stop her, but she just walks past her without so much as a glance.

"Katherine!" Her dad shouts and grabs her.

"No!" She shouts and pushes off his chest. I chase after her, but her dad steps in front of me.

"I… I don't know what just happened. She thinks I was in Vegas on a boys' trip. I need to talk to her." I try to move around him, but he steps in front of me again.

"Let her cool down tonight and talk with her in the morning. Trust me, son." He rubs my shoulder.

"Why would she think I was in Vegas? Who told her that?" Anger churns in the pit of my stomach. One of the women here must have told her I was in Vegas. Who? Why? I sidestep Gamma Earnest, "Who told Kate that I… the guys were on some boys' trip to Vegas? Who?" I roar and let out a wall shaking growl. The room is completely silent, and all eyes are on me. Anger turns into rage that boils just under the surface. I shake and rock my body back and forth, trying to keep Alex from surfacing and ripping this place apart. "No one, huh? Fucking cowards!" I pick up a table and throw it to the ground, and run for the back door of the packhouse. I need to go for a run and clear my head.

Chapter Eighteen

TRUTH HURTS

March 2004

Kate

I'M AWAKENED BY SUNLIGHT peeking through the curtains in my room. Not ready to face the day I lay still with my eyes closed. I hear my bedroom door open and the sounds of my dad's heavy footsteps entering my room. *Great.*

"Hey," the entire bed shifts and shakes as he kicks it, "you going to sleep all day?"

"Maybe," I groan.

"Like hell you are. Up and at 'em. Meet me and your mother downstairs in ten. We need to have a chat." I listen as his heavy feet walk out of my room and down the stairs. He is pissed, and by him referring to my mom as mother, he's pissed at me. I feel like I'm a pup all over again.

I sit up and stretch. To be honest, I'm not in the mood to deal with the parental units this morning. I got very little sleep last night, leaving me just as physically exhausted as I am mentally. I slip on some cutoff shorts, a tank top, and toss my hair into a messy bun.

My phone rings as I start to walk out of my room. I flip open my phone and answer the call.

"Hello?" I sigh out.

"Good Morning, beautiful. I miss you." Darren says.

"Hi, Darren. Um, now's not a good time. I'm getting ready for my brother's wedding." I flop down on my bed. It's not Darren's fault, but I'm annoyed and not in the mood to chat.

"Can we talk later? I don't like how things ended before you left." Darren pleads.

"Sure." I quickly say.

"Great, I'll call you around three, okay?" Darren says excitedly.

"Sure... great." I reply, trying to end the conversation before my dad comes looking for me.

"I love you." Darren coos.

"Ummmm... I got to go, bye." I quickly flip my phone closed and toss it on the bed. For some reason I can't say those words back to him.

I'm not sure why I agreed to talk to him later. Truth be told, I don't want him or Ian at this point. *Did I ever love him?* Hell, I don't know why I'm doing half the shit I'm doing these days. One thing is for sure, I've got to get out of here and back to New York City. My life has gone awry and I'm not liking it at all. I seem to attract chaos with every breath I take. I walk out of my room and down the stairs. *Might as well get this over with.* I can hear my parents mumbling something between themselves.

"Morning." I enter the kitchen and walk straight to the coffeepot without looking at either of them. I pour myself a cup of coffee, then take my seat at the table. Now I'm just waiting to find out what I did to piss my dad off so badly.

"Nine a.m. Nice of you to grace us with your presence today," my dad's voice is harsh as he looks away from his paper to me. I slump down in my chair and sip my coffee. "Want to explain what happened last night?"

"Ian lied to me... again, and I lost it. I'm done with him." I snap, looking between my mom and dad.

"How did he lie to you?" My mom speaks in a soft, calm voice. So, they're playing good cop bad cop, just like when Kelsey and I were pups. This should be fun.

"He told me he had to go on a mission, when in fact he went to Vegas on a boys' trip." I place my cup on the table and stare into the black abyss that is my coffee.

"Vegas? Ha! Who told you that?" My dad slams his paper on the table.

"Does it really matter? The fact is, he lied. I still can't trust him." I narrow my eyes at my dad.

"Let me ask you a question. While you were screaming at him, did you notice what he looked like? Or that he was wearing the same clothes you last saw him in? Or did you notice he stunk to high heaven? Did you?" Dad and I are locked in a staring contest. "Well?"

"No... I didn't take notice. I just..." Dad interrupts me.

"You just what? Focused solely on what some mystery bitch told you. Is that it?" Dad leans into me.

"What's your point?" I snap at my dad and cross my arms.

"My point? You were and are completely in the wrong." Dad leans back in his chair.

"Me?" I stand and shout.

"Sit your ass back down, or I will make you." The chair that dad is sitting in screeches across the floor as he rushes to his feet, meeting my gaze and pointing to my chair. I stand in defiance for a few tense moments before slamming back down in my seat. "Ian, Zane, Kelsey, Beta Charlie, myself, along with one hundred warriors rushed out of here to help protect the Crimson Tide pack from a rogue attack that threatened their very existence." Dad is breathing heavily as the anger rolls off of him. "There was no boys' trip to Vegas!" He shouts before taking his seat.

"Wait, you went on a mission?" I look at my dad and mom.

"Yes, I did. Ya know why? So, your mate could hurry and get back to you!" My dad cups his hands around his mouth and screams at me.

"Sugar, that's why I stayed with Ian's mom. The girls were keeping you busy and occupied, and neither of us wanted to be alone while our mates were on a mission." My mom's soft words and gentle touch pierces my skin like a thousand little needles.

I take in my dad's words, sinking into my chair. *What have I done?* My cheeks flush as the feeling of guilt washes over me, settling into the pit of my stomach. The guilt churns and twists my guts into a thousand knots, and last night's nachos threaten to come back up violently. My breathing is shallow as beads of sweat form on my face and neck.

"I... I..." my dad interrupts.

"Am a complete asshole. Is that what you were going to say?" Dad snarls at me.

"Earnest!" Mom gasps and shouts.

"What? It's the truth. She is the asshole right now. She should have kept her cool and calmly talked with her mate. Instead, she acted like a pup and screamed like a banshee at him in public." Dad looks from mom to me, "You realize *your* mate is the future beta of this pack... and *you're* the future beta female. Those positions hold significant importance in this pack, and as the future beta of this pack, your *mate* deserves respect, and respect starts with you, Kate."

"Respect? You want to talk about respect? Where was his respect towards me when he was cheating on me?" I scrunch my face to hide my quivering lips.

"Ian was the asshole then. He got his ass beat by Alpha, his father, and me multiple times on your behalf. He vowed to do whatever it took to prove to me and this pack that he deserved another chance with you. We all know that the mate bond was not severed. So, tell me Kate, in the over two years you were apart, did you feel him being unfaithful? Because he felt it every time you let that human touch you." Dad shakes his head in disgust and disappointment. Tears stream down my face.

"Earnest!" Mom gasps and shouts.

"Truth hurts, doesn't it, Kate?" Dad leans back in his chair, satisfied with the point he has made. I'm not too sure how he knows so much, but he does.

When my dad is finished, I feel about two inches tall. My dad has never spoken to me this way before, I suppose because I've never given him a reason to. I wasn't a perfect pup, and he has had to *chat* with me before, but never in this manner. He's right though, and I can't argue back with him. I am the asshole. Once again, I've messed everything up; it seems to be an ongoing theme of my life lately. After I mentally digest everything my dad has said, I stand to leave.

"Where do you think you're going?" Dad's voice booms off the walls.

"I need to find Ian," I simply state.

"It won't be hard. He's sleeping on the front porch... been there all night. Poor fool was afraid you'd run away." Dad's voice softens as he shakes his head.

I take a mug from the cupboard and prepare Ian a cup of coffee the way he likes it; two creams and two sugars. I make my way to the front porch, stopping first next to my dad. I look at the ground and fight the tears back. Once I'm fully in control of my emotions, I place the cup of coffee on the table and kiss my dad on his cheek.

"What was that for?" He pulls away and looks me in the eyes.

"Thank you for gut checking me and calling me an asshole." I take a step back and offer him a slight smile.

"Oh, sugar." Dad jumps to his feet and wraps his arms around me. "I'm sorry that I spoke so harshly to you." He squeezes me tight.

"Don't be. I totally deserve it and needed to hear it." I wrap my arms around him and squeeze.

"Listen, you are my priority, not Ian. But I know what he has done to make himself better. He didn't do it because he was made to. He did it because he wanted to." Dad pulls away and looks me in the eyes. "We were all prepared for you not to be his mate or beta female to this pack, but then you agreed to give him a last chance. I just want that to be a fair chance... for both your sakes. This isn't easy for you, and I know that you have trust issues where he is concerned, and for good reason. He hasn't always been the best to you. Sugar if you're going to try to make it work, you can't let the past cloud your judgement now." His tone is soft and loving.

"I know, daddy." I look down. Everything my dad is saying is the truth. If I'm going to give Ian a chance then it needs to be a fair one. This is going to be so hard... learning to trust him again. Ian believed in us, enough to seek help to change. Maybe I should do the same and fight for us.

"Why don't you and Ian go to counseling? It has helped him. I think that would be the best for you both." My dad rubs my arms.

"You know about Ian seeing a therapist?" I look at him in shock. Ian didn't want me to say anything, because he was afraid of the backlash he would receive from our community. There would be some that view his addiction as a weekness and would seek to have him replaced as our future beta. I'm glad my dad is not one of them.

"Of course I do. I know more than you realize." He smiles at me. "I love you sugar, always remember that." He kisses my forehead and hugs me.

"I love you too, daddy." I whisper into his chest. My mom joins us, wrapping her arms around the both of us. I'm truly blessed to have the love and support of both my parents.

I look out the front door sidelight and sure enough, Ian is laying on his side facing the front door. He's only wearing pants; his arm is wrapped around his shirt that is balled up underneath his head like a pillow. Ian's broad shoulders, sculpted arms, and perfectly chiseled chest are on full display for me. Even at his worst, he still is so beautiful. *Am I deserving of his love?* His pants are filthy... is he in the same clothes he came home in? His face is relaxed, but I know he can't be comfortable sleeping on a hard surface like that. After taking a deep breath, I slowly turn the knob and open the door. I don't want to startle him while he is sleeping. I take a few slow steps out, then turn to close the door behind me. Every movement I make is slow. I'm trying not to make too much noise. I turn back to see Ian looking inquisitively at me, then at the mug in my hand.

"You going to throw that at my head again?" He sits up slowly.

"No. I made you coffee... just like you like it." I offer him the mug. He peeks into the mug, then back up to me before taking it. I sit in front of him with my legs crossed.

"Thank you," he takes a large gulp without taking his eyes off of me, "you remembered how I take my coffee?" He smiles and takes another gulp, "no one makes a cup of coffee as good as you." We sit in an awkward silence for a few moments smiling at each other. As I'm mustering the strength and courage, he breaks the silence. "Kate." I place my hand over his mouth.

"No," I shake my head, "don't speak... just listen." There is a lump that is forming in my throat. I gulp it down, take a deep breath in and slowly blow it out. "Ian, I'm so very sorry for the way I treated you last night. You were away saving lives and didn't deserve the disrespect you got from me when you returned. I let someone's words trigger memories of the past... and my emotions got away from me. I promised you another chance, and I let the past sneak in and..."

Before I finish my sentence, Ian grabs the back of my neck, pulling me in for a passionate kiss, wrapping his free hand around my throat. His kiss is deep, demanding, and forceful. He claims my lips and mouth as his own, fully savoring my essence. We're both completely out of breath when we break our kiss. Not ready to let me go, Ian presses his forehead into mine. "You didn't let me finish." I try to control my breathing.

"I heard everything I needed to hear. You are promising me another chance... you've never said that before." Ian kisses my nose.

"Oh... I guess I haven't." I giggle under my breath. "I had more to say."

"There's no need, love. We have a lot of shit to work through because of me. There's a lot to prove. I say we just take it one day at a time. I love you so much... you have no idea." Ian presses his lips into mine. Electricity radiates from our lips.

"You called me love." I say into his mouth.

"Yes, I did." He pulls away and looks into my eyes. "You are the love of my life. It took me too long to figure that out. Now I will remind you every day what you mean to me... love." He nuzzles into the crook of my neck, taking in my scent.

"You smell," I laugh.

"What, you don't like it?" I giggle and shake my head while he sits up and looks at my face, "I rushed off the battlefield to come straight home to you... throwing coffee mugs at my head." We both laugh. I look down and bite my bottom lip.

"Sorry about that." I look back up at him.

"I deserved it... for something, I'm sure. You've got one hell of an arm and impeccable accuracy. Maybe we should start a couple's softball league." I shake my head no and laugh.

Chapter Nineteen

ROYAL HEALER

March 2004

Kate

WE ARE THE FIRST to arrive at the chapel. The white chapel is in the center of the city and is surrounded by a stunning park. The chapel is in a serene and tranquil setting, making it a favorite wedding destination for humans. They come from miles around to be married here. I haven't been here since I was a pup. I'm amazed that this place hasn't changed a bit and is as phenomenal as I remember. The chapel is the only building left standing after the war when Alpha Ezekiel took the land and claimed it as Blue Moon territory. He was planning to tear the chapel down to make way for more modern buildings, but Luna Scarlet saw the beauty in the old simple building and fell in love with it. She loved it so much that Alpha Ezekiel restored the chapel and grounds in her honor. He went so far as to have her favorite roses planted here.

Alpha Ezekiel was ruthless, but the extraordinary stories about his love for Luna Scarlett and how he would stop at nothing to make her happy are what poets write about. One would think the stories about the love they had for each other are nothing more than made up fairytales, but proof is all around. Alpha Ezekiel gave packs back their original territories after he took them, all to make her smile. If that is not love, I don't know what is. Growing up and hearing their love story, I always imagined my fairytale romance would be just like that. Boy, was my bubble burst.

"Wow, that is a lot of reporters." I stare in amazement out the SUV window as we drive past the media area that is roped off and guarded by warriors.

"That's nothing," Rebeka scoffs. "That's probably a quarter that was at mine and Zane's wedding."

"Yeah, Kelsey told me how chaotic it was. That's why he asked his dad to have the press releases scaled back. I'm so thankful for that." Sonia turns to me in the backseat and smiles.

"Mom told me it was insane. Did reporters climb the wall behind the chapel?" I look at Rebeka.

"Yes! They wanted a sneak peek at my dress. One even tried sneaking into the bridal suite. Warriors had to rush from our territory to protect us." Rebeka shakes her head, thinking back. The SUV pulls behind the white chapel to the bridal suite.

"Dad said he tripled security out of an abundance of caution." I say as warriors open the SUV doors for us. We step out of the SUV and I see warriors in their classic black suits and dark sunglasses positioned everywhere. "I should have been here," I place my hand on Rebeka's forearm.

"Yes, you should have been, and I wish you were. We lost so much time that you and I could have been bonding as future luna and beta female. But you're here now." She offers me a warm smile and puts her hand on top of mine. "That's the most important thing... you're here now."

We're escorted into the bridal suite where hair and makeup artists are set up and waiting on us. I'm also excited to see trays of tea sandwiches, fresh fruit, and wine chilling on ice. My mom instructs us to stay in this area and not to venture to the front. They want to keep us out of the sight of the paparazzi. Over the past few weeks, there has been a lot of media speculation about the dress and designer. Everyone wants a sneak peek before the official pictures are given to the media. Honestly, staying hidden away is fine with me. I brought a book and am wearing comfy clothes until it's my turn to get dolled up and dressed.

Sonia and I are the first to get our hair and makeup done. Mine is quick compared to Sonia. She'll probably be in the chair for hours. Just like our dresses, she lets us choose how we want our hair and makeup done. She is probably the most low-key bride in the history of brides. I choose a smokey eye with neutral tone makeup and nude lipstick. I know Ian has never been a fan of wild color lipstick, and I'm more of a clear lip gloss kind of girl, anyway. This will make him happy, and he'll think I'm doing it just for him. *Wait, why do I care what he thinks?* For my hair I go with half up and half down with large bouncing curls. This is perfect hair in case I choose to take a nap. That's a hair trick I learned from my mom. Always opt for large bouncing curls. They're far more forgiving than sleek straight hair.

When my hair and makeup are done, and I get a thumbs up from mom, I fill a plate with tea sandwiches and fresh fruit. I grab my book and head out to the courtyard that is attached to the bridal suite. The chapel surrounds the courtyard and two ten-foot walls with a massive oak tree in the center. Under the tree are a couple of benches. I choose the bench that faces away from the bridal suite and chapel. My view is literally a vine covered white brick wall. Which is fine with me. I don't want any unnecessary distractions from my book that I've been trying to read since Ian showed up in New York.

I stretch my legs out on the bench and make myself comfortable. Opening my book, I take a bite of a cucumber tea sandwich, and just like in New York, my mind drifts to Ian. I think about him and wonder what he is doing right now. Hopefully, he's sleeping, but I doubt it. He's most likely working out. I think about the way I treated him when he got back from his mission, and debate whether or not I should call him. *Why does he consume my thoughts like this?* Frustrated that I can't concentrate on this book long enough to get pulled into, I close it and eat my food in silence. I chew my food slowly and stare at the vine-covered wall, just thinking.

"Hey bitch, move so I can sit down too." A familiar female's voice shouts behind me. I turn to see a very pregnant Jessi waddling her way to me with a huge smile plastered on her face.

My food flies off my lap, landing on the ground as I jump to my feet and run to the arms of my childhood best friend. The two of us embrace, just squeezing each other tight. I think she missed me as much as I missed her.

"Let me look at you." I pull away and take her in. She is still the same beautiful Jessi, only now she has a pregnancy glow about her. "What are you doing here?"

"Ian. Can we please sit? My chankles are killing me." She looks down and laughs.

"Oh gosh, yes, of course." I say as we walk arm in arm to the bench. She sits down and breathes out heavily. "Better?"

"Getting there. You know that I'm due any second. Do you think you can deliver a pup?" She pulls back and tilts her head to the side before laughing.

"Sweetheart?" I turn to see a massive man with jet black hair walking towards us carrying something in his arms.

"Here babe," she waves without looking at him. "He's right on time," she whispers to me. He quickly approaches and puts a stool in front of Jessi, then places a pillow on top before carefully picking up each foot and placing them on the pillow. I watch his rough looking hands delicately touch and rub her feet. I see the love in his rugged sun kissed face as he smiles tenderly while whispering sweet nothings to Jessi. A ping of jealousy hits my chest watching the two of them interact with each other. *This is the kind of love that I want.*

"How's that, sweetheart?" He caresses her jaw.

"Perfect as always," Jessi swoons and leans into his hand. He presses his lips to hers before directing a caring smile my way.

"Hello, you must be Kate, Ian's mate. I've heard so many wonderful things about you from Jessi and Ian. My name is Adam, and if you hadn't guessed it yet, I'm Jessi's mate." He extends his hand to me.

"It's so nice to finally meet you, Adam. I've also heard really great things about you from Jessi." I shake his hand and smile at Jessi. "You've been taking good care of her. Thank you."

"Of course, she's my everything. I waited thirty years to find her, and I want her to know every day exactly what she means to me." Adam's smile turns somber as he looks at the ground for a few moments before looking back at me. "Kate, I meant nothing by that. Please accept my apologies."

"What?" I tilt my head, trying to figure out what he meant. After a few moments, I realize he knows about the history between Ian and me. "No... no. I didn't take it like that at all. No need to apologize." I shake my head. "But you can always go explain to Ian how a mate should be treated." I laugh, trying to ease the tension.

"Thank you," relief washes across Adam's face as he lets out a breath, "and I have spoken to Ian about you... in great detail." He leans in and winks. "I guess you can say I took him under my wing when he came back to the palace alone for combat training. I may have knocked him around the ring a time or four in your honor." He smiles, chuckling lightly, shaking his head.

"My Adam is a palace warrior and will be a guard to the new king; his primary duty is hand to hand combat training in human form." Jessi beams with pride as she talks about Adam. Who is *this* Jessi and where is my fiery childhood friend, the one who wanted to taste life before meeting her mate and settling down?

"Palace warrior and guard to the king? Wow, what an honor and tremendous responsibility." I smile and look between Jessi and Adam. The royal warriors are the best of the best. There is a grueling test to becoming one and most don't make the cut. It's an absolute honor to not only be a part of the royal warriors but chosen to be a guard to the new king and training. This is impressive.

"Well, I come from a long line of them. I guess you can say it's in my blood, and now this one, too." He rubs Jessi's swollen belly.

"Don't wake him. He's been using my rib cage as a trampoline lately." Jessi giggles and stops Adam from rubbing her belly. I enjoy, yet I'm envious of the interactions between the two of them.

"Yes, dear," he kisses her forehead and removes his hand.

Watching the beast of a man be so gentle with Jessi, I can't help but to wonder how he can be a rough and tough royal guard. Then I imagine him knocking Ian around in the ring in my honor and I giggle in my head. *Is that wrong?* For all the crap that Ian put me through, he deserves it. Don't get me wrong, I don't want Ian seriously hurt... but a bump, bruise, or two is just what the doctor ordered, in my opinion. I guess we'll see if it changes him for the better.

"Thank you for talking to him about the way he treated me. Hopefully, it did some good." I smile and nod.

"You're very welcome, Kate. If Ian changed, it wasn't just my doing. Change comes from deep inside a person. They have to want to change, and there's no amount of talking or beating that will change them. You may not realize this, but there were many people who thought the way he treated you was wrong and let him know about it. Our future king being one of them." He looks from me to Jessi, "I need to go check in with Alpha Nathaniel and offer my services... if needed. Are you going to be okay?" He rubs his thumb against Jessi's jawline.

"Of course, babe, because I know you're never too far away." Adam leans in and places a gentle but firm kiss on Jessi's lips. My breath hitches as I watch them, and another ping of jealousy hits my chest. This is what I want, a mate who is loving, caring, and dedicated.

"It was nice meeting you, Kate. Hopefully, I will see you around and get to know you better... as Ian's mate." He bows his head, then walks away. For a large man, I notice how gracefully he moves, just like the other palace warriors I have seen. It must be in their training.

"Jealous, bitch?" Jessi wrinkles her nose and gives me a cocky smile.

"Pfft, no... maybe," I laugh and roll my eyes.

"Yeah, this should be you right now. I should have been the one who ran off to New York." Jessi rubs her belly.

"So weird, you never really wanted pups. What changed?" I lean back.

"I didn't. Adam wanted pups so bad but was willing to wait five years. Even though he's ten years older than me, he understands that I'm young. We both agreed we have a lot of time. Then I started training as a royal healer under his grandmother." She adjusts in her seat.

"Oh, so you're a nurse, like your mom?" I interrupt her.

"Not exactly. Royal healers use herbal potions mixed with a little magic. His grandmother saw a healer within me and took me under her wing. Anyway, at his grandmother's place is where I met Elliot, his four... five-year-old nephew. The more time I spent with Elliot, the more I didn't want to wait for pups. I told Adam and without giving it a second thought, he tossed out my birth control pills and boom, two months later, knocked up." She pats her belly.

"So, you got pup fever from spending time with a pup?" I laugh.

"That shit is contagious, like crazy. You should try it." She pushes my leg.

"Do you know how lucky you are, bitch?" I press my knuckles into Jessi's shoulder, "cute and caters to your every whim."

"Don't forget huge." Jessi holds her hands in front of her about twelve inches apart and pushes them towards me. "Huge!" She continues to hold her hands up, "did I mention HUGE!" She smiles proudly and giggles, watching me blush as I realize she is showing her mate's member's size.

"Oh my goddess, Jessi." I gasp and push her hands down to her lap and look around. My face is flush and I'm sure that I'm beet red.

"Same ol' Kate," Jessi laughs hysterically. "You're acting like a prude little virgin... which I know you're not. You two were pretty hot and heavy in the sack. I'm sure the two of you are back at it like rabbits." She says through her laughter.

"And you're the same ol' Jessi." I laugh, "stop laughing so hard or that pup is going to pop right out." I point at her belly. "And no, we are not going at it like rabbits. There's nothing going on in that department." I purse my lips and sigh out.

"Please, we've been having sex twice a day, trying to get this little fella to come out. I guess he's comfy in there," she pats her belly. "Really? So, tell me, what's really going on with you and the beta?" Her smile and laugh fade to a more serious look and tone.

I spend the next few hours filling Jessi in on everything; Ian showing up in New York for my birthday, still feeling the mate bond with Ian, Darren asking me to marry him, Ian refusing to accept it's over between the two of us. I even tell her what we did in my apartment, and how Ian and I got caught by Darren. Not a single filthy detail was missed. I lay everything out in front of her, including how bad I feel about cheating on Darren with Ian. I end with me throwing a coffee mug at his head and my dad calling me an asshole, before I learned Ian slept on my front porch all night.

"Wow, so after you rejected Ian and all that time you still felt the mate bond?" Jessi breathes out and tilts her head as if she is trying to digest everything that I told her.

"Yes, it was faint in New York, but it was there. It seems to be getting stronger, though." I carefully explain.

"How's that even possible?" Jessi looks confused.

"Luna Martha explained that in order for a rejection to work, both have to accept it. He didn't accept the rejection before I left." I shrug my shoulders.

"Rookie mistake," she laughs. "Moon Goddess must have some cosmic plans for the two of you." Jessi shakes her head and rubs her belly.

"Why do you say that?" I stare at her intently and tilt my head.

"Think about it. She must really want you two together to keep the mate bond intact." Jessi looks like she is in deep thought, as she nods her head.

"Hmmm, I never thought of it like that." Both Jessi and I sit in silence, lost in our thoughts. I think about what Adam said about change coming from inside someone, that they have to want it. So does that mean that Ian really wants me and only me... that he is done with other women?

"But..." Jessi breaks our silence, "if it turns out that he is some master manipulator, Adam has some hot cousins that will treat you right." She winks. "maybe Moon Goddess would bless you a second chance mate... the future king is still unmated," she nudges me with her elbow. I laugh at her antics; she always has a way of making me laugh.

"I guess we'll see." I smile and look down.

"The heart wants what it wants, right?" Jessi lifts my chin with her hand and looks into my eyes. We don't speak, there's no need to. Jessi is my oldest friend and knows me almost as well as I know myself. Deep in the pit of my stomach, the truth is I want Ian. I want Ian and I to have the kind of love Jessi and Adam have... the kind of love that

Alpha Ezekiel and Luna Scarlett had. The kind of love that moves mountains, with a passion that would make one lay their life down for the other. I swallow my emotions down before they form into tears and nod. Jessi smiles and nods along with me, "And that's why I'm rooting for the two of you." She smiles, "I'm glad you're giving him a last chance... one that he doesn't deserve. You deserve to be happy, and I know he can... if he pulls his head out of his ass, he can make you happy. We know that the mate bond still binds you to Ian, and Darren never stood a chance. You would have never been able to give yourself to him fully. Not being excited about marrying Darren should have been a huge red flag."

"Yeah..." I sigh.

"Oh, and didn't I tell you years ago to punch that bitch Nikki right in her stupid, ugly face?" Jessi scowls. "I should have done it for you. I hate her."

"I have missed you... missed talking to you every day." I hug her.

"Me too... me too." She squeezes me back.

Spending time with Jessi is so easy. We can go months, even years, without speaking, but the moment we can talk it's like no time was ever lost. We turn back into the same crazy girls we have always been. That's what I love about Jessi.

Chapter Twenty

THE WHITE CHAPEL

March 2004

Ian

"YOU READY, KELSEY?" I ask, looking out the window of the SUV as the cross on top of the tall white steeple comes into view.

"Ready to get this shit show over with. I hate human media; they always make a big deal out of nothing." Kelsey grumbles from the back seat as we drive down the long driveway that leads to the little white chapel in the center of the city.

"It's not that bad." Zane stops in front of the walkway that leads to the chapel. "Just think of the honeymoon. It makes up for all the craziness," he laughs as he puts the SUV in park.

I can understand where Kelsey is coming from. All eyes on him is not really his thing. Not that Kelsey is shy or anything like that, he's just not a fan of the way human media acts sometimes. That and wedding ceremonies are not normal in our culture. Many don't see the need for human formalities like this. We are bound by the mate bond, which is much stronger than the average human marriage. Since Zane, Kelsey, and I are the next to lead our pack, it is our custom to have a very public wedding ceremony in the city. The Alpha and Beta from different packs will be in attendance, but this event is mostly for the human world associates to witness.

Big events like this bring media in from all around. Local media leaves us alone, mostly. It's the outside media that is the problem. They push their flashing cameras in our faces, forcing their way through the crowd, shout questions, block our paths; some can be real dicks. Since weddings are not normal in our culture, it can be a bit of an annoyance to deal with human tradition and human media. It's not all bad though, through my father I've enjoyed the many perks, like free meals and gifts.

Zane's wedding was a circus, which is understandable since he is the future Alpha. His father sent out a ton of press releases, mostly to introduce him to the business world since he will take over for his father. The three of us, much like our fathers, will have lots of interaction with the human world. Kelsey's father sent out press releases, but not nearly as many as Alpha Nathaniel did for Zane. I think Kelsey secretly asked his father to scale everything back. Like I said, he's not shy, he'd just rather move a little more conspicuous. Like Zane, I won't have that luxury.

"That's the only thing I'm thinking about. One week held up in a mountain cabin with my mate... hell yeah." Kelsey laughs, "Looks like it will be your turn soon, Ian." Kelsey and Zane both look at me.

"I can only hope." I nod my head. Thinking back to the way Kate reacted to a rumor that I was away on a boys' trip and realizing that I'm the one who is responsible for her distrust in me. It was painful for me to see her so angry. I've done more damage than I ever realized. Honestly, I'm not too sure if she will ever fully trust me.

"The paparazzi doesn't look that bad," Zane looks out the driver's side window. "The warriors should be able to handle them."

"Let's do this. I have a plane to catch and a mate to ravage." Kelsey laughs before jumping out of the SUV on the driver's side. As expected, they immediately met him with cameras clicking and questions being shouted by the media. Kelsey adjusts his tuxedo jacket, flashes his pearly whites, and waves at the paparazzi. I wonder how long the cheesy bastard stood in front of his mirror practicing.

I step out the passenger door and am hit with the sweet smell of jasmine mixed with the spicey musky notes of roses. Kate's favorite scents. I stand quietly and take in the scene in front of me, while paparazzi shout at Kelsey behind me.

"Kelsey! Kelsey, right here! Look right here, please?" A female reporter shouts.

"Kelsey, how long have you known Sonia?" A male reporter shouts.

I look at the white chapel and think about Kate. Jasmine vines and small white star-shaped flowers cover the archway at the beginning of the cobblestone path that leads to the simple white building. Jasmine reminds me of Kate's sweet floral scent, something I didn't realize until Kate ran away to New York. They lined the cobblestone path with single black Victorian style lamp posts that are spaced out about ten feet apart. The black lamp posts are ornate, which is a contrast to the simple white building they lead to. The building has two steps that lead to a covered entryway. Both the roof of the building and the porch match and are steep, reminding me of upside-down triangles. The white chapel has clean simple lines, except for the double doors, which are ornate circles within circles. Looking between the Victorian lamp posts and the front doors, I realize that the patterns of both match. *Kate would appreciate details like this.* I look up at the cross on top of the massive steeple that sits high in the sky. The steeple has to be at least twenty feet tall, with a bell at the base. *I wonder if it still works.*

Each side of the pathway is rows of roses with neatly cut grass pathways in between. The rows of roses are so full, they look like short walls. I wonder if Kate has had time to walk around the rose garden and smell each variety of roses in front of the white chapel. She has taken me through the rose garden behind the packhouse, showing me her favorite roses and making me smell each of them. The details she knows about each plant and their smell characteristics, which she calls notes are astounding. Many of the varieties are ones that Luna Scarlett planted years ago. Kate explained to me they're now heirloom varieties and how rare they have become during modern times. The beauty in front of me reminds me of Kate and how special she is to me.

The sound of the SUV pulling away snaps me back to reality. I turn to see the other two standing in front of the roped off media area, with warriors positioned nearby. I walk over and join them, adjusting my tuxedo jacket as I walk. It's hard to make out what is being said since the paparazzi and reporters are shouting over each other. I have to give it to Kelsey; he is doing a great job fielding the questions. I smile while the three of us pose for pictures before turning to walk away.

"Ian!" A female reporter shouts, "you're the only one who's still an available bachelor. How does it feel?"

Normally I wouldn't answer questions, especially since this is Kelsey's show. But I really feel the need to show the world what Kate means to me. A small part of me is hoping that she is watching the coverage on the television.

"Actually," I turn to the reporter, "I'm not a bachelor. I'm engaged. My fiancée, Kate, and I grew up right next to each other. She was the girl next door. That's the things romance books are written about." I smile at the reporter before turning to walk away. I take notice of her swooning at my words, letting her microphone fall to her side.

I can't help but to smile at her reaction to me. Although she is attractive, the thought of being with anyone but my Kate makes my stomach churn, and not in a good way. A few years ago, I would have had my way with this woman in the backseat of the SUV, even after publicly declaring my love for Kate. It was something about the attention from these women that I thrived on. Almost like a drug, I needed hit after hit. Moving from one woman to the next with no remorse for anyone's feelings, especially Kate's. I was a real sick fucking bastard. Now, my drug of choice is Kate, and thinking about just how fucking sexy she is, makes my cock twitch.

Chapter Twenty-One
BREAKING UP

March 2004

Kate

"AHHHHHH!" REBEKA SHOUTS AT the television, "did you just hear what Ian said, Kate?" Everyone turns and looks at me.

"Ummmm... yeah," I stand, shocked, with my mouth wide open. Just hours ago, I was throwing a coffee mug at his head, and swearing that I wanted nothing to do with him. Only to wake up with him sleeping on my front porch, so I couldn't run away. Now he is publicly calling me his fiancée.

Hearing his words fills my soul with so much excitement. I feel like there are a thousand butterflies fluttering around in my chest and belly. The thought of a future with Ian makes my heart race and I feel like I'm floating. For the first time in a long time, I can see a future with him. Pups, family dinners, movie nights at home, making love to him every night for the rest of my life; all of it.

Rebeka and a few of the other bride's maids circle around me and start singing Chapel of Love by the Dixie Cups. I giggle while they dance and sing. Even Sonia joins in. She's only wearing her veil, corset, and thong. She grabs my hands, and we dance, spinning each other around. We're all acting so silly, but it feels good. This... with Ian feels so right.

My phone rings, and everyone laughs as Rebeka and I race for it. I grab it before she does and tuck it into my body, keeping it out of her reach.

"Look girls, Kate's fiancé is calling." Rebeka taunts and giggles.

"Maybe he's wanting to steal her away for a quick make-out session," Sonia puckers her lips, making kissing sounds as she pulls me close to her. The rest of the women join in on the craziness, each of them puckering their lips and making kissing sounds. The sight of them makes me laugh so hard. I flip open my phone and slip away from them.

"Ian, did you really call me your fiancée on national television?" I giggle into the phone.

"Kate?" A familiar male voice whispers.

"Darren," I whisper back. My smile and excitement fade at the sound of his voice. I forgot I told him I'd talk with him today. *Why did I agree with that?* The girls were right. My fiancé is calling me... just not the one they thought it would be. *How did this get to be such a mess?* The excitement I felt hearing Ian call me his fiancée is the same excitement I should have felt when Darren placed an engagement ring on my left hand. Is Jessi right? Darren never stood a chance against the mate bond?

I slip out of the bridal suite and into a quiet hall in the chapel. Swallowing down the lump that is growing in my throat. Poor Darren, he doesn't deserve any of this, and I need to end things with Darren. I feel like I'm leading him on, and it stops now. He might not be for me, but he's a good man and doesn't deserve any of this drama.

"Ian? That's the same guy from New York... the one you go way back with?" Darren sighs.

"Yes," I whisper, fully feeling the guilt of hurting him.

"So... you're with the gym bro?" I can hear the disappointment in his voice. "Let me guess, you're not a virgin either, are you?"

"Yes... I'm seeing Ian. And no, I'm not a virgin." I whisper.

"Ian got that too?" The anger rises in Darren's voice.

"Yes, when I was eighteen." I lean against the wall and press my hand into my belly. I might not have feelings for Darren, but I hate confrontation, especially when I'm the one in the hot seat.

"So, gym bro shows up in New York and you just couldn't wait to spread your legs for him." He snarls out. I know that I'm the one who messed up, but the way he's speaking to me now is just cruel. Darren doesn't know who I really am, or the pull the mate bond has. He will never understand. Even though I hurt him, I don't deserve to be spoken to this way.

"Listen," I snap, "I know you're hurting and it's my fault, but I don't deserve to be spoken to like this. For the record, I had no intentions of rekindling anything with Ian when I met you. Yes, I lied to you about being a virgin, and I'm not too sure why that bothers you so much. Truth is, I developed feelings for you at one point. When Ian showed up in New York, I came to terms with the truth, something that I knew all along... that I had never gotten over him. I found out he never got over me either. Darren, I couldn't give my body to you while I still wanted him." I gasp at how quick the words escape my mouth. My words are harsher than I ever intended them to be, but it infuriated me the way he spoke to me. "I'm sorry you got hurt. That was never my intention." I breathe out heavily. My emotions are somewhere between anger and sadness.

"Wow," he says and laughs.

"I'll send your ring back to you first thing Monday morning." I add, as a wave of relief washes over me.

"Don't bother. Just keep it, and the next time gym bro fucks up... and he will. You look at that pretty little rock and think of what you could have had." The line goes dead.

With my head tilted up, I stand quietly with my back pressed firmly against the wall. The tension from my body is being released by slowly breathing in and out. I see movement from the corner of my eye. I turn my head to see Ian's somber face.

"How much did you hear?" I ask, holding back the tears. All I need is for Ian to have misheard something... I'm not too sure I have the energy to explain my way out of it.

"Enough. Want to talk about it?" Ian moves closer.

"You want to talk to me about breaking up with my ex-boyfriend?" I tilt my head and turn my body towards him, keeping my shoulder pressed against the wall.

"Yeah, well, kind of. I mean... I know that this is hurting you as well, so I want to talk to you about your feelings." He stands close in front of me with his shoulder pressed against the wall.

"My feelings?" I question because Ian has never been concerned with the way anything made me feel.

"Yeah," he laughs out, "look, I know you had some sort of feelings for him, and I know you feel like he got hurt. Which I'm sure he did. I want to talk about how all this has made you feel." He brushes my cheek with his fingers.

"Okay... then let's do this. We'll talk about how this has made me feel." I breathe out, "I hate the fact that I cheated on Darren. I wish I could have done a better job controlling my urges. No one deserves to be cheated on and feel the pain of betrayal. I'll never forgive myself for hurting him like that. But you and I both know the truth... I was not meant for him, and he was not meant for me. As hard as I tried, I just couldn't fully give myself to him." I shake my head. I hate admitting this to Ian, because down deep inside I'm afraid he'll use this against me... to cheat on me again.

"Because the Moon Goddess made us for each other. I wish I would have learned this sooner. I lost so much time with you. We should have been married in a media circus by now, with at least one pup." He smiles and rubs his thumb on my bottom lip.

"Can you imagine... us with a pup?" I laugh.

"Every day, I can't wait until you let me put a pup in here." He rubs the palm of this hand on my belly. "I think about your swollen belly with my pup growing inside every day. It's the only thing that has gotten me through the past two years without you. That and standing by the jasmine vines by the packhouse... they remind me of the way you smell, sweet and floral." I look down at his hand on my belly and place my hand on top of his, then look back into his eyes. Looking deep into his eyes, all I see is sincerity and truth, and for the second time today, I see a future with him. "Wow, you're wearing it. After all this time." He looks at my neck and rubs his fingers on the necklace he gave me for my eighteenth birthday.

"Yeah, and it still fits," I giggle.

"Thank you for giving me the chance that I don't deserve." He wraps his hand around my neck and pulls me in for a kiss. And for the first time, I don't fight the mate bond and wrap my arms around him, kissing him back. Our kiss is slow and full of sweet, beautiful emotions. We melt into each other's bodies as hurt and pain washes away.

"Found her!" Rebeka shouts, "yeah they're making out just like you said, Sonia." I giggle and pull away from Ian's lips.

"Hang on... give me just a minute." Ian says, looking down. I follow his gaze and see his member rising to the occasion, making me laugh a little louder.

"Come on, we're lining up." Rebeka snaps her fingers.

"Yeah... um," I giggle, "I'll be right there."

"Go... it's all good now." Ian laughs, then presses his lips into mine.

Chapter Twenty-Two

MINE

February 2001

Ian

I OPEN MY EYES to the sounds of knocking; but I'm not too sure if I dreamed it or not. I look down and see Kate curled up with her head on my chest and my arm wrapped around her shoulder. She feels perfect pressed into my body. She looks so peaceful, like the angel she is.

Knock **Knock** **Knock**

Someone is knocking on the door, it wasn't a dream. I gently wiggle out from under Kate, trying not to wake her up. I climb out of bed and slip on a tee shirt and basketball shorts before opening the front door to a female omega kitchen worker.

"Sorry to bother you, sir, but Chef Marcy sent dinner for you and your mate." The kitchen worker states, before looking down to the box of food in her arms.

"Oh wow, here I'll take that." I take the box out of her arms and am hit with the wonderful smell of Chef Marcy's famous fried chicken. "Please tell Chef Marcy that Kate and I appreciate this very much." I smile before stepping back to shut the door. I place the box of food on the table and quickly make my way back to the bed I left my Kate in.

Stepping into the bedroom, she is sitting up in bed looking at me. She has a confused look on her face, almost like she doesn't know where she is.

"Hey angel," I pull off my tee shirt and climb back into bed with her.

"I woke up, and you were gone. Where did you go?" Kate pulls away from me. *Does she think I snuck off to be with another woman?*

"There was a knock on the door... Chef Marcy sent food." I wrap my arms around her.

"Do I smell fried chicken?" She says as she sniffs the air.

"I'm pretty sure," I laugh, "although I didn't check it. I couldn't wait to get back to you." Pulling her close to me.

"What time is it?" She asks.

"Quarter until eight." I rub her back.

"We slept through lunch and dinner?" Shock creeps across her face.

"Yes, we did. I didn't sleep much the night before. You went through a lot yesterday and then we ran until the sun came up. Our bodies needed the rest." I pull her onto my lap.

"That's Kelsey's favorite... fried chicken." She laughs.

"Actually, angel, it's mine, Zane, and Kelsey's favorite. We can eat it hot or cold." I nuzzle into the crook of her neck and inhale her delicious, sweet floral scent.

"Really? I didn't know that." She rests her head on mine.

"We still have a lot to learn about each other." I pull away and look into her eyes.

"I guess we do." She nervously looks down.

"Hey, I want you to know that we'll move as fast or as slow as you want. You'll control the speed. I promise you'll never be pressured to do anything you're not ready to do. Okay, angel?" I rub her jaw with my thumb.

"How did you know?" She looks into my eyes.

"You're my mate. We are one. I can feel your emotions and pain." I rub circles on her back.

"You feel my pain? Like you felt the pain last night?" She rubs her fingertips on my chest.

"Yes... I felt all of it. Then Alex and I tracked you." I kiss her shoulder.

"Wow, I didn't know. Thank you, Ian. I'm nervous about what it means to be a mate." She bites her bottom lip and sighs.

"It's okay, angel. Don't be nervous, it's just me." I pull her bottom lip from her teeth and rub it with my thumb. "Earlier. Was that your first kiss?" She smiles and nods yes. "Has anyone touched you like this?" I run my hand from her knee up her inner thigh, stopping inches from her pussy. Her breathing becomes shallow, and I can feel her excitement build. Again, she doesn't speak, only shakes her head no. "Do you like it when I touch you like this?" I rub circles with my nails and fingertips on her inner thigh. Watching her intently, my eyes never leaving her face. Her body relaxes, and she slightly opens her legs, granting me more access to her. "Would you like for me to kiss you, Kate?" I move my hand from her inner thigh to the opposite hip.

"Yes," she squeaks out, then takes a deep breath.

Moving my hand from her hip to her face, I caressing her cheek and jaw. Moving slowly and gently, I bring her lips to mine and kiss her softly. I'm her first everything, which is an immense honor in my book. She has preserved herself just for her mate. I want to make sure each kiss is perfect and exactly what she fantasized it to be. I kiss her slowly, savoring the sweet taste of her lips, moving my hand that's on her back to under her tank top. There is a primal need that I'm fighting, to feel her bare skin on mine, but for now I will settle for feeling her bare skin with my fingertips.

She softly moans into my mouth as sparks radiate from where our skin touches. Both of us are breathing heavily as my cock gets harder by the second. I move my lips from hers and kiss her jaw down to her neck. I kiss, suck, and nip at her neck down to her marking spot. Guiding my tongue over the sensitive area in the crook of her neck, I claim her neck with every lick. Her skin tastes delicious, like a fine delicacy. She lightly gasps at the sensation and moves her head to the side, giving me full access to her exquisite neck. I suck her marking spot and move my hand that's under her tank top to her breast. Gently, I brush my hand against her hard nipples, then pinch it. Kate moans loudly, opening her mouth. I seize the moment and kiss her again, sliding my tongue deep into her mouth.

My tongue strokes hers begging it to dance. Soon her tongue comes to life. Our tongues dance and twist around the other. They explore every inch of the other's mouth. I suck and gently bite her lip, thoroughly enjoying the way her mouth tastes. Our kiss is hot and passionate. Lust and our moans fill the air, I can smell her arousal, and it smells fucking divine.

I tug at the hem of her tank top. When she doesn't stop me, I pull it up, exposing her breasts. She pulls away from my lips and looks down at her exposed breasts, then back at me. Her eyes are black and full of lust. She gives me a grin and nods before pulling her tank top off and tossing it aside.

"Mmmm... MINE." I growl and take her lips again. This time, the kiss is more passionate and slightly rougher. She moans loudly and moves her hips, grinding her ass into my hard cock. I lay us down on our side, our legs are intertwined. I grind my hard-on into her leg. Massaging her ass, I press my leg against her pussy. I can feel her dampness through our clothes, and it's driving me insane. *I want more.*

"You fucking love the way I make you feel, don't you?" I say into her mouth.

"Uh huh," she moans out.

I roll her onto her back and position myself on top. Trapping her hands above her head as she opens her legs wide for me. I kiss and suck her neck; our hips move in unison. Heat rises between us. Both our bodies craving more friction, more contact... simply more.

"We can stop, if you want." I look at her face. I promised her we could take it slow and that I wouldn't pressure her into doing something she wasn't ready for, and I intend to honor that promise.

"No... I don't want to. I want you Ian, so bad." She holds my face between her hands. Her facial expression is somewhere between love and lust. I don't hesitate before plunging my tongue deep into her mouth, grinding my rock-hard dick into her pussy.

I massage her perfect breasts with each hand, pinching each nipple between my thumb and forefinger. She gasps and moans while running her nails down my back. I take one nipple in my mouth, taking my time licking and sucking each one before teasing them with my teeth. Alternating between pleasure and pain, she arches her back while running her nails over my scalp. I love the feeling of her nails digging into my skin.

"I want to taste every inch of your gorgeous body, angel. Can I please taste you?" I look into her eyes.

"Yes," she whispers, then kisses me.

I kiss my way down to her belly. Slowly taking my time, alternating between kissing and licking her flesh. I run my fingers along the waistband of her shorts, gently tugging them down. She lifts her hips, allowing me to remove them. I rise to my knees and bring her legs together, then rest them on my shoulder. Slowly, I pull her shorts and panties off together, tossing them aside. I open her legs and admire her sweet little pussy. Embarrassed, she turns red and covers herself with her hand.

"Never hide yourself from me." I move her hand. "Every inch of you belongs to me, and I want to see what is mine." I look at her from head to toe. "fucking perfection." Her embarrassment turns into a lustful smile.

My lips return to her belly, kissing and licking. My tongue moves from her belly to her inner thigh. I alternate kissing and licking each thigh, teasing her skin with my teeth. I rub my thumb along her slit and rub circles on her hard clit.

Kate

"You smell luscious, angel." Ian whispers before I feel his hot mouth on my entrance.

I throw my head back and close my eyes. His tongue glides up and down my slit, then in and out. I moan and fist the sheets under me. This feels so good. I can't get enough of his hands and mouth on my body. With every stroke of his tongue, every touch from his hands, my body begs for more. I can't get enough of him. His mouth moves up to my nub and his tongue swirls circles around it. I feel something… a pressure building in my pelvic area. I feel like I'm about to explode into a million pieces. My hips move on their own, grinding my core into Ian's mouth. He growls, then sucks on my nub before running his tongue in and out of my entrance. Just when I feel like I can't take anymore, I feel his finger slip inside me. I gasp and moan as the pressure builds inside me. His finger offers a different pleasure all together which compounds the pleasure from his hot mouth.

"Do you like this, angel?" He slowly moves his finger in and out of me.

"Yes, more," I beg.

"Like this?" He inserts a second finger inside me. "Let's get this tight little pussy stretched and ready for my dick."

This time there is a pinching feeling, followed by a small amount of pain. I groan out and shift my hips, trying to ease the discomfort. Ian's hand stops moving, and he looks up at my face.

"You okay, angel? Want me to stop?" I lay still for a moment, trying to decide if we should stop or not. Slowly the pain and discomfort fade and pleasure takes its rightful place.

"No, I'm good." I feel hot liquid pool under me.

Ian's fingers move in and out of me, starting slowly at first, then quickly picking up the pace as his thumb rubs circles on my numb. I move my hips to his rhythm as the pressure inside me builds. Ian's free hand massages my breast. My head spins and my body trembles.

"Oh Ian, that feels so good." I moan out.

"Do you feel you're ready to explode?" His fingers thrust harder.

"Yes, yes," I rock my hips.

"Cum for me, angel. Scream my name. Show me how much you like what I'm doing." I feel his lips wrap around my nub and suck as his tongue flicks the tip.

My body tenses up as the pressure inside me builds higher and higher.

"Oh Ian," I moan out. My head spins as a euphoric wave of pleasure crashes over my body. I can feel my core pulse around his fingers as they continue to move in and out of me as I ride the wave of pleasure.

"Ian," I shout as another wave crashes over me. My body shakes as more hot liquid pools under me. After I come down, Ian removes his fingers and rises to his knees.

I lift my upper body, resting on my elbows, watching as he quickly jumps off the bed, and pulling his shorts and boxer briefs off in one swift move. I giggle as he stumbles, getting his foot stuck in his shorts before kicking them off to the other side of the room. His huge member leaps out towards me, and suddenly I can't take my eyes off it. I'm completely mesmerized. It looks different from what I saw earlier. It's larger, more solid, and standing at full attention. With wide eyes, I watch as he slowly makes his way back on to the bed, pushing my knees apart to take his place between my thighs. I watch with enthusiasm as he runs his hand up and down his shaft, and around the mushroom shaped tip. I'm captivated by how the blue and green veins protrude out further with every stroke from his hand. I feel dampness building as my core throbs for his touch. Ian slowly strokes his member, his hungry eyes are fixed on my face. I lick my lips when I see a clear liquid seep from the top.

"Like what you see, angel?" His tone is low, sending shivers down my spine. Seeing my reaction, he gives me a sly grin. I look from his member to his face and suddenly all shyness is gone. I want him now.

"Very much," I grin back at him.

"Want my dick inside you?" He hovers over me, and I reach my hand out and touch it for the first time.

"Yes," I whisper as I run my hand up and down his smooth shaft, wiping the liquid from the tip.

"Mmmm, that feels good," he groans then kisses me. His lips have a different taste to them, like sweet and salty caramel. Our tongues tangle and dance together.

Ian breaks our kiss and gently pushes me flat on my back, before lining his member up with my entrance. He rubs the tip up and down my slit, dipping it in and out, coating it with the juices from my body. Shockwaves of electric pulses go through my body to my core. Goosebumps form on every inch of my skin as the tip of his shaft massages my core.

"This might hurt a little. Let me know and we stop. Okay, angel?" I nod and he slowly pushes inside me.

My breath hitches and I sink my nails into his shoulders from the discomfort of him entering me for the first time. Ian stops, allowing my body to adjust to him. When he feels my body relax, he withdraws and slowly pushes back in. He repeatedly makes the same move, pushing in a little further each time. Not wanting to hurt me, Ian's moves are slow and gentle. I can feel his member filling and stretching me with each slow movement.

"I'm all the way in. You're doing so good, angel. Are you okay?" Ian stops moving.

"Yes," I whisper. Even though there is some discomfort, I don't want to stop. I like the way he feels inside me... full and connected to each other. Every second he is inside me, the discomfort fades away to pleasure.

Ian and I lock eyes as he slowly withdraws his full length, then slowly pushes back inside me. I open my legs wider, moving my hips to allow him more space to move freely. He continues his soft strokes, and with each slow methodical movement, I feel his love for me. Love and passion takeover as we mold into each other's body. I run my hands up and down his back, feeling his muscle flex as he pushes in and out of me. His arms engulf and concoon my body and I've never felt safer or more loved in my life. He gently caresses my face and rubs my lips with his thumb as we kiss.

Soon the pressure eurupts and my core pulsates around his member, drawing him deeper inside me. Ian's teeth tease the sensitive area in the crook of my neck. He grunts from pure pleasure as he moves in and out of me at a faster pace. My head spins as he pushes deep, holding my hips in place, grunting and growling loudly as his member pulsates filing me with his hot iquid.

I scream his name as I'm hit with wave after wave of euphoric pleasure. I tremble and shake under him as my orgasm crashes over my body, and I feel like I'm flying high in the clouds. When we both come down from our high, I hold his face in the palms of my hands while he still hovers over me. I'm so in love with him.

"Mine," I say with full authority. Ian smiles, crashes his lips into mine for a fiery and passionate kiss.

CHAPTER TWENTY-THREE
THE WAY OF THE DONUT

June 2004

Kate

IT'S A QUARTER UNTIL four in the morning and I'm in my parents' kitchen sipping on my coffee when I hear Ian's SUV pull up next to the house. I stand in the dark kitchen and watch out the window as Ian jumps out of the back passenger seat and walks to the front door. I take my last big gulp of coffee, rinse my cup, and leave it in the sink. Then I grab my day bag and gift for Jessi's pup and walk out the back door. Kelsey quickly greets me with a hug and peck on my cheek before he takes everything from my arms to load into the back of the SUV. Walking towards Ian, I glance at Zane. I'm almost within arm's reach of Ian now. He doesn't sense me. I look back at Zane, who is laughing. I motion for him to be quiet by placing a single finger over my mouth.

'Kate... Kate,' Ian calls through our mindlink. *'Are you up?'* I seize the opportunity to have a little fun at Ian's expense.

"Hey," I say from behind Ian.

"Ahhhh!" He jumps and spins to me. "Where the hell did you come from?" I giggle as he grabs his chest.

"Bro, what the hell? You're slipping," Zane laughs.

"What? Did she sneak up on him?" Kelsey approaches and joins in on the laughter with Zane and me.

"Hahahaha," Ian sarcastically mocks their laughter, "I thought it was you two assholes moving around behind me." He points at them, then turns his attention to me. "You little sneak." He wraps his muscular arms around me and playfully blows raspberries on my neck. I squeal and giggle while trying to squirm my way out of his grip.

"You're slipping," I tease and laugh.

"Only when it comes to you, my love." Ian presses his lips into mine and soon we are lost in each other. Our kiss is slow, sweet, and lingering.

"Aww shit, not this again. Bro, she's still my sister." Kelsey protests behind me. I giggle and break the kiss.

"She's my mate, that supersedes sister. Get used to it. How many times have I watched you two with your tongues down your mates' throats?" Ian says without letting me go. Turning his attention back to me, his face and tone soften. "You ready to go?"

"Yes, Kelsey already loaded my things into the SUV." Ian unwraps his arms from around me and I'm left feeling empty without his touch.

"Good, we need to get on the road, then." He guides me over to the backseat of the SUV.

We've been on the road heading towards the palace for about an hour now and have about another hour of travel left. I watch out the window as we pass through the darkness of the early morning hours. Ian, Zane, and Kelsey have combat training at the palace today, along with about twenty of Blue Moon's top warriors. We are traveling in five different SUVs and will head back to our territory after dinner at the palace tonight.

A few days ago, Ian asked if I would like to join them on this trip, that I could finally meet Jessi's pup. He was born the very next morning after Kelsey and Sonia's wedding. I guess Jessi wasn't kidding when she said she was due any second. Of course, I jump at the opportunity to spend the day with Jessi and her new pup. More so, I'm thrilled that Ian thought enough of my feelings to ask if I wanted to go. It's the little things like this and the way Ian goes out of his way to make me happy. My favorite thing is he never lets me start my day without a good morning mindlink. No matter what he is doing, he stops just to check on me, and it makes me feel so special.

The past two and a half months have been so blissfully perfect and I'm enjoying the time Ian and I have been spending together. Since mine and Ian's relationship is progressing and our future seems bright, I decided not to return to New York for the fall semester. I'm avoiding the fact that I need to go pack my apartment, ending that phase of my life.

I've been spending part of my days apprenticing under both Ian's mom and Luna Martha. I'm learning what it means to be Beta Female, and I have so much to learn. Not only is my relationship with Ian growing, but I'm bonding with Rebeka and Sonia as well. Rebeka and I have become very close, almost like sisters. Which is the bond we will need as Luna and Beta Female. Ian and I spend lots of time with Zane, Rebeka, Kelsey, and Sonia. We eat dinner together with them daily. Every moment Ian and I can, we sneak away to the lake and spend time talking, sometimes for hours on end. We share everything with each other.

Every day that we spend together, the mate bond grows more. When we touch, the sparks that radiate are as strong as they were in the beginning, but our marks are still faded. Luna Martha thinks we will need to mate and mark again to solidify the mate bond as permanent. I'm still living at my parents' home rather than in Ian's quarters in the packhouse. I didn't want to move in with him until I was sure I was ready to mate with him. Our past has made me wary of his actions and I needed for him to prove to me I can trust him with my body, soul, and heart. Now when we are alone together, I fight the need to feel his bare skin on mine and to make love to him. Honestly, I'm not too sure how much longer I can withstand the pull.

"Hey," Ian scooches close to me, wrapping his powerful arms around me, nuzzling into my neck.

"Hey, you," I whisper back, turning my head to kiss his cheek.

"We're about thirty minutes from the palace, and we're going to make a quick pit stop. There's this little hole in the wall donut shop up ahead. It's a dump, but their coffee is good, the bathrooms are clean, and they make the best raspberry filled donuts ever." Ian pecks kisses on my neck.

"Bullshit!" Kelsey objects. "They make the best cinnamon rolls. Kate, it's the kind with the cream cheese icing." Kelsey looks at me and motions swirls with his hands while licking his lips.

"Wrong!" Zane speaks up, looking at me from the rearview mirror. "Don't listen to either of those bozos. They're both clearly wrong. They make the best Bavarian cream donut with the powdered sugar coating. It's so fucking good." Zane hits the steering wheel. I giggle at the three of them and their enthusiasm for pastries.

"It all sounds good, but I love a plain glazed donut all day long." I say, waving my hands out in front of me. All three grunt and groan at this revelation.

"Ian, talk with your mate... set her straight." Kelsey groans out.

"Kelsey, she's your sister. Shouldn't you have taught her about donuts?" Ian sarcastically snaps back.

"Don't worry, Kate, we will bring you from the plain side and teach you the way of the donut." Zane laughs as he pulls into the parking lot of an old run-down white building.

After our bathroom break, we take our coffee and donuts to go. Ian was right. The place is a dump, but the older couple that own the shop are amazing and their coffee and donuts are even better. Ian ate six by himself and insisted that I take a bite of each one before allowing me my plain donut. Even Kelsey insisted I try his cinnamon roll. They were right, plain ended up not being my favorite after all. Glazed chocolate cake is now my favorite, with Boston cream running a close second.

We take ten dozen donuts to-go, arriving at the palace gates at seven thirty. Once we are cleared by palace warriors, we drive for another thirty minutes just past the palace to the large training grounds. The palace grounds are exquisite and are setup similar to Blue Moon with cottages and houses all around. The training grounds are quadruple the size of Blue Moon's. Ian explains that packs from all over the world come here to train. He points out a large white five-story building which is the training guest accommodations, which includes a fully staffed kitchen.

"We're going to go check in for training. Would you like to walk with us or..." I interrupt Ian.

"I'll stay here. This place is enormous, and I really don't feel like walking for miles." I scrunch my nose at the thought of doing so much physical activity so early in the morning.

"Okay, I understand. Here. You can sit back here with the donuts and coffee until we get back." Ian opens the back of the SUV and clears a spot for me to sit.

"You trust me with all these donuts?" I say in a teasing tone.

"Yes, it's coffee that you're not to be trusted with." He laughs, then pecks me on the lips before walking away with Zane, Kelsey, and the warriors that came with us. Watching him walk away, I can't help but to think about how much he has changed and how perfect everything has been.

I fill my cup with coffee from the thermos that Ian filled while we were at the donut shop, and I search for a plain donut. Finding exactly what I'm looking for, I take a large bite and sip my coffee. Enjoying the sounds of the songbirds, the coolness of the damp early morning air, and the smell of sweet gardenias all around me. I take another large bite of donut when I notice a tall, well-toned man approaching. Not really thinking twice about him, I take a sip of my hot coffee. He's not wearing a normal palace uniform, but he is dressed like he is ready to train.

"Good morning." He smiles and leans on the SUV. With a mouthful of donut, I'm not too sure what to do. I don't want to be rude, but I can hear my mom's voice warning me to watch my manners and not to talk with a mouthful of food. I point to my mouth as I chew. The more I chew, the more the donut in my mouth seems to grow. I give the stranger a closed-mouth smile, then cover my mouth with my hand.

"Morning," I say through a mouthful of donut. I can almost hear my mom snapping her lips at me. I swallow and take a large sip of coffee to wash the rest of the donut down.

"I've never seen you around here before. What pack are you from?" The strange man tilts his head and sniffs the air.

"Blue Moon. I've been here a few times over the years for balls and festivals." I smile and nod before glancing down at my half-eaten donut, wishing this strange man would go away so I can eat in peace.

"Oh, I forgot Blue Moon was coming for training today. What's your name? I'm Lazar." He leans a little closer to me and I slide away from him, putting space between the two of us.

"Lazar? Why does your name seem so familiar to me?" I try to place the stranger's name and face but am coming up with blanks. I'm not too sure who he is, but he's giving me slimy creeper vibes.

"Perhaps you've heard my name before, since I'm next in line for the throne." Lazar gives me a cocky smile.

"Prince Lazar?" I put my hand on my chest and choke on air when I realize that the slimy creeper is the next werewolf king. He is a year from taking the throne.

"You can just call me Lazar. We don't need to be so formal, do we?" He chuckles and inches closer to me. "May I have your name?"

"Kate," I nervously sip my coffee, realizing he has ulterior motives than just being friendly.

"Beautiful name for a beautiful woman. It's nice to make your acquaintance, Kate." Lazar offers me his hand. I hesitate for a moment.

I know he is hitting on me, but he is the future king, and I don't want to come off rude. Then again, I don't want to lead him on. Feeling like I'm stuck between a rock and a hard place, I take a deep breath, put my coffee down, and shake Lazar's hand. He shakes my hand, then rubs my knuckles with his thumb. The grin on his face makes me feel more uncomfortable than I already am. *I wish Ian was here right now.*

In one swift move, Lazar pulls my hand up to his lips and open mouth kisses the back of my hand. The kiss is slow, and I can see a string of his saliva in the small space between his mouth and my hand. *Yuck!* I quickly snatch my hand from his grasp and wipe my hand on the SUV's carpet, and narrow my eyes at him. I don't care who he is, what he just did really pisses me off. He took advantage of my kindness.

"I'm sorry," I snap, "but my mate wouldn't approve of the way you're touching me." Keeping my head held high, I confidently say. I may hate confrontations, but this asshole overstepped his bounds.

"Mate?" He laughs. "I don't see a mate anywhere around here." Prince Lazar steps closer and gives me a smug smile.

"I'm right here, Prince Lazar." Ian appears from the side of the SUV and steps between the Prince and I.

Ian gives the prince an icy glare, almost daring him to make a move. The standoff between the two of them is tense and I hate it. I wrap my hand around Ian's bicep to relax him, but it doesn't seem to work. It's quite the opposite. I feel the muscles in his arm tense up. *Oh no, he's angry with me, too. What have I done?*

"Kate, we're so happy you joined us today. Jessi is so excited that you are here." Adam walks up to us with another man at his side. That's when I see Zane and Kelsey approach from the other side of the SUV. Kelsey is angry. Both he and Zane glare at Prince Lazar as well. I'm not liking being in the middle of all this testosterone. A wave of heat hits me as my stomach churns from anxiety.

"What's going on here?" The man standing next to Adam asks sensing the rising tension in the air.

"Ian, please accept my sincerest apology. I did not know that she is your mate." Prince Lazar offers Ian his hand.

"Oh, brother... really?" The man next to Adam sighs out.

"No worries, Prince Lazar, mistakes happen." Ian shakes the prince's hand, but I can tell Ian is still agitated.

"Kate, this is Prince Malachi," Adam introduces the younger prince to me. I don't remove my hand from Ian's arm and just wave at the prince, keeping my eyes fixed on the ground. The uneasy feeling in the pit of my stomach makes me want to vomit. I just hope I can make this right by Ian.

Chapter Twenty-Four

DISDAIN

May 2001

Kate

"THANK YOU SO MUCH for seeing me today, Dr. Patrice." I sit nervously on the examination table in the pack clinic.

"Of course, Kate. Looks like the last time I saw you, we started you on birth control. What brings you in today?" Dr. Patrice sits on a low black stool with thick padding and wheels. She looks over my medical notes attached to a clipboard then up to me.

"I haven't been feeling well, and... there's these pains in my chest." I pat my chest with one hand.

"Chest pains? Eighteen... you're young to be having chest pains." Dr. Patrice writes a note on her clipboard, then looks back up to me. "Tell me about these pains."

"Well... they don't happen all the time." I fidget with my fingers, "they come and go. Sometimes they're mild, other times they knock the wind out of me. When they go away, my energy is zapped. All I want to do is sleep, but I can't." I stretch my shoulders back, trying to ease the tension in them.

"Um hmmm... when did the pains start?" Dr. Patrice continues to write notes without looking at me.

"They started about a week after Ian left to go back to school the second time." I wipe my sweaty palms on my jeans. I'm not too sure why I'm feeling anxious talking to Dr. Patrice about this. Maybe, it's because she's the first person I have spoken to. Maybe, I'm nervous that something medically is seriously wrong with me. Either way, I hate this nervous feeling that's building inside me.

"Ian... Beta Charles' son?" She looks up from her clipboard.

"Yes. I discovered that he is my mate on my eighteenth birthday. We spent the day together, then he left to go back to school. He came back two weeks later, and we spent the weekend together...then he left." I sigh, thinking about how much I miss him and hate that we've been apart so much. "I haven't seen him in two months. Finals and all." I look up at the ceiling, concentrating on the ceiling tiles so I don't start crying.

"And the pain started a week after he left the second time?" Dr. Patrice says looking over her notes.

"Yes." I adjust in my seat.

"Interesting... how often is the pain?" She rolls her stool closer to me.

"Daily... sometimes twice a day." I breathe out heavily.

"How long does the pain last?" Dr. Patrice makes more notes, then flips the page. Her note taking is starting to agitate me. Why so many notes?

"Not long, maybe ten minutes." I turn my head from side to side, popping my neck. The tension that was in my shoulders is now spreading throughout my body.

"Are you okay Kate?" Dr. Patrice sits up straight and takes a deep breath.

"I'm just a little... anxious." I take a deep breath and blow it out.

"You said you hadn't been feeling well. Tell me about that." A nurse walks through the door and hands her a piece of paper, "thank you." She says to the nurse, then reads the paper before looking back at me.

"What's that?" I lean forward trying to get a peek at the paper.

"This?" She holds the paper up, "the results of your blood work and urine sample. First, you're not pregnant, but you probably already knew that. Still, I thought it best to rule it out." She puts the paper under her notes on the clipboard. "Second, all your blood work came back normal. Tell me about how you've been feeling... please." Dr. Patrice's tone is firmer than previously.

"Well... for starters I'm exhausted all the time. I don't have an appetite at all, and I've noticed I've lost some weight... probably because I don't eat. Even though I'm tired I can't sleep," I take a breath and sigh. "When I do sleep, I toss and turn so bad that I don't get any rest. I'm moody and don't want to hang out with my friends. I just want to sit in my room and cry. I'm also having a hard time in school because I can't concentrate." I run my hands through my hair. Hearing that my blood work is normal, I feel like I'm going crazy now.

"Would you say you're restless and get irritated and agitated easily?" Dr. Patrice makes more notes. Maybe she thinks I'm crazy.

"Yes," I close my eyes and breathe.

"Thank you for sharing all this with me today. I know it wasn't easy." She puts the clipboard in her lap. "I don't think you have anything medically wrong with you."

"You think I'm nuts, don't you?" I cringe waiting for her response.

"No," she chuckles under her breath, "I don't think that at all. I'm pretty sure the chest pains and your other symptoms are related to Ian." She tilts her head and offers me a grin.

"How so?" I nervously bite my bottom lip.

"Do you know the story of my mate, Michael?" Dr. Patrice puts her hands on top of the clipboard.

"You met him in medical school and he's human." I pause and think, "that's all." I shrug my shoulders.

"You're correct, I met him in medical school and he's human. When I first met him, I instantly knew he was my mate. I felt the pull... very strongly. I pushed him away, hoping that the bond would diminish. Unfortunately, it did not. Michael had an instant attraction to me, and he pursued me. Relentlessly. I continued to push him away... I even told him that I hated him and thought he was weird looking." She looks up to the ceiling and laughs.

"Why would you push him away?" Leaning towards her, I'm intrigued by her story.

"Fear," she sighs out. "I was afraid that my family and pack would reject our relationship. That I'd be forced to choose between him and those who I love dearly. And if I chose him, I'd have to live away from the pack, and my family." She looks down then back up at me.

"But... our pack doesn't have rules against human mates." I tilt my head.

"I didn't say my thought process was logical," she laughs. "I became so ill, I was hospitalized. I had many of the same symptoms you are having now... plus some. Although I never did have chest pains. I had a battery of tests run on me, and everything came back normal. My doctors finally surmised that my illness was due to stress. When Luna Martha heard of my symptoms, she thought it sounded more like I was dealing with a rejection and took her concerns to her mate. My father came to pick me up from school to bring me back home, to my surprise Alpha Nathaniel was with him. Alpha Nathaniel is not a fan of vanity rejection of mates; he believes that mates are a gift from Moon Goddess herself. He wanted to face the wolf that would spit in the face of Moon Goddess and reject such a precious gift. When I finally told him the truth about Michael and that I was the one who was pushing him away, Alpha Nathaniel just laughed. He thought I was being silly and assured me that the pack would stand behind me and my mate. Human or otherwise. We had a very long discussion about how being mated outside the werewolf community is not taboo at all. He explained that Michael's relentless pursuing of me was due to the mate bond pull. Humans experience the pull differently, but it is just as strong. He also explained that Michael would accept the fact that I'm a werewolf, without hesitation." She explains.

"What happened next?" I'm hanging on to her every word. I've always loved love stories like this.

"They left. My father and Alpha Nathaniel, both thought it would be best if I stopped fighting the mate bond pull, and explore a relationship with Michael. That if they brought me back here, I would just continue to get sicker and sicker until my death. The next day I agreed to get coffee with Michael, and we have been together ever since. After we finished medical school, we moved here." She smiles at me.

"So, you think that I'm feeling this way because I miss Ian?" I look away, trying to process everything.

"In a matter of speaking. The mate bond is very powerful, we are meant to be with our mates always. I think you are feeling his feelings the same as he can feel yours. These negative feelings are fueling each other. Being apart, like you both have been, for long periods of time puts a strain on the mate bond as well. All this combined can manifest itself into a physical illness. Your symptoms should go away when you're both together again. When is he due home?" She gives me a warm smile, which is comforting. Her smile is telling me she completely understands how I'm feeling, and that she doesn't think I'm crazy after all.

"His last final was this morning... so late this evening. I've already moved all my things into a cottage we'll share this summer before we move back to college in the fall." I smile and breathe out. I'm feeling like a weight is being lifted off my shoulders.

"That's wonderful. I think we should wait and see if the pains stop. If not, I can order some tests." Dr. Patrice makes some notes.

"Sounds like a plan. Thank you for seeing me today." I slide off the table and breathe a sigh of relief. Hearing her story gives me hope that something serious is not wrong with me.

"Of course," she stands and shakes my hand when I'm hit with pains in my chest again.

"Ughhh..." I groan while gripping my chest and lean back on the examination table.

"Woah," Dr. Patrice wraps her arms around me, so I don't fall to the floor.

"This one is worse than normal." I breathe heavily through the pain.

"It's ok," she says as two nurses walk through the door. Together the three of them pick me up and lay me down on the examination table. "Get comfortable and rest here. Let me know when the pain stops.

I roll onto my side and apply pressure to my chest with my hands. This is the worst one by far, but the pain remains only in my chest. I breathe in and out slowly. Every time I have one of these pains Sasha cries out for Alex. Her cries are so sorrowful that it makes the pain worse. *I need Ian.* The pain only lasts for five minutes or so, but soon a wave of guilt crashes over me. *What the hell is that about?*

Ian

'This isn't cool, Ian. Kate is my sister.' Kelsey snaps at me through the open mindlink with Zane and me.

'I have to agree with Kelsey.' Zane looks at me through the rearview mirror.

'What? We're just giving a friend a ride back home. Nikki is just my friend.' I look over to see Nikki sleeping soundly pressed up against the SUV's window. Deep inside I know that this is wrong, her sitting so close to me. I should have ended things with her months ago, but every time I tried... I ended up fucking her instead. I'm not even sure why, I don't love her... hell, I don't even like her most of the time. She's

annoying as hell. But somehow, she knows exactly what to do to keep me coming back for more. It's not just her... there's Cindy too. She's a human girl I met a year ago. I don't know why, but I can't stop myself when it comes to them both. I know it's wrong and I feel guilty about it. Maybe it's because I miss Kate, but I wouldn't miss Kate so much if I would go home every weekend like I promised her I would. *Fuck.*

'You need to end this shit with this crazy bitch and the human too. It's just a matter of time before Kate finds out, and shit hits the fan.' Zane mindlinks.

'How will she find out? Kelsey, are you going to tell her?' I look at the back of Kelsey's head.

'No, I promised I wouldn't. You have my loyalty.' Kelsey puts his head down. I know I've put him in a tight place, making him choose loyalty to me over his sister.

'It doesn't matter anyways; I'm done with both Nikki and Cindy.' I mindlink.

'I hope so.' Zane looks at me through the rearview mirror. These two don't understand what it's like being mated so early in life, then being so far away from their mate. They'll never understand the guilt I feel afterwards, knowing I'm betraying someone who loves me.

The rest of the ride back home is quiet... except for the sounds of Nikki's snoring. When we pull up in front of the packhouse, I wake her up before unloading her shit on the front steps of the packhouse.

"What? You're not going to help me bring this up to my room?" Nikki puts her hands on her hips in protest.

"No, I'm not." I snap, closing the back of the SUV. Nikki scoffs and stomps her foot. "You forget, I'm not your boyfriend or mate. You were nothing more than a mediocre fuck... that's it. And we're done. Understand me?" I don't wait for a reply, I turn and get back into the SUV. There's nothing that her and I need to talk about further.

Zane drives me to the cottage that Kate and I are sharing this summer before we go back to college. The cottage is located just outside the training grounds and is usually used as a guest cottage. Luna Martha arranged for us to have it all summer, since we will be moving again in the fall. Walking in I can smell her delicious sweet floral scent. It engulfs me like a warm hug. I take a deep breath and blow it out as a fresh wave of guilt hits me like a pile of bricks.

"Where do you want this shit?" Kelsey snaps.

"Right there is fine," I point to an area by the sofa, "I'll take care of it from here." I snap back. Zane rolls his eyes at the two of us. My relationship with Kelsey is very strained. He's been pissed at me for months, we barely speak anymore. When we do, it's nothing but arguments. He has every right to be pissed, I'm fucking around on his sister. I'd be pissed too. If I'm being honest, Zane is not pleased with me right now either. Really can't say I blame him, he has always treated Kate like a little sister.

As soon as Zane and Kelsey leave, I take note of all the personal things that Kate has put into the living room, including her collection of her favorite movies. I smile then walk into the kitchen. The dishwasher is going, so I know she has been here recently. Looking in the cupboard and fridge, I see that both are fully stocked. I grab my bags of clothes and head for the bedroom. The bed is made and smells so fresh. I put away my clothes and see Kate's clothes are in the closet and chest of drawers. Looks like she has been busy making this a home for the two of us. Seeing everything she has done for us, a pang of guilt hits my chest.

After putting away my things, I head to the packhouse. I need to grab a couple of things from my old room and meet up with my father before Kate gets home from school. She has just a little over a month left of her senior year before she graduates. We have arranged it so that she can live off campus at the boarding school and still attend classes. All high school age pack members attend the boarding school, which is located about twenty minutes from the packhouse. The boarding school prepares us to be more independent of our parents. I haven't lived with my parents since I was fourteen. During summer breaks, I moved into a room on a lower floor in the packhouse. Same with Zane and Kelsey.

"Ian!" My father greets me as I walk into his office.

"Father!" I embrace him.

"Nice to have you back in the territory." He pats my back.

"Nice to be back. I just wanted to check in with you before I grab the last of my things from my old room. I want to get back to the cottage before Kate gets home from school." I take a seat in a chair in front of his desk.

We chat for an hour or so about school, Kate, and life. Normally he's jumping my ass for something, but today his mood seems light. *Odd.* After my meeting with him I head upstairs to my old room to gather the last box of stuff I have in there. Walking in I see the room has been cleaned and is ready for the next occupant. The only thing in here is a single cardboard box of mementos.

"Ian," a familiar high-pitched voice says from the doorway.

"Go away Nikki. I thought I made myself perfectly clear. I'm mated... we're done." I keep my back to her then I hear the door shut and lock.

"I just want five minutes of your time." She runs her hands along my back.

"Stop!" I growl then spin to look at her. I can't stand to even look at this woman. "Leave!" I snarl before grabbing her arm and leading her towards the door.

"Ouch, Ian, you're hurting me." She spins out of my grip. "Five minutes, that's all I ask." She rubs her arm where I grabbed her.

"No. Fuck this... you stay, I'll leave." I grab my box and head to the door. Before I can unlock the door, Nikki slams her body between me and the door. "I don't want to hurt you, but if you force my hand I will." I snap, grinding my teeth.

"Don't be silly, you could never hurt me." She holds the doorknob with one hand while the other runs from my chest down to my abs. I slap her hand away before she reaches the zipper on my jeans. This is the same bullshit she does every single time.

"Move," I demand.

"I have a proposition for you," she whispers seductively.

"Move," I demand again.

"Hear me out, then I'll move." She sticks her breasts out.

"What?" I groan from frustration.

"I know you're mated, but what we have is not mediocre. It's hot. I know how to give you what the virgin can't." She licks her lips and rubs my cock through my jeans. I know I should push her out of the way and leave, but for some selfish reason I can't. "You can have us both. Kate will get the title and all the perks that come with it, and I will be your mistress. The one that will give you what you want."

She removes the box from my hands dropping to her knees. She puts it on the ground next to her then unbuckles my belt. With one quick move my jeans and boxer briefs are at my ankles, and Nikki's mouth is wrapped around my cock. I give in to the moment enjoying the way it feels having her suck my dick. I close my eyes and lean my head back as she moves my shaft in and out of her mouth.

"You like sucking my dick, don't you?" I look down and she looks up at me as her head bobs back and forth. "You're a fucking dirty slut, aren't you?" I grab her hair with both of my hands and push my cock further into her mouth. I roughly move in and out of her mouth as she gags. "This what you want? To be my toy?" I pick up my speed, slamming in and out of her mouth roughly. She gags as I push my cock as far down her throat as I can. Without any warning I shoot hot cum down her throat. I make sure she drinks down every drop before I pull out of her mouth.

I back away and pull my pants back up, looking at her with distain on my face. I can't believe I allowed her to get to me again. *Is she some sort of a witch that has a spell over me?*

"Mmmmm, you taste so good." She purrs with a smile on her face. I finish dressing myself and pain knocks the wind out of me. I stand still for a moment with my eyes closed, breathing through the pain. When I open my eyes, Nikki is on her feet making her way to me. "Let me be your mistress, Ian."

"You," I grab her face with one hand, "are just another filthy whore. You don't compare to my Kate, nor will you ever. You stay away from me and Kate or I will have you thrown in the dungeon. Do you understand me? Leave me the fuck alone!" I growl and snap my teeth at her. I shake her face then release it before grabbing my box and leaving the room.

I'm fucking raging. How could I let this shit happen again? I'm furious at her, but more furious at myself for allowing it to happen. I will do better, not for me, but for my angel on earth.

Chapter Twenty-Five

THIRTY-SECOND CONVERSATION

June 2004

Ian

THE RIDE BACK TO our territory is quiet, and the tension is thick in the air. I know Zane and Kelsey can feel it too. Kate sits on the other side of the SUV, just staring out of the window into the darkness of the night. *I fucking hate this.* For over two months, everything has been perfect, and we've been on the right track. I wish she would talk to me. She must really be angry at me for losing my cool with the prince. I couldn't help it when I saw the sleazy bastard's lips all over her hand. If Zane hadn't been shouting at me to stand down through our mindlink, I would have ripped off that fucker's head right off his shoulders. I could have easily taken him. He doesn't train like the rest of us, never has. He is more of an observer than anything. I need to make this right with her, but how?

Kate hasn't spoken a word to me all day. I have said nothing to her either; I don't want to push any issues with her. We don't exactly have the greatest track record for being at the palace together. I noticed she spent the entire day hidden away in Adam and Jessi's house, which I can see from where we were training. The house is a large two-story home, located right next to the training grounds. So, it was easy for me to watch for her. I was hoping she would come watch me train like she does back home, or that she would walk around the palace gardens. But nothing.

After we ate lunch, I went with Adam to check on them. Walking into the living room, my heart almost leaped out of my chest when I saw Kate holding Jessi's pup. I wanted to rush to her, but my feet stayed firmly cemented to the floor. All I could do was watch my beautiful mate holding the pup. Kate glowed and love radiated from her smile as she held the tiny pup in her arms. Alex howled in my head as I watched as the love of my life rocked, sang, and talk sweet nothings to the pup. I imagined she was holding our pup waiting for me to come home to them. She's going to make a wonderful mother for our children. Not able to take my eyes off her, I stood quietly, observing her without saying a word or making a sound. Watching her with the pup was the highlight of my day, and I can't wait until we have one of our own. At one point, she looked up at me with a huge smile that lit up the room. When our eyes met, her smile faded, and she glanced away from me. *Fuck!*

Dinner at the palace was the same way. She sat quiet and stiff next to me. If others didn't know better, they'd think we were total strangers rather than mates. Now we're on our way home, and I'm not too sure what kind of hell awaits me. The one thing I know for sure is that I can't lose her... I will make this right if it's the last thing I do on this earth. We finally pull up in front of the packhouse. I need to talk with her... alone. As Zane and Kelsey get out of the SUV, Kate reaches for the door handle.

"Please," I beg, wrapping my hand around her forearm. She looks down at my hand, then back up into my eyes and simply nods her head. I don't let go of her arm... I can't let go. It's the first physical contact I've had with her in hours. I've missed her so much. I wait for Zane and Kelsey to get their things from the back of the SUV before speaking a word.

"Kate..." I clear my throat, fearing the worst. "I'm so sorry I upset you earlier today." I slowly scooch closer to her. Kate sits up straight, tilting her head slightly, narrowing her eyes.

"For what? What exactly are you sorry for? What did you do?" Her body stiffens as if she is bracing herself.

"I got jealous and possessive... I almost started a bunch of shit at the palace. I know how much you hate conflicts. Our history at the palace..." Kate puts her hand over my mouth.

"Shhhh... not another word," she holds my face between the palms of her hands, looking deeply into my eyes. "Ian, babe, you didn't do anything wrong. It was me. I was in the wrong. I should have never..." Shocked at what she is saying, I interrupt her.

"You did nothing wrong. Not a thing." I pull her onto my lap, "I felt the way you were feeling... I knew something wasn't right, and I ran back with Zane and Kelsey chasing me. I saw everything. His disgusting mouth on your hand... you snatching your hand away. I heard you tell him you are mated, and he still pressed forward. Why would you think you did anything wrong?" I don't think before I speak, she has to know she did nothing wrong. Before I realize it, the words spill out of my mouth fast. Hopefully, somewhere along the way, my words form some sort of coherent sentence that gets my point across.

"I... I just..." she looks away, then back to me. "After Darren caught us... then when I touched your arm, your muscles got all tight, and I don't want you to think that I'm a cheater." There it is, what she's really thinking. She sees herself as a cheater, something she despises so much. Tears swell up in her eyes.

"Please don't cry." I pull her into my arms and squeeze. She quickly wraps her arms around me and sobs into my neck. The damage I've done to this woman. I hold her, rocking her, allowing her emotions to pour out of her. She has to know the truth.

"Look at me, love." I lift her head from my body and hold it firmly in my hands. "You did nothing wrong today or back in New York. Do you hear me? Not a fucking thing. You are so perfect. Back in New York, that was all me. A long time ago, I learned how to manipulate the mate bond. The mate bond kept you at my side, and I figured out quickly that I could do anything I wanted. I took advantage of it years ago and I tried to do it again in New York. I'm so sorry that I used the mate bond like that. In New York, you couldn't help it. Your body did what it always has... it pulled to me because of the bond. Please, Kate, forgive me? You are not a cheater. I never want you to feel you can't be yourself around people. You are not a cheater. That title is my burden to bear." I fight back the tears, looking into Kate's sad face. I wish I could turn back the hands of time and take all the trauma from her.

"Thank you, Ian." She gulps and takes a deep breath. "I just don't want you to doubt me." her bottom lip quivers.

"Never have and never will. I trust you with my life." I smile. The urge to kiss her is strong, but I don't. I feel like that would be using the mate bond to manipulate her feelings, and I'd rather have her talk to me about her feelings. "So, you thought I was upset with you, and I thought you were upset with me?"

"Seems so." She plays with the hem of her shirt without making eye contact with me.

"You realize that a thirty-second conversation would have cleared everything up right away?" I lift her chin with my fingers, forcing her to look at me.

"Yeah," she squeaks out.

"We have to do better, and implement some of the things we've learned in therapy." I think for a moment before I speak again. "We need to stop walking on eggshells around each other. I say that we never let so much time go by. I don't want to have another misunderstanding to take time away from us. If something is bothering one of us, we talk it out. I missed you so much today." I caress her face.

"Deal." She takes a deep breath and lets it out slowly. This is one of her cleansing breaths she does to help ease her stress. "I missed you too." She relaxes into my body. "Why did you tense up when I touched you?"

"Your fucking brother... when he saw you sitting there upset, he lost it. He wanted to kill the prince. Zane was no help either. They were both so pissed. When you grabbed my arm, my mind relaxed until they showed up. I didn't know what was going to happen... only that it was going to be a bloodbath. I didn't want you in the middle of it."

"I hate that something always happens at the palace with us." She curls up on my lap, putting her head on my chest.

"One good thing happened at the palace today." I rub her ass and thigh.

"Oh, what was that?" She looks up at me.

"I got a glimpse of our future. You glowed holding the pup." I kiss her forehead.

"Really? When I looked at you, your face seemed so serious. Almost... angry." She sits up.

"I was far from angry. I was trying to control the urge to take you right there and put a pup inside of you. You're going to be a wonderful mother." I squeeze her ass with my hand.

"Really? You think so?" She straddles my lap.

"I don't think... I know." I slip my hands under her shirt and rub her back.

"I can see a future with you and it's amazing," she smiles and kisses me.

I groan with pleasure and let her take full control. This is a different side of Kate. I've always been the one who takes the lead. She runs her fingers through my hair, teasing my scalp with her nails. Our tongues dance and mingle together. Having her in control is driving me crazy with desire. She bucks her hips, grinding her sweet pussy into my rock-hard cock. I unhook her bra and massage her breast under her shirt. Shock waves of electricity flow through her body, then to mine. We're both lost in a lust filled haze of the mate bond when all the lights in the SUV turn on.

"What the fuck?" I shout, while Kate ducks her face into my chest. I turn my head at the gaping hole in the back of the SUV that is created when Kelsey opened the door.

"Shit! You two are still in here?" Kelsey chuckles. "I forgot my box of cinnamon rolls."

"Okay, get them and go, you fucking buzz kill." I snarl as Kate giggles before Kelsey slams the door shut.

"Where were we?" I put two fingers under Kate's chin and lift her face to mine.

"Mmmm," she moans out then kisses me.

"Hey," the back door of the SUV opens again, "mom's got cheesecake waiting on us." Kelsey says then stands there like a big dope, staring at us waiting for a response.

"Shut the damn door, Kelsey." Kate snaps, then throws a nearby water bottle at him. Kelsey laughs hysterically, then slams the door closed. "I think he did that on purpose. Asshat." Kate huffs out before climbing off my lap. I can't help but to laugh at my frustrated mate.

We walk back to her parents' house, hand in hand. We talk about our day. She tells me about the day she spent with Jessi and her pup. The pup's name is Joseph, but they call him Joey. She looks radiant talking about Joey and how much she enjoyed playing with him. She asks how training went and apologized for not coming to watch me. Explaining further that she didn't want to be an unwanted distraction because of our misunderstanding earlier. When we reach the front door, I stop her from turning the knob.

"Hey, I have an idea." I pin her against the wall next to the door.

"What's that?" she wiggles her eyebrows at me before wrapping her arms around my neck.

"Let's go on a date... to the city." I excitedly say.

"A date? Like they do in the human world?" She tilts her head and giggles.

"Yes, a date, like we do in our world, too." I press my nose into hers. "There's a brand-new fancy steakhouse that just opened and then we can dance the night away at the new salsa dance club. We'll get those hips moving." I place my hands on her hips and move them from side to side.

"Sounds like fun," she giggles.

"Thank you," I whisper, putting my forehead on hers.

"For what?" She nudges her nose into mine.

"For giving me the chance that I didn't deserve... for trusting me with your heart." I kiss her lips. Our kiss is hot as the emotions flow through us. I love her so much. I deepen the kiss, pressing my body into hers as she softly moans and fists my hair.

"Hey!" Kelsey shouts as the front door flies open. "When you two are done, there's cheesecake in here." Kelsey says through a mouthful of food while holding a plate with a giant slice of cheesecake on it. Kate breaks the kiss and snaps her head to her brother.

"I'm going to kill him," she says in a monotone voice. She pushes me back and lunges for Kelsey, grabbing his fork and cheesecake from his hands. Kate takes a large bite. "Mine now, asshole," she says through a mouthful of cheesecake before walking away.

"Kelsey, my man," I grab his arm with one hand and the back of his neck with the other, and follow Kate inside the house. "Remind me to pay you the same favor one day." I laugh.

"I'm not getting my cheesecake back, am I?" Kelsey frowns.

"Nope, afraid not. You have managed to irritate the shit out of your sister tonight. I'd sleep with one eye open if I were you." We both laugh.

Chapter Twenty-Six

YOURS IN EVERY WAY

June 2001

Kate

WALKING THROUGH THE FRONT door of the cottage, I see candles lit throughout the living room and a rose pedal path. My heart skips a beat at the sight. I smile from ear to ear as I follow the path. It leads down the hall to our bedroom, then continues into the master bathroom. My excitement grows as I see hundreds of red rose pedals on the bed surrounded by the flickering light of candles. I stop in the doorway and stare. It's so beautiful and romantic. My heart skips a beat thinking how amazing Ian is for doing all this. I'm mesmerized by the sight. I've only seen things like this in movies and would have never thought in a million years that a romantic gesture like this would be my reality.

I continue on the rose pedal path to the bathroom where I find Ian sitting on the edge of the garden tub holding a single stemmed red rose.

"Hello, my angel," he stands and slowly walks towards me with a sultry look on his face. He's wearing jeans and a long sleeve black button-up shirt. My breath hitches as I watch him stalk towards me. He's so sexy. His shirt is open, exposing his chest. I can't believe he's really mine.

"Ian, what is all of this?" I look around at the flickering light of dozens of candles lining the bathtub and sink. Ian stands just inches in front of me, his intoxicating fresh scent fills my nose. He brings the rose to his nose, then offers it to me.

"Do you like it?" I take the rose and he closes the small space that divides us.

"I love it," I wrap my arms around his neck, "What's the occasion?" I bite my lower lip and breathe in his essence.

"I figured you might be a little tired from all the hubbub of the graduation ceremony and dinner, that you might need some... relaxing. This seems like the best way to start." He wraps his arms around my waist and brings me in for a kiss. The kiss is sweet and gentle, but full of love and passion. I love the way my body molds and fits into his so perfectly. Everything he does makes me feel so special. I'm sad when he breaks the kiss. "I drew a bubble bath for you." He holds my hand and guides me to the tub.

"Are you joining me?" I wrap my hands around his large bicep and rest my head on his shoulder.

"If that is what you want," He looks down at me and smiles. I love the way he looks at me. With just his smile, he makes me feel like I'm floating on a cloud.

"That's what I want." I step back and undress.

"Your wish is my command, angel." Ian follows my lead and undresses. I watch as he removes his clothes, piece by piece.

I pay special attention when he pulls his jeans off and his member proudly leaps forward. Every time I see it, I'm completely mesmerized, and can't take my eyes off it. I can almost feel it inside me, filling me and bringing me so much pleasure. I lick my lips and wonder what it tastes like... what it would feel like in my mouth. Ian tastes and devours me daily, but I've never returned the favor. Tonight, that changes. I want to know what every inch of him tastes like.

"You can't look at me like that, angel, or we won't make it to the tub." He gently grabs my chin, directing my face up to his.

"Would that be so bad?" I smile, biting my bottom lip, then look away. I'm partially embarrassed about being so forward with him. Every day we spend together, I want him more and more. Even though my appetite for him is insatiable, I usually wait for him to take the lead.

"Don't tempt me, angel." He growls. His voice is lower and deeper in tone and his eyes are black with lust. He looks like a predator ready to pounce on its prey. The way he looks at me takes the air from my lungs and makes my core wet.

Sitting in the tub with my back resting against Ian's chest while he strokes my skin with a washcloth, I'm the most relaxed I've been in my entire life. I'm not too sure if it's the fruity smelling bubbles, the hot water on my skin, or that I'm in the arms of the man I love more than life itself. All my dreams came true a few months back and I couldn't be happier.

Since Ian has been home with me, I've only felt the pain in my chest three times, once in the clinic and two other times shortly after he came back. But nothing in over a month now. I guess Dr. Patrice was right, the strain on the mate bond was making me feel sick. All of my symptoms are also gone, except for a guilty feeling I get from time to time. I think that's from him spending so much time with me, isolating himself from Zane and Kelsey. I don't want to cause trouble in their friendship.

"Mmmm, that feels good." I move my head to the side as Ian trails kisses up and down my neck, settling on my marking spot. That area is so sensitive to his touch. He massages my breasts with both hands while sucking on my neck.

"This is where you'll wear my mark… when you're ready, of course." He continues teasing my skin with his lips and teeth. I can't get enough of him.

"Why haven't you marked me already?" I moan softly.

"I want to make sure you're ready. Marking each other will solidify the mate bond. It's what will connect our two souls into one." He moves one hand from my breast down to my nub. I throw my head back and moan as his fingers rub circles.

"I'm ready to be yours in every way." I whisper out through a heavy breath.

Ian

"I'm ready to be yours in every way." With her words, a wave of guilt hits me. If she knew that I have been unfaithful all these months, would she still love me? Could she see past all my indiscretions? I've messed up three times since I've been home. Each time, Nikki caught me alone and sucked me off. I fucking hate myself for not being able to resist.

It all came to an abrupt stop when I caught Kate coming out of the clinic. When I questioned her, she told me about her chest pains, and I realized her chest pains coincided with each time I was with Nikki. I'm not too sure if it's a coincidence or not, but it was enough to make me want to stop. Kate deserves a faithful mate. But the guilt still eats at me.

"Ian? Where did you go?" Kate looks back at me, snapping me from my thoughts.

"I'm right here, angel. I was just thinking about marking you, and how much I love you." To spare her feelings, I lie. I love her with all my heart. She can never know what I've done . It would devastate her. "Let's get out. The water is getting cold." I whisper in her ear and kiss her neck. We feel the other's feelings, so I need to divert her attention away from my guilt.

As I sit on the bed waiting for Kate to join me, I think about the fact that she is ready for me to mark her, and tonight is the night. I'm excited and nervous at the same time. *Why am I nervous?* She is mine and this will just solidify our bond... bring us closer.

"Ian?" Kate stands between my legs. "Is there something wrong? Do we need to talk about something?" She nervously twists the hem of her tank top, shifting her weight from one foot to the other.

"No angel, why would you ask that?" I wrap my arms around her waist and pull her in to me. Needing to feel her soft skin against mine, I put my hands under her tank top and rub her back.

"You just got... weird after I said I'm ready for you to mark me. Are you sure you even want... for us to mark each other?" She pulls back to look me in the face. I know she felt my emotions earlier, and she knows something is off.

"Of course I am. You're my everything." I pull her back closer into my body.

"It's just that I've been getting the guilty feelings lately." She pulls away and whispers.

"Guilty? What are you guilty about?" My hands are shaking and my palms are sweaty... she knows. *Fuck.*

"Since you've been home, and since you found out about the pains in my chest... you've dedicated so much time to me. You don't spend any time with Zane or Kelsey or anyone else for that fact. I see the strain in your friendship with Zane and Kelsey... you're more like brothers and now nothing. I don't want to come in between your relationship with them." When she finished speaking, she is in tears. She has taken on all of my guilt as her own and is blaming herself for the issues with Zane and Kelsey. I want to tell her the truth and come clean once and for all, but looking at her face, I don't think she could handle the truth.

"Oh, angel... there's no strain in my friendship. I see those two bozos for hours every day. We spend a lot of time together." I pull away, scooting myself onto the bed, pressing my back against the headboard. "Fuck, this is so hard." I put my head in my hands, trying hard to control my breathing. Everything I have done is weighing heavily on me... I need to tell her before we mark each other.

"Ian," she crawls onto the bed and sits facing me, "please talk to me," she begs. I look up and into her beautiful face. She is the purest soul that I have ever met. As much as I want to be truthful with her, I can't. I know it will hurt her and I won't do that to her.

"This is hard juggling a mate and friends, but I'm trying. I hate how you think that you've caused issues with my friendships. It's not true. You are my priority over them. Fuck, now I feel guilty because I know you're feeling guilty, and it hurts me so much." I run my hands through my hair.

"Oh, my Goddess, Ian. I'm so sorry. I didn't realize how hard it's been for you... I know you're trying, babe. Please look at me." She straddles my lap and cups my face in her hands. "I love you so much. Let's not talk about it anymore tonight. You created a romantic night. I don't want to spoil it. Forgive me for bringing it up." She presses her lips into mine.

I take advantage of her willingness to please me and remove her tank top and let the lust of the mate bond take over. Kate takes the lead, kissing me, and with a single kiss, any doubt she may have is washed away. The haze of the mate bond clouds her mind and erases any negative thoughts. She kisses me with fire, almost like she's apologizing. She needs to make me happy, to put my happiness above hers. I like this needy side of her.

She moves her lips down my neck and sucks the area where she will soon leave her mark for everyone to see. Her hips move in circles, grinding her wet pussy into my cock. She scratches her nails down my chest as she trails kisses down to my stomach. I watch her intently as she nears the waistband on my shorts.

"What's on your mind, angel?" I run my fingers through her hair.

"I'm curious," she bites her lip, slipping her body further down.

"Oh?" I lick my lips and press my dick into her breasts.

"I want to know what you taste like." She smiles, then looks down, avoiding eye contact with me.

"So shy for someone so brave." I bend down and kiss her.

"Brave?" She looks up at me, tilting her head.

"You're telling me what you want. You've never done that before, angel." I rub my thumb along her bottom lip.

"I don't know what to do, though." She looks away.

"You want me to teach you, angel?" I push my thumb into her mouth, gliding it over her soft, wet tongue.

"Mmm hmm," she nods her head, closing her lips, gently sucking my thumb.

"Mmmm, I don't think I'll have to teach you much." I remove my thumb from her mouth and slip my shorts off. She watches as my cock jumps out and springs forward towards her. She slides her hand up and down my shaft.

"Go ahead, angel. Taste it with your tongue." I sit up watching her lick up and down my shaft. She moves my cock where she wants it while slowly sliding her hand up and down, tasting every inch with her tongue. "That's it, angel. Taste it." I moan with pleasure, "now, take the head in your mouth."

She follows my directions and wraps her lips around my dick, pausing for a moment before bobbing her head up and down. Each time taking my shaft further into her mouth. I never thought a blow job could feel so fucking good. My cock pops as she takes her mouth off it.

"Am I doing it right?" She continues to slide her hands up and down my shaft.

"So fucking right." I push her head back down . She licks her lips at the sight of clear liquid that has seeped from the head. She quickly laps up every drop with her tongue before wrapping her lips around me again. "Yes, angel, just like that." I moan as I slip my fingers into her hair. "Such a good girl." I thrust my hips up as she sucks harder.

She moans and sucks while her tongue teases my cock with each stroke. I can smell her arousal. Pleasing me is turning her on so much I have to pull out of her mouth before I explode down her throat.

"Come here, angel." I pull her up to me. "Angel, I can smell your arousal, and it's driving me insane. I need your pussy." I push her damp panties down and she quickly takes them off. "Come ride my dick, angel."

I line up with her entrance, she slides down. Impaling herself on my dick. "Fuck, angel, you were ready for me, weren't you?" She nods and moans as she slides up and down.

I watch my angel as she fully enjoys herself. She starts out slow and soft, but each time she rides up, she slides down harder and harder each time. Moaning and throwing her head back, she picks up the pace. I hiss and moan. The way she rides my cock is such a fucking turn on. Her pussy feels so good. I'm about to explode, watching her breasts bounce up and down. She moves her hips... learning what angles bring her the most pleasure. She brings her head forward, looking at me with her canines elongated. Her primal beast is awake, and it's sexy as hell.

"Yes, angel, I'm ready." I wrap my arms tight around her and elongate mine. Her eyes are completely black from lust. She grunts and groans as she moves slowly to my neck. "On the count of three. One…" She grabs my hair with both her hands and forcefully bites down with a growl. A wave of pleasure, like none that I have ever felt before, crashes down hard on me as I cum hard inside her. My cock pulsates and my body shakes. Goosebumps form on my skin and I feel an electric current run through every vein in my body. Her pussy grabs my cock and pulsates, selfishly taking as much of my cum as it can get. "Such a selfish little pussy you have." I grunt as the last drop leaves my body and I come down from the euphoric high.

"I want to feel you come all over my dick. Can you do that for me?" I look her in the eyes. She doesn't speak, only smiles and nods.

Grabbing her hair, I move her head to the side, exposing her delicious neck to me. At the sight of her marking spot, my primal beast awakens, and I sink my canines into her flesh. She hisses at the pain when my teeth enter her skin, but soon the hisses turn to moans as her body shakes and trembles in my arms. I hold her tight, keeping my canines firmly in place. I can feel her soaking wet pussy pulsating on my cock, demanding more cum from it. Her juices flow out of her body onto me, as she continues to moan my name.

CHAPTER TWENTY-SEVEN

SUICIDE MISSION

June 2004

Ian

ZANE, KELSEY, AND I were training when we are called to the Alpha's office. Prince Lazar and Prince Malachi are here and wish to have a meeting with us. *Shit!* I didn't tell my father what happened when we were at the palace. I wonder if that slimy bastard is here because of that. What else could it be?

Walking into Alpha's office, I see the slimy bastard sitting there with a smug look on his face. I look around the room and see ten royal guards, including Adam, who doesn't look my way. *Shit!* I smell trouble.

'You getting a funny feeling about this?' Zane mindlinks Kelsey and me as we take our seats at the small conference table.

'Big time,' I mindlink back.

'We've trained with all the guards; we know how they fight.' Kelsey mindlinks.

'True, but it will be one hell of a fight. Adam is one tough son of a bitch, and his mate is Kate's best friend.' I mindlink.

"Thank you for joining us today, boys," Alpha rests his head on his knuckles.

"Prince Lazar, Prince Malachi, it's nice to see you both again." Zane says, looking between the two princes.

"The princes were just informing us of a potential issue." My father states. I nervously look around the room. Could he be here to claim Kate as his own? He will have to challenge me to a fight... to the death. I know I can beat him in a fight, but will his brother or the palace guards allow that to happen?

"What is that?" Zane sits tall in his chair, locking eyes with Prince Lazar.

"Ian, I hope there are no hard feelings." Prince Lazar looks from Zane to me, then to his watch. He acts as if he doesn't have time for us, but he's the one who came here.

"Not at all," I reply with a smile. Out of the corner of my eye, I see my father tilting his head and narrowing his eyes at me.

"Good," Prince Lazar flashes a cocky smile my way. Prince Malachi breaks the silence by clearing his throat. Of the two princes, I'm more familiar with the younger prince. He trains with the royal guard regularly, and if you didn't know better, you'd have no idea he is a royal. He has a very down-to-earth personality, unlike his douche brother. Prince Lazar seems to think his shit doesn't stink.

"Thank you for joining us today." Prince Malachi leans forward, interlocking his fingers together, and rests them on the table in front of him. "We have received word from the UK about an ongoing issue between a small pack and its neighboring larger pack. Emerald Water is the larger pack with just under a thousand members, and Emerald Cove is the smaller pack with just over two-hundred members. They were once a part of the same pack that broke apart two hundred years ago." Prince Malachi's voice is calm, easing the tension in the room. "Seems the smaller pack has had members come up missing. Fifty so far. At first, they thought they might have a rogue problem. Now it has become clear that this is the work of the neighboring pack."

"And this has piqued the interest of the north American royal palace how?" I direct my full attention to Prince Malachi, ignoring my father's death stares aimed at my head.

"The two packs have been at peace for decades now. Alpha David... from Emerald Water. His mate died during childbirth a year ago. During a routine peace talk meeting in Emerald Cove's territory six months ago, he met Ava, Alpha Oliver's oldest daughter. Captivated by her beauty, he wanted her for his own. Alpha Oliver agreed to the arrangement despite Ava's protest. Last month, Ava turned eighteen and Alpha David came for her, only to find her in the arms of her fated mate. Alpha David demanded that her father honor the agreement and when he didn't, Alpha David promised that he would have Ava in the end. Two months later, pack members started disappearing without a trace. Two weeks ago, they found all fifty pack members' heads on spikes lining the border of the two territories. His demand, hand over Ava and peace will be restored." Prince Malachi leans back in his chair.

"The European royal family contacted us yesterday. They don't want to get involved because of Emerald Water's size and power." Prince Lazar speaks up.

"So, they want to remain neutral because of politics?" Zane looks between the two princes, then back to his father.

"Precisely." Prince Malachi nods his head, looking at his brother.

"Let me guess, the European royal palace doesn't have a problem with someone else going in and cleaning up the mess." I wrinkle my nose and look at Zane.

"Exactly," Prince Lazar replies.

"What would you like us to do?" Zane leans forward, resting his arms on the table.

"We want you and your warriors to join our royal warriors in stopping Alpha David. We have heard from sources that there is a faction in his pack that wants him gone. However, no one has defeated him for the Alpha title." Prince Malachi looks at each of us.

"How many royal warriors will go on this mission?" Alpha Nathaniel sits upright, adcolemang his shoulders.

"One hundred." Prince Lazar answers.

"And which one of you will lead your warriors?" My father asks.

"Neither. Our father feels this mission is much too dangerous for the only two heirs to the throne to go. So, we will send my personal royal guard, Adam, in our place." Prince Lazar looks directly at me. What is he trying to do, get me killed so he can claim Kate?

"Let me get this straight. Your father believes this mission is too dangerous for his sons, but is perfectly fine with me sending mine?" Alpha Nathaniel narrows his eyes at Prince Lazar, wiping the smug look off his face.

"Alpha Nathaniel, with all due respect. This is a dangerous mission, just like the others. But I have it on good authority that over two-thirds of the Emerald Water pack are unhappy with Alpha David and his tyrannical ways. They will stand and fight with us." Prince Malachi sighs out, he knows that Alpha Nathaniel is not happy.

"The numbers are still stacked against us." My father speaks up.

"It's just the three of us and fifty warriors that are trained for these missions. Emerald Water still outnumbers us two to one." Zane shakes his head.

"I will be at your side." Prince Malachi whispers.

"What?" Prince Lazar grabs his brother's arm. "This is a fucking suicide mission!" He shouts at his brother.

"Suicide mission?" I shake my head and scoff, "are your trying to get me... us killed?" I pound my fist on the table.

"I believe in our missions and in our training." Prince Malachi sighs, snatching his arm from his brother's grip. "I would never ask any of you to do something I wouldn't do myself." Prince Malachi looks between Zane, Kelsey, and me. His look is of determination. I admire him. He is not cut from the same spoiled cloth as his brother. In my opinion, he'd make a better King than Prince Lazar. He turns to his brother, "I've spoken to father about this, and he has agreed to let me go, since I'm not the one who'll be taking over the throne. Once again, you can stay safe and out of harm's way." Prince Malachi looks away from his brother with a disgusted look on his face. This is the first time that I've ever seen trouble between the two.

"We will stand beside you, Prince Malachi. Just give us the word." Zane stands and offers his hand to the prince.

"Thank you, Zane." Prince Malachi shakes Zane's hand with enthusiasm. "I won't forget this."

I'm relieved after the princes leave, but I still can't shake the feeling that Prince Lazar is trying to get me killed. I'm grateful that Prince Malachi is a stand-up man, willing to fight side by side with us. *How is he so down to earth and normal?* I'm almost to the door when I hear my father clear his throat, stepping between me and freedom. *Shit.*

"Not so fast." He sucks his teeth, curls his lips, and crosses his arms.

"You three... sit." Alpha slams his hands on his desk, and instantly Zane, Kelsey, and I are like pups in trouble. We take our seats in the chairs in front of Alpha's desk with our shoulders slumped forward. Each of our fathers sits on the edge of the desk in front of us. "Speak," Alpha demands.

Not wanting the other two to catch heat, I take the lead on explaining everything that went down at the palace, with Prince Lazar overstepping his bounds with Kate. I conveniently leave out the fact that Kelsey and Zane had murder on their minds when they saw Kate.

"So, she clearly stated she was mated, and he still made advances?" My father asks and I nod my head in agreement. "Son, that motherfucker is trying to get your ass killed."

"He knows he can't take you on in a fight." Gamma Earnest shakes his head.

"I knew I smelled a rat!" Alpha Nathaniel grinds his teeth. "He probably convinced his father about asking the three of you to go."

"Prince Malachi knows more than he'll ever say, that's why he volunteered to go." Gamma Earnest states.

"Probably has to do with his past." My father states.

"His past?" Zane looks between our fathers.

"Prince Lazar and Prince Malachi are only months apart and are half-brothers." Alpha Nathaniel returns to his seat behind his desk.

"What?" Kelsey shouts.

"This doesn't leave this office, son." Gamma Earnest points to the ground and we shake our head in agreement.

"Prince Malachi is technically his father's illegitimate son. His mother was an omega and the king's true mate. He was in love with her until the day she died. The king's parents put an abrupt stop to their relationship because of her rank within the pack. They went so far as to sell her off to a pack in Europe. In order to take the throne, they forced him to take a chosen mate in an arrangement with the European royal palace. They didn't meet until the mating ceremony." Alpha Nathaniel rubs his chin with his hand.

"Fucking politics," my father scoffs.

"It wasn't a week after taking the throne he went to Europe and bought his mate back, infuriating his parents and the royal council." Alpha Nathaniel laughs quietly.

"He replaced the council shortly after." Gamma Earnest states.

"Honoring the contract with the European royal palace, he produced a male heir with his chosen mate." Alpha Nathaniel adds.

"Luckily for him, it took just once." My father laughs.

"The king never marked his chosen mate, instead he marked his fated mate the omega… Prince Malachi's mother. For years, no one knew of Prince Malachi's existence. His mother feared the queen might have him killed. He was raised out of everyone's sight. The king spent lots of time going between the palace and a large home by the training grounds. Prince Malachi lived there with his mother. The King took an active role in raising Prince Malachi alongside his mother and gave him the best education money could buy. Five years ago, his mother became very ill, and on her deathbed she made the king promise her to continue to look after their son. The day she died, he had young Prince Malachi pack his things and moved him into his rightful place behind the palace walls. After giving his mate the true royal funeral she deserved, he told the world about Prince Malachi and gave him his rightful title of prince." Alpha Nathaniel sighs out.

"So, Prince Malachi has a vested interest in saving Ava from being a political chess piece?" I scoff and shake my head.

"Son, I think he knows his brother's true intentions, and he is saving Kate as well." My father leans down and grabs my shoulder. The thought that Prince Lazar would pull a stunt that could get many killed for his own selfish gains is really pissing me off.

"Best advice Ian, don't get your ass killed." Gamma Earnest looks at me, nodding his head.

"That goes for all three of you." Alpha Nathaniel states, "We'll deal with Prince Lazar after you three get back in one piece."

"I don't get it, Prince Lazar lectured me alongside Adam about what it meant to be a good mate. Why act like this now?" I rub my forehead.

"Simple... he liked what he saw, and you became a pawn in his way." My father says, "Luckily he didn't meet her after she rejected you. He would have had the palace healers formulate some concoction to fully break the bond."

"Shit." I lean forward and rest my head in my hands. The thought of losing her forever sends pains through my chest.

Chapter Twenty-Eight

YOU KNEW

August 2001

Kate

"KATE, I'M HOME." IAN shouts as he walks through the front door of the cottage.

"In here," I yell from the kitchen. The summer has come to an end and tonight is the last night we'll be living in the territory until next summer. Ian and I are headed to college. He'll be in his third year, and I'll be in my first. I decided to start classes, since I won't know what to do with myself while he's in class all day.

"Mmmm, smells good." He pokes his head into the kitchen.

"There you are. You're a little later than normal." I laugh, "what no kiss?" I stick my tongue out teasing.

"No," Ian's tone is sharp. "I'm filthy. Why so much food?" He stands in the kitchen doorway with both hands on each side of the door-jamb, propping himself up.

"Oh," I continue, stirring my gravy without looking at him. I'm not too sure why he does this aloof thing from time to time, but it drives me bonkers. Normally, he wouldn't care how gross or filthy he is. He thinks it's funny watching my reaction to a sweaty hug. "Our parents are coming for dinner tonight... and Kelsey, too. Training must have really been rough. I felt a strong pain in my chest again." The pains, mostly, have gone away, but for the past few weeks they've returned. It only happens once a week, but since we marked each other, the intensity that we feel each other's emotions and pain has increased.

"Yeah, we all got knocked around a bit. I'm going to go shower." Ian states. His mood is getting worse by the second.

"I'll have to talk with Kelsey about hurting my mate." I turn and face him.

"I don't need you to talk to anyone on my behalf." Ian snaps, then walks away.

I'm left standing in the kitchen, not too sure what I did wrong. This summer has been so wonderful. Ian has learned to juggle being mated while preserving his friendships with Zane and Kelsey. I have also learned how to make time for Jessi and a few of my other friends.

Only recently have things changed. Ian is moodier than normal. He snaps at me easier and he's always so defensive. He says there's a lot of stress coming from his father. We don't talk about it because he doesn't want to worry me. I know his father can be tough on him. I've seen it with my own two eyes, but maybe he wouldn't be so stressed if he'd just talk to me about it.

We don't have a dining room here in the cottage, so I set up a table and chairs under a cypress tree in the backyard. I strung up lights and set the table with mixed matched dishes. I love the way everything came together. It's so artistic.

I put the last bit of food in covered serving dishes, and I pull two bottles of wine from the refrigerator, carefully placing them in the wine chillers, then covering them with ice. Looking around, I'm so proud that I pulled this small dinner party off with an hour to spare. I hate how Ian is being so moody. Is he going to be like this when we move away?

Needing something sweet, I head into the large walk-in pantry. I've always thought it was odd that the cottage has such a big pantry, but not a dining room. Looking on the shelves, I spot what I'm after: peanut butter and chocolate chip cookies. Reaching for the bag, I sense Ian behind me and I freeze. I want to turn and wrap my arms around him, but I don't. Not too sure what kind of mood he's in now and not wanting to provoke him anymore, I stand perfectly still. A moment later, I feel Ian's body pressed against mine, his member grinding into my ass.

"I'm sorry I snapped at you, angel." Ian whispers into my ear. He presses his face against my neck and ear. His hot breath teases my skin as he kisses my cheek and neck. My mind is quickly overcome by lust as every bit of hurt feelings are washed away in an instant.

"We have to stop," I breathe out heavily.

"Why?" He lifts my hair and kisses the back of my neck. I love the way the tingles and sparks radiate when his lips touch my skin.

"Our parents..." I try to turn and face him, but he stops me by grabbing my hands and holding them firm on the shelf in front of me. A surge of electricity bolts through my body to my core, dampening my panties. "Five minutes, angel. I need you so bad right now." I can't deny him, not when I need him too. He pushes his hand into my shorts and past my panties, running his fingers up and down my slit. "So wet for me already." He sucks his mark on my neck.

He slips my shorts off my hips, then my panties. I can feel the smooth skin of his shaft rubbing my ass. He tilts my hips up, lining his member up to my entrance, and with one thrust, he pushes completely inside me. We both gasp and moan as he enters me. He doesn't waste any time moving in and out of me. My hips match his rhythm. I feel him unlatch my bra and both his hands move to my breasts. I throw my head back in ecstasy as he nips the tender skin on my neck.

"Oh Ian," I moan as I run my fingers through his hair. I love the way my core is perfectly molded around him, and the way he fills me completely.

"You like that, angel? You like the way my dick feels inside you?" Ian groans in my ear.

"Yes," I moan from the pure pleasure of being connected with him. He withdraws and spins me around, quickly lifting my leg and plunging back deep inside me. His strokes are short and fast as the pressure builds inside me. I take off my shirt and bra, dropping them both to the ground next to me. He growls, watching my breast bounce up and down with each thrust. I tug on the hem of his tee-shirt and he quickly pulls it over his head. One at a time, he takes one of my hard nipples in his mouth, sucking and licking them, savoring their taste before switching to the other. My moans get louder as I run my nails up and down his back.

"I fucking love you," he pushes his tongue into my mouth, claiming it as his own. Our kiss is rough and demanding as our tongues battle for dominance. My core pulsates around his member and my body shakes as I fall off the edge, lost in my euphoric high of pleasure.

Soon Ian follows. He continues to move in and out while he grunts and groans as he fills me completely.

After we both come down, we stand holding each other, completely sated and in love. We don't speak... we don't need to.

"Kate!" I hear my mom's voice shout.

"They're early," I gasp.

"Shit," Ian frustratingly says while pulling out of me. I can't help but to giggle as we both frantically put our clothes back on.

September 2001

Ian and I drive to the royal palace for the Autumn Moon Ball in silence. Silence is our new normal and keeps us from arguing. We've been at school for a month now and share a townhouse off campus with Kelsey and Zane. The first night we were there, I answered the door to a human woman looking for Ian. Her name was Cindy, and she claimed to be his girlfriend for over a year. She was shocked to find out that I'm his fiancée. Ian wasn't home at the time, but said that she was crazy and had been stalking him. He told me to stay away from her because she might be a danger to me. There were a couple of times she chased me, claiming she wanted to talk. Afraid for my life, I'd run away fast.

The stress of it all came crashing down on me and the pains in my chest started again... at least twice a week. Every time I'd try to talk with Ian about it, he'd always dismiss my feelings and tells me that this is what being an adult is... to just deal with it. The past month has not been fun. I'm isolated from women my age and most of the time, I feel like I'm going crazy. Ian and I are more like strangers that share a bed. *I miss home.*

We are traveling in a twenty SUV convoy. As we drive through the palace gates, I sigh, preparing myself mentally to put on a fake smile and pretend that Ian and I are a happily mated couple. As I've led others to think for months now. Ian ignores me. *What's new?* If I wasn't required to be here as Ian's mate and future Beta female, I would have just stayed home. We exit our vehicles and as I wait my turn to be greeted by the royal council; I see a group of twelve being led around the receiving line.

'Mom, why are they skipping the receiving line?' I mindlink.

'They are unranked unmated males and females. Only ranked wolves go through the receiving line.' Mom mindlinks back.

'Why are they here?' I scan the group of faces, stopping when I come across Nikki. Her face is full of hatred and disgust. *What did I ever do to her?*

'Each pack always brings a group of unranked and unmated members to big functions like this. That's how I met your dad.' Mom mindlinks back. I sometimes forget about my mom's humble beginnings. Both her parents were school teachers before they retired, and my mom figured she'd follow in their footsteps.

After we get through the receiving line, we head to the tent in the garden for a formal six-course meal. Everything is very fancy and formal. I didn't recognize half of what I was eating, but still found everything palatable. Watching my dad eat was funny. His facial expressions as he tasted the food in front of him were priceless. This meal is completely out of his comfort zone. He's very much a meat and potato kind of werewolf.

Now and then, I glance at Ian and find that he is off in his own world. If I didn't know better, I'd think he was mindlinking someone. He looks gorgeous in his black tuxedo, and I feel like a princess in my floor length flowing ball gown. We appear to be the ideal couple; too bad I don't feel the love between us.

After dinner, we go to the grand ballroom, which is elaborately decorated with black, gold, and orange flowers and accent pieces. Mom and Luna swoon over every detail of the ballroom's décor. We have yet to see the royal family, but mom assures me they will make their grand entrance soon. Ian and I share a couple of slow dances while photographers capture the moment between the happy couples on the dance floor. Again, I catch death glares from Nikki that are making me uncomfortable.

Shortly after we exit the dance floor, cheering erupts from the back corner of the room, and chants of mate, mate, mate are heard. We watch the area, hoping to catch a glance at the newly mated couple, and soon realize that it is Zane.

"Nathaniel," Luna Martha gasps out, grabbing her chest with tears in her eyes.

"Congratulations, you old dog. Now the race is on to see who will be a grandfather first." My dad pats Alpha Nathaniel on the back and they both laugh.

I smile, watching Zane and his new mate. They already seem so in love. I look at Ian and his face is emotionless. What have I done wrong to deserve this cold treatment from him? After the cheers die down, Zane and his new mate along with her parents make their way to our table. Once again, I turn my fake smile back on.

"Alpha Nathaniel," the large burly man takes Alpha Nathaniel's hand, then pulls him in for a hug, "looks like we're family now."

"Alpha Maxwell, looks that way." Alpha Nathaniel laughs as the two men exchange pleasantries.

We learn that Zane's mate is a daughter of a small pack in Canada, and her name is Rebeka. She's tall, slim, with porcelain skin, and long black hair. She's so pretty and looks like a living doll. I try to get to know her, but Zane is being a little possessive of her, which my mom says is normal.

"Give him a little time. Soon you and Rebeka will have lunches and shopping trips together." Mom whispers in my ear. I'm so happy for the two of them, yet a little jealous at the same time. Kelsey looks a bit annoyed. Maybe because he's not mated yet and the last man standing.

The royal family finally makes their grand entrance, the king, queen, and their two sons. That's funny, I thought they only had one son. Mom says we will make our way to their table shortly, but first we dance and pose for more pictures. *How much longer do I have to be here?* After we return from the dance floor, Ian stands and walks away without a word to me.

"Ian? Where are you going?" I call out, stopping him in his tracks. He slowly turns and walks back over to me.

"If it's okay with you, I have to go to the restroom." He snaps in my ear, "Are we done with the interrogation?" I nod my head and he walks away, leaving me sitting alone.

'Ian,' I call through my mindlink, but his blocks are up. I find that more than odd. Ian said he was going to the restroom and would be right back. That was twenty minutes ago. The pain in my chest is back with a vengeance. This pain is the worst that I have ever felt.

'Ian,' I call out again... still nothing.

"Kelsey?" I walk up to my brother, who is making out with some she-wolf sitting on his lap.

"What?" He snaps, "Can't you see I'm a little busy?"

"Yeah... I see that. I'm looking for Ian. Have you seen him?" I grab my chest and take a deep breath as the pain intensifies.

"He stepped outside to get some fresh air." Kelsey says, before waving me off.

"No wait, Kate." Zane says while holding the hand of his new mate, "he's... um... his father wanted to talk with him. Now that he and I have found our mates." Zane stumbles over his words and my gut is telling me he is lying.

"Oh... that might explain why his blocks are up." I smile, then turn and walk away. I take a few steps before I have to brace myself on a nearby table as the pain continues to intensify.

I'm not too sure why I feel like Zane is lying to me, but something deep inside the pit of my stomach says he is. My gut is telling me that Kelsey is telling me the truth about Ian going outside. I guess he's too distracted by the whore on his lap to think quick. I wait a few seconds until I'm sure that both Kelsey and Zane are not paying attention to me, then I slip out the side door of the ballroom.

'I don't know what is going on, Sasha, but we need to find Ian.' I say to her in my mind.

'It's not good, Kate... he is up to no good. I can feel it.' She sighs out before I give her control of my human body to track down our lost mate.

Before too long, we are walking towards a garden shack about thirty yards from the palace. The pain is extremely intense, but Sasha can push the pain aside. As we get closer to the garden shack, we hear grunting from both a male and female, causing my heart to sink.

'He's in there,' Sasha cries. We both know what is going on behind the garden shack door, but I need to see it with my own eyes. I fling open the door and hit the light switch. The room illuminates up and I come face to face with my worst nightmare.

"What the fuck!" Ian shouts. The shock of the sudden bright lights causes him to close his eyes as he removes his dick from an all too familiar she-wolf's mouth... Nikki. The pain instantly stops, but a new pain in my heart starts, as I realize he's the cause of my pain for all these months.

"How could you?" I whisper as tears spill down my cheek. My entire body shakes, and my breathing becomes shallow as my chest heaves up and down with every breath. My heart races at the sight of the two of them together as bile rises in my throat.

Nikki stands, pulling her dress up covering her breasts followed by her panties, before wiping a white liquid from her chin.

"At least he fucked me this time. Do me a favor... wait a little longer next time so I can at least orgasm before he finishes in my mouth."

My body shakes at the vile words coming from her mouth. I know they were together before Ian and me. The pain that I've felt all these months tells me they never stopped sleeping with each other.

"Nikki, shut the fuck up. Kate," Ian says as he tucks his dick back into his pants, quickly zipping up before rushing to me.

"No!" I shout, backing up. "How could you, Ian?" I say through tears. Any makeup I had on my face was washed away by my own tears.

"What the fuck, Ian? Tell her the truth. We knew she'd find out, eventually. She's your mate and I'm your mistress. This is what we agreed on." Nikki crosses her arms and stomps her foot. I look from Nikki to Ian with shock and disgust on my face.

"Please... let me explain." Ian walks towards me. I feel like I'm going to throw up... I can smell her on him. It's all so clear now. I turn and run, mindlinking to my mom that I need help.

I'm almost back at the palace ballroom when I see Kelsey and Zane walk out the side door, looking around. My guess, Ian mindlinked them and they're looking for me.

"How could you, you bastard?" I run up to Kelsey and hit him in the chest with my fist.

"Kate," my mom says as she and my dad walk out the ballroom side door, followed by Ian's father.

"You lied for him. You knew!" I shout, "you fucking knew he was cheating on me with Nikki. You covered up for him. I'm your sister, Kelsey. Doesn't that mean anything to you?" I shout and sob. Never feeling rage in my life, my body trembles as the rage seeps from my pores.

"Kate, please let me explain," Kelsey grabs my shoulders.

"No!" I pull away from his grip. "You are nothing to me, either of you." I point between him and Zane, "you... you're dead to me." Ian catches up to me at the palace with Nikki quick on his heels. Before he can say anything I run to the safety of the forest.

I make it to the tree line, but I can hear multiple footsteps closing in on me. Positive it's the three bozos coming to talk sense into me, or maybe it's the repulsive whore Nikki. I don't know where I'm going, but anywhere has got to be better than back there. How could I be so foolish, shouldn't I have seen the signs of him cheating? Could that human Cindy be right? She was his girlfriend? He let me believe I was crazy while he treated me like shit.

I run and run, tripping over my ball gown that is tangled around my legs, falling to the ground. The palms of my hands are cut on some rocks, and it becomes clear that I fell right at a cliff's edge. Two more steps and I would have fallen to my death. That doesn't sound bad compared to the hell I'm living right now. I hear footsteps closing in, and I quickly get to my feet.

"Don't come any closer, Ian, or I will jump." I shout and take a step closer to the edge of the cliff.

"Please don't." Ian halts and shouts.

"Go away!" I scream.

"Please talk to me," Ian begs, taking a step closer.

"Go talk to your fucking whore, Nikki!" I shout taking a step closer to the edge.

"Come away from the edge, please." Ian's voice shakes as he takes a step back.

"Why?" I cry. "Wasn't I good enough for you?" I am sobbing so hard that I can't breathe.

"You are. I made a mistake." Ian holds his arms out towards me.

Sasha cries and whines in my head. She and I are both hurting so badly. I see my dad walk past Ian. He has sadness on his face that I've never seen before. He holds his arms out to me. They look so warm and welcoming. All I want right now is to be in my dad's arms and feel the warm touch of my mom's fingers playing with my hair.

"Daddy," I say through tears, then take a step. My gown is tangled around my legs and I slip and start to fall.

Very close to the edge, I don't feel the ground under my feet, only air. My mom gasps and I close my eyes, accepting my fate that I will soon fall to my death. Before I hit the ground, I feel my dad's powerful arms wrap around my body and pull me into his chest. He picks me up in his arms, walking away from the edge of the cliff towards my mom.

"Let's go home, baby girl." My dad whispers and my mom wraps her arms around me, too.

CHAPTER TWENTY-NINE

THE OLD OAK TREE

June 2004

Ian

'IAN, WHERE ARE YOU?' Kate mindlinks.

'Alpha's office,' I mindlink back. She felt my emotions after our meeting with the princes and learning that Prince Lazar might have an ulterior motive, I'm sure of it. How am I going to explain to her I'll be leaving for a mission, and that said mission is more dangerous than the previous ones? I don't want to tell her, but I know I have to. We promised that there will be no secrets between us.

The warriors that are trained for these missions join us in Alpha's office, and like always, we give them the option to stay behind. We explain the risks and that we expect not everyone will come home. The warriors don't blink and not a soul volunteers to stay behind. Our warriors are among some of the best around, and I expect no less from them. Alpha dismisses us after the three of us make plans on how we will tell our mates about the mission. My nerves are on edge, not because of the mission, but because the fear that this will invoke in Kate.

Walking out of Alpha's office, I see Kate leaning against the wall in front of his door. When she sees me, she stands straight, pushing her shoulders back and putting on a brave face.

"Hello, love. How long have you been waiting for me?" I lean down to her and press my lips into hers. Her lips are so soft and sweet, they always leave me wanting more.

"Your emotions are all over the place. What's going on?" She whispers.

"Can't keep anything from you, can I?" I smile and tease.

"Ian?" She tilts her head sideways at me.

"Let's take a walk." I feel like being outside, and in her favorite spot under the oak tree behind the back garden will lessen the sting of learning that I will go away.

Kate

We walk through the back garden to the old oak tree I used to sit and read under when I was younger. As we approach, I see a rope hammock swing, one like I had when I was a pup.

"Ian, what is this?" I smile and run my hands along the swing.

"You like it?" He leans down and whispers in my ear.

"Yes. So much. When did you do this?" I turn and wrap my arms around his neck.

"Earlier today. I ordered it two weeks ago. You should have seen Zane, Kelsey, and me trying to hang the damn thing. It looked like three monkeys trying to hump a football. Maintenance finally had enough of watching the three of us screw around with it and swooped in to finish the project in like five minutes. They said they didn't want you hitting the ground when it fell apart on you." Ian laughs, "get in." he instructs. I climb in and scoot over, giving him room to sit next to me.

"This one is bigger than the one I had as a pup." I curl up to his chest.

"I got one built for two. I know how much you love to read and how this was your favorite spot. From up there, I used to watch you." He points to the upper floor where the beta quarters are.

"You watched me?" I look up at his face, "perv." We laugh and I snuggle back into his chest. I can feel something bubbling under the surface and it's making me nervous and uneasy.

"You know I love you, right?" Ian plays with my hair.

"You're scaring me." I inhale deeply, trying to control my emotions.

"I'm sorry, love. I'm not trying to... I just need you to know that I love you." He runs his fingertips up and down my body. "Prince Lazar and Prince Malachi were here today."

"Oh," knots form in my gut just hearing his name.

"We're leaving to go on a mission." His voice quivers as he speaks.

"What?" I sit up to look at him.

"England," his lip turns up in an attempt to form a smile.

"What?" Heat moves across my body as the shock of it hits me. "When?" I look down and whisper.

"A week... maybe sooner or later. It's hard to say." He brushes my cheek with the back of his hand.

"Is my dad going?" I'm fighting back the tears.

"No, all of our fathers will stay behind." He sighs out, "there's more, but first I need you to promise me you'll be brave."

"Goddess, Ian. You can't say things like that and expect me not to flip out." I shake my head.

"Yes, I can. You're the future Beta female. In reality, if something should happen to me, you'd step up taking my place. So, I need to hear you promise to be brave." He smiles, but I can see the fear in his eyes. I gulp and nod in agreement.

Ian explains that this will be a very dangerous mission, that they are outnumbered two to one, and that not everyone will make it back home. He tells me about the two Emerald packs and how Alpha David is killing off pack members until Ava agrees to be his chosen mate. He doesn't care that Ava is already mated to someone else. To me, Alpha David sounds like a blood hungry monster who's hell bent on destroying the smaller pack.

"Why doesn't the European royal palace do anything?" I nuzzle my nose into the crook of his neck, smelling his intoxicating fresh scent, helping to calm my nerves.

"Politics," he laughs. "It's like our royal palace trying to take us on. We outnumber them, three to one, and our warriors are some of the best trained around. They might defeat us, but there would be a mighty cost to them. I know you have some trust issues. You can go. I will put you up at the royal palace until the fighting is done." He wraps his arms around me.

"No... no matter where I am, I will just be a distraction. I'm learning to trust you again." I hold him tight.

That is the truth. I want to trust him to the fullest. Since he has reentered my life, he hasn't given me a reason to distrust him. I'm also learning how to tell the difference between his emotions and mine. Had I had a handle on that three years ago, I would have realized that the guilt I was feeling was from him and not me. Like earlier today, I felt a pain hit my chest, followed by sadness, and I knew exactly who it was from. The pain in my chest today differed from the infidelity pains I felt years ago. Today, I knew something was deeply troubling him and that I needed to be there for him.

I've also learned the difference between guilt and remorse. Guilt is knowing that you've done something wrong and feeling bad about it. Whereas remorse is the deep regret for doing wrong. I can see through Ian's actions that he knows that he hurt me to my bones, shaking my very existence. He can't change the past or take away the pain I experienced, so he's been on a path of correcting his mistakes and righting his wrongs. This is why I don't need to go or babysit him twenty-four-seven.

"There's one more thing," he sighs out.

"Okay, I'm listening." I feel like he just needs to pull the band aid off quickly, because the way my head is spinning, I don't know how much more I can take.

"Our fathers seem to think that Prince Lazar has his eyes on you and is hoping that I'm killed." Ian says the last part quick. I'm not too sure how to process this bit of news. The future king wants my mate dead so he can claim me as his own.

"This is a lot," I whisper.

"I know. It is for me, too. The last part really isn't relevant, but I wanted you to hear it from me. I promised there would be no secrets between us." He lifts my chin up to his face, "and I meant it." He gives me a soft and gentle kiss that is full of emotion. I hold him tight, getting lost in our kiss. He breaks the kiss with a groan. "Zane wants to get a training session this afternoon, and you have to get ready for our big date tonight." He flashes me the million-dollar smile that I have loved since I was fourteen.

"I think we should wait until you get back. Maybe we should just stay in instead." I sigh out, because after hearing everything he had to say, I'm not really in the going out mood.

"No way. I've been looking forward to a giant steak all day, and I made your brother practice my salsa moves with me this morning." He rests his forehead on mine.

"Did you really?" I laugh, thinking about my brother dancing. Kelsey has zero rhythm like our dad.

"I think we need to enjoy life even more now." He kisses my forehead as a tear escapes my eye.

CHAPTER THIRTY

PROMISE

September 2001

Kate

I'M IN MY BED and haven't seen Ian in a week. I spend my days sitting in my room, staring at the wall. My heart feels like it's shattered in a million pieces as I try to comprehend what has been going on all these months. I'm not too sure when the last time I ate or slept was. I've cried so many tears that I have none left. As hard as I try, I can't wrap my head around why Ian would cheat on me. He did it right under my nose. What does Nikki have that I don't? Why am I not good enough for him? The more I think about it, the more my heart breaks. I'm just a shell of the person I was before.

My parents are worried about my health, so I decide today is the day that I make some sort of effort towards moving forward. Pushing myself to do it for them. I take a shower; the hot water feels amazing on my skin. Almost like I'm washing the past off me. After my shower, I blow dry my hair but put it in a bun on top of my head. I still don't have the energy to do my hair or makeup. Looking at my reflection in the mirror, my skin is dull and I have dark black circles under my eyes. Then I see his mark and my heart breaks all over again. I push forward, throwing on jeans and a tee-shirt. I head downstairs to the kitchen, where my parents are eating breakfast.

My parents are sitting at the table reading the newspaper and eating. I walk past them without saying a word and head for the coffee. Since that fateful night at the palace, I have not spoken a word. I sit at the table and quietly sip my coffee. My mom gets up from the table, but quickly returns with a plate of eggs, sausage, and toast. She sets the plate in front of me, then rubs my back before returning to her seat. My parents don't say a word, but I can feel their love for me. They know I need time to heal and they accommodate that.

I haven't seen or heard from Ian in fourteen days. My brother has called twice, but I don't answer. I haven't had the pains in my chest since the night at the palace. I'm sure he's figured out a way to cheat, so I don't feel the pains. My mom tells me that Nikki's parents removed her from the college that Ian attends and sent her to a college south of our territory. Honestly, I couldn't care less about her. Is it her fault he cheated? I know she played a role in it, especially since she knew he was a mated man, but in the end, he should have been the one to resist.

I've become accustomed to my new normal and have started a job at the pack day care. Although I don't have to work, I need something to keep my mind occupied. I love working with the pups. This might be the closest I get to motherhood, since I have no desire to let my mate touch me, much less have pups with him. After my early morning shift at the day care, I head to the gym and try to kill my emotions with cardio. After running two miles on the treadmill, I walk to the lap pool in the back of the gym.

Walking down the long corridor to the lap pool, someone puts their hand around my mouth and pushes me into a storage room. He locks the door behind us and holds my body tight against his.

"Promise me you won't scream angel and I'll let you go." Ian's voice is just above a whisper and his delicious scent fills my nose. I feel the tears build up in my eyes. My mind races as it's flooded with confused emotions. I nod my head, promising I won't scream. He removes his hand from my mouth and wraps both arms around me, nuzzling his nose into the crook of my neck and inhaling deeply. "Oh angel, I have missed you so much." My body goes limp in his arms, and I cry. "Please don't cry, just say we can start over... please."

"You hurt me." I say through tears.

"I know, and I feel bad that you got hurt." He continues holding me tight in his arms.

"I need to know the truth." I wiggle from his grip, turning to face him.

"Anything. I've wanted to come clean for months." Ian hangs his head.

"Are there more women than just Nikki?" I wipe the tears from my face. He simply nods. "How many?"

"Too many to count." He continues looking at the ground.

"Who is Cindy to you?" My voice is quivering but firm.

"She was a woman that I slept with regularly." He still doesn't make eye contact.

"Your girlfriend?" I cross my arms and he nods his head. "She tried to tell me the truth, and you said she was crazy and dangerous."

"I wanted to spare your feelings." He snaps his head up. His eyes are bloodshot.

"Spare my feelings? You lied to me, Ian. You're only coming clean now because you got caught." My lip quivers as I speak.

"Please," he grabs me, pulling me tight into his body. "I can't live without you. I love you so much." He kisses my neck and the tingles from the mate bond send shivers down my spine. The haze of the mate bond quickly takes over and suddenly I'm lost in him. In an instant, the pain is washed away. "I promise to be a good boy from now on." He continues kissing his way to his mark. "I love you, Kate." He whispers as he sucks on my marking spot, sending a wave of electricity through my body to my core.

"Look at me." I grab him by the hair and lift his head. "Promise that you will not cheat on me ever again. I need to hear you say it."

"I promise," he says as he lowers us to the ground.

We sit on our knees facing each other. I love him so much. Looking into his eyes, I see the guilt and pain he has been living with all these months. I'm choosing to love him and forgive him. Our lips meet and tiny explosions radiate from our kiss. Lust fills the air, and I need to feel his skin on mine. I need to be one with him. I pull up his shirt, jerking it over his head before he takes my lips again. Our tongues dance and intertwine as I savor the sweet taste of his mouth. He breaks the kiss to pull my shirt and sports bra off my body.

I try to unbuckle his belt but end up fumbling around with it instead. We are hungry for each other and can't get our clothes off fast enough. He lays me on my back, snatching my leggings down around my ankles. He is quick and soon I feel his member thrust inside me with a single push. Grabbing my hips, he pounds in and out with short fast strokes. My breasts jump around wildly, and I breathe heavily, trying to control any sounds I make.

He feels amazing inside me, and my body craves more. Just when I think I can't take anymore, he rests my legs on his shoulders, lifting my hips high in the air continuing to push deep inside me. Soon my body shakes and I moan out his name as I fall over the edge. With the next thrust, he follows, and his member pulsates as it fills me with his hot liquid. After we both come down, he rolls off me with a smile on his face.

"Thank you, angel."

Chapter Thirty-One
SAVE AVA

June 2004

Kate

"HEY SUGAR," MOM LOOKS up from her magazine as I walk into the kitchen from the back door. "A delivery came for you," she points to the large flat box propped up against the wall next to the kitchen table.

"A delivery? From whom?" I stand eyeing the box as if it's going to bite me.

"I don't know. Maybe a secret admirer. The only thing I know is if you don't hurry and open it, I am... and I'm claiming whatever is inside it." Mom laughs and points to the scissors on the kitchen table. She has always been like this. She loves surprises, especially from my dad.

Taking a deep breath, I pick up the box, which is lightweight. I didn't expect that, since the box is large. I grab the scissors and watch my mom out of the corner of my eye. She's trying to play it cool, but we both know that she's about ten seconds away from taking over.

There is something wrapped in black tissue paper in the box. The logo on the paper is from a high-end woman's boutique. I open the black tissue paper and see a note on top of solid hot pink fabric. I hand the note to my mom, then remove the fabric from the box.

I smile when I see an elegant hot pink dress. It's short with a plunging V neckline and has long flounced sleeves that are tapered at the wrist. Its high waist is form fitting and flares out just past my hips with a long slit that will surely expose my thigh.

"What does the note say, Mom?" I hold the dress against my body.

"I can't wait to dance the night away with you tonight. Pink has always been my favorite color on you. Love Ian. Awwww... so romantic." My mom swoons after reading his note. She is the reason I'm a hopeless romantic.

"Yeah..." my heart sinks, thinking about the conversation I just had with Ian.

"What's wrong?" She tilts her head, pursing her lips.

"I just found out that Ian and the others will leave for another mission in a few days. This one is very dangerous." I sit in the chair beside her, still holding Ian's gift.

"Yes," she sighs out. "Your dad told me. He is not happy about it."

"What am I going to do? We just started over and..." she places her hand over my mouth.

"First, we don't think about the what if's. We surround them with positive energy only, and that will manifest them returning home safe with minimal injuries. Sugar, none of us are promised eternity on this earth. So, we have to take each day and make the best of it. Dance in the rain like nobody is watching, stop and smell the roses, eat the cake, and love with white hot passion like there's no tomorrow." She squeezes my arm. My breath hitches at my mom's wise words. She's right, there are no guarantees in life, and you never know what tomorrow will bring.

"How did you get so smart?" I smile and lean into her.

"With age, there is wisdom. Now you have a date to get ready for." Mom looks at her watch.

"Mom," I laugh, "Ian won't be here for another five hours."

"Exactly, just enough time for a soak in the tub and nap. You'll appreciate the nap later." She wiggles her eyebrows at me. All I can do is laugh at her antics. I don't know what I'll do without her. She always knows how to brighten my day.

At seven p.m. sharp, Ian mindlinks that he is here to pick me up. I let him know that I'll be right down.

"Mmmmm... damn girl, you're looking fine." Ian leans in the doorway of my bedroom, looking me up and down, biting his bottom lip.

"What are you doing up here?" I laugh while putting in my last earing.

"Your mom told me just to come up." He steps to me, handing me a single red rose. "You look amazing."

"You're pretty damn hot too," I take the rose and wrap my arms around his neck, pulling my body close to his. He's wearing a fitted black suit with a hot pink shirt that is partially buttoned up. His well-defined chest teases my eyes.

"Baby girl, you can't look at me like that. We have reservations." His hands massage my lower back and hips. I'm quickly getting lost in the haze of the mate bond, and all I want is more of him. "We better go," he whispers before softly kissing me.

Ian

Tonight, I pulled out the big guns for this date, borrowing my father's Ferrari F430. This is the life. Beautiful car with a sexy woman sitting next to me, and my hand resting high on her thigh. I push down all the emotions of leaving her in a few days for another mission and focus solely on us. We're just living in the moment. Our conversation is light, which is a good thing, since I'm having a hard time keeping my eyes off her. I thank the Moon Goddess for allowing me a second chance with Kate. She is my world and a true blessing. I was so stupid before, lost in my own selfish ego.

At the restaurant, we're seated in a private area in the back corner. Kate sits next to me with my arm tight around her while her fingertips draw circles on my thigh. She is being very bold and openly flirtatious with me. *Whatever has gotten into her, I like it.* My pants are becoming tighter by the second and the thought crosses my mind to rent a hotel room for the night.

"You can not order salmon." I shake my head. "People normally wait two months for a table here. They have some of the finest steaks around."

"I know, but did you see the salmon that the server carried by? It looked and smelled delicious." Her eyes are wide as she pretends to wipe the drool from her chin. I laugh at her silliness.

"Okay, love. You can have whatever your heart desires." I kiss her nose.

"Really? I can have whatever my heart desires?" She squeezes my thigh with the look of desire in her eyes. "What if I say I want you?" Her tone is low and her breathing is shallow.

"You are making it very hard not to take you on top of this table." I wrap my hand around her throat and pull her in for a kiss. The haze of the mate bond swirls around us. Tiny explosions radiate from our lips.

"Are we ready to o..." our server pauses, then walks away.

"As tempting as you are, I'm starving." Kate says into my mouth.

"Fine, but it looks like I'll be having dessert in my quarters tonight." I watch her smooth, plump lips.

"Mmmmm, can't wait." She presses her lips into mine.

We can't keep our hands off each other, even after our food arrives. She orders the fillet minion, and I order the porter house... and salmon. I couldn't help ordering the salmon for her. The way her eyes lit up when she saw and smelled it. She looked like a pup in a candy store. I made Moon Goddess a promise shortly after Kate rejected me. If she gave me another chance with Kate, I would worship the ground she walks on. That I would do anything just to see her smile, and I intend to do just that as long as there's breath in my lungs.

"You were right, Ian. This steak is amazing." She sips on her cabernet.

"And you were right, this salmon is pretty damn good. You have an amazing nose for food. Here, try this." I cut her a bite of my porter house and feed it to her. I love the way she enjoys food. The way her eyes roll back as she tilts her head back, and the way she moans out the words so good. "Eat up, love. You're going to need lots of energy at the salsa club." I smile and take another bite.

"Do we have to go?" She tilts her head.

"What, you don't want to?" I sip my wine and she sighs loudly.

"I was... just thinking that maybe we could just skip to dessert... for both of us." She bites her bottom lip. I can see her hard nipples through her dress and the smell of her arousal hits my nose, waking my beast.

"Your wish is my command, love." I kiss her lips and flag down our server.

We barely make it to the passenger side of the car before our bodies are tangled up as we kiss passionately. I pressed her between my body and the car and at this rate, we will not make it back to the territory before lust completely overcomes us. I reach my hand in between her legs, pushing her panties aside and rubbing her wet pussy.

"What are you doing?" She whispers in my ear while her hips buck to the rhythm of my fingers.

"Do you like it?" I insert one finger into her tight pussy.

"People…" she moans lightly.

"It's dark and there's no one around." I pick up the pace.

"Your phone," she says as it rings from the front seat.

"Ignore it." I whisper in her ear as she nibbles on my neck. All I want right now is to feel her canine sink into my skin. The ringing stops only to start again.

"Shit." I remove my hand and push her panties back. "That's your phone now." I watch both of our phones ring inside the car. *What the hell is going on?*

We answer our phones. Her father is calling her, and Zane is calling me. We both left our phones in the car and missed twenty calls. Tears of fear fill her eyes as we hang up our phones.

"My dad says Alpha wants you in his office two hours ago." She gulps.

"Zane said the same." I continue holding her, offering her what comfort I can, not knowing what is in store for us.

We arrive back to a chaotic packhouse. Kate holds my arm tight as we watch warriors rushing around checking their gear. *Looks like it's show time.*

"Where the fuck have you been?" My father steps in front of us and snaps. Instinctively, I push Kate behind me and take a protective stance.

"Dinner. I told you earlier, you let me borrow your car." I snap back. He can talk to me however he wants, but I will not allow him to intimidate Kate.

"Where was your phone? I called a hundred times." He calms down a bit, realizing that Kate is frightened.

"My mate and I left our phones in the car. We were enjoying ourselves. What's going on?" My tone is low and my voice is monotone. This is the first time that I'm standing my ground where my father is concerned.

"Ian," Alpha shouts, "my office." I don't let go of Kate and together we walk into Alpha's office. I have no secrets from her. She will be the Beta Female, she will have to learn what the title really means, and how to react under pressure.

"Kate," Alpha greets as she sits down in the chair next to mine. "Ian, from this point on you can't leave your phone anywhere except your blazer pocket when you are out of the territory. Kate, the same goes for you." Alpha speaks in a calm but firm voice, and we acknowledge him with a head nod. "Tonight, we got word that Alpha David has kidnapped Alpha Oliver's Luna." I can hear Kate's light gasp. "He's giving Ava seventy-two hours to reject her mate and pledge her loyalty to him as her Alpha and chosen mate. If Ava doesn't do as he has demanded, he will torture and murder her mother. To make sure they understood he was serious, he sent a vial of the Luna's blood along with her pinky toe. Ava is prepared to meet his demand, but Alpha Oliver is not sure if Alpha David will release his Luna. Inside sources said that Alpha David's actions have become more neurotic and unpredictable in the last twenty-four hours. The team is ready to go now. The palace has arranged private transport for everyone."

I can feel my world crashing down at my feet. I thought I had more time with Kate. More time to fully repair the mate bond I destroyed all those years ago.

"Go save Ava and her mother," Kate squeaks out, putting on her best brave face. I can feel how frightened she is, and I fucking hate it. All I want to do is hold her and tell her everything is going to be okay, but I'm not sure it will be.

"Alpha, I need five minutes to change." I point to my clothes.

"Take fifteen," Alpha nods, looking between Kate and me.

Rushing out of Alpha's office towards the stairs, I'm practically dragging my mate behind me. I stop mid-stride and toss her over my shoulder and run up the stairs two steps at a time until I reach the sixth floor. I burst through the doors of my quarters and carry her straight into my bedroom, putting her down on the bed. She has tears in her eyes and fear on her face. I need to change and grab my battle bag before I stop to talk to her.

She watches every move I make, not taking her eyes off of me. Once I'm changed into my olive-green cargo pants and tee shirt and have my hands on my battle bag, I'm ready to say my goodbyes to Kate. Not knowing what to say, I pull her in for a kiss, taking my time and savoring the way her lips feel and taste before breaking the kiss.

"You're still wearing this old thing." She touches the paracord bracelet she made for me all those years ago.

"Absolutely, it's my good luck charm." I smile. "Love, I have to go. I will call you as often as I can. I love you, no matter what. Never forget that." Holding her head in my hands, I look deep into her eyes. I want her to not only hear my words, but to feel them as well.

"Ian... I," she struggles to get her words out.

"I know, love. You don't have to say a word." I kiss her lips, then for a second time in months, I leave her standing, watching me walk away.

Kate

There's so much I want to say, so many things I want to do with him. We've already lost so much time, and now I may lose him forever. I clutch my chest, watching him walk away. He stops abruptly, sighing loudly, then drops his battle bag on the floor before spinning around and running back to me. He wraps his arms around me and the tears flow. I love this man so much and I know he loves me. He didn't have to change... he wanted to change. To become the man, I can be proud to call my mate. Everything he has done since coming back into my life has proven to me he deserves us and we deserve a future together.

"Ian," I pull away from him and look him in the face. "I... I... I'm proud of the man you're becoming." The tears are trying to surface. I want to tell him that I love him, but I don't have the strength to say those words. Will I ever be able to say them to him? They used to slip from my lips with ease, but now they don't come easy. "I... there's so much..." he interrupts me.

"You just keep thinking about what you want to say and do to me when I get back. Make a list. Stay here. Sleep in my bed and surround yourself with my scent. I expect you to be completely moved in by the time I get back. And yes, I'm coming home safe to you." He kisses me one last time, then leaves.

Watching him walk away, my emotions are mixed; pride, love, fear... it's all there.

CHAPTER THIRTY-TWO

I REJECT YOU

October 2001

Kate

IT'S BEEN THREE WEEKS since I forgave Ian, and so far, everything has been great. No more chest pains at all. I stayed in the territory, because of my job at the day care. Two of the other workers are on extended maternity leave and if I left, they would be short staffed. I don't want the pups to suffer. Ian comes home every Friday and leaves early on Monday morning. It may not be the ideal situation, but we are making it work. We also talk on the phone multiple times a day.

After finishing my shift at the day care I walk to the gym, like I do every day. I'm excited because it's finally Friday and Ian should be home in a few hours. Walking into the gym, I see my dad. It looks like he is finishing up and is leaving.

"Hey dad." Stepping on my tippy toes, I give him a quick peck on the cheek.

"Someone is in a good mood." He smiles, wiggling his eyebrows at me.

"Yes, Ian should be home soon. I wanted to get my workout done, then head home and cook his favorite din..." a sudden pain hits my chest, dropping me to my knees. *Oh Goddess, no, not again.*

"Whoa," my dad kneels next to me. "What's wrong?"

"Not again." I hold my chest and slowly breathe in and out. The pain is intense, the most I have ever felt, with emotions. With shaking hands, I grab my phone and call Ian. After three rings, it goes to voicemail. I hang up and try again... three rings, then voicemail. Desperate to get through to him, I try a third time. I need to remind him what we have. This time, the call goes straight to voicemail.

"What's going on?" I hear Alpha Nathaniel ask.

"Ian... I'm going to kill that motherfucker with my bare hands." My dad growls.

"Charlie, get your son on the phone." Alpha Nathaniel snaps.

"I'm trying. It just keeps going to voicemail." After a brief pause, "Ian, it's your father. Call me immediately." I hear Beta Charlie say.

I have been having crippling chest pains daily for the past week. Ian is refusing to take mine or anyone else's calls. Zane and Kelsey claim that he's not at the townhouse, but I don't believe them at all. They're used to covering for Ian. I called Rebeka and found out she left to go back home on Thursday of last week; her sister gave birth to her first pup. This really can't be happening again; we were making such good progress.

'Kate, we can't keep living like this. This is slowly killing us.' Sasha cries. She and I both have cried every day.

'What do we do?' I close my eyes so I can see her.

'Reject him,' Sasha replies.

'That could kill us.' I state.

'This is killing us, slowly and painfully. If we reject him and it kills us, it will be fast. We can't keep living like this. This hurts so bad.' Sasha cries and I just want to hold her.

'How? Wait until he decides to come home?' I question.

'We go to the townhouse and reject him there.' She demands, her cries turn to anger.

'Then what?' Anything, including death, would be better than this.

'Start over somewhere else... like New York. We've always wanted to go there.' I think for a minute and can't come up with one reason I shouldn't. Ian can't do whatever he pleases and expect me to be waiting for him here.

I tell my parents my plan to reject Ian and move to New York, explaining that I can transfer to the university there and plan on studying art. My parents, who are sticklers about not rejecting your fated mate, have no objection to my plan. They don't blame me for wanting to move on and find happiness.

It took a few days to finalize my plan. I found an efficiency apartment in New York City and transferred to the university. Now all I have to do is execute the plan. Sasha has been giving me pep talks daily and reminding me I'm not a backup plan and I deserve better.

I'm a bundle of nerves driving to the townhouse. I hope I don't cave to the mate bond and back out at the last minute. When I arrive at the townhouse, I park in an inconspicuous spot and wait. I know that Zane and Kelsey have a class earlier than Ian does. We designed our schedules that way so he and I could have some alone time with each other. I don't have to wait long before I see Zane and Kelsey leave. I continue waiting longer, contemplating if I should just go into the townhouse.

Then I spot a familiar face, Cindy. She makes her way down the sidewalk and to the front door. My heart races at the sight of her. This is another bitch that doesn't care whether Ian has a fiancée, she only cares about her needs. I fight the urge to kill her where she stands. Sasha reminds me that the human world operates differently than our world. Soon the door opens, and I see a smiling Ian completely nude grab her and pull her into the townhouse while she giggles wildly. Rage runs through my veins.

I don't waste time before making my way to the townhouse. Standing at the door, I hear music and the two of them talking and laughing. It doesn't take long for the talking and laughing to turn into moans and for the chest pains to start. I take a deep breath and use my key to let myself in.

I push the door open hard. As the door flings open, I catch them both on the couch in the living room, both naked. Cindy is on her knees bobbing her head up and down on Ian's dick. My chests heaves and my body shakes violently with rage at the sight. Ian's eyes are wide. There is fear in his eyes as he pushes Cindy off him. Standing there eye to eye with Ian, my heart races. His fresh scent fills my nose and I'm quickly lost in the haze of the mate bond. What was I thinking? I can't reject him. I love him so much. Suddenly and without warning, Sasha pulls me back and pushes forward.

"I, Kate," Sasha shouts, "of Blue Moon Pack reject you, Ian, of Blue Moon Pack as my mate." Sasha pushes her shoulders back as Ian jumps to his feet, rushing towards us.

"NO!" He screams at the top of his lungs. Watching this play out is chaotic and I feel like I might get sick. We just rejected the only man I have ever loved. The one that I dreamed about being mated to since I was fourteen.

Sasha gives control back to me and before Ian reaches us, we both drop to the ground in pain. This pain is comparable to the pain of my first shift. Ian groans and cries out in pain while Cindy screams for help at the top of her lungs. Sasha helps me push the pain aside so we can leave before Ian recovers. I want to be long gone when he does.

I'm not too sure how long I'm on the ground in pain, but from Cindy's screams, I know Ian is in and out of consciousness. Once I get to my feet, I slowly walk out of the townhouse, and a ping of guilt hits me, thinking that Ian may not survive the rejection. After returning to my car, I sit and process what had just happened. Tears flow down my face, knowing that my dream of a future with Ian is now gone. As I wipe my tears, a wave of relief hits me. Now I can close this chapter of my life, and I feel like I can finally find happiness.

Ian

Seeing Kate bust through the front door was the biggest shock of my life. She doesn't look like her normal sweet self. There is fire and determination in her eyes. Before she started speaking, I knew what she was there for. This thing with Cindy took a life of its own and even though I knew Kate could feel the betrayal, I continued. I figured when I finally got done with Cindy, I could just use the mate bond to win Kate back over. It's worked like a charm every time so far. Why would this time be any different?

Then Kate said the dreaded words, I reject you. I tried to stop her, but I couldn't get to her fast enough. Next thing I know, I'm on the ground dipping in and out of consciousness, with Cindy screaming bloody murder next to me. Shortly after Kate left, I had the strength to pull myself up on the couch. Running my fingers through my hair, I think to myself, *what have I done?* Cindy cries next to me while I sit on the couch, trying to wrap my head around what just happened. I have lost the only woman in the world that I love... the only woman I could ever love. I have felt nothing for the women that I've been fucking on the side. Kate... Kate is different, and I used and abused her... now she's gone.

I see the front door open again. Looking up, I'm hoping it's Kate ready to take me back. Nope. It's something much worse.

"Who the fuck are you?" Cindy shouts.

"Hello son," my father flashes an evil smile at me. Standing beside my father is Alpha Nathaniel, and behind them, three warriors.

"You," Alpha Nathaniel points at Cindy, "you get dressed and get the fuck out of here."

"I'm not going..." Alpha Nathaniel interrupts Cindy.

"Now!" The thunderous roar of his Alpha tone shakes the walls of my small townhouse.

"Please, just go." I'm still trying to catch my breath.

"They look dangerous," Cindy protests.

"That's my father and uncles... get your shit and leave." I snap and growl. Cindy stands and slowly puts her clothes back on, looking between each of us in the room. She grabs her purse and heads to the door.

"Say goodbye," my father grabs her shoulders and spins her to face me. "Tell Ian it was nice knowing you and that you never want to see him again." He shakes her shoulders, and she cries.

"Father, your grievance is with me. Please, just let her go." I run my fingers through my hair, "Cindy it's over... lose my number." I stand and put my jeans back on. She turns away and runs out the door sobbing.

I fully expect what is coming next. My father is furious with me. I can see the rage seething from his face and body. He's so furious his face is red, and he is panting. *Fuck.* The warriors close and lock the door and stand guard. These are the same warriors that I've trained with for years, and now they'll be the ones who help hand out my punishment. Even if I had the strength, I wouldn't fight back. I deserve what I have coming. I just hope for my mother's sake they don't kill me.

My father and Alpha take off their designer suit jackets and roll up their sleeves. They're taking turns telling me what a fucking idiot I am before knocking the shit out of me. They tag team me, taking turns dishing out my punishment. I don't know how long they beat on me, but when they're done, not one part of my body is untouched. Everything hurts and I can't see anything through the blood in my eyes. They leave me on the ground in front of the couch and stand behind the front door. They know Kelsey and Zane should be back from class any moment and they're waiting to ambush them.

"Holy shit, Ian!" Zane shouts, running through the door.

"Bro, what happened?" Kelsey is on Zane's heels. I try to warn them by pointing at my father and Alpha, but by the time they realize that I'm trying to warn them, it's too late, and they're jumped from behind by the three warriors.

I fade in and out of consciousness during the fight between the warriors, Zane, and Kelsey. Kelsey and Zane stay in human form during the fight. They haven't assessed the situation before fists are flying. They don't know if these are humans or shifters. All they know is that I'm on the ground in a bloody mess and someone jumped them from behind.

As the fight rages, Kelsey and Zane start to get the upper hand... until my father and Alpha step in. My father and Alpha have trained together since they were ten, just like Zane and me. Just like the two of us, my father and Alpha are a well-oiled fighting machine. If I wasn't losing so much blood, I'd be watching them with pure admiration. Within minutes, Zane and Kelsey are overtaken by our fathers, and the real punishment begins.

Alpha is angry that his son and Blue Moon's future Alpha would allow such disrespect to happen to a mate, and for not correcting my indiscretions. He's furious that the two of them covered for me, while Kate was slowly dying from the pain I was causing. All three of us were told we didn't deserve our titles for showing disregard to a gift from the Moon Goddess. Zane and Kelsey's punishment is not nearly as bad as mine, but it will still leave a lasting impression on them... hell on all three of us.

When they are done with us, I'm left with broken ribs, nose, fingers, and collarbone. Zane and Kelsey are left black and blue. This by far is the worst punishment any of us have received from Alpha and my father.

Chapter Thirty-Three

THREE LITTLE WORDS

June 2004

Kate

"KATE," SONIA WAVES ME over to the couch where she and Rebeka are sitting drinking their afternoon tea.

"Ladies," I plop down on the couch next to them and pour myself a cup of hot tea. This is a new daily tradition we started last week.

Sonia saw an article in a magazine about high tea and said she wanted to do it. Rebeka told us that her mother and friends would have tea and gossip every day at three p.m. sharp, so here we are. We have fruit, pastries, tea sandwiches, and tea. Most importantly, we bond for an hour every day, shutting the world out. Hopefully, other females in our pack will start the same tradition with their personal circle of friends.

"I'm going to go grab some more cream, I'll be right back." Rebeka says grabbing the porcelain cream carafe and walking to the kitchen.

"Did you hear from Kelsey?" I blow on my hot tea.

"Yes, two days ago. He sounded exhausted." Sonia takes a bite of a pastry.

"Same with Ian. He said there had been no losses or major injuries." I sip my tea.

"Yes, Kelsey is so proud of his warriors." Sonia beams with pride.

Suddenly I'm hit with a sharp pain in my chest. This is a different pain laced with fear. I put my teacup down and bend forward, grabbing my chest. I inhale and exhale slowly.

"Are you okay?" Sonia rubs my back. "Are these the same as before?" I shake my head no. Suddenly there's a loud crash, followed by the sounds of breaking plates.

"No!" Rebeka screams and cries, grabbing the wall for support with one hand and clutching her chest with the other. "Goddess, no! Please no!" Her yowls and sobs are heard throughout the packhouse.

"Go, I'm fine." I instruct Sonia as I catch my breath from my pain.

Everyone comes running, including Alpha, Luna, and my parents. My parents rush to my side when they see me bent over.

"Is it the same pain as before?" My dad asks while he and mom sit on either side of me.

"No... something bad happened." Tears fall down my cheeks as I listen to Rebeka's pain-filled cries.

It's been a long and tortuous four hours since Rebeka and I started experiencing pain. We have heard nothing, not even from Kelsey. My dad says that is normal, that the battlefield can be chaotic, and the last thing anyone thinks is to call home. I wait in the common area of the packhouse, figuring I'll be able to hear any news here first.

They took Rebeka to the clinic and gave her a sedative to calm her nerves, and Sonia is caring for her twins. Now, she is being escorted through the packhouse with Alpha and Luna on either side of her. They're holding her up while she walks. They're being followed by a couple of omegas carrying luggage. My heart sinks watching her walk by and the blank stare on her face. Her face is red and swollen, and her eyes are bloodshot from crying. My gut screams something bad has happened. I feel so helpless.

As I watch Rebeka being escorted through the packhouse my phone rings, startling me. With Shaking hands I fumble with my phone, dropping it in my lap before flipping it open.

"Hello?" My voice shakes from fear.

"Hello, love." He says through heavy breath.

"Ian!" I exclaim as the tears flow. I never thought I'd appreciate hearing his voice as much as I do right now.

Ian

I've never felt so helpless as I do right now, sitting next to my best friend... fuck... he's more like a brother than a friend. Sitting next to my brother as he lays unconscious, hooked up to a thousand tubes, is killing me. Everything happened so fast, and in the blink of an eye, Zane is fighting for his life.

We had moved in and flushed out Alpha David from hiding. He refused to go down without a fight. So, we gave him one hell of a fight. After ten long days of battling, Zane ended it all by ripping Alpha David's heart out. After hearing of his death, his followers began surrendering one by one. The battle was finally over, and we could finally relax. We rescued the Luna, who was on death's door. Her finger was gangrene, and she hadn't been given water or food in three days. The doctors expect her to make a full recovery.

Zane and I were making our way through Emerald Lake's village, along with five warriors from the royal palace and Prince Malachi. Twenty of Alpha David's loyal supporters, who had initially surrendered without incident, ambushed us. These fuckers didn't fight fair, either. They used bows and arrows and knives made from silver and dipped in wolfsbane. Angry that we had killed their precious Alpha, they wanted revenge in his honor.

With arrows whizzing around us, we fight in our wolf form. We quickly take control of the fighting on the ground. This group is not trained fighters, and it shows. Suddenly my wolf, Alex, is hit with a searing pain through his left front leg. We look down and see an arrow hanging out of our flesh and fur. Then I hear Max, Zane's wolf, cry out in pain from behind us. *Shit!* We turn to find Max laying on the ground with an arrow in his side. My heart races. I have to get to him.

Alex shifts back into our human form, giving me full control. I remove the arrow from my arm. Luckily for me, it's just a minor flesh wound, but that silver tip hurts like a motherfucker. When I get to Max, he staggers to his feet while the palace warriors provide cover and protection.

"Here buddy, let me get this out of you." I grab the arrow, and with one swift move, pull it from his side. Like the arrow that hit me, it's just a minor wound. He yelps from the pain, but like the tough bastard he is, he recovers quickly.

I quickly shift, giving Alex full control as we find ourselves surrounded by fifty more werewolves in their human form. They're wielding knives, swords, axes, maces, and other medieval weapons. Where the hell did they get these weapons, the local museum? The fighting is intense and chaotic, as more of our warriors and palace warriors join in on the fight.

I hear Kelsey shout through our open mindlink to find the ones shooting arrows at our heads and destroy them. Max and Alex, along with the original five palace warriors, are getting exhausted and slowing down. Alex is concentrating on the two in front of us and never saw the bastard with the silver dagger aimed right for our chest... but Max did. He jumped in between the dagger wielding bastard and Alex. Max took the full brunt of the dagger to his shoulder, but he made sure to rip that bastard's throat out.

Max suddenly becomes too weak to continue and shifts back to his human form. And that was the moment I knew Zane's life was in danger. Rushing to Zane's side, I was hit with two arrows that stopped me in my tracks and dropped me to the ground. Too weak to continue, Alex shifts back to our human form, giving me control again. That's when it occurred to me, the arrows were dipped in wolfsbane, and Zane just took a huge dose saving me.

I push through the pain and crawl to him when I see a mace wielding lunatic aim for Zane's head. Time slows down, leaving me feeling like I'm watching a movie in slow motion. Zane is too weak to move, and fear spreads across his face. He raises his arms, shielding his face and bracing for impact. I try to crawl faster as I scream and shout for warriors to help, but everyone is in the heat of battle. As the mace makes its way towards Zane's head, Alpha Oliver's ten-year-old son appears out of nowhere, carrying a large wooden medieval shield. He throws his tiny body over Zane's, holding onto the shield with everything he has in him. The force from the mace impacting the shield knocks the boy unconscious. All I can see are his tiny motionless legs between Zane's body and the shield. Somehow, I'm able to scramble to my feet, only to feel the searing pain from two arrows hitting me before my world goes black.

The battle ended as quickly as it started. Even though I'm fading in and out of consciousness, I'm still aware of the chaos surrounding me. All I can think is, I have to get to Zane, who is just mere feet from me. A palace warrior pulls two arrows out of my body, and I flip on to my belly. With every bit of strength I can muster, I push through the pain and crawl through blood saturated ground to Zane's lifeless body. He has six arrows sticking out of his body, and he is not breathing. Warriors rush him and me along with the other wounded to Emerald Lake's hospital for medical treatment, and that's where we are today.

Every arrow that hit him didn't cause significant damage, but was laced with wolfsbane, which made him and Max deathly ill. So far, the doctors have resuscitated him twice. He's had two seizures that caused him to convulse violently, and I haven't left his side. I forced them to treat my wounds right here, next to Zane. I won't give anyone a chance to kill him.

After the final skirmish with Alpha David's most loyal followers, all one hundred lay dead. Sadly, over half were young teens, around thirteen years old. I'm sickened over that fact, that so many young ones had to die, and for what? A blood hungry alpha hell bent on destroying a smaller territory, for his own selfish gains. We lost two warriors, and the palace lost five. *Please, Moon Goddess, please let Zane pull through.*

"Hey," Kelsey steps next to me, offering me a coffee. "It's typical hospital shit, but it's hot and has caffeine in it."

"Thank you." I take the coffee. "How are you?" I ask, looking him over. He's covered in blood.

"Nothing major. Rebeka, Alpha, and Luna are on their way. I talked with Sonia," he sighs. "Please call my sister. She knows you got hurt... she felt it. The same way Rebeka felt when Zane stopped breathing. She's worried sick." He squeezes my shoulder.

"Shit! You're right," I sigh out running my hand through my hair. "I forgot... I," Kelsey interrupts me before I can finish my thought.

"Had your hands busy?" He smiles, "yeah, I know, and she knows too. Go. It's my turn to be by his side."

I step out of Zane's room into the hall. My fucking nerves are shot and my hands are trembling. I grab my phone and dial Kate's number. My stomach churns in antsicipation of her answering the phone. All I want is to hear the sound of her sweet voice. The ringing stops and I hear her fumbling with her phone.

"Hello?" Kate's voice is trembling.

"Hello, love." I say, fighting back the emotions and tears.

"Ian!" She shouts and cries. Tears escape down my cheek, hearing her excitement. I miss her so much. Her voice is like a breath of fresh air to me.

"Yes, love." I cry. This is the first time in my life, crying in front of someone. I was raised to be tough and tough meant sucking it up, dealing with it, and absolutely no fucking crying. But here I am, crying on the phone at the sound of my mate's voice.

"How bad are you hurt?" I can hear the love and genuine concern for my safety in her voice.

"Not too bad, still weak from the wolfsbane in my system." I sniffle back the tears.

"Oh, Ian... I felt it and I was so scared I'd never see you again. How's Zane?" Her voice once again trembles. Emotions build in my chest hearing her say she was afraid she'd never see me again. I love this woman with every ounce of my being.

"He's hurt real bad, love. Real bad." I slowly inhale and exhale, trying to control my emotions.

"But he's alive?" She whispers.

"Barely." I close my eyes and drop my head to the floor. I don't want to worry her. Zane is like a brother to her. We all grew up together, and she has always been the one tagging along in everything that we did.

"Oh Goddess," she gasps. "I knew it was bad, because Rebeka collapsed in pain about the same time that I felt yours, and she kept screaming please no, please no. Alpha, Luna, and her... they left about twenty minutes ago."

"That's good. Zane needs his mate if he's going to recover fully. Listen, love... I need to get back to Zane. I'll check in with you daily, okay?"

As much as I don't want to end the call with her, it's physically painful talking with her right now. Goddess, I want her here next to me. I need to feel her arms wrapped around me, holding me tight, letting me know everything is going to be alright. I'm hit with the guilt of knowing that I'm fine and Zane may never feel the warmth of his mate's touch. All because he saved me. I don't deserve to be saved. So much of the past was me being a selfish prick, and Zane protecting me. Why Zane? It should be me laying on that fucking hospital table, not him. I don't deserve to be fine; I deserve to be dead.

"Of course, please take care of Zane. Give my brother a hug for me." She says through hitched breath.

"Yes, love, I will. I'll talk to you soon. Kate, I love you to the moon and back." I wipe the tears that have escaped down my cheek. Never in a million years could I have ever imagined that Kate would have such an effect on me.

"Ok. I... I... I will talk to you soon." She pauses, then hangs up the phone. I felt like she was going to say something else, and I'm saddened that she didn't. Will she ever be able to say those three little words that used to come so easy to her? The words that I abused and tossed around at will. Those same three little words have so much more meaning now than they ever did.

CHAPTER THIRTY-FOUR

THE SITUATION

July 2004

Kate

JUST AS IAN PROMISED, he has called me twice a day every day. Rebeka, along with Alpha and Luna, has been by Zane's side for fourteen days now. Day three, he opened his eyes and spoke. Ian says he has improved so much in a short amount of time for a guy who died twice. They're all coming home today, and the pack is getting ready to greet them with a huge dinner of fried chicken... Ian, Zane, and Kelsey's favorite.

Three days ago, I started running a temperature and having full body aches. Two days ago, I let my parents know what was going on, and the first thing my dad ask was the pain the same as before when Ian was cheating on me. I told him no, that I don't think that this has anything to do with Ian. It's a fair question though, since Ian doesn't have the best track record.

Yesterday my fever spiked, and I began having full body pain. They would last for a few minutes, then go away. When I spoke with Ian yesterday, he asked if I was ok, because he was feeling off, and had the feeling he needed to be home immediately. I told him I wasn't feeling good, that I thought the mate bond was strained, making me ill. He offered to come home a day early, but I told him no, that I'd be fine and am staying at my parents' house until he comes home.

Today, I can't get out of bed because of the fever and body pain. Dr. Patrice came by and took some blood so she could run tests. I just want Ian home... I need him.

Ian

"You've had enough of a nap, mister." I whisper in Zane's ear. "Today your father and I both noticed Rebeka's scent has changed ever so slightly. We both think she's with pup." I take a deep breath and blow out slowly. Smiling, I think of Kate and her calming breaths she does when she's feeling anxious. They really work. I'm ready to get home to her. "So, you better wake the fuck up, or some other son of a bitch is going to raise your pups." I state through gritted teeth. It's been four long days since I've seen his eyes or heard his voice.

"Like hell he will." Zane mumbles so quietly I can barely make out his words, even with my exceptional hearing.

"That's it, bro," I fight back the tears. "Now open your eyes." My heart skips a beat as I watch his eyes flutter back to life.

"You better not being lying about her scent change." He slightly turns his head to look at me. I laugh. This fucker was at death's door, and now all he cares about is the pup his mate is carrying.

"I'd never lie about that. Your parents took her to get something to eat. Your mother told her, and I quote, you both need to be healthy when my son wakes up." I hold his hand in mine. He just smiles and nods his head.

"Help me sit up, please." I lift the top of the hospital bed until he signals that it's good enough. I hold a cup with a straw for him so he can drink some water. He's still so weak, but he's alive... I can't believe he's alive. "Where's Kelsey?"

"He is building your reputation for ruthlessness. We have burned all loyal followers alive. A few adults using young teens to do their dirty work orchestrated the attack on us." I put my head down. This is the part of war that I hate.

"Zane!" Kelsey shouts, running through the door. He leaps and lands on Zane, squeezing him in a tight bear hug.

"Bro! He's been awake for five minutes. Get your big ass off him before you suffocate him." I laugh while trying to pull Kelsey off Zane.

Soon Rebeka rushes into the room, leaping into Zane's arm. She is crying hysterically, so relieved to see her mate is awake and talking. It's a beautiful sight when she tells him he is going to be a father again. All of this is making me want Kate so much more.

Like I do everyday, I check in with my Kate. After two rings she quickly answers.

"Hello handsome," Kate's voice is such music to my ears. I can't wait until I'm holding her in my arms.

"Hello beautiful," I sigh and lay back on my bed. "Are you ready for me to be home?"

"Yes, it's been almost a month since I've seen you." She says through heavy breath.

"Love, are you okay? I've had the feeling something is wrong the past couple of days." I sit up. I've had this nagging feeling that something is wrong with Kate. Hearing her breathe heavy, my feelings are confirmed.

"I'm fine. I think it's just the strain on the mate bond making you feel that way." She sighs. I have a feeling there is more that she is not telling me, but I don't want to push her.

"I can come home today... I'm just an eleven-hour flight and a two-hour car ride away from you." I open my laptop to search for flights.

"Don't be silly. Everyone is planning a huge fried chicken dinner in the packhouse tomorrow to welcome you all home. Get a good night's sleep. Your flight is at six a.m. tomorrow." She giggles, but even that feels forced.

"Okay, love. I can't wait to see you tomorrow." I hang the phone up and as the worry sets in, I wonder if I should just jump a flight now. Fuck, the shit I put her through in the past. How will I ever make it up to her?

Alex has been unsettled the last thirty minutes of our drive back to our territory. He has begged to be let out so he can just run home. He's not normally like this. We've taken many trips to Europe, and he's never wanted to run the rest of the way home. This is odd behavior, even for him. He howls in my head as we drive through the front gates of our territory. Truthfully, the asshole is giving me a headache.

I get out of the SUV in front of the packhouse and stretch my legs. It's so good to be home. I'm just feet away from holding her in my arms. I reach into the SUV and grab the bouquet and box of chocolates that I picked up for her at the airport. As I turn to go to the back of the SUV to grab my battle bag, I'm hit by what feels like a fucking dump truck and slammed up against the side of the SUV. It knocks the wind out of me as the flowers and candy hit the ground.

I hear gasps and shouting from all around, and when I can focus, I realize that I'm staring into the raging face of Gamma Earnest.

"What the fuck have you done now, boy?" He shouts and slams me against the SUV again. "I trusted you with my daughter. You gave me your fucking word that you'd do right by her this time." He shouts and snaps in my face as my father and Alpha try to pull him off me.

"What are you talking about? I haven't done shit to anyone!" I shout, trying to remove his forearm from my throat. This bastard is strong. He's like a brick wall.

"My daughter is sick, and this is your fault. I'm going to fucking kill you, just as I promised I would." He applies pressure to my throat.

"Sick! Kate's sick?" I land a right hook to the side of his face, knocking him back just enough to free myself from his grasp. "Why the fuck didn't you lead with the fact that *my* mate is sick?" I shove him back and take off for Gamma Earnest's house... to my Kate.

"Kate! Kate!" I shout, running through the front door. Her heavenly scent hits my nose and I follow it upstairs to her bedroom.

She's laying there on the bed, pale white, and drenched in sweat.

"Ian!" Her mom shouts, "You need to leave!" She steps in between Kate and me, stomping her foot and pointing to the door.

"I'm not going anywhere. Kate is my mate and my responsibility. I've done nothing wrong." I raise my voice and growl, much like my father does when he is in Beta mode. A shocked look crosses her face. I've never spoken to her like this before. As she stares into my eyes, her face softens and I can see understanding in her eyes. Without speaking a word to one another, she knows that I'm telling her the truth. I haven't so much as looked at another woman. Her bottom lips quivers as tears roll down her cheek before she steps out from between Kate and me. "Thank you," I touch her arm and whisper before rushing to Kate's side.

'Zane... Kelsey, please keep Gamma Earnest from getting between us.' I mindlink them both.

'Done. Take care of your mate.' Zane mindlinks back.

"Ian..." Kate opens her eyes and smiles at me. "I'm so glad you're home." She flinches in pain.

"I am, love. You're burning up." I rub the palm of my hand across her forehead and face.

"Has Dr. Patrice seen her?" I ask without taking my eyes off Kate.

"Yes. Her bloodwork shows everything is normal. We've given her medicine to bring her temperature down, but nothing is working. She just keeps asking for you." Her mom sniffles, fighting her emotions and fears.

I understand why Kate's parents had the nasty reaction now. They've ruled out any medical issues, so the only logical choice would be that I must have been unfaithful again. I hate that my history with Kate will always be in the back of everyone's mind, but it's no one's fault but my own.

The only thing I'm thinking is I need to bring her body temperature down... and quick. Scooping Kate up in my arms, I head for the bathroom. There's a commotion downstairs, multiple male voices shouting, with Gamma Earnest being the loudest. I really don't blame his anger. I have not always had Kate's best interest at heart, and I've done some real shitty things to his daughter. But now, she is the only one who is important.

In the bathroom, I turn a cold shower on and lay down in the tub, with Kate on top of me. She gasps as the cold water hits her flesh.

"I'm sorry, love, but we have to get your body temperature down." I rub her face and arms with my hands and soon she relaxes in my arms, allowing the cold water to do its magic.

"Thank you, Ian." She rolls on to her side and looks up at me. "I'm feeling better." She coos and rubs her hands along my arm and up the sleeve of my tee shirt. "Did you know that I'm an arm girl?" She giggles, as Kate's mom, Gamma Earnest, Zane, and Kelsey rush into the bathroom.

"Earnest, stop." Kate's mom shouts. I do my best to not focus on the chaos at the door. If I have to, I will fight Kate's father right here and right now to protect my mate.

"Move!" Luna Martha commands. She uses her Luna tone to gain everyone's attention, commanding them to follow orders. Whenever she uses this tone, Alpha is never too far away.

"Kate, sweetheart." She kneels beside the tub and runs her hand across Kate's forehead. "Look at me, please." Kate does as she's told, and Luna Martha looks into her eyes and mouth. She watches as Kate coos in my arms and takes notice of her hand up my sleeve. She smiles sweetly and rubs her cheek. "Better now that you're in your mate's arms?"

"Mine," Kate nods her head, then rolls back onto her side, tucking her head back into my chest.

"Yes, he is, sweetheart." She stands, turning the shower off. "Ian, you'll need to get your mate to the fishing cabin. Gamma Earnest, please see they are guarded by *mated* warriors." I lie still with my mate on my chest, not quite understanding why Luna told me to take Kate to the fishing cabin.

"What's going on, Martha?" Kate's mom asks casually, which is rarely done in public, but she is not asking her Luna a question, she is asking her friend and confidant.

"Honey, she's in heat." Luna Martha replies.

"What?" Kate's mom sounds shocked. "I've been in heat multiple times, and I've never had an experience like this."

"Neither have I, but I assure you that Kate is in heat. Our heats have never gotten like this, because our mates have always been right there to... to... take care of the situation." Luna Martha replies, and Kate giggles.

"You have to take care of my situation, Ian." She whispers and we both laugh.

"Tough job, but someone has to do it," I kiss her forehead.

"My daughter is not going anywhere with him." Gamma Earnest's voice is harsh and demanding. I hear heavy footsteps enter the small bathroom; I don't even have to look up to realize who it is.

"It's okay, Nathaniel." She pauses, probably mindlinking her mate to calm him. Gamma Earnest just made a grave mistake by being disrespectful to his Luna in front of her overprotective mate. "Earnest." Luna Martha takes a deep breath before she continues talking to her friend. "I know that you only have your daughter's best interest in mind, and you feel it's your duty as a father to protect your pup until your last breath. The truth is, Ian has done everything he can to prove to everyone that he is worthy of Kate's love. We all know that these two have a past... a dark one that many don't overcome. Look at your daughter. Being in her mate's arms has made her pains and high body temperature more bearable. No one is going to stop nature or Moon Goddess' plans for them. Not you, nor I... no one." The room is so silent that you could hear a pin drop.

"Why though?" Kate's mom asks, "Why did her heat come on like this?"

"My guess is that they have not fully repaired the damaged mate bond." She sighs, turning to me, "Ian, you two have not mated since you've reconnected... correct?"

"Correct Luna." I answer. This is probably one of the more humiliating conversations I've had with Luna.

"My guess," she turns away from me and continues her conversation about Kate and me like we aren't even here. "To fully repair the damaged mate bond after that one," she points at me, "damaged it so bad, they'll need to complete the mating and marking all over again. It's just a theory, but that's what I believe will have to happen. Right now, their marks are so faded, they're not visible... not like any of ours anyway." Luna Martha turns back to me. "Why are you still here?"

"I promised Kate we would wait until..." Luna Martha interrupts me before I can say another word.

"Time is up, nature decided for the two of you. I hope you realize now that you're here Kate's fever has broken. Kate will now go into a phase of heat that we," she points between Kate's mom and herself, "understand. She will be the one who will aggressively take what she wants." She pauses and sighs, "she will also emit a pheromone that will alert all unmated males of her heat. Are you looking to battle again so soon?" Zane and Kelsey giggle like schoolgirls. "Knock it off, you two. Gamma Earnest... warriors... SUV. Time is of essence here. You don't want what is going to happen under your roof in the room right next to you, do you?" Luna Martha's words cause Alpha to laugh.

"SUV is downstairs now." Gamma Earnest says in defeat. I stand and step out of the bathtub.

"I have done nothing to Kate. I made you a promise to do right by your daughter, and I intend to do just that." Looking Gamma Earnest in his eyes, I speak frankly to him. Like a man protecting his mate... like the beta that I am. He nods, then I turn and pick my mate up to carry her downstairs.

"Wait!" Luna Martha demands. "Kate honey, where is that cheap piece of glass... and yes, that's all it is. That's all that the human thought you are worth. Where is it?" I put Kate down and she disappears into her room, returning seconds later, placing the ring that frat boy gave her in the palm of Luna's hand. "Thank you." I pick Kate back up.

"I can walk, Ian." Kate protests.

"I know... I would just rather carry you right now." She doesn't argue, just nods. I'm about halfway down the stairs when I hear Luna Martha speak again.

"Zane, Kelsey, make sure this gets back to its rightful owner." There is disgust in Luna Martha's voice.

"Yes, mother." Zane replies.

Chapter Thirty-Five

YOU WANT ME

July 2004

Ian

"Wait, Kate, wait." I grab her hands from the hem of my soaking wet tee-shirt. Pushing her hands back into her body and stopping her from pulling the tee-shirt off me.

"What?" She frustratingly sighs out. Annoyed at me, she throws herself down on the bed in the fishing cabin, crossing her arms, and glaring at me. I bite my bottom lip to keep from laughing out loud at the little fit she is throwing. All I can think is, once again after returning home from a mission, she's mad at me. This time she's throwing herself at me instead of coffee mugs. I'll take it as a win. She is so damn cute right now, with her wet hair and wet clothes. Damn, she's so fucking hot.

"Listen, this is not how I wanted this to go. I want you to want me, not because nature is forcing this." I wave my hands in front of me. The fact is, I want her so badly, I can taste it, but I don't want her thinking that I'm using the mate bond to manipulate her feelings about me. I don't want her regretting anything.

"What did you say to me when you left?" She tilts her head.

"Ummm…" I try to think back.

"Think about what you want to say and *do* to me." She licks her lips and pushes her breasts out. "I've slept in your bed, surrounded by your scent every day since you've been gone. All I've done is think about the things I want to do to you. Especially when I… touched myself in the middle of the night." She rubs her breasts through her wet tee-shirt. "Hell, I probably caused this heat because of all the things I was thinking." I'm fixated on her hard nipples poking through her wet shirt. "I had already decided that I wanted to mate with you, and if we didn't get interrupted… we would have… that night." She opens her legs slightly and leans back. "Now get over here and handle my situation like a good mate."

I stand in complete shock. It feels like my feet are cemented to the floor. I watch my mate with my mouth agape and my cock twitching to be released. Her eyes are black with lust and her full pink lips are begging to be kissed. Kate has never been this bold and demanding with me. Some men might want to run and hide, but I've never been so turned on.

"You want me?" I point to myself. "Not because nature is forcing you?" My breathing is heavy as excitement builds within me.

"Yes. I want you, Ian." She tilts her head back, exposing her neck to me. Her chest heaves up and down as the mate bond swirls around us.

"You touched yourself?" I whisper and gulp. My body slowly moves on its own towards her, as if the tethers of the mate bond are tightening and drawing me closer to her.

"Yes," her face and chest become red and flush as she flinches in pain. Her sweet floral scent hits my nose along with a slight earthy scent, driving my primal beast crazy with lust.

"Show me." I'm just inches from ravishing her.

"You want to watch me play with it?" Her tone is low and sultry as she scoots towards the headboard.

"Yes. Show me how you played with it while I was gone." I crawl onto the bed.

Smiling, she removes all her clothes and leans back on the headboard, spreading her legs wide for me. I position myself at her feet, my eyes fixed on her glistening, wet pussy. Putting her middle and ring fingers in her mouth, she coats them with her saliva. She bites her lower lip and runs her slick fingers up and down her entrance. With her other hand, she massages her breast and pinches her nipple, letting out a loud moan and hiss. Captivated, I can't take my eyes off her and the show she is giving me. I pull my tee-shirt over my head as she continues, dipping her fingers in and out, soaking them with her delicious juices.

"Ooooo," her fingers rub circles around her clit, before sliding back down between the folds of her entrance. She bucks her hips wildly as her fingers thrust in and out of her pussy.

I lick my lips and slip out of my wet jeans. I can't take it anymore and position myself between her thighs. She looks so fucking delicious. I'm having a hard time not cumming all over the place watching her play with herself.

"Mine," I growl, sucking her juices off her slick fingers. "Mmmm, so fucking good." I run my nose along her entrance, savoring the delicious scent of her arousal.

Forcefully, I plunge my tongue deep into the lips of her entrance. Fully claiming her as my own with every stroke of my tongue. She grabs my hair while her moans and groans get louder as I devour her. I suck on the slick folds of her entrance and tease her clit with my teeth. Flipping us over, I seat her firmly on my face.

"I want you to ride my face." I hold her hips down, forcing her full weight on me as my tongue continues its attack on her.

She grinds her wet pussy on my face as I lick and suck her clit. Her body shakes and trembles. She is close to climaxing. Her moans turn to screams before she pulls herself off my face, landing next to me.

"You're not getting away that easy." I plunge two fingers into her and attack her clit with my mouth. She fists my hair and screams my name as she climaxes hard.

"I need you," she says through heavy breath. "I need you inside me now." She spreads her legs wide for me.

"You want me to fuck you?" I grab her hips and I plunge my rock-hard cock deep inside her with one thrust. We both gasp and hiss at the sensation of me entering her. I pause, relishing in this moment being fully connected with her again. Being inside her feels like heaven. She moans as I pull out almost completely before slamming back inside her. Her breasts bounce with each forceful thrust. "You like it when I fuck you like this?" I continue plunging in and out with long, slow strokes.

"Yes," she gasps, "faster," she demands. I pick up the pace. "Faster," she repeats.

Following her commands, I grab her hips, holding them tight and continue to thrust in and out of her at a rapid pace. Her breasts bounce wildly as both our moans fill the surrounding air. With each thrust, our skin slaps together, making music of their own. Kate's juices spill out of her and down her ass as she climaxes again. I love the way she constricts and pulsates on my dick as she cums. I continue to rapidly plunge in and out of her, allowing her to ride out her orgasm, prolonging her euphoric high. Watching her while she climaxes brings me so much pleasure.

When she comes down from her high, I pull out, flipping her on her knees. I close her legs and enter with a single thrust. I pull her upper body up and into mine. She leans back, wrapping her arms around my neck and leans on my chest and slides up and down on my shaft. I match her rhythm and wrap one hand around her throat and the other pinching her nipples.

"You fucking love riding my dick, don't you?" I whisper in her ear, biting her neck with my front teeth.

"Yes… harder." She moans out.

I push her back down on all fours and pull her to the edge of the bed. Standing up behind her, I lift one of her legs and thrust in and out.

"I'm so close," I groan out while rubbing circles on her clit.

Her pussy pulsates as her body shakes and with one final hard thrust, we both fall over the edge. My head spins and my vision blurs as my cock shoots hot liquid inside her. She feels so good that I don't want to pull out of her.

"Lay down. I'll be right back." I lightly slap her ass before rushing off to the bathroom for a warm washcloth.

When I return, she is laying on her side with her head on the pillows, sound asleep. I laugh and think to myself that guys have the terrible reputation of falling asleep after sex. I clean her up with the warm washcloth, then lay down next to her. If this is any sign of what I have in store for me over the next seven days, I better get rest while I can.

Chapter Thirty-Six

SIX

July 2004

Kate

TODAY IS DAY EIGHT and I'm woken up by someone knocking on the door of the cabin. Ian and I haven't left the cabin, spoken to anyone, or left the bed in seven days. Slipping from Ian's grip, I climb out of bed and throw on his tee-shirt that has been laying on the ground for seven days. I open the door to find one red and one blue cooler. I look around. Whoever dropped these off is nowhere to be found. Bringing them both into the cabin, I open the red cooler first.

Immediately, the smell of pancakes and bacon hits my nose and my stomach growls so loud I swear the walls shake. Exploring the red cooler further, I also find sausage and cheese omelets, biscuits, honey, and warm syrup. All this mouthwatering food looks and smells delicious. For a moment, I contemplate just digging in before Ian wakes up. He wouldn't mind too much, right?

I close the red cooler, so the food stays warm. Opening the blue cooler, I discover water, orange juice, milk, creamer, sugar, coffee grounds, and a note.

Welcome back to the world.

Enjoy the food, fill up.

Lunch starts at noon.

We will have several protein-packed

foods perfect for expecting mothers.

Hopefully the heat took,

and we will have pups from all our

future leaders born at the same time.

Chef Marcie

After reading the note, excitement hits my chest. Are Rebeka and Sonia pregnant? I hope it's true. Rebeka is a wonderful mother to her twin girls, and I know she wants a huge family. Sonia is so amazing with the pups I've seen her around; I know she will be a perfect mother as well. Kelsey will make a good father; all he has to do is follow our dad's lead. I smile, thinking about my mom as a grandmother and the excitement she must feel right now, knowing there will be a pup for her to spoil soon.

Then I think about myself, and I get a little sad. The heat won't take because I'm on the pill. I've been on them since just after Ian and

I found out we were mates, and I never forget... wait. Shit, I haven't taken my pill since the fever started. *I FORGOT! Shit!*

Ian and I have never really talked about when we should start a family. Both of us want pups, but we just got back together. Are we ready? Am I ready? *Shit!* This stupid heat. *Why* did nature have to step in and complicate things? I know why because I wanted to take it slow... then I didn't... then I did... then I didn't. Since I couldn't seem to decide, nature stepped in and said, *'hold my beer, hun, I've got this.' Shit!* Will Ian be pissed, thinking I'm trying to trap him? Wait, trap him. How exactly? He found me, he pursued me, and...

My head is spinning. I've put myself into full panic mode doing the overthinking thing I do and am having a hard time breathing. I need to calm myself down before I pass out from a panic attack. Sitting down in a chair at the table, I take a deep breath in, hold it for a count of ten, then blow it out slowly. I do this several times before I feel the tension leave my body. Ian is my mate, the other half of my soul... whatever happens, we will get through it together. I continue sitting and practice my calming breaths.

I peek in at him and watch him sleep from the doorway of the bedroom. He looks so beautiful and blissful, like he is finally at peace. I watch as his chest rises and falls with each breath he takes. He has changed so much in the last two and a half years. He was a rotten boy in a man's body doing whatever he wanted, not caring who he hurt. The guilt he felt was only because he knew what he was doing was wrong. The man he has become is caring, loving, thoughtful, and truly remorseful about what he did in the past. He wants to be a better man... for me.

I turn the shower on and step under the hot water. We did nothing but have sex and sleep in our bodily fluids for the past seven days. A shower is definitely in the cards for this morning. Letting the hot water flow over my head and down my body, washing seven days of sex, sweat, and our bodily fluids down the drain. I can't believe my appetite for him was insatiable. I couldn't get enough... still can't. Even this morning, I want him.

Heat for me is finally over, but I still find my core throbbing and craving him this morning. *How can that be?* There was no time for eating, only sex. Rough sex at that. I had the desire to feel pain each time he thrust in and out of me, which is not normal for me. *Maybe it was the heat.* I usually like slow and soft... but now... I feel different somehow. More confident, almost, something about the heat changed me. I think I like it.

"There you are." Ian pulls the shower curtain back and joins me in the shower.

"Did you think I ran away?" I stick my tongue out, teasing him.

"Nope." He spins us so he is under the water, "I know neither of us will ever be too far from the other again." He kisses my nose then lifts his head up, letting the hot water wash over him. "Oh, hell yeah."

"Same," I laugh. Watching his body and the way the water rolls off his muscular build, my core throbs harder. How does this magnificent man belong to me?

"How are you feeling?" He puts shampoo in his hair, then hands the bottle to me.

"Heat is over and I'm feeling normal again." I wash my hair.

"And your body?" He rinses his hair.

"A little stiff... I'm a little sore down there." I point to my core before he puts me under the water.

"I'm sure you are. I didn't know you liked it so rough." He puts conditioner in my hair, then puts himself back under the water.

"I don't... didn't..." I laugh, "I like it now." He washes his body.

"So, you want more?" He fills the washcloth with more body wash then washes my body.

"Yes, I want more." I move his hand to my core, "and more," I rub his fingers along my slit, "and more." He dips his fingers in and out, then up to my nub, rubbing circles around it.

"Mmmm, you're a little sex kitten, aren't you?" He growls and lifts my leg. "So fucking wet already for me."

"Always," I moan and gasp as his member enters me.

"Slow is still good." His hot breath teases my skin as he whispers in my ear. "Slow and steady, so I can feel every inch of you." He presses me up against the shower wall while slowly pumping in and out of me. "Slow, so I can enjoy your wetness." He moves my hips, and he takes small strokes up and forward. Goosebumps form across every inch of my body. His shaft is rubbing my sweet spot inside and I feel like I'm going to explode. "I fucking love being inside you, filling every inch of you with me." I moan as he bites and sucks my neck.

"Ian." I moan. "Please mark me. I want to be yours in every way." I hold on to his biceps as he continues slowly pumping in and out.

Each move he makes feels like our souls are melting into one. The connection I feel with him is on a spiritual level, on a plane that I have never felt with him before. He pulls me tight to his body and licks my marking spot. Then I feel the hot pain as his canines enter my flesh. The pain is brief before turning in to pure bliss. My head becomes dizzy and my legs tremble as I'm hit with the most wonderful earth shattering orgasm. This climax is like none I've ever felt, a true transcendent experience. Ian holds me tight, my body shakes as electric pulses move through my body like lightening bolts. My body feels weightless like I'm soaring high in the sky. My core massages his shaft begging to be filled with his seed.

Still in a euphoric state I elongate my canines and sink them into Ian's neck. He growls and groans, his muscles tensing up with each thrust into me. Ian's grunts echo off the walls. He presses my body hard against the shower wall and fills me with his hot cum. With each grunt, I can feel his shaft pulsate as it releases. His release is so hard that it causes me pain as his member pulsates, releasing his hot liquid inside me. The pain turns to pleasure and my core squeezes his member tight, demanding every drop from him. When he fully comes down, I remove my canines and lick the spot, sealing the wound.

We stand still looking into each other's eyes, still connected to each other. The lust has turned to love. A love so strong that it can move mountains. A love that stories are written about. A love worth fighting for. Our souls have finally joined together, becoming one. As we stare into the windows of our soul, we both say "Mine."

After getting dressed, I walk out of the bathroom to find Ian making coffee. He has unpacked all the food and made a simple place setting for each of us, complete with a glass of orange juice.

"Where did the clothes come from?" I watch him move around the tiny kitchen.

"I had Kelsey drop some clothes off for us." Ian points to a seat at the table.

"Good thinking." I take a sip of orange juice.

"Everything okay, love?" He looks into my eyes, placing my coffee in front of me.

"I should probably tell you... but I don't want you to get mad." I take a sip of my coffee while he puts an omelet on my plate.

"Go ahead." He nods and looks at me inquisitively.

"I forgot to take my pill... it's been eleven days." I fidget with my fork.

"That's why you're afraid I'll get mad?" He kneels next to me. "I was going to flush them today, anyway." He rubs my cheek and winks. "I told you I couldn't wait until you let me put a pup in here," he places his hand on my stomach. "I wasn't lying. You're going to make a great... no... phenomenal mom."

"Oh, Ian." I sigh. This man just gets more and more perfect, and my heart is so full right now.

"I've been practicing the *look* I'm giving our daughters' future mate." He narrows his eyes, purses his lip, then curls one corner of his mouth up. I laugh, looking at the face he is making. "It needs to be perfected." He takes a bite of bacon.

"How many do you want?" I take a bite of my omelet.

"Six," he nods his head while sipping his coffee.

"Six?" I cough, almost choking on a piece of egg. "I was thinking two."

"Two? Nah... how about we meet in the middle, four?" He wiggles his eyebrows and rubs my thigh.

"You secretly wanted four the entire time, didn't you?" I tilt my head and raise my eyebrow.

"Maybe," he takes a large bite of pancake.

"What if I'm stuck on two?" I lean into him.

"Then I will wear you down until you give me four." We both laugh. I have as much of a desire to please him as he has for me. We both know that we will be happy whether the number is two or four.

"I love you, Ian. With all my heart, I love you so much. The way you've changed, not just for me, but for us. My heart is just so full." I put my hand on his thigh as tears of happiness roll down my face. Ian looks like I've knocked the wind out of him. My chair screeches across the floor as he pulls me close to him. He cups the back of my neck with one hand and my face with the other.

"You have no idea how long I've waited to hear you say those words." Tears form in his eyes. "They're like music to my ears. I love you more than life itself. You'll never have to wait to hear me say those words to you. Everything I do until the day I die will make you feel love... so much more than words can ever describe." I'm holding on to his every word and we both have tears rolling down our face. It looks like after so much time and hardship we have finally made it. We have beat all odds despite what anyone else thought. He pulls me onto his lap for an emotional kiss. The type of kiss you feel in your soul. The type of kiss that assures you that not everyone is a lost cause.

CHAPTER THIRTY-SEVEN

THAT'S MY GIRL

July 2004

Kate

AFTER IAN AND I spend more quality time alone in the cabin, I notify the house manager that we are done with the fishing cabin, and it needs to be cleaned. We walk into the busy dining hall at the packhouse hand in hand. We join our families for lunch with Alpha and Luna. It thrills everyone to see us both with fresh marks on our necks.

I squeal with excitement as Rebeka and Sonia both confirm they're pregnant, and their due dates are just days apart. I smile, watching Zane, Kelsey, and Ian have their own reunion as Ian congratulates them both on the pups. It feels so good to smile and laugh with the most important people in my life.

"I know you said you were on the pill, but you stopped when the fever started. There's still a chance the heat took." Rebeka says as she rubs my belly as if she is willing a pup in there.

"Yeah. My cousin's friend's sister's best friend stopped taking the pill and boom, pregnant two weeks later. I think it took too." Sonia nods her head then joins Rebeka in rubbing my belly.

"Why are you both rubbing my belly?" I laugh and look between the two of them.

"Because this is contagious." Rebeka says, pointing at her belly.

"Can you imagine all of us being pregnant together?" Sonia squeals with excitement.

"Well, I guess we'll just have to wait and see." I sigh, hoping that the heat took. Looking down, I place my hand on my belly and rub circles around it. Wondering if there is a life growing inside me. Ian places his hand on top of mine and gently squeezes.

"There is a life in there. Don't ask me how I know, but I just do. I love you both so much." Ian whispers in my ear, then kisses my neck.

Looking around this table at the smiling faces of the most important people in my life, my heart overflows with love. I honestly never thought that I'd be back here, sitting next to Ian as his mate. Everything that Ian and I have been through was absolute hell, and I don't wish it on my enemies. Ian's indiscretions broke us, like a shattered ceramic vase. His desire to change... to be a better man, has pieced us back together. And like a ceramic vase that has been pieced back together, we are whole again. Even though we are whole, we are not without imperfections and scars. Together, we are perfectly imperfect, and that's what will make our love unique. I admire how he has learned from his mistakes and grown so much in a short amount of time. Even when I was reluctant to give him a last chance, he never gave up on us. I'm so glad he didn't, because look at everything I'd be missing out on right now.

After a long, lingering lunch, the six of us head to the gym and training grounds. The guys want to get some training in, and us girls want to get some cardio in together before Rebeka and Sonia are too big and pregnant.

"We're just going to be upstairs for an hour. Are you sure you'll be okay?" Ian pulls me into his chest.

"I'll be fine. I've been here a million times by myself. How about you, Mr. Cling?" I laugh and wrinkle my nose at him.

"I'm sweating bullets over here," Ian wipes his forehead and we both laugh.

"Come on, big guy, the first time is the toughest." Kelsey laughs, pulling him away from me.

Rebeka, Sonia, and I do more talking and laughing than cardio, but I don't care. I'm just enjoying being with the two of them, without needing to distract each other from not knowing where our mates are or if they will make it home safe. There's something comforting in knowing that our men are just upstairs training. After an hour, we spot the guys lifting weights and decide ogling some eye candy is much better than cardio and head for our mates.

We take a seat on the floor a few feet from the guys and continue chatting amongst ourselves, while each of our mates flex and pose for us. In between the chatter and laughter I hear a familiar high-pitched, nails on the chalkboard voice that causes my heart to race. Nikki.

"I mean, it looks like everything has worked out." Nikki says to the woman sitting next to her.

I could go a lifetime without hearing her voice or seeing her obnoxious face. I don't put all the blame on her for what went down between Ian and me, but she definitely played a role in it all. The worst part is that she has no remorse for what she did to me. Quite the opposite. She enjoyed tormenting me.

'It was Nikki who said I was in Vegas, wasn't it?' Ian mindlinks me.

'Yes... I overheard a phone conversation she was having with Dante about being on a boys' trip to Vegas.' I mindlink and look up at him.

'Bitch! She knew exactly what she was doing. I'll have a word with Dante about his mate.' Ian mindlinks. The weights make a loud crash as he frustratingly drops them on the floor.

'No, don't. I won't let her get to me anymore. Now get back to your workout and pay me no attention.' I mindlink and smile.

"Ya know, if she would have just asked how to please him. I mean she knew our history, why not just ask how he is in bed?" Nikki says loud enough for everyone to hear. Is she trying to get my attention? *Why?* Rebeka and Sonia get awkwardly quiet and watch me.

"I'm going to go to the restroom." I pat Sonia on the leg and smile at Rebeka. They both nod and smile.

"Hey, I'll be right back. I need some air." I mindlink Ian before standing and walking away. As I pass Nikki and her friend, she speaks to me.

"Oh hey, Kate. I didn't see you there. Nice mark." Nikki's voice sends shivers down my spine as she and her friend laugh.

Hearing them laugh at my expense makes my blood boil and stops me in my tracks. I slowly turn towards her. As rage flows through my veins like a poison, I can feel heat rising throughout my body. I feel like something in me has finally had enough and snapped. I'm sure she thinks I'll run, just like I used to when it came to confrontation. Not this time. All the years of torment, animosity, resentment, irritation, bitterness, and raw emotions boil just below the surface. Every ill feeling I have pushed down and suppressed over the years erupts within me in a violent explosion of fury and rage.

I scream and leap on top of her, punching her as hard as I can, right in the middle of her nose. Feeling my fist make contact with her face brings me so much joy. Hearing the sounds of bones cracking, Sasha shouts, 'More', in my head. I pull my arm back and slam my fist into her face again. Her nose bursts open, splattering blood on my face which sends me into a wrath filled frenzy.

Laughing, I grab her hair with one hand and lock my thighs around her waist and punch her again and again. Words are coming from my mouth, but in my rage filled fury, I can't hear anything past the sounds of my knuckles connecting with her flesh.

There're more screams and shouts coming from all around me, but I continue to punch her mercilessly. I want to hurt her as much as she has hurt me. She needs to feel the pain she inflicted on me for so many years. I continue punching and laughing when someone tries pulling me off her, but I'm locked in tight. I'm nowhere near done with her. Today is the day she will feel my wrath.

"Kathrine," my dad's voice booms behind me, but I'm not done rearranging this bitch's face, and I hit her again.

I feel multiple hands on me, stopping my fist from flying. They finally rip me off Nikki, but not before I take a handful of hair from her head. My entire body shakes uncontrollably and tears roll down my cheek from the rush of adrenalin as years of bitterness leave me. I look to my left and right and see that my dad and Beta Charles are on either side of me with my feet dangling in the air as they carry me away from the chaos I created.

"About fucking time, kiddo." Beta Charles whispers in my ear.

"How'd that feel, sugar?" My dad whispers in the other.

"Fucking great, daddy." I smile.

"That's my girl," he shakes my arm. "That's my girl," his voice is low and filled with pride.

Ian

Hearing Nikki's voice and seeing Kate tense up, I put two and two together. After all these years, Nikki is still harassing Kate. I wish I would have seen Nikki for what she was back then... a bully. Nikki never loved me, but continued a sexual relationship with me, just to spite Kate.

For example, the night that Kate caught us together at the Autumn Moon Ball. Nikki was pissed that she and the other unmated wolves were ushered around the receiving line. She kept mindlinking me the entire night, telling me the same things she had been saying for months. How much she loves me and that I need to reject Kate, because she is a better match for me. She promised she'd stop mindlinking me if I joined her in the garden shack for five minutes.

I'll never understand why I just didn't block her out. In the garden shack, she put a condom on me, explaining how Kate wouldn't feel the infidelity. Stupid, I know.

After Kate ran out, Nikki laughed hysterically. She kept saying how the virgin deserved what she got. That's when I saw the true Nikki. Furious, I told her I never wanted to see her again and would try to have her banished from our territory. She thought that was hilarious and called me a pussy.

What I don't understand is why Nikki and her friend is here in the first place. They're not lifting weights and their mates are nowhere around us. Is she purposely trying to get a reaction from Kate? *Bitch.*

'It was Nikki who said I was in Vegas, wasn't it?' Watching Kate's body tense up, I mindlink her.

'Yes... I overheard a phone conversation she was having with Dante about being on a boys' trip to Vegas.' She mindlinks back and looks up at my face. I should have known that Nikki was behind that. She's still trying to break us up after all this time.

'Bitch! She knew exactly what she was doing. I'll have a word with Dante about his mate.' Irritated, I mindlink and drop my weights on the floor.

'No, don't. I won't let her get to me anymore. Now get back to your workout and pay me no attention.' She mindlinks and smiles. "Hey, *I'll be right back. I need some air.*" I nod as she stands and walks away.

"Bro, spot me." Zane says, shaking his head at Kelsey. We laugh, watching the cheesy bastard flex and show off for Sonia.

"Bro, I hope one day you have two just like you," I laugh before turning to spot Zane as he benches. A second later a commotion erupts behind me.

"Kate!" Kelsey shouts, sending a shock wave through my body. All I can think is that my Kate is in trouble and needs me. I can't get the weights racked fast enough.

I turn to find Kate... my sweet, non-confrontational Kate on top of Nikki punching the shit out of her. I stand with my mouth open in shock for a few seconds. My brain needs a minute to comprehend what I'm seeing. Kate's body shakes and trembles as she unleashes her wrath on Nikki's face.

"Bitch!" Kate shouts, as her fist connects with Nikki's face. "Why?" She screams as her fists fly again. Nikki's nose burst and blood flies everywhere. Seeing Nikki's blood sends her into a killing frenzy, the same frenzy you see on the battlefield. I need to stop her before she makes a mistake she will regret.

"What the fuck did I ever do to you?" With each word, Kate's fist connects with Nikki's face. She lets out a menacing evil laugh. I'm nervous because I've never heard Kate laugh like this.

"I hate you!" Kate continues, punching and laughing.

I grab Kate and pull. She doesn't budge. She has Nikki locked between her thighs and has a death grip on her hair. It's like she's anchored to the floor. I pull again but am knocked off balance by someone bumping into me.

"Fucking watch it!" I shout and get in the bastard's face, only to realize that it is my father. He quickly turns, averting his attention to Kate.

He's quickly joined by Gamma Earnest and Alpha Nathaniel. They form a barrier between me and Kate. I'm sure to some, their actions look like they are trying to break the fight up. Not to me. They look more like they are dancing and bumping into each other. They're doing one hell of a job blocking me from my mate.

Zane and Kelsey join me, trying to get through the impenetrable wall made of our fathers. They're blocking everyone from breaking up the fight. *What the hell?* After a few more punches, Gamma Earnest and my father pull Kate off Nikki, while Alpha shouts to take Kate to his office. The sound of Alpha's voice seems off... this entire thing feels off.

Walking behind Kate and our fathers, I see my father whisper something in her ear, then her dad whispers something in her other ear, followed by an arm shake.

'That looks like someone being congratulated after winning a fight.' Zane catches up to me and mindlinks.

'Did those three bastards run interference for Kate?' Kelsey stands on my other side and mindlinks.

'I think so,' I mindlink in absolute shock.

'Those fuckers are us!' Zane shouts through our mindlink.

'No way!' Kelsey shouts through our mindlink.

What the hell did we just witness? All these years, we've never seen the fun-loving side of our fathers. Sure, there was laughter, but that was few and far between. They were busy trying to raise the three of us to fit in the perfect box they designed for the future leaders of this pack. Our sisters never have understood our issues with our fathers. They saw our fathers in an entirely different light. Seeing them in action today makes me wonder what trouble the three of them got into when they were younger. I wonder if they ever felt they weren't good enough for their fathers, too.

Behind the closed doors of Alpha's office, I hold Kate tight in my arms.

"I'm so sorry, Ian. I didn't mean to embarrass you." Kate says through tears.

"Embarrassed? For what? You're not the one who got her ass handed to her." Alpha says handing Kate a glass of whiskey. "Drink it. It will calm your nerves and stop the adrenalin shakes."

At this point, I'm not even sure I know Alpha. What happened? Did the three of them get abducted and replaced by aliens?

"Listen, love. You didn't embarrass me or anyone. If I hadn't..." I'm interrupted by my father.

"Shut up, son. Stop being a pussy. Your mate just got the justice she deserved for the shit *that* she-wolf put her through for years." He exchanges air-punches with Earnest Gamma, leaving me completely speechless.

"Who the fuck are you three?" Zane looks between the three of them with a confused look on his face. Kate breaks the silence by laughing, causing the rest of us to laugh as well.

CHAPTER THIRTY-EIGHT

HIS PAIN

August 2004

Kate

IT'S BEEN TWO WEEKS since the fight. I'm not too sure what came over me, but I just snapped. I remember little of the fight past seeing Nikki's blood splatter on my face. It's like I have amnesia or something like that. Ian had to explain what happened, including how our fathers ran interference for me. Today I'm in Alpha's office with Ian at my side, because Dante has requested that Alpha punish me for attacking his mate. Standing on either side of Alpha are Beta Charlie and my dad. Zane and Kelsey are also present.

Dante is not from our territory and as far as I know, doesn't know any of Nikki's history. He is from the Hidden River pack down in Texas. They met a year after Nikki transferred to his college. I've met him at the training grounds a couple of times, and he seems nice enough. Of course, after the fight, he looks at me with disdain.

"Thank you for allowing us this meeting, Alpha." Dante sits tall in his chair, next to Nikki. Her face is almost completely healed. Normally, we heal fast. I must have caused more damage than I realized. Good.

"Of course. I'll let you start." Alpha Nathaniel stoically states.

"Alpha Nathaniel, as you know, my mate was brutally attacked two weeks ago in the gym by Kate. The attack came out of nowhere and was unprovoked. During Kate's assault, she broke Nikki's nose, cheekbone, and dislocated her jaw." Dante wraps his arm around Nikki's shoulder. She is playing victim very well, keeping her eyes down and her shoulders slumped forward.

Sasha and I giggle in my mind when we hear Nikki's injuries. Is it wrong to laugh at someone else's pain and suffering? Yes, but this is Nikki. She never cared about causing me pain, and now I feel the same about her.

"Alpha, I'm asking that Kate be publicly punished for her crime against Nikki." Dante finishes and looks directly at me with pure disgust.

"Hmmm, I see." Alpha Nathaniel leans forward, resting his chin in his hand.

The office is quiet, and the silence is deafening. Dante is right, I did attack Nikki. However, it was not unprovoked. Nikki has always bullied me, and I have always run away. I'm guessing that she assumed that day would be no different, but it was. I snapped.

"Fine. For Kate's crimes, she will be given ten lashes with a whip... publicly." Alpha Nathaniel leans back in his chair and I gasp.

"Alpha!" Ian shouts. His body immediately tenses up.

"I. Am. Not. Done. Careful boy, or I will double her lashes." Alpha Nathaniel whips his head to Ian.

"My apologies Alpha Nathaniel." Ian bows his head. "I have a request. Please allow me to take Kate's punishment for her, since I'm the reason for all of this mess."

"What's that supposed to mean?" Dante glares at Ian.

"Speak up now, woman." My dad demands, but Nikki remains silent.

"Nikki, baby, what are they talking about?" Dante leans down to look Nikki in the eyes. With tears in her eyes, she remains silent.

"Enough! Let's talk about Nikki's punishment for interfering in a mated pair's relationship, with the sole purpose of breaking it apart." Alpha Nathaniel narrows his eyes to Nikki.

"What?" Dante gasps, "she has done no such thing." He looks around the room.

"Oh, you're unaware of your mate's history." Alpha Nathaniel looks between Dante and Nikki. Nikki continues to look at the floor. "Would you like to tell your mate the truth now, or shall I?" Nikki gulps but doesn't look up or address Alpha at all. "Dante, your mate has a long history with Ian. One that started in high school, when they became sexually involved with each other." Dante looks at Ian in shock.

"Is that why you wanted to move back here after college? To be close to him?" It's apparent that he didn't know. She didn't tell Dante, which is to be expected. I'm sure he didn't tell her about all the women before her. That would just be weird, in my opinion. Nikki doesn't respond, and Dante removes his arm from around her.

"Two years later, when Kate turned eighteen, we all learned that Ian and Kate were mates. This didn't stop Nikki. She continued to pursue Ian, and like a dumbass, he continued his affair with her." Dante is now pale as he scoots away from Nikki. "Son, I will spare you the details, however the affair stopped only after Kate caught the two of them together." Alpha Nathaniel pauses, looking around the room. Dante looks like he might throw up any second.

"Why Nikki? Why did you continue to sleep with Ian after you found out about us being mated? Why did you bully me through school? What did I ever do to you?" I look directly at her and ask in a firm voice.

"I hate you." She mumbles without looking up.

"What was that? If you're going to speak, then lift your fucking head and speak!" Beta Charlie growls.

"I hate you!" Nikki snaps her head to me and shouts. "I have always hated you as far back as I can remember."

"Why?" I lower my gaze to meet hers. I'm done cowering down to her. Any power she had over my life, I'm taking it back.

"No reason in particular. I just fucking hate you." She says through gritted teeth.

"Your hatred for me almost killed me! I felt a crippling pain in my chest every time you and Ian would hook up." I shout and point at her. The rage is flowing through my veins once more.

If she felt some sort of remorse, I could forgive her, just like I have forgiven Ian. She feels nothing but hate. She has hated me since we were pups for no reason. How could someone hate another for no reason?

"What did you say?" Dante looks at me. "Pains in your chest?"

"Yes." I take a deep breath and sigh. "Every time they were intimate, I had pains in my chest. Sometimes minor other times crippling." I nod and look down.

"Who, Nikki? Who have you been fucking behind my back?" Dante grabs her face, forcing her to look at him. "Fuck!" He shouts and slams his fists on his legs.

Tears swell up in my eyes, watching Dante unravel. I know exactly what he is feeling. The pain from betrayal is like no other. Dante glares at Ian.

"Don't look at me. I haven't touched her in over three years." Ian waves his hands and shakes his head.

"I thought I was going crazy." Dante stands and walks to the door. "I knew something was off." He paces between the door and Nikki. "Is that my pup?" He points to her belly.

"Yes. You're the only one that I've never used protection with." Nikki stands and sobs.

"I don't get it. I've given you everything you've ever wanted. Do you hate me too?" With tears rolling down his face, Dante leans down to Nikki.

"No, Dante! I love you so much." Nikki puts her hands on her chest and sobs. I know I shouldn't, but I feel bad for her. Watching her, I believe she loves him. She knows she did wrong, but does she truly have remorse for what she has done?

"I gave up everything for you. Everything! My alpha title... fucking everything, and for what? To be lied to and cheated on."

"Please Dante!" She pleads, "I made a mistake. Please!" She attempts to wrap her arms around him, but he pushes her away.

"No! Do not touch me. You never get to touch me again!" Dante screams in Nikki's face, then steps back, gaining his composure. "Earnest Gamma, may I be excused from my warrior duties? Alpha Nathaniel, I need to go home... back to Hidden River. Alone." Dante pushes his shoulders back, looking Alpha in the eyes.

"Of course, son. Take all the time you need." Alpha Nathaniel nods his head.

"Alpha... please do not punish Kate. Considering everything I've learned; she doesn't deserve it." Dante gulps, then directs his attention to me. "Kate, please forgive me. I grossly misjudged you."

I nod my head and Dante walks out of Alpha's office. My heart breaks for him. I know his pain. To hear that he gave up everything, including his alpha title for Nikki... his fated mate, makes me sick to my stomach.

"No!" Nikki shouts and runs for the door as it slams shut.

"Nikki, I'm not done with you." Alpha shouts in his alpha tone as Nikki's body hits his door. "Your lover, is he in this pack?" Alpha Nathaniel stands.

"No, Alpha. He is from the New Moon pack." She sniffles and wipes her face.

"Our neighboring pack?" Alpha Nathaniel shakes his head and scoffs. "The pup you are carrying, is it your mate's or lover's?"

"There is no pup, Alpha. Dante detected another scent on me, and I told him I was pregnant." Nikki wraps her arms around her body.

"You have really made a mess of things, haven't you? What you have done is punishable by death, but death is too easy for you. Instead, your punishment will be to live with the memory of what you have done and the pain you have caused. However, you will not continue to be a member of this pack. Do you understand?"

"Yes, Alpha." Nikki pushes her shoulders back and lifts her head high. She doesn't beg or plead for Alpha to change his mind.

"Very well. Nikolina Raine, I, Alpha Nathaniel Roberts, renounce you as a member of the Blue Moon pack. You are permanently banned from Blue Moon territories. Punishment for entering any of the Blue Moon territories will be immediate death. I will allow you twenty-four hours to gather your things and say your goodbyes."

Chapter Thirty-Nine

I BELIEVE YOU

August 2004

Ian

I HATE WHAT HAPPENED in Alpha's office today. Dante is a good man and doesn't deserve what Nikki is putting him through. I did not know that he is of alpha descent. Dante is larger than our normal warriors, but I would have never guessed he was an alpha. I don't know too much about the Hidden River pack, except they're a small pack of about one-hundred located in central Texas.

I can't understand why Nikki would give up a chance at being Luna. The entire situation is just bizarre. It doesn't surprise me that Nikki has a lover on the side. She had several when she and I were messing around. It didn't bother me, because she did her thing, and I did mine. Nikki likes sex and the power over men it gives her.

"Hey you," Kate stands next to the bed, wearing a tank top and thong.

"There is the love of my life. Did you have a nice shower?" I pat the bed next to me.

"It was so good." Kate climbs onto the bed and settles in next to me. "What are you thinking about?"

"How Dante doesn't deserve what happened to him. Just like you didn't." I wrap my arm around her, pulling her tight into my body. Burying my face into the crook of her neck, I breathe in her delicious scent. Sweet floral, I will never get enough of it.

"True. Just like Darren, and my friend Melissa..." Kate stops talking when she hears me sigh. "Why do you always act like that when I mention Melissa's name? I mean, I understand why you would when I say Darren's name, but why Melissa?" She looks up at me with that look that screams, *I know you're not telling me everything.*

"Ugh." With an exasperated sigh, I run my hand through my hair then pull Kate on to my lap. "Listen, I don't know how to tell you this, but I promised that there would be no secrets between the two of us." I hold her tight because I'm not too sure how she'll react. Will I become the bad guy again?

"Okay. Go on." Her body tenses up, and her heart races.

"The night of your twenty-first birthday party. Kelsey and I heard two guys talking at the bar before you arrived. It was Darren and some blonde guy with a beard." I take a breath and watch her.

"Coleman. That's his best friend." She adds, nodding her head.

"Darren told him you were still a virgin, saving yourself for marriage. He showed him the ring and said it was just a cheap piece of glass. He planned on asking you to marry him, just so he could take your virginity and then dump you. His parents don't approve of you, something about not being in the same circle of people." I gulp and rub circles on her back.

"Oh, I see." Her right eye twitches as thoughts run through her head.

"Why did you tell him you were a virgin?" I rub her jaw.

"Well," she gulps, "I really don't know. He was pressuring me, and I couldn't bring myself to sleep with him. Which sounds completely hypocritical, because you were in town for like a day and we got tangled up together." She wrinkles her nose and looks down. "I guess I couldn't because we were still bound since the mate bond wasn't severed completely."

"Maybe." I nod my head.

"What about Melissa?" She tilts her head.

"She is sleeping with Darren and Coleman. They bragged that they see her at least once a week." I rub my hand along the outside of her thigh.

"What?" She gasps. "Are you serious?" Her mouth falls open and her hands shake.

"Ask Kelsey." I rub her cheek.

"I don't have to… I believe you." She squeaks out, then nuzzles into my chest.

Kate

"Why did you wait so long to tell me about Darren?" I look up at his face.

"I wanted to tell you at breakfast the next morning, but I thought if I did, it would just make me look like a jealous ex that would say anything to win you back. Since you hated me at that point, I thought it would push you further into his arms. After you agreed to give me a last chance, it didn't seem important." Ian caresses my cheek and looks lovingly into my eyes.

He's right. I wouldn't have believed him or Kelsey back in New York. Ian was the bad guy, Kelsey too. I wouldn't have believed either of them. Things are different now. What would Ian have to gain by telling me this? Nothing.

It should hurt me hearing how Darren only wanted me for sex, but I'm numb. Maybe because of everything I've been through with Ian. Or maybe I feel like he got what he deserved when I cheated on him with Ian. Or maybe it's because we never belonged to each other. Who knows? I still feel remorse for my part in all of it.

What hurts the worse is what I'm hearing about Melissa. How could she betray me like that? I told her all about Ian and how he cheated on me. She knew how hurt and traumatized it left me. Melissa counseled me and gave me advice about Darren. I know her entire family. She acted like she hated him so much. How could she betray our friendship like that?

"Melissa is the one who told me to tell Darren I was a virgin and was saving myself for marriage. She said I shouldn't sleep with Darren until I was sure he was the one. I guess she just wanted to save him for herself alone." I'm in shock and heartbroken. Melissa and I were so close.

"There's more." Ian inhales sharply. "Melissa caught me coming out of the men's room and tried to get my hotel key, promising me a good time." He cringes.

"What?" I pull away from him and look at him in disbelief. "I told her who you were. She knew all about you!" My hands shake as I feel anger building up inside. Technically speaking, Ian and I were broken up. He was fair game. It's just the audacity that she was sleeping with my current boyfriend while trying to hook up with my ex. I didn't realize she was so sexually active, which is not a bad thing. It's just that she always led me to believe that she was done with relationships after she caught her boyfriend with another woman.

"Nothing happened. I told her to stay the fuck away from me and that she is a horrible friend." Ian pulls me back into his body.

"Is that why you were stuck at my side all night?" I put my head on his bare chest and breathe in his intoxicating fresh scent.

"Not really. After I decided to work on myself and earn you back, no woman affected me. I have full control over my urges... except when it comes to you." He lifts my head and presses his lips into mine. "I wanted to be close to you so the mate bond would work its magic on you. That, and it bugged the shit out of frat boy." He laughs and I playfully slap his chest.

"Darren led me to believe he was so hurt and that I was some horrible person. Hopefully, he'll see what it feels like to be cheated on and change his ways."

"I doubt he will." Ian runs his fingers through my hair.

"Why do you say that?" I straddle his lap.

"Listening to the frat boys' conversation led me to believe their fathers keep women on the side. It's a learned behavior." He slips his hands under my tank top, igniting my skin with tingles everywhere he touches.

"I'm so glad you came back into my life." I run my fingers through his hair and move my hips.

"Careful, woman. I told you I have no control where you are concerned." Ian growls.

"You saved me from more heartache." I kiss his neck.

"Mmmmm, damn." He grabs my ass and grinds my core harder into him.

"I want to lose control with you every day." I suck on his earlobe.

"Mine." Ian growls. With both hands he grabs my hair, cocking my head to the side, and attacks my neck with his mouth.

His lips on my skin send an electric pulse through my body to my core, setting my skin on fire with desire. He slips my tank top over my head before pulling me in for a passionate kiss. Our bodies melt together as our tongues dance. Lust fills the air as the haze of the mate bond takes over our minds. Dampness builds between my legs as my core throbs for him.

"Ian." I moan, "fuck me, please." I hiss and beg.

"No." He flips me on my back and hovers over me. With love in his eyes and a soft face, he brushes my hair with his fingers, then caresses my face. He smiles as he strokes my lips and jawline with his thumb. "Not tonight, love. Tonight, I want to make love to you. Soft, slow, and full of passion."

He kisses me, massaging my breasts. Taking his time, giving each one his full attention before taking a nipple into his mouth. He flicks his tongue as he sucks and licks each one before switching to the other. Tingles radiate off our skin, elevating us to another plane of existence.

His lips work their way down my chest to my belly. He tugs at my thong, and I lift my hips so he can slip them off me. Positioning himself between my legs, he kisses and licks up and down the inside of each thigh. His movements are slow, methodical, and full of love. My entire body buzzes with anticipation of where his touch might go next.

I feel the warmth of his mouth as it invades my core. I move my hips to his rhythm as the pressure builds inside me with every lap of his magnificent tongue. He rigorously devours my core, and I fist the sheets and moan.

"Does that feel good, love?" He takes my nub into his mouth, teasing it with his tongue, and nibbling it with his teeth. A lustful haze clouds my mind, and I can't form a coherent thought or sentence, so I moan louder.

He slips two fingers inside me, slowly pumping and rubbing my sweet spot. I close my eyes and throw my head back. My body shakes and trembles as I fall off the edge with an explosive orgasm.

"Yes, Ian!" I shout, as I'm hit with wave after wave of pleasure.

"I love when you cum for me." He continues to pump in and out while his thumb rubs circles on my nub. He watches my body with a smile, knowing that he's the only one who can take me to such an ecstatic state.

He slips off his boxer briefs, then rubs the tip of his shaft up and down my entrance. Dipping it in and out of my folds, thoroughly coating the tip with my juices. The need to feel him inside me rises and I reach for him. Grabbing his ass, I pull him close to me, begging for him to enter. He chuckles at my eagerness, and with a single slow push; he obliges my request.

We both hiss and moan as he enters me. He is completely inside. We are one. Still, he's too far away from me. I need him closer, close enough that our hearts beat in unison. His tongue invades my mouth, exploring every inch, and claiming it as his own. I lock my legs around him, and I can feel his smooth shaft as he slowly pumps in and out of me. Each thrust feeling better than the last.

I pull him close, wrapping my arms around him, molding myself into his body. We are like two perfectly matched puzzle pieces. Our moans grow louder as his hands explore my body, sending it into a buzzing frenzy.

"I'm so in love with you, Kate." He whispers in my ear, sending me spiraling out of control.

My vision blurs and my head spins as I'm hit with the most amazing climax. I feel like we are floating on thin air as I shake under him. My appetite for him can never be satisfied. I'm simply insatiable. The more he touches me, the more I crave. He pumps a few more times before pushing in as deep as he can. He grunts; I can feel his member pulsate and throb as he fills me with his hot liquid. I love the grunts and groans he makes when he climaxes. Knowing that I'm able to please him sets my soul ablaze with desire.

He doesn't pull out, but continues to slowly pump in and out. We stare deep into each other's eyes and smile. I've never felt so connected to him as I do right now.

"I'm in love with you, too." I whisper. He really is the other half of my soul. My true one and only.

CHAPTER FORTY

A NEW REIN

September 2006

Ian

"IAN?" KATE CALLS OUT from the bedroom, "help!"

"Be right there." I walk down the hall to our room, passing packed boxes along the way. Our wedding photo still hangs on the wall. I stop to adjust it, making it level again. Every time I see this photo, I get emotional. I think about how much we overcame, and how we didn't almost exist. Our wedding was two short months after we re-marked each other. It was a beautiful day for the private ceremony in front of the glass greenhouse at the arboretum in the city. Kate looked so beautiful in her simple yet elegant white dress. Our garden wedding was perfectly Kate, and she was in her element amongst the roses and jasmine. We spent two blissful weeks in Tahiti on our honeymoon.

"Hey, love. What can I help you with?" I walk into our room.

"I can't get this zipped up and I'm feeling like a beached whale." She puts her hand on her swollen belly and sighs.

"Dada, mama pretty." Our year and a half year old daughter says from my arms.

"You hear that, mama? Our little sugar thinks you're pretty." Kate walks up to us both.

"Oh, thank you, sugar. Mama thinks you're pretty too." Kate kisses our daughter's hand before I sit her on the bed.

"If my opinion matters, I think mama is smoking hot. Especially with my little sweet pea growing inside here." I kiss Kate and rub her belly. Still, to this day, I can't get enough of her, and I let her know every chance I get. "Turn around. Let me get you zipped up and help you into your shoes."

Tonight, a new rein at Blue Moon will take over, as we are all sworn into our respective positions. Zane will take over as Alpha, I will become Beta, Kelsey will become Gamma, Rebeka will become Luna, Kate will become Beta Female, and Sonia will become Gamma Female. As our parents step down and we step up in their places, we know we each have huge shoes to fill as leaders in this massive pack.

Kate sits on the edge of the bed and plays with our daughter while I slip on her shoes. Before I do, I take a moment to rub her swollen legs and feet. She is due any moment. We're just hoping she gets through the ceremony before the new pup's arrival. I watch her play with our daughter and smile. She really is an amazing mom.

"It's time to go. Are you ready, love?" She flashes me the most beautiful smile and nods her head. I pick up our daughter then help Kate to her feet, and as a family, we head down to the ceremony.

I think back to when it all started, the day I found out she was my mate. Watching her walk down the stairs, I saw the most beautiful woman where a little girl once stood. She was no longer just the girl next door and my best friend's little sister. Looking into her eyes, I saw love. She was and is the most beautiful woman in the world. I felt love when she helped me into the paracord bracelet that she made me. That was the moment my life changed, and I knew she was mine.

What started out as a fairytale romance went sour so quickly, due to me. My selfishness and immaturity almost cost me all of this. She is the only woman I will ever belong to. I wish it didn't take me losing her to realize that. We beat every odd stacked against us the day she agreed to give me a final chance, and every day our love grows stronger and stronger.

Despite what I did, what anyone thought, we made it. I look at the life we share, the life we created in my arms, and the one she is still carrying... I almost lost all of this. I'm so glad we made it. We might have taken the long route, but we got here, and I'm forever grateful for Kate and the chance that I didn't deserve. After all this time, she is my one and only true love, the only one I want to kiss goodnight and wake up next to in the morning. As long as we have each other, we can overcome whatever life throws at us.

The End

EPILOGUE

August 2004

Zane

"THIS PLACE IS A shit hole." I say in disgust, looking around this tiny apartment that Kate lived in for over two years. "Why wouldn't your father put his princess in a penthouse or something like that?" I watch the movers work packing up her belongings.

"My parents never visited her, or they would have had a fit. Kate loved the neighborhood, and the university is just a few blocks away. All this furniture is being donated; we're only taking personal belongings." Kelsey instructs the movers.

"What about all these books?" I walk up to the two bookcases in the living room.

"She will kill me if she loses her collection. They come with us." Kelsey stands next to me.

"I didn't realize she reads so much." I thumb through the books.

"She always has." Kelsey nods his head.

"What the hell is this? Warrior by Krys Strong?" I look at the cover of a half-naked man with tattoos.

"Kinda looks like you." Kelsey laughs. "She is a fan of romance." Curiosity gets the better of me and I read the back of the book.

"Werewolves?" I flip through the pages of the book. "The growl is so loud the room falls silent. Remove your hands from what is MINE before I remove them for you," I read out loud. Kelsey and I stare at each other for a few moments before bursting out in a fit of uncontrollable laughter. "This shit is so unbelievable. Who says things like that?" I toss the book into a box.

"Who the hell are you?" A man appears in the doorway with a bouquet of carnations.

"Ah, you must be the frat boy. What's with the funeral flowers?" I laugh, wondering what the hell Kate ever saw in this loser. Ian is an eight or nine, this dork is a two... maybe a three on a good day.

"Oh, hey Darren, remember me? Kelsey, Kate's older brother." Kelsey, being ever so diplomatic, walks over to him.

"Yeah, I remember you. Last time I saw you, I was hung over for a week. Who's he?" Frat boy points at me.

"Is that really important?" I look between him and Kelsey and sigh. "Fine. I'm Zane." I cross my arms.

"Are you another one of Kate's boyfriends?" Frat boy asks nervously.

"What, you think there's a group of us pulling a train on her every night?" I snap. This little fucker is bugging the shit out of me.

"Bro!" Kelsey shouts and snaps his head at me.

"I'm her... cousin. Happy frat boy?" I roll my eyes.

"Kate!" Frat boy calls out towards the bedroom, then looks back at me. "Where's Kate?" He asks suspiciously.

"That's one room you've never gotten to see up close and personal, isn't it?" I laugh, pointing at the bedroom door. "Kate is back home with her ma... man... Ian... fiancé. They're in a fishing cabin right now, fucking each other's brains out." I say as a matter of fact. I'm having fun messing with this piece of shit.

"Bro! She's my sister." Kelsey snaps.

"Sorry, but I mean facts are facts, right?" I shrug my shoulders and lift my palms up.

"Still, you want me talking about one of your sisters like that?" Kelsey puts his hands on his hips.

"Alright, I get it." I pause and think. "Kate is currently unavailable. She is locked away in a fishing cabin with her fiancé. He is taking care of business... handling a personal situation for Kate. Better bro?" I look at Kelsey.

"Fucking a... I need a beer." Kelsey walks to the fridge.

"Oh..." I pull the ring frat boy gave Kate from my blazer pocket. "She wanted me to give this back to you and wishes you luck on your next conquest. You'll need it giving out cheap pieces of glass like that." I place the ring in the palm of his hand.

"Ummm, excuse me? Is Kate here?" A woman steps through the doorway and stands next to Darren.

"Melissa, hey, remember me?" Kelsey points to himself, "I'm Kate's older brother."

"Kelsey... yeah, I remember you. Where's Kate? I got this weird written message on my cell phone asking me to meet her here."

"Oh yeah, that was from me. It's called a text message. They've been around for a little while, but not super popular yet. I have a feeling that in the future people will be text messaging rather than calling each other." Kelsey explains.

"That's the stupidest bunch of bullshit I've ever heard. Do you realize how long it would take to send one of those messages on your cell phone?" I shake my head at Kelsey.

"You'll see, bro." He looks away from me back to Melissa, "Kate is not here, she's at home with her fiancé."

"Ian... you know the guy. The muscular guy that showed up with that one for Kate's party. You know, the one you tried rubbing your ass against at the bar." I put my hands on my hips.

"That's... umm... it was crowded. I may have bumped into him." Melissa shifts nervously.

"Oh... so you didn't follow him to the bathroom and promise him a blowjob? That wasn't you? You're also not the one he told to stay away from him, and you're a pathetic excuse for a friend? Still not you?" I tilt my head.

"That's disgusting Melissa." Darren looks at Melissa curling his lip up at her.

"Shut the fuck up, Darren." She snaps at him.

"Anyway, I asked you here today because I know you and my sister were close, and I wanted to make sure that you could get any of your personal effects before we pack everything up." Kelsey's voice is soft and soothing. I wonder if he'll read me a bedtime story later.

"No, I don't have anything here." Melissa snaps.

"You sure about that?" I question.

"I'm sure." Her Bronx accent really gets stronger when she's irritated.

"Maybe a boyfriend?" Kelsey points at Darren.

"Hey frat boy, now's your chance. Give her that ring you gave Kate." I point between Melissa and Darren.

"What?" She shouts, turning to face Darren. "You fucking proposed to Kate? You mother fucker! We were going to be together because you said you were ending it with her." Melissa crosses her arms and stomps her foot.

"Shit, this is getting good. Hey Kelsey, beer me. I'd offer you one frat boy, but we all know you can't handle your liquor." I catch the beer Kelsey tosses across the room.

"Shut up, Melissa! You're totally fucking Coleman, too." Darren faces Melissa.

"Whoa, I didn't expect that." I open my beer.

"Hey, was that the guy you were bragging to at the bar the night of Kate's party?" Kelsey asks.

"Yeah, they're always together; fucking glued at the hips those two. I wouldn't be surprised if they were blowing each other." Melissa snaps at Darren.

"This is bullshit. Tell Kate I never want to hear from her again. Fuck this, fuck that, and fuck you," Darren points at Melissa. "I'm getting the fuck out of here." He throws the carnations on the ground.

"Hey!" I shout, "you forgot your funeral flowers." I laugh. "Word of advice, Melissa..." I direct my attention to her. "Stop betraying your friends by fucking their boyfriends, fiancés, and husbands. No one will want to make a housewife out of a whore." I can see the tears swelling up in her eyes. Sometimes the truth stings.

"And." Kelsey narrows his eyes at me then turns his attention to Melissa. "Darren and Coleman, to them, you're only a piece of ass and nothing more. You're from the wrong borough and your family is not connected enough. You will never be more than a side piece, just good enough to sneak around with in the shadows, but never good enough to show off in public. Be a better friend and person, and good things will come to you." Kelsey looks her in the eyes.

"It's not too late for you to change your ways." I take a page from Kelsey's book and soften my tone. She nods her head, then walks away.

About an hour later, Kate's apartment is packed up and loaded into trucks, either destined for our territory or the donation center, thus ending this chapter of her life.

"Alright bro let's get our pregnant wives and get some food in them before Sonia rips my head off." Kelsey turns the light off and shuts the door behind us as we walk out.

"Yeah, Rebeka told me about some restaurant near the hotel that she wants to try." We continue down the hall towards the front door.

ABOUT AUTHOR

Born in Thailand, Krys currently lives in Texas . She has been an aspiring writer for years who finally took the plunge and publish her first book. She loves all things romance with paranormal and fantasy as her favorite. Krys loves to write books that take you on an emotional ride and are plot driven.

In her spare time, she enjoys spending time outdoors exploring the Texas Hill Country, tending to her gardens, chickens, and cuddling with her rescue pup.